THE BESTSELLING NOVELS
OF
TOM CLANCY

EXECUTIVE ORDERS

Jack Ryan has always been a soldier. Now he's giving the orders.

"AN ENORMOUS, ACTION-PACKED, HEAT-SEEKING MISSILE OF A TOM CLANCY NOVEL."
—*Seattle Times*

DEBT OF HONOR

It begins with the murder of an American woman in the back streets of Tokyo. It ends in war . . .

"A SHOCKER CLIMAX SO PLAUSIBLE YOU'LL WONDER WHY IT HASN'T YET HAPPENED!"
—*Entertainment Weekly*

THE HUNT FOR RED OCTOBER

The smash bestseller that launched Clancy's career—the incredible search for a Soviet defector and the nuclear submarine he commands . . .

"BREATHLESSLY EXCITING!"
—*Washington Post*

continued . . .

RED STORM RISING

The ultimate scenario for World War III—the final battle for global control . . .

"THE ULTIMATE WAR GAME . . . BRILLIANT!"
—*Newsweek*

PATRIOT GAMES

CIA analyst Jack Ryan stops an assassination—and incurs the wrath of Irish terrorists . . .

"A HIGH PITCH OF EXCITEMENT!"
—*Wall Street Journal*

THE CARDINAL OF THE KREMLIN

The superpowers race for the ultimate Star Wars missile defense system . . .

"*CARDINAL* EXCITES, ILLUMINATES . . . A REAL PAGE-TURNER!"
—*Los Angeles Daily News*

CLEAR AND PRESENT DANGER

The killing of three U.S. officials in Colombia ignites the American government's explosive, and top secret, response . . .

"A CRACKLING GOOD YARN!"
—*Washington Post*

THE SUM OF ALL FEARS

The disappearance of an Israeli nuclear weapon threatens the balance of power in the Middle East—and around the world . . .

"CLANCY AT HIS BEST . . . NOT TO BE MISSED!"
—*Dallas Morning News*

WITHOUT REMORSE

The Clancy epic fans have been waiting for. His code name is Mr. Clark. And his work for the CIA is brilliant, cold-blooded and efficient . . . but who is he really?

"HIGHLY ENTERTAINING!"
—*Wall Street Journal*

Tom Clancy's Op-Center

BALANCE OF POWER

Created by
Tom Clancy and Steve Pieczenik

B

BERKLEY BOOKS, NEW YORK

TOM CLANCY'S OP-CENTER: BALANCE OF POWER

A Berkley Book / published by arrangement with
Jack Ryan Limited Partnership and S&R Literary, Inc.

PRINTING HISTORY
Berkley edition / May 1998

All rights reserved.
Copyright © 1998 by Jack Ryan Limited Partnership and S&R Literary, Inc.
This book may not be reproduced in whole or in part,
by mimeograph or any other means, without permission.
For information address: The Berkley Publishing Group,
a member of Penguin Putnam Inc.,
200 Madison Avenue, New York, New York 10016.

The Penguin Putnam Inc. World Wide Web site address is
http://www.penguinputnam.com

ISBN: 0-425-16556-6

BERKLEY®
Berkley Books are published by The Berkley Publishing Group,
a member of Penguin Putnam Inc.,
200 Madison Avenue, New York, New York 10016.
BERKLEY and the "B" design
are trademarks belonging to Berkley Publishing Corporation.

PRINTED IN THE UNITED STATES OF AMERICA

10 9 8 7 6 5 4 3 2 1

Acknowledgments

We would like to thank Jeff Rovin for his creative ideas and his invaluable contributions to the preparation of the manuscript. We would also like to acknowledge the assistance of Martin H. Greenberg, Larry Segriff, Robert Youdelman, Esq., Tom Mallon, Esq., and the wonderful people at The Putnam Berkley Group, including Phyllis Grann, David Shanks, and Elizabeth Beier. As always, we would like to thank Robert Gottlieb of The William Morris Agency, our agent and friend, without whom this book would never have been conceived. But most important, it is for you, our readers, to determine how successful our collective endeavor has been.

      —Tom Clancy and Steve Pieczenik

Tom Clancy's

Op-Center

BALANCE
OF
POWER

ONE

"You were way out of line," Martha Mackall said. She was openly disgusted with the young woman standing beside her and it took a moment for her to calm down. Then she bent close to Aideen's ear so the other passengers wouldn't hear. "You were out of line and reckless. You know what's at stake here. To be distracted like that is inexcusable."

The statuesque Martha and her slight assistant, Aideen Marley were holding a pole in the aisle near the front door of the bus. Aideen's full, round cheeks nearly as red as her long hair, she tore absently at the moist towelette she clutched in her right hand.

"Do you disagree?" Martha asked.

"No," Aideen said.

"I mean, good lord!"

"I said no," Aideen repeated. "I don't disagree. I was wrong. Totally and completely wrong."

Aideen believed it, too. She had behaved impulsively in a situation that she probably should have ignored. But like Aideen's own overreaction a few minutes before, this dressing-down from Martha was excessive and punitive. In the two months since

Aideen had joined Op-Center's Political and Economics Office, she'd been warned more than once by the other three staff members to avoid crossing the boss.

Now she saw why.

"I don't know what you needed to prove," Martha went on. She was still bent close to Aideen. There was anger in her clipped tone. "But I never want you doing it again. Not when you're touring with me. Do you understand?"

"Yes," Aideen said contritely. *God*, she thought, *enough already*. Aideen had a flashback to a brain-washing seminar she'd once attended at the U.S. embassy in Mexico City. The prisoners were always dunned by their captors when they were at their weakest emotionally. Guilt was an especially effective doorway. She wondered if Martha had studied the technique or came by it naturally.

And almost at once, Aideen wondered if she were being fair to her boss. After all, this *was* their first mission together for Op-Center. And it was an important one.

Martha finally looked away—but only for a moment. "It's unbelievable," she said, turning back. Her voice was just loud enough to be heard over the powerful engine. "Tell me something. Did it ever occur to you that we might have been detained by the police? How would we have explained that to our Uncle Miguel?"

Uncle Miguel was the code name for the man they were here to see, Deputy Isidro Serrador. Until the women arrived for their meeting at the Congreso de los Diputados, the Congress of Deputies, that was how they were supposed to refer to him.

"Detained by the police for what?" Aideen asked. "Frankly, no. That did not occur to me. We were simply protecting ourselves."

"Protecting ourselves?" Martha asked.

Aideen looked at her. "Yes."

"From whom?"

"What do you mean?" Aideen asked. "Those men—"

"Those *Spanish* men," Martha said, still bent close to Aideen. "It would have been our word against theirs. Two American women crying harassment to police*men* who probably do their own share of harassing. The *policía* would have laughed at us."

Aideen shook her head. "I can't believe it would have gone that far."

"I see," Martha said. "You know that for sure. You can guarantee it wouldn't have."

"No, I can't," Aideen admitted. "But even so, at least the situation would have been—"

"What?" Martha asked. "Ended? What would you have done if we'd been arrested?"

Aideen looked out the window as the stores and hotels of Madrid's commercial center passed by. She'd recently partaken in one of Op-Center's computerized WaSPs—War Simulation Projects—a mandatory exercise for members of the diplomatic staff. It gave them a feeling for what their colleagues had to endure if diplomacy failed. Casualties greater than the mind could process. That exercise was easier than this one.

"If we'd been arrested," Aideen said, "I would

have apologized. What else could I have done?''

''Not a thing,'' Martha said, ''which is exactly my point—though it's a little late to be thinking about it.''

''You know what?'' said Aideen. ''You're right. You're *right*!'' She looked back at Martha. ''It's too late. So what I'd like to do now is apologize to you and put this behind us.''

''I'm sure you would,'' Martha replied, ''but that's not my style. When I'm unhappy, I let it out.''

And out and out, Aideen thought.

''And when I get real unhappy,'' Martha added, ''I shut *you* out. I can't afford charity.''

Aideen didn't agree with that policy of excommunication. You build a good team, you fight hard to keep it; a wise and effective manager understands that passion needs to be nurtured and channeled, not crushed. But this was a side of Martha she'd simply have to get used to. As Op-Center's Deputy Director, General Mike Rodgers, had put it when he hired her, *Every job has politics. They just happen to be more pronounced in politics.* He went on to point out that in every profession, people have agendas. Often, only dozens or hundreds of people are affected by those agendas. In politics, the ramifications from even tiny ripples are incalculable. And there was only one way to fight that.

Aideen had asked him how.

Rodgers's answer had been simple. *With a better agenda.*

Aideen was too annoyed to contemplate what Martha's agenda was right now. That was a popular topic of discussion at Op-Center. People were divided as to whether the Political and Economics Liaison worked hard doing what was best for the nation or for Martha Mackall. The truth, most felt, was that she was looking out for both.

Aideen looked around the bus. She could tell that some of the people gathered around her were also unhappy, though that had very little to do with what was going on between the young woman and Martha. The bus was packed with people returning to work after the afternoon lunch break—which lasted from one o'clock to four—as well as camera-carrying tourists. A number of them had seen what the young woman had done at the bus stop. Word had spread very rapidly. The riders nearest Aideen were pressing away from her. A few of them cast disapproving glances at the young woman's hands.

Martha remained silent as the brakes ground noisily. The large red bus stopped on Calle Fernanflor and the two women got off quickly. Dressed as tourists in jeans and windbreakers, and carrying backpacks and cameras, they stood on the curb of the crowded avenue. Behind them, the bus snarled away. Dark faces bobbed in the windows, looking down at the women.

Martha regarded her assistant. Despite the reprimand, Aideen's gray eyes still had a glint of steel beneath her lightly freckled lids.

"Look," Martha said, "you're new in this arena. I brought you along because you're a helluva linguist and you're smart. You have a lot of potential in foreign affairs."

"I'm not exactly new at it," Aideen replied defensively.

"No, but you're new on the European stage and to my way of doing things," Martha replied. "You like frontal assaults, which is probably why General Rodgers hired you away from Ambassador Carnegie. Our Deputy Director believes in attacking problems head on. But I warned you about that when you came to work for me. I told you to turn down the heat. What worked in Mexico is not necessarily going to work here. I told you when you accepted the position that if you work for me you have to do things my way. And I prefer end runs. Skirt the main force. Finesse the enemy rather than launch an assault. Especially when the stakes are as high as they are here."

"I understand," Aideen said. "Like I said, I may be new at this type of situation. But I'm not green. When I know the rules I can play by them."

Martha relaxed slightly. "Okay. I'll buy that." She watched as Aideen tossed the tattered towelette into a trash can. "Are you okay? Do you want to find a restroom?"

"Do I need one?"

Martha sniffed the air. "I don't think so." She scowled. "You know, I still can't believe you did what you did."

"I know you can't and I'm truly sorry," Aideen said. "What else can I possibly say?"

"Nothing," Martha said. She shook her head slowly. "Not a thing. I've seen street fighters in my day, but I have to admit I've never seen that."

Martha was still shaking her head as they turned toward the imposing Palacio de las Cortes, where they were scheduled to meet very unofficially and very quietly with Deputy Serrador. According to what the veteran politician had told Ambassador Barry Neville in a very secret meeting, tension was escalating between the impoverished Andalusians in the south and the rich and influential Castilians of northern and central Spain. The government wanted help gathering intelligence. They needed to know from which direction the tension was coming—and whether it also involved the Catalonians, Galicians, Basques, and other ethnic groups. Serrador's fear was that a concerted effort by one faction against another could rend the loosely woven quilt of Spain. Sixty years before, a civil war, which pitted the aristocracy, the military, and the Roman Catholic Church against insurgent Communists and other anarchic forces, had nearly destroyed Spain. A modern war would draw in ethnic sympathizers from France, Morocco, Andorra, Portugal, and other nearby nations. It would destabilize the southern flank of NATO and the results would be catastrophic—particularly as NATO sought to expand its sphere of influence in Eastern Europe.

Ambassador Neville had taken the problem back to the State Department. Secretary of State Av Lincoln decided that the State Department couldn't afford to become involved at this early stage. If the matter exploded and they were shown to have had a hand in it, it would be difficult for the United States to help negotiate a peace. Lincoln asked Op-Center to make the initial contact and ascertain what, if anything, the United States could do to defuse the potential crisis.

Martha zipped her blue windbreaker against the sudden chill of night. "I can't stress this enough," she said. "Madrid is not the underbelly of Mexico City. The briefings at Op-Center didn't cover this because we didn't have time. But as different as the various peoples of Spain are, they all believe in one thing: honor. Yes, there are aberrations. There are bad seeds in any society. And yes, the standards aren't consistent and they definitely aren't always humanistic. There may be one kind of honor among politicians and another kind among killers. But they always play by the rules of the profession."

"So those three little pigs who insisted that they show us around when we left the hotel," Aideen said sharply, "the one who put his hand on my butt and kept it there. They were acting according to some kind of honorable sexual harassers' code?"

"No," Martha said. "They were acting according to a street extortionists' code."

Aideen's eyes narrowed. "Excuse me?"

"Those men wouldn't have hurt us," Martha said. "That would have been against the rules. And the rules are that they follow women, pester them, and keep at it until they get a payoff to leave them alone. I was about to give them one when you acted."

"You were?"

Martha nodded. "That's how it's done here. As for the police you would have gone to, many of them collect kickbacks from the street extortionists to look the other way. Get it through your head. Playing the game, however corrupt it seems, is still diplomacy."

"But what if you hadn't known about their 'profession,' their code? I didn't." Aideen lowered her voice. "I was worried about having our backpacks stolen and our covers blown."

"An arrest would have blown our covers a whole lot faster," Martha said. She took Aideen by the arm and pulled her aside. They stood next to a building, away from pedestrian traffic. "The truth is, eventually someone would have told us how to get rid of them. People always do. That's how the game is played, and I believe in obeying the rules of whatever game or whatever country I'm in. When I started out in diplomacy in the early 1970s on the seventh floor of the State Department, I was excited as hell. I was on the seventh floor, where all the real, heavy-duty work is done. But then I found out *why* I was there. Not because I was so damn talented, though I hoped I was. I was there to deal with the apartheid leaders in South Africa. I was State's 'in-your-face' figure. I was a wagging finger that said, 'If you want to deal with the U.S., you'll have to deal with blacks as equals.' " Martha scowled. "Do you know what that was like?"

Aideen made a face. She could just imagine.

"It's not like having your fanny *patted,* I can tell you that," Martha said. "But I did what I was supposed to do because I learned one thing very early. If you infract the rules or bend them to suit your temperament, even a little, it becomes a habit. When it becomes a habit you get sloppy. And a sloppy diplomat is no use to the country—or to me."

Aideen was suddenly disgusted with herself. The thirty-four-year-old foreign service officer would be the first to admit that she wasn't the diplomat her forty-nine-year-old superior was. Few people were. Martha Mackall not only knew her way around European and Asian political circles—partly the result of summers and vacations she'd spent touring the world with her father, popular 1960s soul singer and Civil Rights activist Mack Mackall. She was also a summa cum laude MIT financial wizard who was tight with the world's top bankers and well connected on Capitol Hill. Martha was feared but she was respected. And Aideen had to admit that in this case she was also right.

Martha looked at her watch. "Come on," she said. "We're due at the palace in less than five minutes."

Aideen nodded and walked alongside her boss. The younger woman was no longer angry. She was disgusted with herself and brooded, as she usually did when she screwed up. She hadn't been able to screw up much during her four years in army intelligence at Fort Meade. That was paint-by-numbers courier work, moving cash and top secret information to operatives domestically and abroad. Toward the end of her tenure there she interpreted ELINT—electronic intelligence— and passed it on to the Pentagon. Since the satellites and computers did all the heavy lifting there, she took special classes on elite tactics and stakeout techniques—just to get experience in those areas. Aideen didn't have a chance to mess things up either when she left the military and became a junior political officer at the U.S. Embassy in Mexico. Most of the time

she was using ELINT to help keep track of drug dealers in the Mexican military, though occasionally she
was permitted to go out in the field and use some of
the undercover skills she'd acquired. One of the most
valuable aspects of the three years Aideen had spent
in Mexico was learning the ploy that had proved so
effective this afternoon—as well as offensive to Martha and the busload of commuters. After she and her
friend Ana Rivera of the Mexican attorney general's
office were cornered by a pair of drug cartel muscle-
men one night, Aideen discovered that the best way
to fight off an attacker wasn't by carrying a whistle or
knife or by trying to kick them in the groin or scratch
out their eyes. It was by keeping moist towelettes in
your handbag. That's what Ana used to clean her
hands and arms after tossing around some *mierda de
perro*.

Dog droppings. Ana had casually scooped them off
the street and flung them at the toughs who were following them. Then she'd rubbed some on her arms to
make sure no one grabbed them. Ana said there wasn't
an attacker she'd ever encountered who stuck around
after that. Certainly the three "street extortionists" in
Madrid had not.

Martha and Aideen walked in silence toward the
towering white columns of the Palacio de las Cortes.
Built in 1842, the palace was the seat of the Congreso
de los Diputados; along with the Senado, the Senate,
it comprised the two houses of the Spanish parliament.
Though the sun had set, spotlights illuminated two
larger-than-life bronze lions. Each lion rested a paw
atop a cannonball. The statues had been cast using

guns taken from the enemies of Spain. They flanked the stone steps that led to a high metal door, a door used only for ceremonies. To the left of the main entrance was a very tall iron fence, which was spiked along the top. Beside the fence gate stood a small guardhouse with bulletproof windows. This was where the deputies entered the halls of parliament.

Neither woman spoke as they walked past the imposing granite facade of the palace. Though Aideen had only worked at Op-Center a short while, she knew that in spirit her boss was already at the meeting. Martha was quietly reviewing things she'd want to say to Serrador. Aideen's own role was to draw on her experience with Mexican insurrectionists and her knowledge of the Spanish language to make sure nothing was misstated or misinterpreted.

If only we'd had a little more time to prepare, Aideen thought as they walked around snapping pictures, acting like tourists as they slowly made their way to the gate. Op-Center had barely had time to catch its breath from the hostage situation in the Bekaa Valley when this matter had been relayed to them from the U.S. Embassy in Madrid. Relayed so quietly that only Deputy Serrador, Ambassador Neville, President Michael Lawrence and his closest advisors, and the top people at Op-Center knew about it. And they would keep quiet. If Deputy Serrador were correct, tens of thousands of lives were at risk.

A church bell rang in the distance. To Aideen, it somehow sounded *holier* in Spain than it did in Washington. She counted out the tolls. It was six o'clock. Martha and Aideen made their way to the guardhouse.

Nosotros aqui para un viaje todo comprendido, Aideen said through the grate in the glass. "We're here for a tour." Completing the picture of the excited tourist, she added that a mutual friend had arranged for a private tour of the building.

The young guard, tall and unsmiling, asked for their names.

Señorita Temblón y Señorita Serafico, Aideen replied, giving him their cover identities. Before leaving Washington Aideen had worked these out with Serrador's office. Everything, from the airplane tickets to the hotel reservations, was in those names.

The guard turned and checked a list on a clipboard. As he did, Aideen looked around. There was a courtyard behind the fence, the sky a beautiful blue-black above it. At the rear of the courtyard was a small stone building where auxiliary governmental services were located. Behind that was a new glass-covered building, which housed the offices of the deputies. It was an impressive complex that reminded Aideen just how far the Spanish had come since the death in 1975 of El Caudillo, "the leader," Francisco Franco. The nation was now a constitutional monarchy, with a prime minister and a largely titular king. The Palacio de las Cortes itself spoke very eloquently of one of the trying times in Spain's past. There were bullet holes in the ceiling of the Chamber of Sessions, a remnant and graphic reminder of a right-wing coup attempt in 1981. The palace had been the site of other attacks, most notably in 1874 when President Emilio Castelar lost a vote of confidence and soldiers opened fire in the hallways.

Spain's strife had been mostly internal in this century, and the nation had remained neutral during World War II. As a result, the world had paid relatively little attention to its problems and politics. But when Aideen was studying languages in college her Spanish professor, Señor Armesto, had told her that Spain was a nation on the verge of disaster.

Where there are three Spaniards there are four opinions, he had said. *When world events favor the impatient and disaffected, those opinions will be heard loudly and violently.*

Señor Armesto was correct. Fractionalization was the trend in politics, from the breakup of the Soviet Union and Yugoslavia to the secessionist movement in Quebec to the rising ethnocentrism in the United States. Spain was hardly immune. If Deputy Serrador's fears were correct—and Op-Center's intelligence had corroborated it—the nation was poised to suffer its worst strife in a thousand years. As Intelligence Chief Bob Herbert had put it before Martha left Washington, "This will make the Spanish Civil War look like a brawl."

The guard put his list down. "*Un momento,*" he said, and picked up the red telephone on the console in the back of the booth. He punched in a number and cleared his throat.

As the sentry spoke to a secretary on the other end, Aideen turned. She looked toward the broad avenue, which was packed with traffic—*la hora de aplastar,* or "crush hour," as they called it here. The bright lights of the slow-moving cars were blinding in the dark twilight. They seemed to pop on and off as pedestrians scurried past. Occasionally, a flashbulb would fire as a tourist stopped to take a picture of the palace.

Aideen was blinking off the effects of one such flash when a young man who had just taken a picture put his camera in the pocket of his denim jacket. He turned toward the booth. She couldn't see him clearly beneath the brim of his baseball cap, but she felt his eyes on her.

A street extortionist posing as a tourist? she wondered impertinently as the man ambled toward her. Aideen decided to let Martha handle this one and she started to turn away. As she did, Aideen noticed a car pulling up to the curb behind the man. The black sedan didn't so much arrive as edge forward, as though it had been waiting down the block. Aideen stopped turning. The world around her suddenly seemed to be moving in slow motion. She watched as the young man pulled what looked like a pistol from inside his jacket.

Aideen experienced a moment of paralytic disbelief. It passed quickly as her training took over.

"Fusilar!" she shouted. "Gunman!"

Martha turned toward her as the gun jerked with booming cracks and dull flares. Martha was thrown against the booth and then dropped to her side as Aideen jumped in the opposite direction. Her thinking was to draw the man's fire away from Martha. She succeeded. As Aideen dove for the pavement, a startled young mailman who was walking in front of her stopped, stared, and took a bullet in his left thigh. As his leg folded and he pitched forward, a second bullet

hit his side. He landed on his back and Aideen
dropped flat beside him. She lay as low as she could
and as close to him as she could as he writhed in
agony. As bright blood pumped from his side, she
reached over and pressed her palm to the wound. She
hoped that pressure would help stanch the bleeding.

Aideen lay there, listening. The popping had
stopped and she raised her head carefully. As she
watched, the car pulled from the curb. When people
began to scream in the distance, Aideen rose slowly.
She kept up pressure on the man's wound as she got
on her knees.

"*Ayuda!*" she yelled to a security guard who had
run up to the gate at the Congress of Deputies.
"Help!"

The man unlocked the gate and rushed over. Aideen
told him to keep pressure on the wound. He did as he
was told and Aideen rose. She looked back at the
booth. The sentry was crouched there, shouting into
the phone for assistance. There were people across the
street and in the road. The only ones left in front of
the palace were Aideen, the man beside her, the
guard—and Martha.

Aideen looked at her boss in the growing darkness.
Passing cars slowed and stopped, their lights illumi-
nating the still, awful scene. Martha was lying on her
side, facing the booth. Thick puddles of blood were
forming on the pavement beneath and behind her
body.

"Oh, Jesus," Aideen choked.

The young woman tried to rise but her legs
wouldn't support her. She crawled quickly toward the

booth and knelt beside Martha. She bent over her and looked down at the handsome face. It was utterly still.

''Martha?'' she said softly.

Martha didn't respond. People began to gather tentatively behind the two women.

''Martha?'' Aideen said more insistently.

Martha didn't move. Aideen heard the sound of running feet inside the courtyard. Then she heard muted voices shouting for people to clear the area. Aideen's ears were cottony from the shots. Hesitantly, she touched Martha's cheek with the tips of two fingers. Martha did not respond. Slowly, as though she were moving in a dream, Aideen extended her index finger. She held it under Martha's nose, close to her nostrils. There was no breath.

''God, oh God,'' Aideen was muttering. She gently touched Martha's eyelid. It didn't react and, after a moment, she withdrew her hand. Then she sat back on her heels and stared down at the motionless figure. Sounds became louder as her ears cleared. The world seemed to return to normal motion.

Fifteen minutes ago Aideen was silently cursing this woman. Martha had been caught up in something that had seemed so important—so very damned important. Moments always seemed important until tragedy put them in perspective. Or maybe they *were* important because inevitably there would be no more. Not that it mattered now. Whether Martha had been right or wrong, good or bad, a visionary or a control freak, she was dead. Her moments were over.

The courtyard gate flew open and men ran from behind it. They gathered around Aideen, who was staring vacantly at Martha. The young woman touched Martha's thick, black hair.

"I'm sorry," Aideen said. She exhaled tremulously and shut her eyes. "I'm so very, very sorry."

The woman's limbs felt heavy and she was sick that the reflexes that had been so quick with those street kids had failed her completely here. Intellectually, Aideen knew that she wasn't to blame. During her week-long orientation when she first joined Op-Center, staff psychologist Liz Gordon had warned Aideen and two other new employees that if and when it happened, unexpectedly facing a weapon for the first time could be devastating. A gun or a knife pulled in familiar surroundings destroys the delusion that we're invincible doing what we do routinely every day—in this case, walking down a city street. Liz had told the small group that in the instant of shock, a person's body temperature, blood pressure, and muscle tone all crash and it takes a moment for the survival instinct to kick in. *Attackers count on that instant of paralysis,* Liz had said.

But understanding what had happened didn't help. Not at all. It didn't lessen the ache and the guilt that Aideen felt. If she'd moved an instant sooner or been a little more heads-up—by just a heartbeat, that's all it would have taken—Martha might have survived.

How do you live with that guilt? Aideen asked herself as tears began to form.

She didn't know. She'd never been able to deal with coming up short. She couldn't handle it when she found her widower father crying at the kitchen table after losing his job in the Boston shoe factory where he'd worked since he was a boy. For days thereafter she tried to get him to talk, but he turned to scotch instead. She went off to college not long afterward, feeling as though she'd failed him. She couldn't handle the sense of failure when her college sweetheart, her greatest love, smiled warmly at an old girlfriend in their senior year. He left Aideen a week later and she joined the army after graduation. She hadn't even attended the graduation ceremony; it would have killed her to see him.

Now she'd failed Martha. Her shoulders heaved out the tears and the tears became sobs.

A young, mustachioed sergeant of the palace security guard raised her gently by the shoulders. He helped her stand.

"Are you all right?" he asked in English.

She nodded and tried to stop crying. "I think I'm okay."

"Do you want a doctor?"

She shook her head.

"Are you sure, *señorita*?"

Aideen took a long, deep breath. This was not the time and place to lose it. She would have to talk to Op-Center's FBI liaison, Darrell McCaskey. He had remained at the hotel to await a visit from a colleague with Interpol. And she still wanted to see Deputy Serrador. If this shooting had been designed to prevent the meeting, she'd be damned if she was going to let that happen.

"I'll be fine," Aideen said. "Do you—do you have the person who did this? Do you have any idea who it was?"

"No, *señorita*," he replied. "We'll have to take a look and see what the surveillance cameras may have recorded. In the meantime, are you well enough to talk to us about this?"

"Yes, of course," she said uncertainly. There was still the mission, the reason she'd come. She didn't know how much she should tell the police about that. "But—*por favor?*"

"*Sí?*"

"We were to be met by someone inside. I would still like to see him as soon as possible."

"I will make the necessary inquiries—"

"I also need to contact someone at the Princesa Plaza," Aideen said.

"I will see to those things," he said. "But Comisario Fernandez will be arriving presently. He is the one who will be conducting the investigation. The longer we wait, the more difficult the pursuit."

"Of course," she said. "I understand. I'll talk to him and meet with our guide after. Is there a telephone I can use?"

"I will arrange for the telephone," the sergeant said. "Then I will personally go and see who was to meet you."

Aideen thanked him and rose under her own power. She faltered. The sergeant grabbed one of her arms.

"Are you sure you wouldn't like to see the doctor first?" the man asked. "There is one in residence."

"*Gracias, no,*" she said with a grateful smile. She wasn't going to let the attacker claim a second victim. She was going to get through this, even if it were one second at a time.

The sergeant smiled back warmly and walked with her slowly toward the open gate.

As Aideen was being led away the palace doctor rushed by. A few moments later she heard an ambulance. The young woman half turned as the ambulance stopped right where the getaway car had been. As the medical technicians hurriedly unloaded a gurney, Aideen saw the doctor rise from beside Martha's body. He'd only been there a moment. He said something to a guard then ran over to the mailman. He began opening the buttons of the man's uniform then yelled for the paramedics to come over. As he did, the guard lay his jacket over Martha's head.

Aideen looked ahead. That was it, then. It took just a few seconds, and everything Martha Mackall had known, planned, felt, and hoped was gone. Nothing would ever bring that back.

The young woman continued to hold back tears as she was led into a small office along the palace's ornate main corridor. The room was wood-paneled and comfortable and she lowered herself into a leather couch beside the door. She felt achy where her knees and elbows had hit the pavement and she was still in an acute state of disbelief. But a countershock reflex was going to work, replenishing the physical resources that had shut down in the attack. And she knew that Darrell and General Rodgers and Director Paul Hood and the rest of the Op-Center team were behind her. She might be by herself at the moment, but she was not alone.

"You may use that telephone," the sergeant said,

pointing to an antique rotary phone on a glass end table. "Dial zero for an outside line."

"Thank you."

"I will have a guard posted at the door so you will be safe and undisturbed. Then I will go and see about your guide."

Aideen thanked him again. He left and shut the door behind him. The room was quiet save for the hissing of a radiator in the back and the muted sounds of traffic. Of life going on.

Taking another deep breath, Aideen removed a hotel notepad from her backpack and looked down at the telephone number printed on the bottom. She found it impossible to believe that Martha was dead. She could still feel her annoyance, see her eyes, smell her perfume. She could still hear Martha saying, *You know what's at stake here.*

Aideen swallowed hard and entered the number. She asked to be connected with Darrell McCaskey's room. She slipped a simple scrambler over the mouthpiece, one that would send an ultrasonic screech over the line, deafening any taps. A filter on McCaskey's end would eliminate the sound from his line.

Aideen did know what was at stake here. The fate of Spain, of Europe, and possibly the world. And whatever it took, she did not intend to come up short again.

TWO

Monday, 12:12 P.M.
Washington, D.C.

When they were at Op-Center headquarters at Andrews Air Force Base in Maryland or at Striker's Base in the FBI Academy in Quantico, Virginia, the two forty-five-year-old men were Op-Center's Deputy Director, General Michael Bernard Rodgers, and Colonel Brett Van Buren August, commander of Op-Center's rapid-deployment force.

But here in Ma Ma Buddha, a small, divey Szechuan restaurant in Washington's Chinatown, the two men were not superior and subordinate. They were close friends who had both been born at St. Francis Hospital in Hartford, Connecticut; who had met in kindergarten and shared a passion for building model airplanes; who had played on the same Thurston's Apparel Store Little League team for five years—and chased home run queen Laurette DelGuercio on the field and off; and who had blown trumpet in the Housatonic Valley Marching Band for four years. They served in different branches of the military in Vietnam—Rodgers in the U.S. Army Special Forces, August in Air Force Intelligence—and saw each other infrequently over the next twenty years. Rodgers did two tours of Southeast Asia, after which he was sent to Fort Bragg, North Carolina, to help Colonel "Chargin' Charlie" Beckwith oversee the training of the U.S. Army's 1st Special Forces Operational Detachment—the Delta Force. Rodgers remained there until the Persian Gulf War, where he commanded a mechanized brigade with such Pattonesque fervor that he was well on his way to Baghdad while his backup was still in Southern Iraq. His zeal earned him a promotion—and a desk job at Op-Center.

August had flown eighty-seven F-4 spy missions over North Vietnam during a two-year period before being shot down near Hue. He spent a year as a prisoner of war before escaping and making his way to the south. After recovering in Germany from exhaustion and exposure, August returned to Vietnam. He organized a spy network to search for other U.S. POWs and then remained undercover for a year after the United States withdrawal. At the request of the Pentagon, August spent the next three years in the Philippines helping President Ferdinand Marcos battle Moro secessionists. He disliked Marcos and his repressionist policies, but the U.S. government supported him and so August stayed. Looking for a little desk-bound downtime after the fall of the Marcos regime, August went to work as an Air Force liaison with NASA, helping to organize security for spy satellite missions, after which he joined the SOC as a specialist in counter-terrorist activities. When Striker commander Lt. Colonel W. Charles Squires was killed on a mission in Russia, Rodgers immediately contacted Colonel August and offered him the commission.

August accepted, and the two easily resumed their close friendship.

The two men had come to Ma Ma Buddha after spending the morning discussing a proposed new International Strike Force Division for Op-Center. The idea for the group had been conceived by Rodgers and Paul Hood. Unlike the elite, covert Striker, the ISFD unit would be a small black-ops unit comprised of U.S. commanders and foreign operatives. Personnel such as Falah Shibli of the Sayeret Ha'Druzim, Israel's Druze Reconnaissance unit, who had helped Striker rescue the Regional OpCenter and its crew in the Bekaa Valley. The ISFD would be designed to undertake covert missions in potential international trouble spots. General Rodgers had been quiet but attentive for most of the meeting, which was also attended by Intelligence Chief Bob Herbert, his colleagues Naval Intelligence Chief Donald Breen and Army Intelligence head Phil Prince, and August's friend Air Force Intelligence legend Pete Robinson.

Now Rodgers was simply quiet. He was poking his chopsticks at a plate of salt-fried string beans. His rugged face was drawn beneath the close-cropped salt-and-pepper hair and his eyes were downturned. Both men had recently returned from Lebanon. Rodgers and a small party of soldiers and civilians had been field testing the new Regional Op-Center when they were captured and tortured by Kurdish extremists. With the help of an Israeli operative, August and Striker were able to go into the Bekaa Valley and get them out. When their ordeal was over and an attempt to start a war between Turkey and Syria had been averted, General Rodgers had drawn his pistol and executed the Kurdish leader out of hand. On the flight back to the United States, August had prevented a distraught General Rodgers from turning the handgun on himself.

August was using a fork to twirl up his pork lo mein. After watching the prison guards eat while he starved in Vietnam, if he never saw a chopstick again it would be too soon. As he ate, his blue eyes were on his companion. August understood the effects of combat and captivity, and he knew only too well what torture could do to the mind, let alone the body. He didn't expect Rodgers to recover quickly. Some people never recovered at all. When the depth of their dehumanization became apparent—both in terms of what had been done to them and what they may have been forced to do—many former hostages took their own lives. Liz Gordon had put it very well in a paper she'd published in the *International Amnesty Journal*: *A hostage is someone who has gone from walking to crawling. To walk again, to face even simple risks or routine authority figures, is often more difficult than lying down and giving up.*

August picked up the metal teapot. "Want some?"

"Yes, please."

August kept an eye on his friend as he turned the two cups rightside up. He filled them and then set the pot down. Then he stirred a half packet of sugar into his own cup, raised it, and sipped. He continued to stare at Rodgers through the steam. The general didn't look up.

"Mike?"

"Yeah."

"This is no good."

Rodgers raised his eyes. "What? The lo mein?"

August was caught off guard. He grinned. "Well, that's a start. First joke you've made since—when? The twelfth grade?"

"Something like that," Rodgers said sullenly. He idly picked up his cup and took a sip of tea. He held the cup by his lips and stared down into it. "What's there been to laugh about since then?"

"Plenty, I'd say."

"Like what?"

"How about weekend passes with the few friends you've managed to hold on to. A couple of jazz clubs you told me about in New Orleans, New York, Chicago. Some damn fine movies. More than a few nice ladies. You've had some real nice things in your life."

Rodgers put the cup down and shifted his body painfully. The burns he'd suffered during torture at the hands of the Kurds in the Bekaa were a long way from healing, though not so long as the emotional wounds. But he refused to lie on his sofa and rust.

"Those things are all diversions, Brett. I love 'em, but they're solace. Recreation."

"Since when are solace and recreation bad things?"

"Since they've become a *reason* for living instead of the reward for a job well done," Rodgers said.

"Uh oh," August said.

"Uh oh is right," Rodgers replied.

August had sunk a hose into a cesspool and Rodgers had obviously decided to let some of the raw sewage out.

"You want to know why I can't relax?" Rodgers

said. "Because we've become a society that lives for
the weekend, for vacations, for running away from responsibility. We're proud of how much liquor we can
hold, of how many women we can charm our way into
bed with, of how well our sports teams are doing."

"You used to like a lot of those things," August
pointed out. "Especially the women."

"Well, maybe I'm tired of it," Rodgers said. "I
don't want to live like that any more. I want to *do*
things."

"You always have done things," August said.
"And you still found time to enjoy life."

"I guess I didn't realize what a mess the country
was becoming," Rodgers said. "You face an enemy
like world Communism. You put everything into that
fight. Then suddenly you don't have them anymore
and you finally take a good look around. You see that
everything else has gone to hell while you fought your
battle. Values, initiative, compassion, everything. Now
I've decided I want to work harder kicking the asses
of those who don't take pride in what they do."

"All of which is very heartfelt," August said. "It's
also beside the point, Mike. You like classical music,
right?"

Rodgers nodded. "So?"

"I forget which writer it was who said that life
should be like a Beethoven symphony. The loud parts
of the music represent our public deeds. The soft passages suggest our private reflection. I think that most
people have found a good and honest balance between
the two."

Rodgers looked down at his tea. "I don't believe

that. If it were true, we'd be doing better.''

"We've survived a couple of world wars and a nuclear cold war,'' August replied. "For a bunch of territorial carnivores not far removed from the caves, that ain't bad.'' He took a long, slow sip of tea. "Besides, forget about recreation and weekends. What started this all was you making a joke and me approving of it. Humor ain't weakness, pal, and don't start coming down on yourself for it. It's a deterrent, Mike, a necessary counterbalance. When I was a guest of Ho Chi Minh, I stayed relatively sane by telling myself every bad joke I could remember. Knock-knocks. Good news, bad news. Skeleton jokes. You know: 'A skeleton walks into a bar and orders a gin and tonic . . . and a mop.' ''

Rodgers didn't laugh.

"Well,'' August said, "it's amazing how funny that seems when you're strung up by your bleeding goddamn wrists in a mosquito-covered swamp. The point is, it's a bootstrap deal, Mike. You've got to lift yourself out of the muck.''

"That's you,'' Rodgers said. "I get angry. Bitter. I brood.''

"I know. And you let it sit in your gut. You've come up with a third kind of symphonic music: loud passages that you keep inside. You can't possibly think that's good.''

"Good or not,'' Rodgers said, "it comes naturally to me. That's my fuel. It gives me the drive to fix systems that are broken and to get rid of the people who spoil it for the rest of us.''

"And when you can't fix the system or get back at

the bad guys?'' August asked. ''Where does all that high octane go?''

''Nowhere,'' Rodgers said. ''I store it. That's the beauty of it. It's the far eastern idea of *chi*—inner energy. When you need it for the next battle it's right there, ready to tap.''

''Or ready to explode. What do you do when there's so much that you can't keep it in anymore?''

''You burn some of it off,'' Rodgers said. ''That's where recreation comes in. You turn it into physical exertion. You exercise or play squash or call a ladyfriend. There are ways.''

''Pretty lonely ones.''

''They work for me,'' Rodgers said. ''Besides, as long as you keep striking out with the ladies I've got you to dump on.''

''Striking out?'' August grinned. At least Rodgers was talking and it was about something other than misery and the fall of civilization. ''After my long weekend with Barb Mathias I had to take a sabbatical.''

Rodgers smiled. ''I thought I was doing you a favor,'' he said. ''She loved you when we were kids.''

''Yeah, but now she's forty-four and all she wants is sex and security.'' August twirled noodles around his fork and slid them into his mouth. ''Unfortunately, I'm only rich in one of those.''

Rodgers was still smiling when his pager beeped. He twisted to look at it then winced as his bandages pulled at the side.

''Those pagers are made to slip right off your belt,'' August said helpfully.

"Thanks," Rodgers said. "That's how I lost the last one." He glanced down at the number.

"Who wants you?" August asked.

"Bob Herbert," Rodgers said. His brow knit as he took his napkin from his lap. He rose very slowly and dropped it on the chair. "I'll call him from the car."

August leaned back. "I'll stay right here," he said. "I'm told that there are three women to every man in Washington. Maybe one of them will want your plate of cold-growing string beans."

"Good luck," Rodgers told him as he moved quickly through the small, crowded restaurant.

August finished his lo mein, drained his cup, and poured more tea. He drank it slowly as he looked around the dark restaurant. This state of mind Rodgers was in would not be easy to dispel. August had always been the more optimistic of the two. It was true, he couldn't glance at the Vietnam Veterans Memorial or flip past a cable documentary about the war or even pass a Vietnamese restaurant. Not without his eyes tearing or his belly burning or his fists tensing with the desire to hit something. August was usually upbeat and hopeful but he was not entirely forgiving. Still, he didn't hold on to bitterness and disappointment the way Mike did. And the problem here was not so much that society had let Mike down but that Mike had let himself down. He wasn't about to let that go without a serious struggle.

When Rodgers returned, August knew at once that something was wrong. The bandages and pain notwithstanding, the general moved assertively through the crowded restaurant, weaving around waiters and customers instead of waiting for them to move. He did not rush, however. The men were in uniform and both foreign agents and journalists paid close attention to military personnel. If they were called away in a hurry, that told observers which branch and usually which group within that branch was involved in a breaking event.

August rose calmly before Rodgers arrived. He stretched for show and took a last swallow of tea. He dropped a twenty-dollar bill on the table and moved out to greet Rodgers. The men didn't speak until they were outside. The mid-fall air was biting as they walked slowly down the street to the car.

"Tell me more about the good things in life," Rodgers said bitterly. "Martha Mackall was assassinated about a half hour ago."

August felt the tea come back into his throat.

"It happened outside the Palacio de las Cortes in Madrid," Rodgers went on. His voice was clipped and low, his eyes fixed on something in the distance. Even though the enemy was still faceless, Rodgers had found a place to put his anger. "The status of your team is unchanged until we know more," Rodgers went on. "Martha's assistant Aideen Marley is talking to the police. Darrell was in Madrid with her and is heading over to the palace now. He's going to call Paul at fourteen hundred hours with an update."

August's expression hadn't changed, though he felt tea and bile fill his throat. "Any idea who's responsible?"

"None," Rodgers said. "She was traveling incognito. Only a few people even knew she was there."

They got into Rodgers's new Camry. August drove. He started the ignition and nosed into traffic. The men were silent for a moment. August hadn't known Martha very well, but he knew that she was no one's favorite person at Op-Center. She was pushy and arrogant. A bully. She was also damned effective. The team would be much poorer for her loss.

August looked out the windshield at the overcast sky. Upon reaching Op-Center headquarters, Rodgers would go to the executive offices in the basement level while August would be helicoptered over to the FBI Academy in Quantico, Virginia, where Striker was stationed. Striker's status at the moment was neutral. But there were still two Op-Center personnel in Spain. If things got out of hand there they might be called upon to leave in a hurry. Rodgers hadn't told him what Martha was doing in Spain because he obviously didn't want to risk being overheard. Bugging and electronic surveillance of cars belonging to military personnel was not uncommon. But August knew about the tense political situation in Spain. He also knew about Martha's involvement in ethnic issues. And he assumed that she was probably involved in diplomatic efforts to keep the nation's many political and cultural entities from fraying, from becoming involved in a catastrophic and far-reaching power struggle.

He also knew one thing more. Whoever had killed her was probably aware of why she was there. Which raised another question that transcended the shock of the moment: whether this was the first or the last shot in the possible destruction of Spain.

THREE

Monday, 6:45 P.M.
San Sebastián, Spain

Countless pieces of moonglow glittered atop the dark waters of La Concha Bay. The luminous shards were shattered into shimmering dust as the waves struck loudly at Playa de la Concha, the expansive, sensuously curving beach that bordered the elegant, cosmopolitan city. Just over a half mile to the east, fishing vessels and recreational boats rocked in the crowded harbor of *Parte Vieja,* the "old section." Their masts creaked in the firm southerly wind as small waves gently tapped at the hulls. A few stragglers, still hoping for a late-day catch, were only now returning to anchor. Seabirds, active by the score during the day, roosted silently beneath aged wharfs or on the high crags of the towering Isla de Santa Clara near the mouth of the bay.

Beyond the nesting birds and the idle boats, slightly more than a half mile north of the coast of Spain, the sleek white yacht *Verídico* lolled in the moonlit waters. The forty-five-foot vessel carried a complement of four. Dressed entirely in black, one crewman stood watch on deck while another had the helm. A third man was taking his dinner in the curving dining area beside the galley and the fourth was asleep in the forward cabin.

There were also five passengers, all of whom were gathered in the very private midcabin. The door was shut and the heavy drapes were drawn over the two portholes. The passengers, all men, were seated around a large, ivory-colored table. There was a thick, over-sized leather binder in the center of the table and a bottle of vintage Madeira beside it. The dinner plates had all been cleared away and only the near-empty wineglasses remained.

The men were dressed in expensive pastel-colored blazers and large, loose-fitting slacks. They wore jeweled rings and gold or silver necklaces. Their socks were silk and their shoes were handmade and brightly polished. Their haircuts were fresh and short. Their cigars were Cuban and four of them had been burning for quite some time; there were more in a humidor in the center of the table. The men's hands were soft and their expressions were relaxed. When they spoke their voices were soft and warm.

The owner of the *Verídico*, Señor Esteban Ramirez, was also the founder of the Ramirez Boat Company, the firm that had built the yacht. Unlike the other men, he did not smoke. It wasn't because he did not want to but because it was not yet time to celebrate. Nor did he reminisce about how their Catalonian grandparents had raised sheep or grapes or grain in the fertile fields of León. As important as his heritage was, he couldn't think about such things right now. His mind and soul were preoccupied with what should have happened by now. His imagination was consumed with everything that was at stake—much as it had been during the years of dreaming, the months of planning, and the hours of execution.

What was keeping the man?

Ramirez reflected quietly on how, in years gone by, he used to sit in this very room of the yacht and wait for calls from the men he worked with at the American CIA. Or wait to hear from the members of his *"familia,"* a very close and trusted group comprised of his most devoted employees. Sometimes the *familia* henchmen were on a mission to deliver packages or to pick up money or to break the bones of people who didn't see the sense of cooperating with him. Some of those unfortunate people had worked for one or two of the men who sat at this table. But that was in the past, before they were united by a common goal.

Part of Ramirez yearned for those more relaxed days. Days when he was simply an apolitical middleman making a profit from smuggling guns or personnel or learning about covert activities by the Russians or Moslem fundamentalists. Days when he used *familia* muscle to obtain loans that the banks didn't want to give him, or to get trucks to carry goods when no trucks were available.

Things were different now. So very, very different.

Ramirez did not speak until his cellular phone rang. At the beep, he moved unhurriedly and slipped the telephone from the rightside pocket of his blazer. His small, thick fingers trembled slightly as he unfolded the mouthpiece. He placed the telephone to his ear.

After speaking his name he said nothing. He simply listened as he sat looking at the others.

When the caller had finished, Ramirez closed the telephone gingerly and slipped it back into his pocket. He looked down at the clean ashtray in front of him. He selected a cigar from the humidor and smelled the black wrapper. Only then did a smile break the flat smoothness of his soft, round face.

One of the other men took the cigar from his mouth. "What is it, Esteban?" he asked. "What has happened?"

"It is accomplished," he said proudly. "One of the targets, the primary target, has been eliminated."

The tips of the other cigars glowed richly as the four men drew on them. Smiles lit up as well and hands came together in polite but heartfelt applause. Now Ramirez clipped the tip of his cigar into the ashtray. He toasted the tip with a generous flame from the antique butane gas lighter in the center of the table. After rolling the cigar back and forth until the edges glowed red he puffed enthusiastically. Ramirez allowed the smoke to caress his tongue. Then he rolled it around his mouth and exhaled.

"Señor Sanchez is now at the airport in Madrid," Ramirez said. He was using the name the killer had assumed for this mission. "He will reach Bilbao in one hour. I will ring the factory and have one of my *familia* drivers meet him there. And then, as planned, he will be brought out to the yacht."

"For a short stay, I trust," one of the men said anxiously.

"For a very short stay," Ramirez replied. "When

Señor Sanchez arrives I will go on deck and pay him.'' He patted his vest pocket, where he had an envelope stuffed with international currency. ''He will not see anyone else so there is no way he can ever betray you.''

''Why would he?'' asked the man.

''Extortion, Alfonso,'' Ramirez explained. ''Men like Sanchez, former soldiers who have come into money, tend to live lavishly, only for the day. When they run out of money, sometimes they come back and ask for more.''

''And if he does?'' asked Alfonso. ''How will you protect yourself?''

Ramirez smiled. ''One of my men was present with a video camera. If Sanchez betrays me, the tape will find its way into the hands of the police. But enough of what could be. Here is what will be. After Sanchez has been paid he will be escorted back to the airport and will leave the country until the investigation has been closed, as agreed.''

''What of the driver in Madrid?'' asked another of the men. ''Is he leaving Spain as well?''

''No,'' said Ramirez. ''The driver works for Deputy Serrador. He wants very much to rise so he will be silent. And the car used by the killers has already been left at a garage for dismantling.'' Ramirez drew contentedly on his cigar. ''Trust me, my dear Miguel. Everything has been thought out very carefully. This action will not be traced to us.''

''I trust you,'' sniffed the man. ''But I'm still not certain we can trust Serrador. He is a Basque.''

''The killer is also a Basque and he did as he was

instructed," said Ramirez. "Deputy Serrador will also do as he was told, Carlos. He is ambitious."

"Then he is an ambitious Basque. But he is still a Basque."

Ramirez smiled again. "Deputy Serrador does not wish to be a spokesman for the fishermen, shepherds, and miners forever. He wants to lead them."

"He can lead them over the Pyrenees into France," said Carlos. "I won't miss any of them."

"I wouldn't either," said Ramirez, "but then who would fish, herd, and mine? The bank managers and accountants who work for you, Carlos? The reporters who work for Rodrigo's newspapers or Alfonso's television stations? The pilots who work for Miguel's airline?"

The other men smiled, shrugged, or nodded. Carlos flushed and acceded with a gracious nod of his head.

"That's enough about our curious bedfellow," said Ramirez. "The important thing is that America's emissary has been slain. The United States will have no idea who did it or why, but they will be extremely wary about becoming involved in local politics. Deputy Serrador will caution them further when he meets with the rest of the contingent later this evening. He'll assure them that the police are doing everything they can to apprehend the killer, but that the prevention of further incidents cannot be guaranteed. Not in such troubled times."

Carlos nodded. He turned to Miguel. "And how is your part going?"

"Very well," said the portly, silver-haired airline executive. "The discount air fares from the United

States to Portugal, Italy, France, and Greece have proven extremely popular. Travel to Madrid and Barcelona is down eleven and eight percent respectively from the levels of last year. Hotels, restaurants, and car services are feeling the loss. The ripple effect has hurt many local businesses.''

"And revenues will fall even further," Ramirez said, "when the American public is told that the slain woman was a tourist and that this was a random shooting.''

Ramirez drew on his cigar and smiled. He was particularly proud of that part of the plan. The United States government could never expose the identity of the dead woman. She had come from an intelligence and crisis management center, not from the State Department. Nor could the United States reveal the fact that she had gone to Madrid to meet with a powerful deputy who feared a new civil war. If Europe ever learned that an American representative of this type had been scheduled to meet with Serrador, America would be suspected of trying to position the players to its own advantage. Which was exactly why Serrador had asked for her. With one shooting, Ramirez and his group had managed to gain control of both the White House and Spanish tourism.

"As for the next step," Ramirez said, "how is that coming, Carlos?''

The black-haired young banker leaned forward. He placed his cigar in the ashtray and folded his hands on the table. "As you know, the lower and middle classes have been hurt very seriously by the recent employment cutbacks. In the past six months, Banquero Cedro has restricted loans so that our partners in this operation"—he indicated the other men at the table—"as well as other businesspeople, have been forced to raise consumer prices nearly seven percent. At the same time they've cut back production so that there has been an eight-percent drop in trade of Spanish goods throughout Europe. The workers have been hit hard although, thus far, we haven't curtailed their credit. We've been extraordinarily generous, in fact. We've been extending credit to repay old debts. Of course, only some of that money goes to relieve debt. People make new purchases, assuming that credit will be available to them again. As a result, interest on loans has compounded to levels eighteen percent higher than they were at this time last year."

Ramirez smiled. "In conjunction with a fall in tourism, the financial blow will be severe when that credit is not made available."

"It will be extremely severe," said Carlos. "The people will be so deeply in debt they will agree to anything to be out of it."

"But the blow is one you're certain you can control," said Alfonso.

"Absolutely," Carlos replied. "Thanks to cash reserves and credit with the World Bank and other institutions, the money supply at my bank and at most others will remain sound. The economy will be relatively unaffected at the top." He grinned. "It's like the plague of blood which befell Egypt in the Old Testament. It did not affect those who had been forewarned and had filled their jugs and cisterns with fresh water."

Ramirez sat back. He drew long and contentedly on his cigar. "This is excellent, gentlemen. And once everything is in place, our task is simply to maintain the pressure until the middle and lower classes buckle. Until the Basques and the Castilians, the Andalusians and the Galicians acknowledge that Spain belongs to the people of Catalonia. And when they do, when the prime minister is forced to call for new elections, we will be ready." His small, dark eyes moved from face to face before settling on the leather binder before him. "Ready with our new constitution—ready for a new Spain."

The other men nodded their approval. Miguel and Rodrigo applauded lightly. Ramirez felt the weight of history past and history yet to come on his shoulders, and it felt good.

He was unaware of a disheveled man who sat an eighth of a mile away with a different sense of history on his shoulders—and a much different weapon at his disposal.

FOUR

Monday, 7:15 P.M.
Madrid, Spain

Aideen was still sitting in the leather couch when Comisario Diego Fernandez arrived. He was a man of medium height and build. He was clean-shaven with a ruddy complexion and carefully trimmed goatee. His black hair was longish but neat and he peered out carefully from behind gold-rimmed spectacles. He wore black leather gloves, black suede shoes, and a black trenchcoat. Beneath the open coat was a dark gray business suit.

An aide shut the door behind him. When it had clicked shut, the inspector bowed politely to Aideen.

"Our deepest sympathy and apologies for your loss," he said. His voice was deep, the English accent thick. "If there's anything I or my department can do to help you, please ask."

"Thank you, Inspector," Aideen said.

"Be assured that the resources of the entire Madrid metropolitan police department as well as other government offices will be applied to finding whoever was responsible for this atrocious act."

Aideen looked up at the police inspector. He couldn't be talking to her. The police department couldn't be looking for the killer of someone she knew. The TV announcements and newspaper headlines wouldn't be about a person she had been dressing with in a hotel room just an hour before. Though she had lived through the killing and seen Martha's body on the street, the experience didn't seem real. Aideen was so accustomed to changing things—rewinding a tape to see something she'd missed or erasing computer data she didn't need—that the irreversibility of this seemed impossible.

But in her brain Aideen knew that it *had* happened. And that it was irreversible. After being brought here, she'd called the hotel and briefed Darrell McCaskey. McCaskey had said he would inform Op-Center. He'd seemed surprisingly unshocked—or maybe Darrell was always that collected. Aideen didn't know him well enough to say. Then she'd sat here trying to tell herself that the shooting was a random act of terrorism and not a hit. After all, it wasn't the same as in Tijuana two years earlier when her friend Odin Gutierrez Rico had literally been blasted to death by four gunmen with assault rifles. Rico was the director of criminal trials in Baja California. He was a public figure who had regularly received death threats and had continued to defy the nation's drug traffickers. His death was a tragic loss but not a surprise. It was a very public statement that the prosecution of drug dealers would not be tolerated by the underworld.

Martha was here with a cover story known only to a handful of government officials. She had come to Madrid to help Deputy Serrador work out a plan to keep his own people, the Basques, from joining with the equally nationalistic Catalonians in an effort to break away from Spain. The Basque uprisings in the 1980s had been sporadic enough to fail but violent enough to be remembered. Martha and Serrador both believed that an organized revolt by two of the nation's five major ethnic groups—especially if those groups were well armed and better prepared than in the 1980s—would not only be enormously destructive but would have a good chance of succeeding.

If this were an assassination, if Martha had been the target, it meant that there was a leak in the system somewhere. And if there were a leak then the peace process was in serious danger. It was a cruel irony that only a short time before, Martha had been insisting that nothing must be allowed to interfere with the talks.

You know what's at stake. . . .

Then, of course, Martha had been worried about Aideen's overreaction in the street.

If only that had been our worst roadblock, Aideen thought. *We sweat the details and end up missing the big picture—*

"*Señorita?*" the inspector said.

Aideen blinked. "Yes?"

"Are you all right?"

Aideen had been looking past Comisario Fernandez, at the dark windows. But she focused on the inspector now. He was still standing a few feet away, smiling down at her.

"Yes, I'm fine," she said. "I'm very sorry, Inspector. I was thinking about my friend."

"I understand," the inspector replied quietly. "If it

would not be too much for you, might I ask you a few questions?''

"Of course," she replied. She'd been slumping forward but now she sat up in the chair. "First, Inspector, would you mind telling me if the surveillance cameras told you anything?"

"Unfortunately, they did not," the inspector said. "The gunman was standing just out of range."

"He knew what that range was?"

"Apparently, he did," the inspector admitted. "Unfortunately, it will take us a while to find out everyone who had access to that information—and to interrogate them all."

"I understand," Aideen said.

The inspector drew a small, yellow notebook from his coat pocket. The smile faded as he studied some notes and slipped a pen from the spiral binder. When he was finished reading he looked at Aideen.

"Did you and your companion come to Madrid for pleasure?" the inspector asked.

"Yes. Yes, we did."

"You informed the guard at the gate that you came to the Congreso de los Diputados for a personal tour."

"That's right."

"This tour was arranged by whom?"

"I don't know," said Aideen.

"Oh?"

"My companion set it up through a friend back in the States," Aideen informed him.

"Would you be able to provide me with the name of this friend?" the inspector asked.

"I'm afraid not," Aideen replied. "I don't know

who it was. My coming on this trip was rather last-minute."

"Possibly it was a coworker who arranged it," he suggested. "Or else a neighbor? A local politician?"

"I don't know," Aideen insisted. "I'm sorry, Inspector, but it wasn't something I thought I'd need to know."

The inspector stared at her for a long moment. Then he lowered his eyes slowly and wrote her answers in his notebook.

Aideen didn't think that he believed her; that was what she got from the disapproving turn of his mouth and the stern knot of flesh between his eyebrows. And she hated stonewalling the investigation. But until she heard otherwise from Darrell McCaskey or Deputy Serrador, she had no choice but to continue to play this by the cover story.

Comisario Fernandez turned slowly and thoughtfully to a fresh page of the notebook. "Did you see the man who attacked you?"

"I didn't see his face," she said. "He fired a flash picture just before he reached for his weapon."

"Did you smell any cologne? Aftershave?"

"No."

"Did you notice the camera? The make?"

"No," she said. "I wasn't close enough—and then there was the flash. I only saw his clothes."

"Aha," he said. He stepped forward eagerly. "Can you tell me what they looked like?"

Aideen took a long breath. She shut her eyes. "He was wearing a tight denim jacket and a baseball cap. A dark blue or black cap, worn with the brim in front.

He had on loose khaki trousers and black shoes. I want to say that he was a young man, though I can't be entirely certain.''

"What gave you that impression?"

Aideen opened her eyes. "There was something about the way he stood," she replied. "His feet planted wide, his shoulders squared, his head held erect. Very strong, very poised."

"You've seen this look before?" the inspector asked.

"Yes," Aideen replied. The killer had reminded her of a Striker, though of course she couldn't say that. "Where I went to college there was ROTC," she lied. "Reserve Officers' Training Corps. The killer had the bearing of a soldier. Or at least someone who was skilled in handling firearms."

The inspector made an entry in his notebook. "Did the gunman say anything to you?"

"No."

"Did he shout anything—a slogan or a threat?"

"No."

"Did you notice the kind of weapon he used?"

"I'm sorry, I did not. It was a handgun of some kind."

"A revolver?"

"I wouldn't know," she lied. It was an automatic. But she didn't want the inspector to know that she knew enough to tell the difference.

"Did he pause between shots?"

"I believe so."

"Was it loud?"

"Not very," Aideen said. "It was surprisingly

quiet.'' The gun had been silenced but she didn't want to let him know that she knew that.

"It was probably silenced," the inspector said. "Did you see the getaway car?"

"Yes," Aideen said. "It was a black sedan. I don't know what kind."

"Was it clean or dirty?"

"Average."

"Where did it come from?" the inspector asked.

"I believe it was waiting for the killer down the street," Aideen said.

"About how far?"

"Maybe twenty or thirty yards," Aideen said. "It seemed to creep up along the curb a few seconds before the man opened fire."

"Did any of the shots come from the car?"

"I don't think so," she replied. "The only flashes I saw came from the one gun."

"You were behind the other victim, the postman, for part of the attack. You were very conscientiously attending to his wound. You might have missed a second gunman."

"I don't think so," she said. "I was only behind him at the very end. Tell me—how is the gentleman? Will he recover?"

"Sadly, *señorita*, he has died."

Aideen glanced down. "I'm sorry."

"You did everything you could to help him," the inspector said. "There is nothing you should regret."

"Nothing," she muttered, "except moving in that direction. Did he have a family?"

"Sí," said the inspector. "Señor Suarez supported a wife, a baby son, and a mother."

Aideen felt her temples grow tight as fresh tears formed behind her eyes. Not only had she failed to do anything to help Martha, but her instincts to draw the gunman's fire had cost an innocent man his life. In retrospect, she should have jumped toward Martha. Maybe she could have put her body between the gunman and Martha or tried to pull the wounded woman behind the goddamn sentry booth. She should have done anything but what she'd done.

"Would you like a glass of water?" the inspector asked.

"Thank you, no. I'm all right."

The inspector nodded. He paced for a moment, staring at the floor, before looking back at Aideen. *"Señorita,"* he said, "do you believe that you and your companion were the gunman's targets?"

"I believe we were," she replied. She had expected the question and now she wanted to be very careful about how she answered it.

"Do you know why?" he asked.

"No," she said.

"Have you any suspicions? Are you involved in any kind of political activity? Do you belong to any groups?"

She shook her head.

There was a knock on the door. The inspector ignored it. He regarded Aideen harshly and in silence.

"Señorita Temblón," he said, "Forgive me for pressing you at this time, but a killer is free in the streets of my city. I want him. Can you think of no reason that someone would want to attack you or your friend?''

"*Comisario,*" she replied, "I have never been to Spain nor do I know anyone here. My companion was here years ago but she has—she *had*—no friends or enemies that I know of."

There was a second knock. The inspector went to the door and opened it. Aideen couldn't see who was standing outside.

"*Sí?*" the inspector asked.

"*Comisario,*" said a man, "Deputy Serrador wishes for the woman to be brought to his office at once."

"Does he?" the inspector asked. He turned and looked at Aideen. His eyes narrowed slightly. "Perhaps, *señorita*, the deputy wishes to apologize in person for this terrible tragedy."

Aideen said nothing.

"Or perhaps there is some other reason for the audience?" the inspector suggested.

Aideen rose. "If there is, Comisario Fernandez, I won't know that until I see him."

The inspector folded away his notebook and bowed courteously. If he were annoyed with her he didn't show it. He thanked Aideen for her assistance, apologized again for what had happened, then extended an arm toward the open door. Aideen left the room. The sergeant who had brought her inside was waiting. He greeted her with a bow and they walked down the corridor together.

Aideen felt bad for the inspector. He had an investigation to oversee and she hadn't given him anything to go on. But as Martha had pointed out, there were rules for every society and for every stratum of that society. And whatever the country, despite the constitutions and the checks and balances, the rules were always different for government. Phrases like "need-to-know" and "state secrets" effectively shut out otherwise legal inquiries. Unfortunately, in many instances—this one among them—the obstructions were necessary and legitimate.

Deputy Serrador's office was located a short walk down the corridor. The office was the same size and had largely the same decor as the room Aideen had just left, though there were a number of personal touches. On three walls were framed posters of the bullring of Madrid, the Plaza de las Ventas. On the fourth wall, behind the desk, were framed newspaper front pages describing Basque activities during the 1980s. Family photographs were displayed on shelves around the room.

Deputy Serrador was seated behind the desk when Aideen entered. Darrell McCaskey was sitting on the sofa. Both men rose when she entered. Serrador walked grandly from behind the desk, his arms outstretched and a look of deep sympathy on his face. His brown eyes were pained under his gray eyebrows. His high, dark forehead was creased beneath his slicked-back white hair and his wide mouth was downturned. His soft, large hands closed gently around Aideen's.

"Ms. Marley, I am so, so sorry," he said. "Yet in my grief I am also relieved that you are unharmed."

"Thank you, Mr. Deputy," Aideen said. She looked at McCaskey. The short, wiry, prematurely gray Deputy Assistant Director was standing stiffly, his hands folded in front of his groin. He was not wearing the kind of diplomatic sympathy that was all over Serrador: his expression was grave and tight. "Darrell," she said. "How are you?"

"I've been better, Aideen. You all right?"

"Not really," she said. "I blew it, Darrell."

"What do you mean?"

"I should have reacted . . . differently," Aideen said. Emotion caused her to choke. "I saw what was happening and I blew it, Darrell. I just blew it."

"That's insane," McCaskey said. "You're lucky you were able to get out of the way at all."

"At the expense of another man's life—"

"That was unavoidable," McCaskey said.

"Mr. McCaskey is correct," Serrador said. He was still holding her hands within his. "You mustn't do this to yourself. These things are always much clearer in—what do you call it? Hindsight."

"That's what we call it," McCaskey said with barely concealed irritation. "Everything is always much clearer after the fact."

Aideen gave McCaskey a questioning look. "Darrell, what's wrong?"

"Nothing. Nothing except that Deputy Serrador is disinclined to hold any discussions at the moment."

"What?" Aideen said.

"It would be most inappropriate," Serrador stated.

"We don't agree," McCaskey replied. He looked at Aideen. "Deputy Serrador says that the arrangement was made with Martha. That it was her experience and her ethnic background that enabled him to convince the Basques and Catalonians to consider possible U.S. mediation.''

Aideen regarded Serrador. "Martha was a respected and highly skilled diplomat—"

"A remarkable woman," Serrador said with a flourish.

"Yes, but as gifted a negotiator as Martha was, she was not indispensible," Aideen went on.

Serrador stepped back. His expression was disapproving. "You disappoint me, *señorita.*"

"Do I?"

"Your colleague has just been murdered!"

"I'm sorry, Mr. Deputy," Aideen said, "but the issue is not my sense of occasion—"

"That is true," said Serrador. "The issues are experience and security. And until I'm convinced that we have both, the talks *will* be postponed. Not canceled, Señor McCaskey, Señorita Marley. Merely delayed."

"Deputy Serrador," McCaskey said, "you know as well as I that there may not be time for a delay. Before Ms. Marley arrived I was telling you about her credentials, trying to convince you that the talks can go ahead. Ms. Marley has experience and she isn't timid, you can see that."

Serrador looked disapprovingly at the woman.

"We *can* carry on," McCaskey said. "As for security, let's assume for the moment that word of this meeting did get out. That Martha was the target of an assassination. What does that mean? That someone wants to scare away American diplomats. They want to see your nation come apart."

"Perhaps the goal isn't even a political one," Aideen said. "Martha thinks—Martha *thought* that perhaps someone is hoping to make money on an armed secession."

Serrador cleared his throat. He looked away at his desk.

"Mr. Deputy, please," McCaskey said. "Sit down with us. Tell us what you know. We'll take the information back with us and help you put a plan in place before it's too late."

Serrador shook his head slowly. "I have already spoken with my allies in the Congress. They are even more unwilling than I am to involve you now. You must understand, Señor McCaskey. We were talking with the various separatist parties before this—and we will do so again. It was my personal hope that if the United States could be brought into the discussions unofficially, and the leaders of both sides could be persuaded to make concessions, Spain could be saved. Now I'm afraid we'll have to try and solve the problem internally."

"And how do you think that will end?" Aideen demanded.

"I don't know," Serrador replied. "I only know, regrettably, how your association with this process must end."

"Yes," she said. "Thanks to the death of one who was brave enough to lead . . . and the retreat of one who wasn't."

"Aideen!" McCaskey said.

Serrador held up a hand. "It's all right, Señor

McCaskey. Señorita Marley is overwrought. I suggest you take her back to the hotel."

Aideen glared at the deputy. She wasn't going to be bullied into silence and she wasn't going to do an end run. She just wasn't.

"Fine," she said. "Play it cautiously, Mr. Deputy. But don't forget this. When I dealt with revolutionary factions in Mexico the results were always the same. The government inevitably relied on muscle to crush the rebels. But it was never enough to destroy them completely, of course, and the insurrectionists went underground. They didn't flourish but they didn't die. Only people who were caught in the crossfire died. And that's what's going to happen here, Deputy Serrador. You can't tamp down centuries of resentment without a very big boot."

"Ah. You have a crystal ball?"

"No," she replied sharply. "Just some experience in the psychology of oppression."

"In Mexico," Serrador pointed out. "Not in Spain. You'll find that the people are not just—what do you call them? Haves and have-nots. They are also passionate about their heritage."

"Aideen," McCaskey said, his voice stern, edgy. "That's enough. No one knows what's going to happen anywhere. That's what these meetings were supposed to be about. They were supposed to be fact-finding, sharing ideas, a chance to find a peaceful resolution to the tensions."

"And we may yet have those explorations," Serrador said, once again the diplomat. "I mean no disrespect to the loss of your colleague but we've lost just one opportunity. There will be other ways to avoid spilling blood. Our immediate concern is to find out who was responsible for this crime and how the information got out of my office. Then—we will see.''

''That could take weeks, months,'' McCaskey said.

''While haste, Señor McCaskey, may cost us more lives.''

''I'm willing to take that risk,'' Aideen muttered. ''The cost of retreat and inactivity may be much higher.''

Serrador walked behind the desk. ''Prudence is neither of those.'' He pressed a button on the telephone. ''I sought the help of the distinguished Señorita Mackall. She has been taken from us. I sought and may still seek the help of the United States. Is that still available, Señor McCaskey, should I call on it?''

''You know it is, Mr. Deputy,'' McCaskey answered.

Serrador dipped his head. *''Gracias.''*

''De nada,'' McCaskey replied.

The door opened. A young aide in a dark suit took a step into the office. He stood with his arms stiffly at his sides.

''Hernandez,'' said the deputy, ''please take our guests out through the private entrance and tell my driver to see that they get safely back to their hotel.'' He looked at McCaskey. ''That is where you wish to go?''

''For the moment, yes. If possible, I'd like to go wherever the investigation is being handled.''

''I see. You have a background in law enforcement, I recall.''

"That's right," said McCaskey. "I spent a lot of time working with Interpol when I was at the FBI."

Serrador nodded. "I'll look into it, of course. Is there anything else I can do for either of you?"

McCaskey shook his head. Aideen did not move. She was seething. Again, politics. Not leadership, not vision. Just a cautious "T-step," as they used to call a little dance move back in Boston. She wished she'd saved some of the *mierda de perro* for this meeting.

"My automobile is bulletproof and two of the guards will accompany you," Serrador said. "You will be safe. In the meantime, I will speak with those of my colleagues who were scheduled to participate in today's meeting. I will contact you in a few days—in Washington, I imagine?—to let you know how and if we wish to proceed."

"Of course," McCaskey replied.

"Thank you." Serrador smiled thinly. "Thank you very much."

The deputy extended his hand across the large mahogany desk. McCaskey shook it. Serrador swung his hand toward Aideen. She shook it as well, very briefly. There was no warmth in the short look they exchanged.

McCaskey had eased his hand onto Aideen's back. He half-guided, half-pushed her out the door and they walked the corridor in silence.

When they were inside the deputy's limousine, McCaskey turned to Aideen. "So."

"So. Go ahead. Tell me I was out of line."

"You were."

"I know," she replied. "I'm sorry. I'll take the next

plane home.'' This was becoming the theme of the
day. Or maybe it was something larger, the wrong fit
of Aideen Marley and ivory tower diplomacy.

''I don't want you to do that,'' McCaskey said.
''You were out of line but I happen to agree with what
you were saying. I don't think our accidental good-
cop, bad-cop routine worked, but it's got potential.''

She looked at him. ''You agreed with me?''

''Pretty much. Let's wait until we can call home
and see what the rest of the clan has to say,''
McCaskey continued.

Aideen nodded. She knew that that was only part
of the reason McCaskey didn't want to talk. Limousine
drivers were never as invisible as passengers pre-
sumed: they saw and heard everything. And putting
up the partition wouldn't guarantee privacy. Chances
were good that the car was bugged and their conversation was being monitored. They waited until they
had returned to McCaskey's hotel room before continuing. He'd set up a small electromagnetic generator
designed by Matt Stoll, Op-Center's technical wizard.
The unit, approximately the size and dimensions of a
portable CD player, sent out a pulse that disrupted
electronic signals within a ten-foot radius and turned
them to ''gibberish,'' as Stoll described it. Computers,
recorders, or other digital devices outside its range
would be unaffected.

McCaskey and Aideen sat on the side of the bed
with the Egg, as they'd nicknamed it, between them.

''Deputy Serrador thinks that there isn't much we
can do without cooperation on this end,'' McCaskey
said.

"Does he," Aideen said bitterly.

"We may be able to surprise him."

"It might also be *necessary* to surprise him," Aideen said.

"That's true," McCaskey said. He looked at Aideen. "Anything else before I call the boss?"

Aideen shook her head, though that wasn't entirely true. There was a great deal she wanted to say. One thing Aideen's experiences in Mexico had taught her was to recognize when things weren't right. And something wasn't right here. The thing that had pushed her buttons back in the deputy's office wasn't just the emotional aftermath of Martha's death. It was Serrador's rapid retreat from cooperation to what amounted to obstruction. If Martha's death were an assassination—and her gut told her that it was—was Serrador afraid that they'd target him next? If so, why didn't he take on extra security? Why were the halls leading to his office so empty? And why did he assume—as clearly he did—that simply by calling off the talks word would get back to whoever did this? How could he be so certain that the information would get leaked?

McCaskey rose and went to the phone, which was outside the pulse-radius. As Aideen listened to the quiet hum of the Egg, she looked through the twelfth-floor window at the streetlights off in the distance. Her spirit was too depleted, her emotions too raw for her to try to explore the matter right now. But she was certain of one thing. Though these might be the rules by which the Spanish leaders operated, they'd crossed the line into three of her own rules. First, you don't shoot people who are here to help you. Second, if shooting them is designed to help you, then you're going to run into rule number three: Americans—especially this American—shoot back.

FIVE

Monday, 8:21 P.M.
San Sebastián, Spain

The hull of the small fishing boat was freshly painted. The smell of the paint permeated the cramped, dimly lighted hold. It overpowered the bite of the handrolled cigarette Adolfo Alcazar was smoking as well as the strong, distinctive, damp-rubber odor of the wetsuit that hung on a hook behind the closed door. The paint job was an extravagance the fisherman couldn't really afford but it had been necessary. There might be other missions, and he couldn't afford to be in drydock, replacing rotted boards. When he'd agreed to work with the General, Adolfo knew that the old boat would have to last them for as long as this affair took. And if anything went wrong, that could be a while. One didn't undermine one takeover and orchestrate a counterrevolution in a single night—or with a single strike. Not even with a big strike, which this one would be.

Although the General is going to try, Adolfo thought with deep and heartfelt admiration. And if anyone could pull it off, a one-day coup against a major world government, it was the General.

There was a click. The short, muscular man stopped

staring into space. He looked down at the tape recorder
on the wooden table beside him. He lay his cigarette
in a rusted tin ashtray and sat back down into the
folding wooden chair. He pushed PLAY and listened
through the earphones, just to make sure the remote
had picked up the sounds. The General's technical officer from Pamplona, the man who had given him the
equipment, had said the equipment was extremely precise. If properly calibrated, it would record the voices
over the slosh of the ocean and the growl of the fishing
boat's engine.

He was correct.

After nearly a minute of silence Adolfo Alcazar
heard a mechanical-sounding but clear voice utter, *"It
is accomplished."* The voice was followed by what
sounded like crackling.

No, Adolfo realized as he listened more closely. The
noise wasn't static. It was applause. The men in the
yacht were clapping.

Adolfo smiled. For all their wealth, for all their
planning, for all their experience at managing their
bloodthirsty *familias,* these men were unsuspecting
fools. The fisherman was pleased to see that money
hadn't made them smart—only smug. He was also
glad because the General had been right. The General
was always right. He had been right when he tried to
arm the Basques to grease the wheels of revolution.
And he was right to step back when they began fighting among themselves—the separatists battling the antiseparatists. Killing themselves and drawing attention
from the real revolution.

The small dish-shaped "ear" the fisherman had

placed on top of his boat's cabin, right behind the navigation light, had picked up every word of the conversation of that *altivo,* the haughty Esteban Ramirez, and his equally arrogant *compadres* on board the *Verídico.*

Adolfo stopped the cassette and rewound it. The smile evaporated as he faced another unit directly to the right. This device was slightly smaller than the tape recorder. It was an oblong box nearly thirteen inches long by five inches wide and four inches deep. The box was made of Pittsburgh steel. In case it were ever found, there would be metallurgic evidence pointing to its country of origin. Ramirez, the traitor, had ties to the American CIA. After seizing power, the General could always point to them as having removed a collaborator who had outlived his usefulness.

There was a green light on the top of the box face and a red light beneath it. The green light was glowing. Directly below them were two square white buttons. Beneath the topmost button was a piece of white tape with the word ARM written in blue ink. That button was already depressed. The second button was not yet depressed. Below it was a piece of tape with the word DETONATE written on it. The General's electronics expert had given this device to Adolfo as well, along with several bricks of U.S. army plastique and a remote detonator cap. The fisherman had attached two thousand grams of C-4 and a detonator below the waterline of the yacht before it left the harbor. When the blast occurred, it would rip through the hull at a velocity of twenty-six thousand feet per second—

nearly four times faster than an equivalent amount of dynamite.

The young man ran a calloused hand through his curly black hair. Then he looked at his watch. Esteban Ramirez, the wealthy son of a bitch who was going to bring them all under the iron heel of his monied Catalonian cohorts, had said that the assassin would be arriving at the airport in an hour. When Adolfo had heard that, he'd used his ship-to-shore radio to pass the information along to his partners in the northwestern Pyrenees, Daniela, Vicente, and Alejandro. They'd hurried out to the airport, which was located outside of Bilbao, which was seventy miles to the east. Just two minutes ago they'd radioed back that the airplane had landed. One of Ramirez's petty thugs would be bringing him out here. The other members of the *familia* would be rounded up and dealt with later. That is, if they didn't panic and disperse of their own accord. Unlike Adolfo, so many of those bastards were only effective when they worked in big, brutal gangs.

Adolfo picked up his cigarette, drew on it one last time, then ground it out. He removed the audiocassette from the recorder and slipped it into his shirt pocket, beneath his heavy black sweater. As he did so, his hand brushed the shoulder holster in which he carried a 9mm Beretta. The gun was one that had been used by U.S. Navy SEALs in Iraq and retrieved by coalition forces. It had made its way to the General through the Syrian weapons underground. Adolfo slipped in a tape of native Catalonian guitar music and pressed PLAY. The first song was called "Salou," a song for two guitars. It was a paean to the magnificent illuminated fountain in the beautiful town south of Barcelona. The young man listened for a moment, humming along with the lilting tune. One guitar played the melody while the other made pizzicato sounds like water droplets hitting the fountain. The music the instruments made was enchanting.

Reluctantly, Adolfo turned off the tape. He took a short breath and grabbed the detonator. Then he doused the battery-powered lantern that swung from an overhead hook and went upstairs to the deck.

The moon had slid behind a narrow bank of clouds. That was good. The crew of the yacht probably wouldn't pay attention anyway to a fishing boat over six hundred feet off their portside stern. In these waters, fishermen often trolled for night-feeders. But the men on the yacht would be less likely even to see him if the moon were hidden. Adolfo looked at the boat. It was dark save for its navigation lights and a glow from behind the drawn curtain of the midcabin porthole.

After several minutes Adolfo heard the muffled growl of a small boat. The sound was coming from behind him, from the direction of the shore. He turned completely around and watched a small, dark shape head toward the yacht. It was traveling about forty miles an hour. From the light slap of the hull upon the water Adolfo judged it to be a small, two-person runabout. He watched as it pulled up to the near side of the yacht. A rope ladder was unrolled from the deck. A man stood unsteadily in the passenger's seat of the rocking vessel.

That had to be the assassin.

The detonator felt slick in Adolfo's perspiring hand. He gripped it tightly, his finger hovering above the lower button.

The seas were unusually active. They seemed to be reflecting the times themselves, uneasy and roiling below the surface. There were only four or five seconds from the peak of one uproll to the peak of the next. But Adolfo stood at the edge of the rolling deck with the sure poise of a lifelong fisherman. According to the General, he needed to be in a direct and unobstructed line with the plastique. Though they could have given him a more sophisticated trigger than the line-of-sight transmitter, these were more commonly available and less easy to trace.

Adolfo watched as the yacht rocked gently from side to side. The assassin started uncertainly up the short ladder and the runabout moved away to keep from being rocked by the yacht's swells. A man appeared on deck. He was a fat man smoking a cigar—clearly not one of the crewmen. Adolfo waited. He knew exactly where he'd placed the explosives and he also knew the precise moment when they'd be exposed by the roll of the boat.

The yacht tilted to port, toward him. Then it rolled away. Adolfo lowered the side of his thumb onto the bottom button. One more roll, he told himself. The ship was inclined toward the starboard for just a moment. Then gently, gracefully, it righted itself for a moment before angling back to port. The hull of the yacht rose, revealing the area just below the waterline. It was dark and Adolfo couldn't see it, but he knew that the package he'd left was there. He pushed hard with his thumb. The green light on the box went off and the red light ignited.

The portside bottom of the hull exploded with a white-yellow flash. The man on the ladder evaporated as the blast followed a nearly straight line from prow to stern. The fat man flew away from the blast into the darkness and the deck crumpled inward as the entire vessel shuddered. Splinters of wood, shards of fiberglass, and torn, jagged pieces of metal from the midcabin rode the blast into air. Burning chunks arced brightly against the sky while broken fragments, which had been blown straight along the sea, plopped and sizzled in the water just yards from Adolfo's fishing boat. Smoke rose in thick sheets from the opening in the hull until the yacht listed to port. Then it became steam. The yacht seemed to stop there for a moment, holding at an angle as water rushed through the huge breach; Adolfo could hear the distinctive, hollow roar of the sea as it poured in. Then the yacht slowly rolled onto its side. Less than half a minute after the capsizing, the wake caused the fishing boat to rock quickly from side to side. Adolfo easily retained his balance. The moon returned from behind the clouds then, its bright image jiggling on the waves with giddy agitation.

Dropping the detonator into the water, the young man turned from the sea and hurried back into the cabin. He radioed his associates that the job had been accomplished. Then he walked to the controls, stood behind the wheel, and turned the boat toward the wreckage. He wanted to be able to tell investigators that he had raced to the scene to look for survivors.

He felt the weight of the 9mm weapon under his sweater. He also wanted to make sure there weren't any survivors.

SIX

Monday, 1:44 P.M.
Washington, D.C.

Intelligence Chief Bob Herbert was in a gray frame
of mind as he arrived in Paul Hood's bright, windowless basement office. In contrast to the warm fluores-
cence of the overhead lights, the gloomy mood was
much too familiar. Not long ago they'd mourned the
deaths of Striker team members Bass Moore, killed in
North Korea, and Lt. Col. Charles Squires, who died
in Siberia preventing a second Russian Revolution.

For Herbert, the psychological resources he needed
to deal with death were highly refined. Whenever he
learned of the demise of enemies of his country—or
when it had been necessary, early in his intelligence
career, to participate in some of those killings—he
never had any problems. The life and security of his
country came before any other considerations. As Herbert had put it so many times, "The deeds are dirty
but my conscience is clean."

But this was different.

Although Herbert's wife, Yvonne, had been killed
nearly sixteen years ago in the terrorist bombing of
the U.S. Embassy in Beirut, he was still mourning her
death. The loss still seemed fresh. *Too fresh,* he

thought almost every night since the attack. Restaurants, movie theaters, and even a park bench they had frequented became shrines to him. Each night he lay in bed gazing at her photograph on his night table. Some nights the framed picture was moonlit, some nights it was just a dark shape. But bright or dark, seen or remembered, for better or for worse, Yvonne never left his bedside. And she never left his thoughts. Herbert had long ago adjusted to having lost his legs in the Beirut explosion. Actually, he'd more than adjusted. His wheelchair and all its electronic conveniences now seemed an integral part of his body. But he had never adjusted to losing Yvonne.

Yvonne had been a fellow CIA agent—a formidable enemy, a devoted friend, and the wittiest person he'd ever known. She had been his life and his lover. When they were together, even on the job, the physical boundaries of the universe seemed very small. It was defined by her eyes and by the curve of her neck, by the warmth of her fingers and the playfulness of her toes. But what a rich and full universe that had been. So rich that there were still mornings when, half-awake, Herbert would reach his hand under her pillow and search for hers. Not finding it, he'd squeeze her lumpy pillow in his empty fingers and silently curse the killers who'd taken her from him. Killers who had gone unpunished. Who were still permitted to enjoy their own lives, their own loves.

Now Herbert had to mourn the loss of Martha Mackall. He felt guilty. Part of him was pleased that he wasn't the only one grieving now. Mourning could be an oppressively lonely place to be. Less guiltily,

Herbert also wasn't willing to laud the dead just because they were dead, and he was going to have to listen to plenty of that over the next few days and weeks. Some of the praise would be valid. But only some of it.

Martha had been one of Op-Center's keystones since the organization's inception. Regardless of her motivation, Martha had never given less than her utmost. Herbert was going to miss her intelligence, her insights, and her justified self-confidence. In government, it didn't always matter whether a person was right or wrong. What mattered was that they led, that they roused passions. From the day she arrived in Washington Martha certainly did that.

Yet in the nearly two years that he had known Martha Mackall, Herbert had found her to be abrasive and condescending. She often took credit for work done by her staff—a common enough sin in Washington, though a rare occurrence at Op-Center. But then, Martha wasn't devoted solely to Op-Center. Since he'd first encountered her when she worked at State, she had always applied herself to the advancement of the cause that seemed most important to her: Martha Mackall. For at least the last five or six months she'd had her eyes on several ambassadorial positions and had made no secret of the fact that her position at Op-Center was simply a stepping stone.

On the other hand, Herbert thought, *when patriotism isn't enough to drive you to do your best, ambition is a workable substitute.* As long as the job got done, Herbert wasn't one to throw stones.

Herbert's cynicism burned off quickly, though, as

he crossed the threshold into Hood's small, wood-paneled office. "Pope" Paul had that effect on people. Hood believed in the goodness of humankind and his conviction as well as his even temper could be contagious.

Hood finished pouring himself a glass of tap water from a carafe on his desk. Then he rose and walked toward the door. Herbert had been the first to arrive, and Hood greeted him with a handshake and tight-lipped solemnity. Herbert wasn't surprised to see the director's dark eyes lacking their usual spirit and vigor. It was one thing to get bad news about an operative on a covert mission. Reports like that were statistical inevitabilities and a part of you was always braced for that kind of loss. Each time the private phone or fax line beeped, you half-expected a coded communiqué with a heart-stopping phrase like "The stock market is down one" or "Lost a charge card—cancel account."

But to hear about the death of a team member who was on a quiet diplomatic mission to a friendly nation during peacetime—that was another matter. It was disturbing regardless of what you thought about the person.

Hood sat on the edge of his desk and folded his arms. "What's the latest from Spain?"

"You read my e-mail about the explosion off the coast of San Sebastián, up north?"

Hood nodded.

"That's the last thing I have," Herbert replied. "The local police are still pulling body parts and pieces of yacht from the bay and trying to ID the people. No one has claimed responsibility for the attack. We're also monitoring commercial and private broadcasts in case the perps have something to say.''

''You wrote that the yacht blew up midship,'' Hood said.

''That's what two eyewitnesses onshore said,'' Herbert replied. ''There hasn't been any official word yet.''

''And there isn't likely to be,'' Hood said. ''Spain doesn't like to share its internal matters. Does the midship location mean anything?''

Herbert nodded. ''The blast was nowhere near the engines, which means we're almost certainly looking at sabotage. The timing may also be significant. The explosion occurred soon after Martha was shot.''

''So the two events could be related,'' Hood said.

''We're looking into it,'' Herbert replied.

''Starting where?''

Hood was pushing more than usual, but that wasn't surprising. Herbert had felt that way after Beirut. Apart from wanting the killer found and punished, it was important to keep one's mind active. The only other option was to stop, mourn, and have to deal with the guilt.

''The attack on Martha does adhere to the modus operandi of the Homeland and Freedom group,'' Herbert said. ''In February of 1997 they killed a Spanish Supreme Court judge, Justice Emperador. Shot him in the head at the front door of his building.''

''How does that tie in to Martha?''

''Judge Emperador heard labor law cases,'' Herbert

said. "He had nothing to do with terrorists or political activism."

"I don't follow."

Herbert folded his hands on his waist and answered patiently. "In Spain, as in many countries, judges involved in terrorist matters are given bodyguards. Real bodyguards, not just for show. So Homeland and Freedom typically goes after friends and associates in order to make a point to the principals. That's been their pattern in a half-dozen shootings since 1995, when they tried to murder King Juan Carlos, Crown Prince Felipe, and Prime Minister Aznar. The failure of that operation had a chilling effect."

"No more direct frontal assaults," Hood said.

"Right. And no more prime targets. Just attacks on the secondaries to rattle the support structure."

Two other people had arrived as Herbert was speaking.

"We'll talk about all this in a minute," Hood said. He took a swallow of water and rose as staff psychologist Liz Gordon and somber-looking press officer Ann Farris walked in. Herbert saw Ann's eyes catch Hood's for a moment. It was an open secret along the executive corridors of Op-Center that the young divorcée was more than fond of her married boss. Because Hood was so unreadable—a talent he had apparently developed as mayor of Los Angeles—no one was quite sure how Hood felt about Ann. However, it was known that the long hours he spent at Op-Center had put a strain on his relationship with his wife, Sharon. And Ann was attractive and attentive.

Martha's shell-shocked number-two man, Ron

Plummer, arrived a moment later with Op-Center attorney Lowell Coffey II and Deputy Assistant Secretary of State Carol Lanning. The slim, gray-haired, sixty-four-year-old Lanning had been a very close friend and mentor to Martha. Officially, however, that wasn't the reason she was here. Hood had asked Lanning to come to Op-Center because an American "tourist" had been shot abroad. It was now a matter for her division of the State Department, the Security and Counselor Affairs—the nuts and bolts group which dealt with everything from passport fraud to Americans imprisoned abroad. It was the job of Lanning and her staff to work as liaisons with foreign police departments to investigate attacks on American citizens. Like Hood, Lanning was temperate by nature and an optimist. As she sat down beside Herbert, the intelligence chief found it extremely unsettling to see Lanning's bright eyes bloodshot and her thin, straight mouth pulled into a deep frown.

Mike Rodgers was the last to arrive. He strode through the door quickly, his eyes alert and his chest expanded. His uniform was smartly pressed, as always, and his shoes were brightly polished.

God in Heaven bless the general, Herbert thought. Outwardly, at least, Rodgers was the only one who seemed to have any fight in him. Herbert was pleased to see that Rodgers had regained some of the grit he had lost in Lebanon. The rest of them would need to draw upon that if they were going to carry on here and revitalize Darrell McCaskey and Aideen Marley in Spain.

Hood went back to his desk and sat down. Everyone

else took seats except for Rodgers. The general folded his arms, squared his shoulders, and stood behind Carol Lanning's chair.

"As you all know," Hood began, "Martha Mackall was murdered in Madrid at approximately six P.M. local time."

Although Hood was addressing everyone in the room, he was looking down at the desk. Herbert understood. Eye contact could do him in. And he had to get through this.

"The shooting happened as Martha and Aideen Marley were standing at a guard booth outside the Palacio de las Cortes in Madrid," Hood went on. "The lone gunman fired several shots from the street and then escaped in a waiting car. Martha died at the scene. Aideen was not hurt. Darrell met her at the palace. They headed back to their hotel with a police escort."

Hood stopped and swallowed hard.

"The police escort was made of handpicked operatives attached to Interpol," Herbert continued for him, "and Interpol will continue to look over their shoulders for as long as they remain in Spain. The laxness of palace security has got us wondering if at least some of the guards weren't in on the plot—which is why we turned to Darrell's friends at Interpol for security, rather than relying on government-appointed police. We've got a lot of background data on the Interpol crew, due to the time agent María Corneja spent working with Darrell here in Washington," Herbert added. "We're very comfortable with how Darrell and Aideen will be looked after from this point forward.''

''Thank you, Bob,'' Hood said. He looked up. His eyes were glistening. ''Martha's body is en route to the embassy. It will be flown back as soon as possible. At the moment, we have a service scheduled at the Baptist Evangelical Church in Arlington for Wednesday morning, ten A.M.''

Carol Lanning looked away and shut her eyes. Herbert's hands were still folded on his waist and he glanced down at his thumbs. Before Herbert had attended Op-Center's annual sensitivity training seminar, he would have thought nothing about leaning over and putting his arms around the Deputy Assistant Secretary of State. Now if he wanted to comfort her, all he was supposed to do was ask if she wanted anything.

Hood beat him to it. ''Ms. Lanning,'' he asked, ''would you care for some water?''

The woman opened her eyes. ''No, thank you. I'll be all right. I want to get on with this.''

There was a surprising edge in her voice. Herbert snuck a glance at her. Carol's lips were straight now, her eyes narrow. To him, it didn't look like she wanted water. What Carol Lanning seemed to crave was blood. Herbert knew exactly how she felt. After the Beirut embassy bombing, he would have had no trouble nuking the entire city just to get the bastards who killed his wife. Grief was not a merciful emotion.

Hood looked at his watch. He sat back in his chair. ''Darrell will be calling in five minutes.'' He looked at Plummer. ''Ron, what do we do about the mission? Is Aideen qualified to continue?''

Plummer leaned forward and Herbert looked at him. Plummer was a short man with thinning brown hair and wide eyes. He wore thick, black-framed glasses on a large hooked nose. He had on a dark gray suit badly in need of dry cleaning and scuffed black shoes. The tops of his socks were falling over his ankles. Herbert hadn't had many dealings with the former CIA intelligence analyst for Western Europe. But Plummer had to be good. No one who dressed so carelessly could get by on anything but talent. Besides, Herbert had had a look at the psych workup Liz Gordon had done of Plummer before he was hired. Herbert and Plummer had both detested the CIA director Plummer had worked under. That was enough of a character endorsement for Herbert.

"I can't answer for Aideen's state of mind," Plummer said, with a nod to Liz Gordon. "But apart from that I'd say that Aideen is very capable of continuing the mission."

"According to her file," Carol said, "she hasn't had a great deal of diplomatic experience."

"That's very true," Plummer said. "Ms. Marley's methods are rather less diplomatic than Martha's were. But you know what? That just may be what's needed now."

"I like the sound of that," Herbert said. He looked at Paul. "*Have* you decided to continue the mission?"

"I won't decide that until I talk to Darrell," Hood said. "But my inclination is to keep them over there."

"Why?" Liz Gordon asked.

Herbert couldn't decide whether it was a question or a challenge. Liz's manner could be intimidating.

"Because we may not have a choice," Hood said. "If the shooting was random—and we can't dismiss that possibility, since Aideen is alive and a Madrid postal worker was the other victim—then the killing was tragic but not directed at the discussions. If that's the case, there's no reason not to keep the talks on-line. But even if the shooting was directed at us we can't afford to back down."

"Not back down," Liz said, "but wouldn't it be wise to step back until we're sure?"

"American foreign policy is determined by the Administration, not by the barrel of a gun," Lanning said. "I agree with Mr. Hood."

"Darrell can arrange for security with his people at Interpol," Hood said. "This won't happen again."

"Paul," Liz pressed, "the reason I mention this has nothing to do with logistics. There's one thing you need to consider before deciding whether Aideen should be a part of this process."

"What's that?" asked Hood.

"Right about now she's probably coming out of the first stage of alarm reaction, which is shock," Liz told him. "That's going to be followed almost immediately by countershock, a quick increase in the adrenocortical hormones—steroid hormones. She's going to be pumped."

"That's good, no?" Herbert asked.

"No, it isn't," Liz replied. "After countershock, a resistance phase settles in. Emotional recuperation. Aideen's going to be looking for someplace to turn that energy loose. If she was not too diplomatic before, she may become an unguided missile now. But even that's not the worst of it."

"How so?" Hood asked.

Liz rolled her broad shoulders forward. She leaned toward the group, her elbows on her knees. "Aideen survived a shooting in which her partner died. A lot of guilt comes along with that. Guilt and a responsibility to see the job through at any cost. She won't sleep and she probably won't eat. A person can't maintain those countershock and resistance levels for long."

"What's 'long'?" Herbert asked.

"Two or three days, depending on the person," Liz said. "After that, the person enters a state of clinical exhaustion. That brings on a mental and physical breakdown. If countershock is left untreated for that long, there's a good chance our girl's in for a long, long stay in a very quiet rest home."

"How good a chance?" Herbert asked.

"I'd say sixty-forty in favor of a crash," Liz said.

Hood's phone beeped as Liz was speaking. As soon as she was finished Hood picked it up. His executive assistant, "Bugs" Benet, said that Darrell McCaskey was on the line. Hood put McCaskey on the speakerphone.

Herbert settled back into his wheelchair. Until recently, a call like this wouldn't have been possible over an unsecured line. But Matt Stoll, Op-Center's Operations Support Officer and resident computer genius, had designed a digital scrambler that plugged into the data port of public telephones. Anyone listening in over the line would hear only static. A small speaker attached to the scrambler on McCaskey's end filtered out the noise and enabled him to hear the conversation clearly.

"Darrell, good evening," Hood said softly. "I've got you on speaker."

"Who's there?" he asked.

Hood told him.

"I've gotta tell you," McCaskey said, choking, "you can't imagine what it means to have a team like you back there. Thanks."

"We're in this together," Hood said.

Hood rolled his lips together. It was the closest Herbert had seen the boss come to losing it.

Hood collected himself quickly. "How are you both? Do you need anything?"

The compassion was real. Herbert had always said that when it came to sincerity in government Hood was in a category all by himself.

"We're still pretty shaken up," McCaskey answered, "as I'm sure you are. But I guess we'll be all right. As a matter of fact, Aideen seems to be in a pretty combative mood."

Liz nodded knowingly. "Countershock," she said softly.

"How so?" Hood asked.

"Well, she kind of took Deputy Serrador apart for getting cold feet," McCaskey said. "I called her on the carpet for it but I have to say I was actually pretty proud of her. He had it coming."

"Darrell," Hood asked, "is Aideen there?"

"No, she isn't," said McCaskey. "I left her in her room with Deputy Ambassador Gawal from the Amer-

ican embassy. They're on the phone with my friend
Luis at Interpol, discussing security measures if you
decide to keep us here. Like I said, she's pretty worked
up and I wanted her to have time to settle down a
little. But I also didn't want her to feel left out of the
process."

"Good thinking," Hood said. "Darrell, are you
sure *you* feel up to talking now?"

"It's got to be done," McCaskey said, "and I'd
rather do it now. I'm sure I'll feel a lot lower when
all of this sinks in."

Liz gave Hood a thumbs-up.

Herbert nodded. He knew the feeling.

"Very good," Hood said. "Darrell, we were just
discussing the idea of you two staying. How do you
feel about that—and what's the problem with Deputy
Serrador?"

"Frankly," McCaskey said, "I'd feel fine about
staying. Only the problem isn't me. Aideen and I just
came from Serrador's office. He's made it pretty clear
that he doesn't want to continue."

"Why?" Hood asked.

"Cold feet," Herbert suggested.

"No, Bob, I don't think it's that," McCaskey said.
"Deputy Serrador told us that he wants to talk to the
investigators and to his colleagues before he decides
whether to proceed with our talks. But it seemed to
me—and this is only a former G-man's hunch—that
that was bull. Aideen had the same feeling. I think he
wanted to shut us down."

"Darrell, this is Ron Plummer. Deputy Serrador
was the one who initiated these exploratory talks

through Ambassador Neville. What does he possibly gain by terminating them?''

"Terminating them?" Herbert muttered. "The son of a bitch didn't even start them!"

Hood motioned the intelligence chief to silence.

"I'm not sure what he gains, Ron," McCaskey replied. "But I think that what Bob just said—that was you grumbling, Bob, wasn't it?"

"Who else?"

"I think that what he said is significant," McCaskey said. "From the time Av Lincoln first put Serrador in touch with Martha—at Serrador's request, remember—the deputy has insisted that he only wanted to talk with Martha. She's murdered and now Serrador doesn't want to talk. One conclusion, the obvious conclusion, is that someone who has access to Serrador's political agenda—as well as his calendar—killed her to intimidate him."

"Not just to intimidate him," Plummer pointed out, "but to shut down everyone who's a member of his pronationalism team."

"That's right," said McCaskey. "Also, by attacking Martha, they send a message to our diplomats to stay out of this matter. But I still feel that those are the things we're supposed to think. I don't believe that they're the real reason behind the killing."

"Mr. McCaskey, this is Carol Lanning with State." Her voice was composed, though just barely. "I'm coming in a little late on all of this. What else is going on here? What does somebody want our diplomats to stay out of?"

"I'll take this one, Darrell," Hood said. He fixed

his eyes on Lanning. "As you know, Ms. Lanning, Spain has been going through some serious upheavals over the last few months."

"I've seen the daily situation reports," Lanning replied. "But it's mostly separatist Basques attacking antiseparatist Basques."

"Those are the very public disputes," Hood confirmed. "What you may not know is how concerned some of Spain's leaders are about other recent events involving violent attacks on members of the country's largest ethnic groups. The government has conspired to keep these very, very quiet. Ann, you've got some intel on this."

The slender, attractive, brown-haired press liaison nodded professionally but her rust-colored eyes smiled at Hood. Herbert noticed; he wondered if "Pope" Paul did.

"The Spanish government has been working very hard with journalists to keep the news out of the press and off the air," Ann Farris said.

"Really?" Herbert said. "How? Those ambulance chasers are even worse than the Washington press corps."

"Frankly, they're paid off," Ann said. "I know of three incidents in particular that were hushed. A Catalonian book publisher's office was burned after distributing a new novel that seriously bashed the Castilians. An Andalusian wedding party was attacked leaving a church in Segovia in Castile. And a Basque antiseparatist—a leading activist—was killed by Basque separatists while he was a patient in the hospital."

"Sounds like a lot of brushfires," Plummer said.

"They are," Hood agreed. "But if those fires should ever join up they could consume Spain."

"Which is why local reporters have been bribed to bury these stories," Ann went on, "while foreign reporters have been kept away from crime scenes altogether. UPI, ABC, the *New York Times*, and the *Washington Post* have all filed complaints with the government but to no effect. That's been going on for a little over a month now."

"Our own hands-on involvement in Spain began just about three weeks ago," Hood continued. "Deputy Serrador met secretly with Ambassador Neville in Madrid. It was a very quiet backdoor get-together at the U.S. Embassy. Serrador told the ambassador that a committee had been formed, with himself as the chair, to investigate this growing tension between Spain's five major ethnic groups. He said that during the previous four months, in addition to the crimes Ann mentioned, over a dozen ethnic leaders had been murdered or kidnapped. Serrador wanted help obtaining intelligence on several of the groups. Neville contacted Av Lincoln, who brought the matter to us, and to Martha."

Hood's eyes lowered slowly.

"And if you remember correctly," Herbert said quickly, "as soon as Deputy Serrador had a look at our diplomatic roster he asked for Martha specifically. And she couldn't wait to get her arms around this situation and make it hers. So don't even think about second-guessing what you did."

"Hear, hear," Ann Farris said quietly.

Hood looked up. He thanked them both with his eyes then looked at Carol Lanning. "Anyway," he said, "that was the start of our involvement."

"What do these groups want?" Lanning asked. "Independence?"

"Some do," Hood said. He turned to his computer screen and accessed the file on Spain. "According to Deputy Serrador, there are two major problems. The first is between the two factions of Basques. The Basques comprise just two percent of the population and are already battling among themselves. The bulk of the Basques are staunch antiseparatists who want to remain part of Spain. A very small number of them, less than ten percent, are separatists."

"That's point two percent of the population of Spain," Lanning said. "Not a very considerable number."

"Right," Hood said. "Meanwhile, there's also a long-simmering problem with the Castilians of central and northern Spain. The Castilians make up sixty-two percent of the population of Spain. They've always believed that they *are* Spain and that everyone else in the country isn't."

"The other groups are regarded as squatters," Herbert said.

"Exactly. Serrador tells us that the Castilians have been trying to arm the separatist factions of the Basques to begin the process of tearing the Spanish minorities apart. First the Basques, then the Galicians, the Catalonians, and the Andalusians. As a result, Serrador had intelligence that some of the other groups might be talking about joining together for a political or military move against the Castilians. A preemptive strike.''

''And it isn't just a national issue,'' McCaskey said. ''My Interpol sources tell me that the French are supporting the antiseparatist Basques. They're afraid that if the separatist Basques get too much power, the French Basques will act to form *their* own country as well.''

''Is there a real danger of that?'' Herbert asked.

''There is,'' said McCaskey. ''From the late 1960s through the middle 1970s, the quarter-million Basques in France helped the two million Basques in Spain fight the repression of Francisco Franco. The camraderie between the French Basques and the Spanish separatist Basques is so strong that the Basques— Spanish and French alike—simply refer to the region as the northern and southern Basque country, respectively.''

''The Basques and the Castilians are the two groups Serrador wanted us to investigate immediately,'' Hood said. ''But in addition to them, there are the Catalonians, also of central and northern Spain, who make up sixteen percent of the population. They're extremely rich and influential. A large portion of the Catalonians' taxes go to supporting the other minorities, especially the Andalusians in the south. They would be just as happy to see the other groups disappear.''

''How happy would they be?'' Lanning asked. ''Happy enough to make that happen?''

''As in genocide?'' Hood asked.

Lanning shrugged. ''It doesn't take more than a few loud men to fan suspicion and hate to those levels.''

"The men on the yacht were Catalonian," McCaskey said.

"And the Catalonians have always been separatists," Lanning said. "They were a key force in spurring on the Spanish Civil War sixty years ago."

"That's true," Ron Plummer said. "But the Catalonians also have a bunker mentality regarding other races. Genocide is usually the result of an already dominant force looking to turn widespread public anger against a specific target. That's not what we have here."

"I'm inclined to agree with Ron," Hood said. "It probably would have been easier for the Catalonians to exert financial pressure on the nation than to resort to genocide."

"We'll be able to check this out more thoroughly after we find out who else was on the yacht," Herbert said confidently.

Hood nodded and turned back to the computer monitor. "In addition to the Basques, Castilians, and Catalonians, we've got the Andalusians. They comprise roughly twelve percent of the population and they'll side with any group in power because of their financial dependency. The Galicians are roughly eight percent of the population. They're an agricultural people— very Spanish, traditionally independent, and likely to stay out of any fray that might erupt."

"So," Lanning said, "they've got a complex situation over there. And given the volatile history of the interrelations I can understand them wanting to keep the disputes quiet. What I don't understand is something Mr. Herbert said—why this Deputy Serrador wanted to see Martha specifically.''

"Deputy Serrador seemed comfortable with her due to her familiarity with Spain and the language,'' Hood said. "He also liked the fact that she was a woman who belonged to a racial minority. He said he could count on her to be both discreet and sympathetic.''

"Sure,'' Herbert said. "But I've been sitting here thinking that she also happened to be the perfect victim for one of those ethnic groups.''

Everyone looked at him.

"What do you mean?'' Hood asked.

"To put it bluntly,'' Herbert said, "the Catalonians are male-supremacists who hate black Africans. It's an animosity that goes back about nine hundred years, to the wars with the Moors of Africa. If someone wanted to get the Catalonians on their side—and who wouldn't want the folks with the money in their camp?—they'd pick a black woman as a victim.''

There was silence for a moment.

"That's a bit of a reach, don't you think?'' Lanning asked.

"Not really,'' the intelligence chief replied. "I've seen longer shots pay off. The sad truth is, whenever I go looking for muddy footprints in the gutter of human nature, I'm rarely disappointed.''

"What ethnic group does Serrador belong to?'' Mike Rodgers asked.

"He's Basque, General,'' McCaskey's voice came from the speakerphone, "with absolutely no record of antinationalist activity. We checked him out. To the contrary. He's voted against every kind of separatist legislation.''

"He could be a mole," Lanning said. "The most damaging Soviet spy we ever had at State was raised in whitebread Darien, Connecticut, and voted for Barry Goldwater.''

"You're catching on," Herbert said, grinning. He had a feeling what was coming: there was no one more passionate than a convert.

Lanning regarded Hood. "The more I think about what Mr. Herbert just said, the more troubled I am by all of this. We've had situations before where we've been set up by foreign interests. Let's assume for the moment that that's what happened. That Martha was lured to Spain to be assassinated, for whatever reason. The only way we'll ever find that out is if we have access to all aspects of the investigation. Do we have that, Mr. McCaskey?''

"I wouldn't count on it," McCaskey replied. "Serrador said he's going to look into it, but Aideen and I were both shuttled off to our hotel rooms and we haven't heard anything since.''

"Yeah, the Spanish government isn't always very forthcoming about their private activities," Herbert said. "During World War II, this supposedly neutral nation rode shotgun on train- and truckloads of Nazi booty sent from Switzerland to Portugal. They did it in exchange for future favors, which, luckily, they never got to collect on.''

"That was Francisco Franco," Ron Plummer said. "Professional courtesy, dictator-to-dictator. It doesn't mean that Spanish people are that way.''

"True," Herbert said, "but the Spanish leaders are still at it. In the 1980s the defense minister hired drug smugglers as mercenaries to kill Basque separatists. The government purchased guns for the team in South Africa. They let them keep the weapons afterward, too. No," he said, "I wouldn't count on any Spanish government to help the United States with anything."

Hood held up both hands. "We're getting off the subject here. Darrell, for the moment I'm not concerned about Serrador, his motives, or his intelligence needs. I want to find out who killed Martha and why. Mike," Hood looked at Rodgers—"you recruited Aideen. What's she made of?"

Rodgers was still standing behind Carol Lanning. He unfolded his arms and shifted his weight. "She stood up to some pretty tough dealers in the drug trade in Mexico City. She's got iron in her back."

"I see where you're going, Paul," Liz said, "and I want to caution you. Aideen's under a lot of emotional stress. Throw her into a covert police action right now and the pressure could break her."

"It could also be just what she needs," Herbert said.

"You're absolutely right," Liz replied. "Everyone is different. Only the question isn't just what Aideen needs. If she goes undercover and cracks, she could be the nail that cost the horse that cost the kingdom."

"Besides," Herbert said to Hood, "if we send someone else over to follow the muddy footprints, we lose time."

"Darrell," Hood asked, "did you hear that?"

"I heard."

"What do you think?"

"I think a couple of things," McCaskey said. "Mike's right. The lady's got backbone to spare. She wasn't afraid to get right in Serrador's face. And my gut tells me the same thing as Bob's: I'm inclined to let her loose on the Spaniards. But Liz has also got a solid point. So if it's okay with you, let me talk to Aideen first. I'll know pretty quick whether she's up to it."

Hood's eyes shifted to the staff psychologist. "Liz, if we decide to go ahead with something and Aideen's involved, what should Darrell look for? Any physical signs?"

"Extreme restlessness," Liz replied. "Rapid speech, foot tapping, cracking the knuckles, heavy sighing, that sort of thing. She's got to be able to focus. If her mind wanders into guilt and loss, she's going to drop down a hole and not be able to get out."

"Any questions, Darrell?" Hood asked.

"None," McCaskey said.

"Very good," Hood said. "Darrell, I'm going to have Bob and his team look over any new intelligence that's come in. If there's anything useful, they'll get it over to you."

"I'm also going to make a few calls over here," McCaskey said. "There are some people at Interpol who might be able to help us."

"Excellent," Hood said. "Anyone else?"

"Mr. Hood," Carol Lanning said, "this is not my area of expertise but I do have a question."

"Go ahead," Hood said. "And please—it's Paul."

She nodded and cleared her throat. "Might I ask if

you're looking to gather intelligence to turn over to the Spanish authorities or—'' She hesitated.

''Or what?''

''Or are you looking for revenge?''

Hood thought for a moment. ''Frankly, Ms. Lanning, I want both.''

''Good,'' she said. Rising, she smoothed her skirt and squared her shoulders. ''I hoped I wasn't the only one.''

SEVEN

Monday, 10:56 P.M.
San Sebastián, Spain

No one had survived the explosion of the Ramirez yacht.

Adolfo hadn't expected anyone to be left alive. The blast had flipped the ship onto its side before anyone could get out. The men who weren't killed in the explosion itself were drowned when the yacht capsized. Only the pilot of the runabout had escaped. Adolfo knew about the man. He was Juan Martinez, a leader of the Ramirez *familia*. He had a reputation for being resourceful and devoted to his boss. But Adolfo wasn't worried about Martinez—or any other Ramirez thugs. Very soon the *familia* would no longer exist as an adversarial force. And with their demise other *familias* would stay out of the General's way. It was funny how power didn't matter so much when one's survival was threatened.

The fisherman and two other late-night trawlers had waited at the scene to provide police with eyewitness accounts of the explosion. When two young officers with the harbor patrol boarded Adolfo's boat, he acted as though he were very upset by the evening's events. The officers told Adolfo to calm down, which he did—

but only slightly. He informed them that he had been looking toward the harbor when the ship exploded. Adolfo said that all he saw was the dying fireball and then the wreckage showering down, the shards sizzling and steaming as they hit the water. He said that he had sailed for it immediately. One of the investigators wrote rapidly, taking notes, while the other asked questions. They both seemed excited to have something so dramatic occur in their harbor.

The police officers took Adolfo's name, address, and telephone number and allowed him to leave. By that time Adolfo had pretended to calm enough to wish them well on the investigation. Then he went to the wheelhouse of his fishing boat and throttled up. The engine chugged deeply as Adolfo turned the old vessel toward the harbor.

As Adolfo sailed the choppy waters, he plucked one of the handrolled cigarettes from his pants pocket. He lit it and drew deeply, feeling a greater sense of satisfaction than he had ever known. This was not his first mission for the cause. In the past year he had prepared a letter bomb for a newspaper and had rigged a TV reporter's car to explode when the gas cap was removed. Both of those had been successful. But this was his most important job and it had gone perfectly. Even better, he'd pulled it off alone. The General had asked Adolfo to do it by himself for two reasons. First, if Adolfo had been caught the cause would only have lost one soldier in the region. Second, if Adolfo had failed then the General would know who to blame. That was important. With so many important tasks ahead there was no room for incompetency.

Adolfo guided the boat swiftly toward shore, his right hand on the wheel and his left hand holding the well-worn string of the old bell that hung outside the wheelhouse. He'd fished these waters since he was a small boy working on his father's vessel. The low, foggy sound of that bell was one of the two things that brought those days back to him vividly. The other was the smell of the harbor whenever he drew near. The ocean smell intensified the closer Adolfo came to shore. That had always seemed odd to him until he mentioned it to his brother. Norberto explained that the things that cause the smells—the salt, the dead fish, the rotting seaweed—always wash toward the land. That was why beaches smelled more like the sea than the sea did.

"Father Norberto," Adolfo sighed. "So learned yet so misguided." His older brother was a Jesuit priest who had never wanted to be anything else. After his ordination seven years ago he was given the local parish, St. Ignatius, as his ministry. Norberto knew a lot about many things. The members of his parish lovingly called him "the Scholar." He could tell them why the ocean smelled or why the sun turned orange when it set or why you could see clouds even though they were made of drops of water. What Norberto didn't know much about was politics. He had once joined a protest march against the Spanish government, which was accused of financing death squads that killed hundreds of people in the middle 1980s. But that wasn't so much a political crusade as a humanistic one. He also didn't know about church politics. Norberto hated being away from his parish. Two or three times a year Father General González—the most powerful Jesuit prelate in Spain—held audiences or hosted dinners for church dignitaries in Madrid. Norberto did not go to these functions unless commanded, which he seldom was. Norberto's disinterest in his own advancement allowed the power and funding in this province to go to Father Iglesias in nearby Bilbao.

Adolfo was the expert in politics, something Norberto didn't admit. The brothers rarely argued about anything; they had looked out for one another since they were boys. But politics was the one area where they disagreed passionately. Norberto believed in a unified nation. He had once said bitterly, "It is bad enough that Christendom is divided." He wished for what he called "God's Spaniards" to live in harmony.

Unlike Norberto, Adolfo did not believe in either God or Spaniards. If there were a God, he reasoned, the world would be doing better. There wouldn't be conflict or need. As for that creature called a "Spaniard," Spain had always been a fragile tapestry of different cultures. That was true before the birth of Christ, when the Basques, Iberians, Celts, Carthaginians, and others were first united under the rule of Rome. It was true in 1469, when Aragon and Castile were joined in an uneasy alliance by the marriage of Ferdinand II to Isabella I. It was true in 1939, when Francisco Franco became El Caudillo, leader of the nation, after the devastating Civil War. It was true today.

It was also true that within this confederacy the Castilians had always been victimized. They were the largest group and so they were feared. They were always the first to be sent into battle or exploited by the wealthy. The irony was that if there were a "real" Spaniard, the Castilian was it. His nature was industrious and fun-loving. His life was filled with the honest sweat of hard work and passion. His heart was filled with music, love, and laughter. And his home, the land of El Cid, was one of vast plains dotted with windmills and castles beneath an endless blue sky.

Adolfo savored the pride of his heritage and the blow he'd struck for both of those tonight. But as he entered the harbor, he turned his attention to the boats moored there. The harbor was located behind the enormous nineteenth-century Ayuntamiento, the town hall. Adolfo was glad it was night. He hated coming back when it was light and all the gift shops and restaurants were visible. Catalonian money was responsible for transforming San Sebastián from a fishing village to a tourist spot.

Adolfo maneuvered carefully and skillfully around the numerous pleasure boats moored there. The fishermen usually kept their vessels out of the way, near the wharf. It made unloading the fish easier. But the pleasure boats dropped anchor wherever their owners chose. The crews then rowed to shore on dinghies. For Adolfo the pleasure boats were a daily reminder that the needs of working men did not matter to the rich. The requirements of the fishermen didn't matter to the powerful and wealthy Catalonians, or to the tourism they encouraged to benefit their hotels and restaurants and airlines.

When Adolfo reached the wharf he tied his boat in

the same spot as always. Then, slinging his canvas grip over his shoulder, he made his way through the groups of tourists and locals who had gathered when they heard the explosion. A few people near the wharf, who had watched him come in from the bay, asked what had happened. He just shrugged and shook his head as he walked along the gravel path, through a row of gift shops and past the new aquarium. It was never a good idea to stop and talk to people after completing a job. It was only human to want to lecture or to boast and that could be deadly. Loose lips not only sink ships: they can undo those who sink them.

Adolfo continued along the path as it turned into Monte Urgull, the local park. Closed to automobile traffic, the park was the site of ancient bastions and abandoned cannon. It was also home to a British cemetery from the duke of Wellington's 1812 campaign against the French. When he was a boy, Adolfo used to play here—before the ruins were promoted from weed-covered wreckage to protected historical relics. He used to imagine that he was a cavalry soldier. Only he was not fighting the imperious French but the "*bastardos* from Madrid," as he knew them. The exporters who drove his father to an early grave. They were men who bought fish by the ton to ship around the world and who encouraged inexperienced fishermen to ply the waters off San Sebastián. The exporters didn't want to develop a regular team of suppliers. Nor did they care whether they destroyed the ecological balance of the region. Bribes to officials made certain that the government didn't care either. All they wanted was to fill a new and unprecedented demand for fish as it replaced beef on tables throughout Europe and North America. Five years later, in 1975, the exporters began buying fish from Japan and the opportunists left. The coastal waters were theirs again. But it was too late for his father. The elder Alcazar died a year later, having struggled long and hard to survive. His mother died just a few months after that. Since then, Norberto was the only family Adolfo had.

Except, of course, for the General.

Adolfo left the park after the Museum of San Telmo, a former Dominican monastery. Then he walked briskly along dark, quiet Calle Okendo. The only sounds were the distant waves and muffled voices from television sets coming through open windows.

Adolfo's tiny second-floor apartment was located on a small side street two blocks to the southeast. He was surprised to find the door unlocked. He entered the one-room apartment cautiously. Had someone been sent by the General or was it the police?

It was neither. Adolfo relaxed when he saw that it was his brother lying on the bed.

Norberto closed the book he was reading. It was *The Moral Discourses of Epictetus*.

"Good evening, Dolfo," Norberto said pleasantly. The old bedsprings complained as he sat up. The priest was slightly taller and heavier than his brother. He had sandy brown hair and kind brown eyes behind wire-frame glasses. Because Norberto wasn't constantly exposed to the sun like his brother, his skin was paler and unwrinkled.

"Good evening, Norberto," Adolfo said. "This is a pleasant surprise." He tossed his threadbare bag on the small kitchen table and pulled off his sweater. The cool air coming through the open window felt good.

"Well, you know," Norberto said, "I hadn't seen you in a while so I decided to walk over." He looked over at the ticking clock on the kitchen counter. "Eleven-thirty. Isn't this rather late for you?"

Adolfo nodded. He dug into his bag and began pulling out dirty clothes. "There was an accident on the bay. An explosion on a yacht. I stopped to assist the police."

"Ah," Norberto said. He stood. "I heard the blast and wondered what it was. Was anyone hurt?"

"Unfortunately, yes," Adolfo said. "Several men were killed." He said no more. Norberto knew about his brother's political activism, but he didn't know anything about his involvement with the General or his group. Adolfo wanted very much to keep it that way.

"Were the men from San Sebastián?" Norberto asked.

"I don't know," Adolfo said. "I left when the police arrived. There was nothing I could do." As he spoke he began throwing the wet clothes over a line strung by the open window. He always brought spare clothes on the boat so he could change into something dry. He did not look at his brother.

Norberto walked slowly toward the old iron stove. There was a small pot of stew on top. "I made some *cocido* at the rectory and brought it over," he said. "I know how you like it."

"I wondered what smelled so good. Not my clothes." He smiled. "Thanks, Berto."

"I'll warm it for you before I head back."

"It's all right," Adolfo said. "I can do that. Why don't you go home? I'm sure you've had a long day."

"So have you," Norberto said. "A long day and a long night."

Adolfo was silent. Did Norberto suspect?

"I was reading just now that in the same way as God is beneficial, *good* is beneficial," Norberto said with a smile. "So let me be good. Let me do this for you." He went to the stove and lit the flame with a wooden match. He shook the match out and removed the lid from the pot.

Adolfo smiled cautiously. "All right, *mi hermano*," he said. "*Be* good. Even though if you ask anyone in town, you are already good enough for the two of us. Sitting with the sick, reading to the blind, watching children at the church when both parents are away—"

"That's my job," Norberto said.

Adolfo shook his head. "You're too modest. You'd do those things even if the priesthood weren't your calling."

The smell of lamb filled the room as the stew began to warm. The deep popping of the bubbles sounded very cozy. They reminded Adolfo of when he and Norberto were boys and they ate whatever their mother had left for them on the stove. When they were together like this, it didn't seem so very long ago. Yet so much had happened to Spain . . . and to them.

Adolfo kept his movements unhurried. Even though he didn't have time for this now, he didn't want to give Norberto a reason to worry about him.

Norberto looked over at his brother as he stirred the stew. The priest appeared wan and tired in the yellow light of the bare overhead bulb. His shoulders were more and more rounded every year. Adolfo had long ago decided that doing good must be a draining experience. Taking on the sorrows and pain of others without being able to pour out your own—except to God. That required the kind of constitution Adolfo did not have. It also required a kind of faith Adolfo did not have. If you were suffering on earth you took action on earth. You didn't ask God for the strength to endure. You asked God for the strength to make things right.

''Tell me, Adolfo,'' Norberto asked without turning. ''What you said a moment ago—was it true?''

''I'm sorry?'' Adolfo said. ''Was what true?''

''Do I need to be good enough for you and me?''

Adolfo shrugged. ''No. Not as far as I'm concerned.''

''What about as far as God is concerned?'' Norberto asked. ''Would He say that you are good?''

Adolfo draped his wet socks over the line. ''I wouldn't know. You'll have to ask Him.''

''Unfortunately, He doesn't always answer me, Dolfo.'' Norberto turned now. ''That's why I'm asking you.''

Adolfo wiped his hands on his pants. ''There is nothing on my conscience, if that's what you mean.''

''Nothing?''

''No. Why are you really asking me this? Should I be worried about something?''

Norberto took a mug from the shelf and ladled stew

into it. He brought it over to the table and pointed. "Eat."

Adolfo walked over. He picked up the stew and sipped it. "Hot. And very good." As he sipped more he continued to watch his brother. Norberto was acting strangely.

"Did you catch anything tonight?" Norberto asked.

"Quite a bit," Adolfo replied.

"You don't smell of fish," Norberto said.

Adolfo chewed on a thick chunk of lamb. He pointed to the clothesline. "I changed."

"Your clothes don't smell of fish either," Norberto said. He looked down.

Suddenly, Adolfo realized what was wrong. He was the fisherman but Norberto was doing the fishing. "What brought this on?" he asked.

"The police telephoned a while ago."

"And?"

"They told me about that terrible explosion on a yacht," Norberto said. "They thought I might be needed to give the last sacraments. I came here so I could be closer to the wharf."

"But you weren't," Adolfo said confidently. "No one could have survived that explosion."

Norberto looked at him. "Do you know that for certain because you *saw* the blast? Or is there another reason?"

Adolfo looked at him. He didn't like where this conversation was heading. He put the mug down and dragged the back of his hand across his mouth. "I really must get going."

"Where?"

"I'm meeting friends tonight."

Norberto stepped over to his brother. He put his hands on Adolfo's shoulders and looked into his eyes. Adolfo was very aware that his face was closed to his brother. A blank mask.

"Is there anything you want to tell me?" Norberto asked.

"About what?"

"About—anything," Norberto replied uneasily.

"About anything? Sure. I love you, Berto."

"That isn't what I meant."

"I know," Adolfo said. "And I know you, Norberto. What's troubling you? Or should I help you? You want to know what I was doing tonight? Is that what this is about?"

"You've already said you were fishing," Norberto said. "Why shouldn't I believe you?"

"Because you knew exactly what the explosion was and yet you pretended not to," Adolfo said. "You didn't come here to be closer to the sea, Berto. You came here because you wanted to see if I was home. All right. I wasn't. You also know that I wasn't fishing."

Norberto said nothing. He removed his hands from Adolfo's shoulders. His arms fell heavily.

"You've always been able to see inside me," Adolfo said. "To know what I was thinking, feeling. When I was a teenager I'd come back from a night of whoring or cockfights and lie to you. I'd tell you I was playing soccer or watching a movie. But you always looked in my eyes and saw the truth, even though you said nothing."

"You were a boy then, Dolfo. Your activities were a part of growing up. Now you're a man—"

"That's right, Norberto," Adolfo interrupted. "I'm a man. One who barely has time for cockfighting, let alone whoring. So you see, brother, there's nothing to worry about."

Norberto stepped closer. "I'm looking in your eyes again now. And I believe there *is* something to worry about."

"It's my worry, not yours."

"That isn't true," Norberto said. "We're brothers. We share pain, we share secrets, we share love. We always have. I want you to talk to me, Dolfo. Please."

"About what? My activities? My beliefs? My dreams?"

"All of it. Sit down. Tell me."

"I don't have time," Adolfo said.

"Where your soul is concerned you must make the time."

Adolfo regarded his brother for a moment. "I see. And if I did have time would you be listening to me as a brother or as a priest?"

"As Norberto," the priest replied gently. "I can't separate who I am from what I am."

"Which means you would be my living conscience," Adolfo said.

"I fear that that position may be open," Norberto replied.

Adolfo looked at him a few seconds longer. Then he turned away. "You really want to know what I was doing tonight?"

"Yes. I do."

"Then I'll tell you," Adolfo said. "I'll tell you because if anything happens I want you to know why I have done what I've done." He turned back and spoke in a low voice lest the neighbors hear through the thin walls. "The Catalonian men on the boat that sank, Ramirez and the rest of them, planned and carried out the execution of an American diplomat in Madrid. In my pocket I have their taped conversation about the murder." The cassette rattled as he patted it through his sweater. "The tape is in effect a confession, Norberto. My commander, the General, was right about these men. They were the leaders of a group that is attempting to bankrupt our nation in order to take it over. They killed the diplomat to make sure that the United States does not become involved in their conquest of Spain."

"Politics do not interest me," Norberto said quietly, "you know that."

"Perhaps they should," Adolfo replied. "The only help that ever reaches the poor of this parish comes from God and that doesn't put food on the table. It isn't right."

"No, it isn't," the young priest agreed. "But 'Blessed are the poor in spirit for theirs is the kingdom of Heaven.'"

"That's true in your profession, not mine," Adolfo said angrily.

He went to go but Norberto grasped his arm. He held it firmly. "I want you to tell me, Adolfo. What part did you have in the killing?"

"What part did I have?" Adolfo said quietly. "I

did it," he blurted out. "I'm the one who destroyed the yacht."

Norberto recoiled as though he'd been slapped.

"Millions of our people would have suffered had those monsters lived," Adolfo said.

Norberto made the sign of the cross on his forehead. "But they were men, Adolfo. Not monsters."

"They were ruthless, unfeeling *things,*" Adolfo snapped. He didn't expect his brother to understand what he had done. Norberto was a Jesuit, a member of the Society of Jesus. For over five hundred years the order's adherents had been trained to be soldiers of virtue, to strengthen the faith of Catholics and to preach the Gospel to non-Catholics.

"You are wrong." Norberto trembled as he squeezed Adolfo's arm even tighter. "These 'things,' as you call them, were people. People with immortal souls created by God."

"Then you should thank me, brother, for I have returned their immortal souls to God."

There were tears in the priest's eyes. "You take too much on yourself. Only God has the right to take a soul."

"I have to leave."

"And those millions you speak of," Norberto continued, "their suffering would only have been in this world. They would have known perfect happiness in the presence of God. But you—you risk damnation for eternity."

"Then pray for me, brother, for I intend to continue my work."

"*No,* Adolfo! You mustn't."

Adolfo gently pulled away his brother's fingers. He squeezed them lovingly before dropping them.

"At least let me hear your confession," Norberto urged.

"Some other time," Adolfo replied.

"Some other time may be too late." Norberto's voice, like his eyes, were now full of emotion. "You know the punishment if you die unrepentant. You will be estranged from God."

"God has forgotten me. Forgotten all of us."

"No!"

"I'm sorry," Adolfo said. The fisherman looked away from his brother. He didn't want to see the hurt in his kind eyes. And he didn't want to face the fact that he'd caused it. Not now. Not with so much left to do. He took another swallow of stew and thanked his brother again for bringing it. Then he pulled a cigarette from the crushed pack in his pants pocket—his last, he noted. He'd have to stop and buy pre-mades. Lighting it, he headed toward the door.

"Adolfo, please!" Norberto grabbed his brother's shoulder and turned him around. "Stay here with me. Talk to me. Pray with me."

"I have business up on the hill," he replied evenly. "I promised the General I'd deliver the taped conversation to the radio station there. They are Castilians at the station. They will play the tape. When they do, all the world will know that Catalonia has no regard for life, Spanish or otherwise. The government, the world will help end the financial oppression they've forced on us."

"And what will the world think of the Castilian who

killed these men?'' Norberto managed to lower his voice on the word *killed* lest he be overheard. ''Will they pray for your soul?''

''I don't want their prayers,'' Adolfo said without hesitation. ''I only want their attention. As for what the world will think, I hope they'll think that I had courage. That I didn't resort to shooting an unarmed woman in the street to make a point. That I went right to the heart of the devils' conspiracy and cut that heart out.''

''And when you have done that,'' Norberto said, ''the Catalonians will try to cut *your* heart out.''

''They may try,'' Adolfo admitted. ''Perhaps they will even succeed.''

''Then where does it end?'' Norberto asked. ''When every heart has been cut out or broken?''

''We didn't expect that one strike would end their ambitions or that Castilian lives would not be lost,'' Adolfo said. ''As for when the bloodshed will end, it should not be very long. By the time the Catalonians and their allies mobilize it will be too late to stop what is coming.''

Norberto's broad shoulders slumped and he shook his head slowly. The tears rolled easily from his eyes. He suddenly seemed spent.

''Dear God, Dolfo,'' he sobbed. ''What is coming? Tell me, so that at least I can pray for your soul.''

Adolfo stared at his brother. He rarely saw Norberto cry. It had happened once at their mother's funeral and another time over a young parishioner who was dying. It was difficult to see it and be unmoved.

''I and my comrades are planning to give Spain

back to its Castilian people,'' Adolfo said. "After a thousand years of repression, we intend to reunite the body of Spain with its heart."

"There are other means with which to accomplish that goal," Norberto said. "Nonviolent means."

"They've been tried," Adolfo said. "They don't work."

"Our Lord never raised a sword nor took a life."

Adolfo lay a hand on his brother's shoulder. "My brother," he said as he looked into Norberto's tear-glossed eyes, "if you can arrange for His help, then I will not take another life. I swear."

Norberto looked as if he wanted to say something but stopped. Adolfo patted his cheek and smiled. Turning, he opened the door and stepped out. He stopped and lowered his head.

Adolfo believed in a just God. He did not believe in a God who punished those who sought freedom. He couldn't let his brother's beliefs affect him. But this *was* Norberto, a good man who had worried about him man and boy and cared for him and loved him whatever he did. He couldn't leave him in pain.

Adolfo looked back. He smiled at his brother and touched his soft cheek. "Don't pray for me, Norberto. Pray for our country. If Spain is damned, my salvation will be unhappy—and undeserved."

He drew on the cigarette and hurried down the steps leaving a trail of smoke and his weeping brother behind him.

EIGHT

Paul Hood took his daily late-afternoon look at the list of names on his computer monitor. Just a few minutes before he had put his thumb on the five-by-seven-inch scanner beside the computer. The laser unit had identified his fingerprint and had asked for his personal access code. One point seven seconds later it brought up the closed file of HUMINT personnel reporting to Op-Center from the field. Hood used the keyboard to enter his wife's maiden name, Kent. That opened the file and the names appeared on the screen.

There were nine "human intelligence" agents in all. Each of these men and women was a national on Op-Center's payroll. Beside the names were their present whereabouts and assignments; a summary of their last report, which had been prepared by Bob Herbert (the full report was on file); and the location of the nearest safe house or exit route. If any of the operatives were ever found out, Op-Center would look for them at those places and make every effort to extricate them. To date, none of the agents had ever been compromised.

Three of the operatives were based in North Korea.

Their mission was an ongoing follow-up to the Striker team's destruction of the secret missile site in the Diamond Mountains. The agents' job was to make sure that the missile launchers weren't rebuilt. Even though a traitorous South Korean officer had masterminded the construction of the base originally, no one put it past the opportunistic North Koreans to take advantage of the equipment that had been left behind by attempting to build a new missile installation.

Two Op-Center agents were located in the Bekaa Valley in Lebanon and two others were working in Damascus, Syria. Both teams were based in terrorist hideouts and were reporting on the political fallout due to Op-Center's activities there. The fact that Op-Center operatives had helped to avert a war between Syria and Turkey was not being looked upon favorably: the feeling in the Middle East was that nations there took care of their own problems, even if that solution was war. Peace brought by outside forces, particularly by the United States, was looked upon as illicit and dishonorable.

The last two agents were in Cuba, keeping an eye on developing political situations in that nation. The reports were that the aging Castro's hold was beginning to fray. Whatever the dictator's drawbacks—and they were considerable—his iron heel had ironically kept the entire Caribbean more or less stabilized. Whatever tyrant came to power in Haiti, Grenada, Antigua, or on any of the other islands still needed the approval of Castro to run arms or drugs or even maintain a sizeable military force. They knew that the Cuban leader would have rivals assassinated before he let them become too powerful. The concensus was that as soon as Castro was gone, chaos and not democracy would come to the island and to the region. The United States had a contingency plan, Operation Keel, to fill and control that power vacuum using the military and economic incentives. Op-Center's agents were key parts of the EWAP network—early warning and preparedness—which was designed to pave the way for the plan.

Nine lives, Hood thought. And for each of those lives there were maybe two, three, or four dependents. That was not a responsibility to be taken lightly. He examined the afternoon reports and saw that the situations were relatively stable and unchanged. He closed the file.

These foreign operatives counted on their files and their communications with Op-Center to be absolutely secure. They contacted Op-Center by calling a telephone number at an office in Washington, an office that rented space to executives. The number was registered to Caryn Nadler International Travel Consultants. The operatives spoke in their native languages, though each word they used was assigned a different meaning in English. ''Can I book a flight to Dallas?'' in Arabic could mean ''The Syrian President is gravely ill'' in English. Though the translation files were all dedicated, seven people other than Paul Hood had access to them . . . and also to the identities of the operatives. Bob Herbert and Mike Rodgers were two of them and Darrell McCaskey was the third. Hood trusted them completely. But what about the other four people, two of them in Herbert's office, one in

McCaskey's group, and one on Rodgers's team? All of them had passed standard background checks, but were those checks thorough enough? Were the codes themselves sufficiently secure in the event that foreign surveillance picked them up? Unfortunately, one never knew the answer to that until someone disappeared or a mission was sabotaged or a team was ambushed.

There was peril in espionage and intelligence work. That was a given. For the operatives, the danger was also part of the excitement. Despite what had happened to Martha in Spain, Op-Center was doing everything it could to minimize the risks. At the moment, the shooting of Martha Mackall was being investigated by Darrell McCaskey, Aideen Marley, and Interpol in Spain. Mike Rodgers and Bob Herbert were studying intelligence reports here and Ron Plummer was talking to foreign diplomats in Washington and abroad. Carol Lanning was conferring with State Department contacts. Whether it was NASA, the Pentagon, or Op-Center, the cleanups were always so damn thorough.

In retrospect, why didn't the preparations ever seem as careful? Hood asked himself. *Because it* was *retrospect, dammit.* They had the luxury of hindsight to see what they did wrong.

What had they done wrong here? Op-Center had had no choice about sending Martha. After Av Lincoln had suggested her name and Serrador had approved her, she had to go. As for Aideen working as her assistant instead of Darrell—it made complete sense. Aideen spoke the language, which Darrell did not. Serrador had risen from a working-class family and so had Aideen—Hood thought that might help them.

And even if Darrell had been there with them, that probably wouldn't have helped Martha. Not if she was the target.

Still, Hood was ashamed that the system had failed on his watch. Ashamed and also angry.

He was angry at so much right now he couldn't focus on any one thing for long. He was angry at the cavalier way in which a life had been ended. Hood abhorred murder for any reason. When he had first come to Op-Center, he'd read a closed CIA file about a small assassination squad created during the Kennedy administration. Over a dozen foreign generals and diplomats were executed from 1961 to 1963. The justification for the existence of such a team was politically valid, Hood supposed. However, he had trouble accepting it morally—even if lives were saved in the long run.

But that was the tragedy about Martha's death. It wasn't as if a despot had been removed to improve the life of others, or a terrorist had been taken out to prevent a bombing or shooting. Someone had gunned down Martha to make a point. A *point*.

He was angry at the Spanish government. They had asked for help with satellite surveillance, to watch terrorist activities, and they'd gotten it. But when it came to giving help they were less than forthcoming. If they had any information about the shooting they weren't sharing it. What little information Op-Center possessed had come from Darrell McCaskey, who had gotten it from his sources at Interpol. No one had claimed responsibility for the killing. Herbert's surveys of the airwaves and fax transmissions to govern-

ment and police offices had confirmed that. The
getaway car had not been found either by ground or
helicopter surveillance, and the National Reconnaissance Office at the Pentagon had been unable to spot
it by satellite. The Spanish police were searching for
a *cortacarro,* the Spanish equivalent of a chop shop.
But if the car had been driven to one, no one expected
to find the vehicle before it was dismantled. The bullets were undergoing chemical tests to see if their point
of origin could be determined. By the time they were
traced, and assuming whoever bought them could be
identified, the trail would be cold. Finally, McCaskey
reported that the mail carrier who had died had no
criminal background. He appeared to be an unfortunate bystander.

Hood was also angry at himself. He should have
had enough foresight instead of hindsight not to have
let Martha and Aideen undertake what amounted to an
undercover operation without a shadow or two, someone to watch their backs. Perhaps the gunman couldn't
have been stopped but maybe he could have been captured. Just because the job was clean—an office meeting instead of open surveillance or espionage—he'd
let them go in alone. He hadn't anticipated trouble. No
one had. The congressional security office had a solid
reputation and there was no reason to doubt their efficiency.

Martha had paid for his carelessness.

The office door was open and Ann Farris walked
in. Hood looked up. She was dressed in an oyster-
colored pantsuit, her brown hair bobbed chin-length.
Her eyes were soft and her expression was compas-

sionate. Hood glanced back at the computer monitor just to look away.

"Hi," he said.

"Hi," Ann replied. "How're you doing?"

"Lousy," Hood said. He opened a file Herbert had transmitted about Serrador. "What's doing on your end?"

"A couple of reporters have connected Martha with Op-Center," Ann said, "but only Jimmy George at the *Post* has figured out that she probably wasn't there as a tourist. He agreed to hold the story for a day or two in exchange for some exclusives."

"Fine. We'll give him the morgue shots," Hood said bitterly. "That'll sell a few papers."

"He's a good man, Paul," Ann replied. "He's playing fair."

"I suppose he is," Hood replied. "At least there was a dialogue between you two. You spoke and reason prevailed. Remember reason, Ann? Remember reason and talk and negotiation?"

"I remember them," Ann said. "And the truth is, a lot of people still practice them."

"Not enough," Hood said. "When I was mayor of L.A. I had a feud with Governor Essex. Lord Essex, we called him. He didn't like what he called my unorthodox way of doing things. He said he couldn't trust me." Hood shook his head. "The truth is, I cared about the quality of life in Los Angeles while he dreamed of being President. Those two goals didn't mix. So he stopped talking to me. We had to communicate through Lieutenant Governor Whiteshire. The joke is, L.A. didn't get the money it needed and

Essex didn't get reelected as governor. Freakin' baby. Politicians don't communicate, sometimes families don't communicate, and then we're surprised when things come apart. I'm sorry, Ann. I congratulate you for talking to Mr. George.''

Ann walked over and leaned across the desk. She reached out her right hand and touched the back of Hood's hand with her fingertips. They felt gentle and very, very feminine. "Paul, I know how you feel.''

"I know that,'' Hood said softly. "If anyone does, you do.''

"But you've got to believe that no one could have anticipated this,'' Ann said.

"There you're wrong,'' Hood replied. He withdrew his hand from under hers. "We screwed up. *I* screwed up.''

"Nobody screwed up,'' she said. "This was unforeseeable.''

"No,'' he replied. "It was just unforeseen. We have combat simulations, terrorist simulations, and even assassination simulations. I can push a button on this computer and it'll show us ten different ways to capture or kill the warlord-of-the-month. But the process of anticipating simple security problems wasn't built into our system and Martha is dead as a result.''

Ann shook her head. "Even if we'd had security people watching her, Paul, this couldn't have been prevented. They couldn't have moved in in time. You know that as well as I do.''

"At least they might have gotten the killer.''

"Maybe,'' Ann said. "And Martha would still be dead.''

Hood wasn't convinced, though he would know more when his own cleanup analysis was completed. "Is there anything else we have to take care of, press-wise?" he asked as his phone beeped twice. That meant it was an internal call. Hood glanced at the caller code. It was Bob Herbert.

"Not a thing," Ann said. She rolled her lips together as though she wanted to say more, but she didn't.

So much for communication, Hood thought cynically as he picked up the phone. "Yes, Bob?"

"Paul," he said urgently, "we've got something."

"Go ahead."

"We picked this recording up from a small commercial radio station in Tolosa. I'm sending it over on the Vee-Bee. We haven't been able to verify the authenticity of the tape you're about to hear, though we'll be able to do that in about an hour. We're getting sound bites of the speaker from a Spanish television station here in order to compare the voices. My gut tells me they're real but we'll know for sure in an hour or so.

"The first voice you're going to hear is the local radio announcer introducing the tape," Herbert went on. "The second voice is from the tape itself. I'm e-mailing the translation over as well."

Hood acknowledged as he closed the Serrador file and brought up Herbert's e-mail. Then he hit the Vee-Bee key on the keyboard. The Vee-Bee, or Voice Box, was the equivalent of audio e-mail. The sounds were digitally scanned and cleaned by one of "Miracle" Matt Stoll's computer programs. The audio delivered by the Vee-Bee simulator was as close to real life as possible. Thanks to the digital encoding, the listener could even isolate background or foreground sounds and play them separately.

Ann came around the desk and leaned over Hood's shoulder. Her warmth, her closeness were comforting. He concentrated on reading the translation as the message played.

"Ladies and gentlemen, good evening," said the announcer. "We interrupt the supper club troubador to report about further developments in the explosion of the yacht tonight in La Concha Bay. A few minutes ago, a tape recording was delivered to our studio. It was brought by a man who represented himself as a member of the First People of Spain. This recording is reportedly of a conversation which took place on-board the yacht, identified as the *Verídico*, moments before it blew up. With the delivery of this tape, the FPS claims responsibility for the attack. They also declare Spain as the province of Spaniards, not of the elite of Catalonia. We will play the recording in its entirety."

A parenthetical comment from Herbert read: *The FPS is a group of Castilian pure-bloods. They've been publishing broadsides and recruiting members for two years. They've also claimed responsibility for two acts of terrorism against Catalonian and Andalusian targets. Their size and the identity of their leader(s) is unknown.*

His jaw tightening, Hood continued reading the transcript as the recording began to play. He listened to the cool, quiet voice of Esteban Ramirez as he spoke about the Catalonian plans for Spain and boasted about the involvement of his group in the murder of Martha Mackall. His group—with the help of Congressional Deputy Isidro Serrador.

"Lord Jesus," Hood said through his teeth. "Bob— is this possible?"

"Not only is it possible," Herbert said, "but it explains Serrador's unwillingness to continue the talks with Darrell and Aideen. That son of a bitch set us up, Paul."

Hood looked at Ann. He'd seen many of her darker moods during their nearly two years together but he'd never seen anything like the way she looked now. The compassion had faded completely from her face. Her lips were pressed tightly together and he could hear her breathing through her nostrils. Her eyes were hard and her cheeks were flushed.

"What do you want to do, Paul?" Herbert asked Hood. "And before you answer, keep in mind that the Spanish courts are not going to throw the book at a leading political figure because of an illegal tape recording made by someone whose hands are probably as dirty if not dirtier than Serrador's. They'll have a long, tough talk with him and investigate the hell out of him. But if he's got friends—and I'm sure he has— they're going to say he was framed. They'll do everything they can to stall the machinery of justice."

"I know," Hood said.

"I know you know," Herbert replied. "But they could let him plea-bargain, just to keep his constituents happy. Or they may let him off. Or they may let him 'escape' the country when no one's looking. What I'm saying is, we may have to take this matter into our own hands. If Serrador turns out to be a terrorist sponsor, we should fight fire with fire.''

''I hear you,'' Hood said. He thought for a moment. ''I want the bastard, and if I can't have him legally at least I want him dead-to-rights.''

So much for higher morality, Hood told himself. He thought for a moment more. He didn't want Serrador to slip away. Unfortunately, he had only two HUMINT resources on the scene, Darrell and Aideen. And he didn't know if they were up to keeping tabs on him until Striker or some third party group could get in and have a heart-to-heart talk with the bastard. He'd have to talk to Darrell about that. In the meantime, he needed more intelligence.

''Bob,'' Hood said, ''I want you to set up whatever electronic recon you can on the deputy.''

''It's already done,'' Herbert said. ''We're getting on top of his office and home phones, fax lines, modem, and mail.''

''Good.''

''What do you plan on doing with Darrell and Aideen?'' Herbert asked.

''I'm going to talk to Darrell and then leave the decision in his hands. He's onsite; it should be his call. But before I do I want to talk to Carol Lanning, see if State can give us the big picture of what's really going on in Spain.''

''What do you think is going on?'' Ann asked.

''Unless I miss my guess,'' Hood said, ''the death

of Martha and her killers probably weren't just warning shots.''

"What were they?'' she asked.

Hood looked at her as he rose. "I believe they were the opening salvos of a civil war.''

NINE

Monday, 11:30 P.M.
Madrid, Spain

During the months that Congress was in session, Deputy Isidro Serrador lived in a two-bedroom apartment in the very fashionable Parque del Retiro section of Madrid. His small seventh-floor rooms overlooked the spectacular boating lake and beautiful gardens. If one leaned out the window and glanced toward the southwest, Europe's only public statue of the devil was visible. Sculpted in 1880, the statue commemorated the only place where eighteenth-century Spanish ladies were permitted—by tradition, not by law—to defend their own honor in duels. Very few women had ever done so, of course. Only men were vain enough to risk their lives in order to reply to an insult.

Serrador was sitting in a divan and looking out the window at the lamplit park. He had come home after working on congressional business for the rest of the day, content in the knowledge that things had gone exactly as planned. Then he had taken a hot bath and briefly fallen asleep in the tub. When he got out, he turned on the oven to heat the dinner left for him by his housekeeper. He enjoyed a brandy while his pork shoulder, boiled potatoes, and chickpeas warmed.

While he ate, on the hour, he would watch television and see how the news channel interpreted the shooting of the American "tourist." Then he would check his answering machine for calls and return them if it wasn't too late. He just didn't feel like dealing with people right now. He simply wanted to savor his triumph.

Watching the news, he thought, *will be very amusing.*

The experts would talk about the impact of the shooting on tourism without having any idea what was truly going on—or what was going to happen over the next few weeks. It was astonishing how little political and economic forecasters ever really knew. For everyone who said *this,* someone else said *that.* It was all just an exercise, a game.

His back was settled comfortably in the thick pillows and his bare feet lay crossed on the coffee table in front of him. The last of the brandy was settled comfortably in the back of his throat and reflections of the day's developments were resting comfortably in his head.

The plan was ingenious. Two minorities, the Basques and the Catalonians, would unite to take over Spain. The Basques would contribute their arms, muscle, and experience at terrorist tactics. The Catalonians would use their influence over the economy, winning political converts by threatening a massive depression. Once control over the nation was established, the Catalonians would grant autonomy to the Basque country, allowing those—like Serrador—who wanted self-rule to have it. And the wealthy Catalonians would continue to run Spain, keeping the other nonautonomous groups in check by controlling commerce.

It was ingenious—and foolproof.

The telephone rang a moment before there was a knock on the door. Serrador started as his reverie was interrupted—on two fronts, no less. Grumbling unhappily, the politician slid his feet into his slippers and rose. As he shuffled toward the telephone he shouted roughly for whoever was at the door to wait a minute. No one could come upstairs without being announced by the concierge. So he wondered which of the neighbors wanted a favor at this hour. Was it the owner of the grocery chain who needed to expand his stores? Or the Castilian bicycle manufacturer who wanted to ship more units to Morocco, the bastard. At least the grocer paid for favors. The bicycle maker asked for them just because he happened to live on the same floor. Serrador helped them because he didn't want to make an enemy. One never knew when the neighbors might see or hear something that could be compromising.

Serrador wondered why he was never visited by one of the beautiful concubines who lived here. There were at least three that he knew of, kept by government ministers who went home to their wives each night.

The antique telephone sat on a small drop-leaf table in the carpeted foyer. Serrador finished tying the red sash of his smoking jacket and picked up the receiver. Let them wait at the door another minute, whoever it was. He'd had a long and exhausting day.

"*Sí?*" he said.

The pounding on the door grew more insistent.

Someone outside was calling his name but he didn't recognize the voice.

Serrador couldn't hear whoever was speaking on the telephone. Annoyed, he turned from the mouthpiece and yelled at the door. "Just a moment!" Then he scowled down at the phone. "Yes? What is it?"

"Hello?" said the caller.

"Yes?"

"I'm calling on behalf of Mr. Ramirez."

Serrador felt a chill. "Who is this?"

"My name is Juan Martinez, *señor,*" said the caller. "Are you Deputy Serrador?"

"Who is Juan Martinez?" Serrador demanded. *And who is at the door? What the* hell *is going on?*

"I'm a member of the *familia,*" Martinez said.

A key clattered against the door. The bolt was thrown back. Serrador glared over as the door opened. The superintendent stood in the hallway. Behind him were two police officers and a sergeant.

"I am sorry, *Señor Deputy,*" said the concierge as the other men entered around him. "These men I had to let up."

"What are you doing?" Serrador demanded of them. His voice was indignant, his eyes unforgiving. Suddenly, he heard the phone click off, followed by the dial tone. He froze with the buzzing phone pressed to his ear, realizing suddenly that something had gone terribly wrong.

"Deputy Delegado Isidro Serrador?" asked the sergeant.

"Yes—"

"You will please come with us."

"Why?"

"To answer questions regarding the murder of an American tourist."

Serrador pressed his lips together. He breathed loudly through his nose. He didn't want to say anything, ask anything, do anything until he'd had a chance to speak with his attorney. And think. People who didn't think were doomed before they started.

He nodded once. "Permit me to dress," he said. "Then I will come with you."

The sergeant nodded and sent one of the men to stand by the bedroom door. He wouldn't let Serrador shut it but the deputy didn't make an issue of it. If he let his temper go there'd be no getting that genie back in the bottle. It was best to suffer the humiliation and stay calm and rational.

The men took Serrador down to the cellar and out through the garage of the building—so he wouldn't have to suffer the embarrassment of being arrested, he assumed. At least they didn't handcuff him. He was placed in an unmarked police car and driven to the municipal police station on the other side of the park. There, he was escorted into a windowless room with a photo of the king on the wall, a hanging fixture with three bulbs in white tulip-shaped shades, and an old wooden table beneath it. There was a telephone on the table and he was told he could use it to make as many calls as he wished. Someone would come to speak with him shortly.

The door was shut and locked. Serrador sat in one of the four wooden chairs.

He phoned his attorney, Antonio, but he was not in.

Probably out with one of his young women, as a wealthy bachelor should be. He didn't leave a message. He didn't want Antonio coming home and some talkative nymph overhearing the message. There hadn't been any press waiting outside so at least this was being done quietly.

Unless they were at the front of my apartment? he thought suddenly. Maybe that was why the police had taken him out through the garage door. Maybe that was what the concierge had meant: *These men I had to let up.* The press often tried to get to people who lived in the building, and the staff was good about insulating celebrity tenants from reporters. And his telephone number was changed regularly so they wouldn't be able to bother him.

But the caller had had it. He still wondered who that was and what he had tried to warn him about. No one could have known that he was involved with the people who had killed the American. Only Esteban Ramirez knew that and he wouldn't have told anyone.

It occurred to him then to telephone the answering machine in his office. It also occurred to him that this telephone might be bugged, but that was a chance he was willing to take. He didn't have much of a choice.

But before he could place the call, the door opened and two men walked in.

They were not police.

TEN

Tuesday, 12:04 A.M.
Madrid, Spain

The International Crime Police Organization—popularly referred to as Interpol—was established in Vienna in 1923. It was designed to serve as a worldwide clearinghouse for police information. After the Second World War, the organization was expanded and rechartered to focus on smuggling, narcotics, counterfeiting, and kidnapping. Today, one hundred seventy-seven nations provide information to the organization, which has offices in most of the major cities of the world. In the United States, Interpol liaises with the United States National Central Bureau. The USNCB reports to the Undersecretary for Enforcement of the U.S. Treasury Department.

During his years with the FBI, Darrell McCaskey had worked extensively with dozens of Interpol officers. He had worked especially closely with two of them in Spain. One was the remarkable María Corneja, a lone wolf special operations officer who had lived with McCaskey in America for seven months while studying FBI methods. The other was Luis García de la Vega, the commander of Interpol's office in Madrid.

Luis was a dark-skinned, black-haired, bear-large,

two-fisted Andalusian Gypsy who taught flamenco dancing in his spare time. Like the dance style, the thirty-seven-year-old Luis was spontaneous, dramatic, and spirited. He ran one of the toughest and best-informed Interpol bureaus in Europe. Their efficiency and effectiveness had earned him both the jealous loathing and deep respect of local police forces.

Luis had intended to come to the hotel right after the shooting, but the events in San Sebastián had caused him to delay his visit. He arrived shortly after eleven-thirty P.M., as McCaskey and Aideen were finishing dinner.

Darrell greeted his old friend with a long embrace.

"I'm sorry about what has happened," Luis said in husky, accent-tinged English.

"Thank you," McCaskey said.

"I'm also sorry to be so late," Luis said, finally breaking the hug. "I see that you have adapted the Spanish way of dining. Eat very late at night and then sleep well."

"Actually," said McCaskey, "this is the first chance we've had to order room service. And I'm not sure either of us will be able to sleep tonight, however much we eat."

"I understand," Luis remarked. He squeezed his friend's shoulders. "A terrible day. Again, I'm very sorry."

"Would you care for something, Luis?" McCaskey asked. "Some wine, perhaps?"

"Not while I am on duty," Luis replied. "You should know that. But please, you two go ahead." His eyes fell on Aideen and he smiled. "You are Señorita Marley."

"Yes." Aideen rose from the table and offered her hand. Though she was physically and emotionally exhausted, something came alive when she touched the man's hand. He was attractive, but that wasn't what had stimulated her. After everything that had happened today she was too numb, too depleted to care. What he gave her was the sense of not being afraid of anything. She had always responded to that in a man.

"I'm sorry about your loss," Luis said. "But I'm glad that you are all right. You *are* all right?"

"Yes," she said as she sat back down. "Thanks for your concern."

"Mi delicia," he said. "My pleasure." Luis pulled over an arm chair and joined them at the table.

McCaskey resumed eating his spicy partridge. "So?"

"That smells very good," Luis said.

"It is," McCaskey said. His eyes narrowed. "You're stalling, Luis."

Luis rubbed the back of his neck. *"Sí,"* he admitted. "I'm stalling 'big time,' as you say in America. But it's not because I have something. It's because I have nothing. Only thoughts. Ideas."

"Your thoughts are usually as good as someone else's facts," McCaskey said. "Would you care to share them?"

Luis took a drink from McCaskey's water glass. He gestured vaguely toward the window. "It's terrible out there, Darrell. Simply terrible. And it's getting worse.

We've had very small anti-Basque and anti-Catalonian riots in Ávila, Segovia, and Soria.''

"All Castilian regions," Aideen said.

"Yes," Luis remarked. "It doesn't appear as if the police there are doing everything they can to prevent these outbursts."

"The police are standing along racial lines," McCaskey said.

Luis nodded slowly. "I've never seen such—I'm not even certain what to call it."

"Collective insanity," Aideen said.

Luis regarded her. "I don't understand."

"It's the kind of thing psychologists have been warning about regarding the coming millennium," Aideen said. "The fear that we're all going into it but most of us won't be coming out alive. Result: a sense of mortality which brings out panic. Fear. Violence."

Luis looked at her and pointed. "Yes, that's right. It's as though everyone has caught some kind of mental and physical fever. My people who have gone to those regions say there's a sense of hatred and excitement you can almost feel. Very strange."

McCaskey frowned. "I hope you're not saying that Martha's shooting is part of a mass psychotic episode."

Luis waved his hand dismissively. "No, of course not. I'm merely remarking that something strange is happening out there. Something I've never felt before." He leaned forward, toward the Egg. "There is also something brewing, my friends. Something that I think is very well planned."

"What kind of 'something'?" McCaskey asked.

"The ship that sank in San Sebastián was destroyed with C-4," Luis said. "Traces were found on some of the debris."

"We heard that from Bob Herbert," McCaskey said. He regarded Luis expectantly. "Go on. There's an 'and' in your voice."

Luis nodded. "One of the dead men, Esteban Ramirez, was at one time a CIA courier. His company's yachts were used to smuggle arms and personnel to contacts around the world. There have been whisperings about that for a while, but those whisperings are bound to become louder now. People here will say he was hit by American agents."

"Do you believe that the CIA was involved in the attack, Luis?" Aideen asked.

"No. They wouldn't have done something so public. Nor would they have been so quick to retaliate for the murder of your colleague. But there will be loud gossip about that in political circles. No one talks more than people in government. You know that, Darrell."

McCaskey nodded.

"And the Spanish people will hear about it," Luis continued. "Many will believe it and turn on Americans here."

"According to Bob Herbert, who I spoke with earlier," McCaskey said, "the Agency is as surprised by the attack on the yacht as everyone else is. And Bob always gets through the bureaucratic double-talk over there. He knows when they're bullshitting him."

"I agree that the CIA probably isn't behind this," Luis said. "So here is a possible scenario. An American diplomat is murdered. That sends a message to your government to stay out of Spanish affairs. Then the men who killed her are murdered. The tape recording tells all of Spain that the Catalonian dead and their Basque accomplice, Deputy Serrador, are ruthless assassins. That turns the rest of the nation against those two groups.''

''To what end?'' McCaskey asked. ''Who benefits from a civil war? The economy is ravaged and everyone suffers.''

''I've been considering that,'' Luis said. ''By law, treason is punishable by capital punishment and a seizure of assets. The taking of Catalonian businesses would help to distribute power more evenly among other groups. Conceivably, the Castilians, Andalusians, and Galicians would all benefit.''

''Back up a moment,'' Aideen said. ''What would the Catalonians and Basques gain by joining forces?''

''The Catalonians control the heart of Spain's economy,'' Luis said, ''and a core group among the separatist Basques are highly experienced terrorists. These are very complementary assets if one is looking to paralyze a nation and then take it over.''

''Attack the physical and financial infrastructure,'' McCaskey said, ''then come in and save it like a white knight.''

''Exactly. A cooperative effort supports intelligence we have had—not first hand and not enough to act upon—that they have been planning a combined action of some kind.''

''How'd you come by this information?'' McCaskey asked.

''Our source was a longtime hand on the Ramirez

yacht,'' Luis said. ''A good man. Reliable. He was killed in the explosion. He reported on frequent meetings between Ramirez and key members of industry, as well as regular trips along the Bay of Biscay.''

''Basque Country,'' remarked McCaskey.

Luis nodded. ''With frequent disembarkments by Ramirez. Our informant reported that a bodyguard always went with him, some member of his *familia*. He had no idea who Ramirez met there or why. He only knew that over the last six months the meetings increased from once-monthly to once-weekly.''

''Is there any chance that your informant was double-dipping?'' McCaskey asked.

''You mean selling this information to someone else?'' Luis asked.

''That's right.''

''I suppose it's possible,'' Luis said. ''Obviously, some outside person or group learned what Ramirez and his people were planning and made sure that things went wrong. The question is who. To begin with, whoever stopped Ramirez and his group knew that the assassination of your diplomat was going to happen.''

''How do you know that?'' McCaskey asked.

''Because the yacht was bugged and booby-trapped before the assassination,'' Luis informed him. ''They obtained the taped confession, the man who shot Martha arrived, and they blew the yacht up.''

''Right,'' McCaskey said. ''Very neat and professional.''

''The whole thing has been very neat and professional,'' Luis agreed. ''You know, my friends, talking about civil war—there are those who believe that the last one never really ended. That differences were merely patched over with—what do you call them?''

"Band-Aids?" Aideen offered.

Luis pointed at her. "That's right."

Aideen shook her head. "Can you imagine," she said, "the enormous impact that a person—not a group, but an individual—would make by bringing a final and lasting end to the strife?"

Both men looked at her.

"The new Franco," Luis said.

"Right," said Aideen.

"That's a helluva thought," McCaskey agreed.

"It's like the old Boston election racket my father used to talk about when I was a kid," Aideen continued. "A guy hires thugs to terrorize shopkeepers. Then one day that same guy picks up a baseball bat and stands guard at a fish store or shoe shop or newsstand and chases the thugs away—which he'd also paid them to do in the first place. Next thing you know he's running for public office and gets the workingman's vote."

"The same thing could be happening here," Luis said.

Aideen nodded slowly. "It's possible."

"Anybody you know who might fit that profile, Luis?" McCaskey asked.

"*Madre de Dios,* there are so many politicians, officers, and business figures who could do that job," Luis said. "But what we have decided is this. Someone in San Sebastián destroyed the yacht. Someone else delivered the tape to the radio station. Whether these people are still in the village or not, there has to be a trail. We have asked someone to go up there tonight and have a look. She's being helicoptered up"—he looked at his watch—"in two hours."

"I'd like to go with her," Aideen said. She threw her napkin on the table and rose.

"I'll be happy to send you," Luis said. He regarded McCaskey warily. "That is, if you don't mind."

McCaskey gave him a funny look. "Who's going up there?"

"María Corneja," Luis answered softly.

McCaskey quietly placed his knife and fork on his plate. Aideen watched as a strange discomfiture came over the normally stoic former G-man. It started with a sad turn of the mouth then grew to include the eyes.

"I didn't realize she was working with you again," McCaskey said. He touched his napkin to his lips.

"She returned about six months ago," Luis said. "I brought her back." He shrugged. "She needed the money so she could keep her small theater in Barcelona going. And I needed her because—*pues, she is* the best."

McCaskey was still looking away. Far away. He managed a weak smile. "She is good."

"The best."

McCaskey finally raised his eyes. He looked at Aideen for a very long moment. She couldn't imagine what was going through his mind.

"I'll have to clear it with Paul," he said, "but I'm in favor of having our own intel from the site. Take your tourist papers." He looked at Luis. "Will María be going as an Interpol officer or not?"

"That will be her call," he replied. "I want her to have the freedom to act."

McCaskey nodded. Then he fell silent again.

Aideen looked at Luis. "I'll get a few things together. How are we going to San Sebastián?"

"By helicopter from the airport," he said. "You'll have a rental car when you arrive. I'll phone María to let her know that you will be accompanying her. Then I will take you over."

McCaskey looked at Luis. "Did she know I was here, Luis?"

"I took the liberty of informing her." He patted the back of his friend's hand. "It's all right. She gave you her best."

McCaskey's expression grew sad again. "That she did," he replied. "That she most surely did."

ELEVEN

Tuesday, 12:07 A.M.
San Sebastián, Spain

When Juan Martinez maneuvered the runabout away from the Ramirez yacht, the twenty-nine-year-old sailor and navigator had no idea that he'd be saving his own life.

Idling roughly twenty-five meters from the boat, Juan was rocked from his feet by the explosion. But his small boat was not overturned. As soon as the main blast had died, the muscular young man threw the small boat ahead, toward the listing ship.

He had found Esteban Ramirez—who was his employer as well as the father of their powerful *familia*—lying face-up in the water. His severely burned body was floating some fifteen meters from the yacht. Holding on to a mooring rope, Juan jumped into the choppy waters. Dog-paddling toward Ramirez with his free hand and feet, he reached the man and pulled him toward the boat.

His employer was still breathing.

"Señor Ramirez," Juan said. "It's Juan Martinez. I'm going to bring you onto the runabout and get you to a—"

"*Listen!*" Ramirez wheezed suddenly.

Juan started. A moment later Ramirez's groping hand latched onto his sleeve. His grip was surprisingly strong.

"Serrador!" Ramirez said. "Warn . . . him."

"Serrador?" Juan said. "I don't know him, sir."

"Office—" Ramirez choked. "Reading glasses."

"Please, sir," Juan said. "You mustn't exert yourself—"

"*Must call!*" Ramirez said. "Do . . . it!"

"All right," Juan said, "I promise to call."

Just then, Ramirez began to tremble violently. "Get them . . . or they . . . will . . . get us."

"Who will?" Juan asked.

Suddenly, Juan heard the chugging of an engine on the other side of the yacht. He saw the edges of a bright white light creeping around it, playing across the water. A searchlight. A boat was approaching. Juan didn't know much about his boss's business affairs but he did know that their company's powerful *familia* had many enemies. The boat might not belong to one of them, but he wasn't sure he wanted to take that risk.

Before Juan could get his employer onto the runabout, Ramirez opened his mouth but did not close it again. Air hissed softly from deep in his throat as his mouth hung frozen, agape.

Juan shut his employer's eyes. He decided to leave his body there. Doing so was a sign of disrespect and that bothered him. But whoever was responsible for the explosion might still be in the vicinity. Perhaps even on the boat that was approaching. Juan didn't think it was prudent to be found here. Climbing back onto the runabout, he engaged the engine and sped away before the boat arrived. He headed out to sea where he wouldn't be seen, then cut the engine. He remained until he saw the police arrive. Then he set out again, giving the accident a wide berth as he headed toward shore.

Upon reaching the dock, Juan went to a pay phone. Wet and chilly, he called the night watchman at the factory and asked him to send a car for him. Upon arriving, Juan went directly to Señor Ramirez's office. He forced open the door and sat behind his desk.

His employer had mentioned something about his reading glasses. Juan found the pair in the top drawer. He looked at them. Printed inside the frames—innocuously, like serial numbers—was a series of four telephone numbers and identifying letters.

Ingenious, Juan thought. His boss didn't need glasses—*hadn't* needed glasses, he thought bitterly—but no one would ever think to check them for coded messages or phone numbers.

He called the number with the *S* next to it. Serrador answered—whoever that was. The man was indignant, brusque, and in trouble, judging from the sounds Juan heard over the telephone. He decided to hang up before the call could be traced.

He remained behind the desk in the large second-floor office. He looked out the bank of windows at the large yacht factory. Esteban Ramirez had been good to him for many years. Juan hadn't been an intimate but he was a member of Señor Ramirez's *familia.* And that loyalty continued even after death.

Juan looked at the eyeglasses. He called the other numbers. Housekeepers answered using the family name: they were all men who had been on the ship. Juan knew because he had ferried them there.

Something evil was afoot, as Señor Ramirez had warned. Someone had been careful to wipe out everyone who was involved with the boss and his new project. It was a matter of honor, nothing else, that Juan find that someone and avenge the murders.

The night crew at the factory was already talking about the rumors of the death of their employer. They were also talking about a tape recording that had just been played at the local radio station. A tape that reportedly had their boss revealing his involvement in the murder of the American tourist.

Juan was too angry to allow himself to be overcome by grief. Rounding up several other members of the *familia*—two watchmen and a night manager—he decided to go to the radio station to find out if there were such a tape.

And if there were, find out who had brought it to them.

And whoever it was, cause him to regret that he had.

TWELVE

Paul Hood was unhappy. That was occurring a lot lately, and usually for the same reason.

Hood had phoned his wife to tell her that he'd be missing dinner with the family tonight.

"As usual," Sharon reminded him before leaving him with a curt goodbye and hanging up.

Hood tried not to blame his wife for being disappointed. How could he? She didn't know he'd lost Martha in the field. He wasn't permitted to discuss Op-Center matters with anyone over an open line. Anyway, Sharon was more upset for the two kids than for herself. She said that even though it was spring vacation, eleven-year-old Alexander had gotten up early and set up his new scanner by himself. He was burning to show his father some of the computer-morphs he'd created. By the time Hood got home most nights, Alexander was too drowsy to boot the system and talk him through the steps of whatever he'd been working on, which was what the boy liked to do. Thirteen-year-old Harleigh practiced her violin for an hour after dinner each night. Sharon said that for the past few days, ever since she'd mastered her Tchaikovsky piece, the house at sunset had been a magical place to be. Sharon said it would be more magical for them all if Paul were there once in a while.

A part of Hood felt guilty. Sharon and also Madison Avenue were responsible for that. Family-first was the advertising mantra of the nineties. But Pennsylvania Avenue made him feel guilty too. He had a responsibility to the President and to the nation. He had a responsibility to the people whose lives and livelihoods depended upon his industry, his judgment. His focus.

He and Sharon both knew what the rules were when he took this job. Wasn't it she who had wanted him to get out of politics? Wasn't she the one who had hated the fact that being the family of the mayor of Los Angeles had entitled them to zero privacy even when they were together? But the truth was, whatever he did Hood wasn't a high school principal with summers off like her father. He wasn't a banker anymore, who worked from eight-thirty to five-thirty with the occasional client dinner. Or an independently wealthy yachtsman like that rugged, self-impressed Italian winemaker Stefano Renaldo with whom she'd sailed the world before marrying Hood.

Paul Hood was a man who enjoyed his work and the responsibility of it. And he enjoyed the rewards, too. Each morning he woke up in the quiet house and went downstairs to make his coffee and sat there drinking it in the den and looking around and thinking, *I did this.*

They all enjoyed the rewards. There wouldn't *be* a computer or violin lessons or a nice house for them to miss him at if he didn't work hard. Sharon would have to work full-time instead of being able to appear semiregularly on a cable TV cooking show. She didn't have to thank him but did she have to damn him? She didn't have to enjoy his absence—he didn't—but she could make it easier.

His hand was still on the phone. His eyes were on his hand. It had taken only a moment for the pros and cons to flash through his brain. He lifted his hand and sat back, a sour look on his face.

These weren't exactly new or deeply buried feelings. Neither was the bitterness, which set in next. If only Sharon supported him instead of condemning him. It wouldn't make him try any harder to be home earlier. He couldn't. His hours were what they were. But it would make him feel like he had a real home to go to instead of a seminar on What's Wrong with Paul Hood.

He thought of Nancy Bosworth again. Not long before, he'd bumped into his old flame in Germany. Never mind that she'd been the one who ran out on him years before. Never mind that she'd shattered his heart. When he saw her again he felt drawn to her because she was someone who wanted him, uncritically. She had only kind and flattering things to say.

Of course, Hood said, his conscience taking Sharon's side, *Nancy can afford to be generous. She doesn't have to live with you and raise two kids and hurt for them when Dad's not there.*

But that didn't change the fact that he'd wanted to hold Nancy Jo Bosworth tightly and he'd wanted to be held *by* her. That he'd yearned to crawl into her arms because she wanted him there, not as a reward for being good to his kids. That was passionless.

Then he thought about Ann Farris. The beautiful and sexy press liaison liked him. She cared about him. She made him feel good about himself. And he liked her. There were many times when he'd had to fight the urge to reach across the desk and touch her hair. But he knew that if he ever crossed that line, even a bit, there would be no going back. Everyone at Op-Center would know. Washington would know. Eventually Sharon would know.

So what? he asked himself. *What's wrong with ending a marriage that isn't working the way you want it to anyway?*

The words hung in his brain like a medical diagnosis he didn't want to hear. He hated himself for even flirting with the notion of divorce, for despite everything he loved Sharon. And she had thrown in her lot with him, not with Renaldo. She had committed to building a life *with* him, not around him. And there were some things women would always be more possessive of than men. Like kids. That didn't make her right and him wrong, her good and him bad. It made them different, that's all. And differences could be worked out.

The bitterness was softened by the reminder that he and Sharon were vastly different people. She was a dreamer and he was a pragmatist. He was being judged by a standard that was more romantic wishfulness than reality. It was time to shelve those concerns for now because reality had to be dealt with. Besides, *because* they were family, his wife and children would forgive him.

At least, that's how it was supposed to work in the World According to Paul.

Mike Rodgers, Bob Herbert, and Ron Plummer arrived for a 5:15 update. Hood was ready for them, his conscience relatively clear and his mind almost entirely focused. Plummer had been named the acting diplomatic officer until an official review process for Martha's replacement could take place. That would not happen until the current crisis had passed. If Plummer had the chops for the job they'd know soon enough and the review would be a simple formality.

"Grim news," Herbert said as he rolled in on his automated wheelchair. "The Germans just canceled a big soccer match they were supposed to play tomorrow in Barcelona at the Olympic Stadium. Said they're concerned about the 'air of violence' in Spain."

"Will the cancellation be recorded as a forfeit for Germany?" Hood asked.

"That's a good question," Herbert said, "to which the answer is no, unfortunately." He pulled a printout from a pouch on the side of his chair. "The Federation of International Football Associations has ruled that in a nation where—and I quote—'there is a substantial disturbance of services or a reasonable fear for security, a visiting team may request a postponement for the duration of said unrest.' What's going on in Spain certainly fits that requirement."

"Which will probably cause more unrest among soccer fans," Plummer said, "which will help the situation unravel further."

"In a peanut shell, yeah," Herbert replied. "The prime minister is going to go on TV in the morning to urge everyone to stay calm. But the military has already been sent into major cities in three Castilian provinces to keep peace where the police have been sitting on their hands. The people there have always had a real dislike for the Catalonians and Basques who work there. The stuff with Serrador and the group in San Sebastián really sent them over the edge."

"The question is, where does it go from here?" Hood asked.

"We'll know more after the prime minister speaks," Plummer replied.

"What's your sense of things?" Hood pressed.

"The situation will probably deteriorate," Plummer said. "Spain has always been a patchwork of very different people—not unlike the Soviet Union was. Something like this, which polarizes ethnic groups, is a very tough fix."

Hood looked at Rodgers. "Mike?"

The general was leaning against the wall. He shifted slowly, still obviously in pain. "The military people I spoke with in Portugal are extremely concerned. They can't remember a time when tensions were so openly high."

"I'm sure you know that the White House has contacted our ambassador in Spain," Herbert said. "They've been told to button the embassy up tight."

Hood nodded. National Security Chief Steve Burkow had phoned a half hour earlier to tell him that the embassy in Madrid was being put on alert. Passes for the military staff had been revoked and all nonmilitary personnel were ordered to remain on the compound. There was some fear about further attacks against Americans. But there was a more general concern that Americans might get caught in the overall violence that seemed to be brewing.

"Does NATO have any jurisdiction here?" Hood asked.

"No," Rodgers replied. "They're not a domestic police force. I checked with General Roche, Commander-in-Chief of Allied Forces in Central Europe. He's pretty conservative. Doesn't want to plant a toe outside the charter."

"With Basques being attacked, the French Basques might not let it remain a domestic matter for long," Plummer said.

"That's true," said Rodgers. "But NATO still won't want to break their primary mandate, which is to resolve disputes between member nations peaceably."

"I know William Roche," Herbert said, "and I don't blame him. NATO still has egg on its face from the Serbian-Bosnian conflict in ninety-four. The Serbs violated designated safe havens all over the place despite the threat of limited NATO air strikes. If you don't intend to go in with everything you've got, stay on the sidelines."

"Anyway," Rodgers said, "there's a larger issue. If Portugal or France or any local government puts troops on alert it might help to precipitate a crisis."

"The Spanish are kinda ornery that way," Herbert said. "Groups of 'em will get together and start something because they're insulted that someone would *think* they'd start something."

"Are we talking about lynch mobs?" Hood asked.

"They might look for Portuguese or French nationals to beat up on," Herbert said. "Then, of course, those governments will have to respond."

Hood shook his head.

"Welcome to the world of precipitating crises," Herbert said. "From my kinfolk firing on Fort Sumter to blowing up the battleship *Maine*, from shooting Archduke Ferdinand to the bombing of Pearl Harbor. Give people a spark and you usually end up with a fire."

"That's the old way," Hood said tensely. "Our job is to figure out how to manage these things, to defuse crises." That came out sounding harsher than Hood had intended and he took a long, slow breath. He had to be careful not to let frustration with his personal crisis seep into his professional crisis. "Anyway," he said, "this brings us to the matter of Darrell and Aideen. Darrell has recommended sending Aideen to San Sebastián with an Interpol agent. I've okayed this. They're going to go undercover to try and find out how the tape from the yacht was made, by whom, and why."

"Who's the Interpol agent?" Herbert asked.

"María Corneja," Hood told him.

"Ouch," Herbert said. "That's got to sting a bit."

Hood thought back to his own brush with his former lover. "They'll have very minimal contact. Darrell will be able to handle it."

"I meant it's gonna sting her," Herbert said. "She

may handle it like the Castilians are handling the Catalonians.''

It was a joke but a nervous one. María had been infatuated with McCaskey. Their romance, two years before, had caused almost as much conversation as Op-Center's first crisis, finding and defusing a terrorist bomb onboard the space shuttle *Atlantis*.

''I'm not worried about it,'' Hood said. ''I *am* worried about giving Aideen an exit strategy in case something goes wrong. They're flying up to San Sebastián tonight. Darrell says that Interpol is worried about the same thing that's been hounding police all over Spain: ethnic loyalties within the organization.''

''Meaning that Aideen and María are on their own,'' Rodgers said.

''Pretty much,'' Hood agreed.

''Then I think we need Striker over there,'' Rodgers continued. ''I can set them down at the NATO airfield outside Zaragoza. That'll put them about one hundred miles south of San Sebastián. Colonel August knows that region well.''

''Get them going,'' Hood said. ''Ron, you'll have to take this to the CIOC. Get Lowell to work with you on it.''

Plummer nodded. Martha Mackall had always handled the Congressional Intelligence Oversight Committee pretty much on her own. But Op-Center's attorney Lowell Coffey knew his way around the group and would give Plummer an assist as needed.

''Is there anything else?'' Hood asked.

The men shook their heads. Hood thanked them and they agreed to meet again at six-thirty, just before the night shift came on. Though the day team officially remained in charge as long as they were on the premises, the presence of the backups allowed them to get rest if the situation dragged on through the night. Until things stabilized or got so far out of control that crisis management gave way to open war, Hood felt it was his duty to be onsite.

My duty, he thought. Everyone had a different idea about what duty was and to whom allegiance was owed. To Hood, the bottom line was that he owed it to his country. He'd felt that way ever since he first watched Davy Crockett die at the Alamo on a Walt Disney TV show. He'd felt that when he watched the astronauts fly into space on TV during Project Mercury, Project Gemini, and Project Apollo. Without that kind of devotion and sacrifice there was no nation. And without a safe and prosperous nation the kids had no future.

The trick was not so much convincing Sharon of that. She was a smart, smart lady. The trick was convincing her that his sacrifice mattered.

He couldn't let it rest. Against his better judgment Hood picked up the phone and called home.

THIRTEEN

Tuesday, 12:24 A.M.
Madrid, Spain

Isidro Serrador's small eyes were like stones as he watched the men walk into the room.

The congressional deputy was nervous and wary. He was unsure why he had been brought to the police station and had no idea what to expect. Had they somehow connected him with the death of the American diplomat? The only ones who knew were Esteban Ramirez and his comrades. And if they betrayed him he'd betray them right back. There was no point to that.

Serrador didn't recognize these men. He knew from the chevrons on the sleeves of the sharp brown uniforms that one was an army general and the other was a major general. He knew from the general's swarthy coloring, dark hair, flat black eyes, and lithe build that he was of Castilian ancestry.

The major general stopped several paces away. When the general was finally near enough so that Serrador could read the white letters on the small black name-tag attached to his breast pocket he knew his name: AMADORI.

Amadori raised a white-gloved hand. Without turning, he motioned crisply toward the major general. The officer set an audiotape player on the table. Then he left, shutting the door behind him.

Serrador looked up at Amadori. He couldn't read anything in the general's face. It was set perfectly and inexpressively. All formal lines like the creases in his uniform.

"Am I under arrest?" Serrador finally asked, quietly.

"You are not." Amadori's voice and manner were rigid—just like his lean face, like his unwrinkled uniform, like the taut, creaking leather of his new boots and twin holsters.

"Then what's going on?" Serrador demanded, feeling bolder now. "What is an army officer doing at the police station? And what is this?" He flicked a fat finger disdainfully at the tape recorder. "Am I being interrogated for something? Do you expect me to say something important?"

"No," Amadori answered. "I expect you to listen."

"To what?"

"To a recording that was broadcast on the radio a short time ago." Amadori stepped closer to the table. "When you're finished, you will have the choice of walking out of here or using this." He removed the Llama M-82 DA pistol, a 9 × 19mm Parabellum. He tossed it casually to Serrador, who caught it automatically, noted that there was no clip in it, and set it on the table between them.

There was a sudden queasiness in Serrador's groin. "Use that?" he said. "Are you insane?"

"Listen to the tape," Amadori said. "And when

you do, keep in mind that the men you hear have joined the American diplomat in the abode of the blessed. You are apparently a dangerous man to know, Deputy Serrador." Amadori stepped closer and smiled for the first time. He leaned toward Serrador and spoke in a voice that was barely above a whisper. "Keep this in mind as well. Your attempt to capture the government of Spain has failed. Mine will not."

"Yours," Serrador said warily.

Amadori's thin smile broadened. "A Castilian plan."

"Let me join you," Serrador said urgently. "I am Basque. Those other men, the Catalonians—they never wanted me to be part of their plan. I was convenient because of my position. I was an expeditor, not an equal. Let me work with you."

"There is no place for you," Amadori said coldly.

"There must be. I'm well connected. Powerful."

Amadori straightened and tugged down the hem of his jacket. He nodded toward the tape player. "You were," he said.

Serrador looked at the machine. Perspiration collected under his arms and along his upper lip. He jabbed a thick finger at the PLAY button.

"What of the driver in Madrid?" he heard someone say. It sounded like Carlos Saura, head of Banco Moderno. *"Is he leaving Spain as well?"*

"No. The driver works for Deputy Serrador." That was Esteban Ramirez, the bastard. Serrador listened for a few moments more as the men on the tape talked about the car and about the deputy being a Basque.

An *ambitious* Basque and willing to do anything to further the cause and himself.

The stupid, careless bastard, Serrador thought. He stopped the machine and folded his hands. He looked up at Amadori. "This is nothing," Serrador said. "Don't you see? This is designed to discredit me because of my heritage. It's blackmail."

"The men did not know they were being taped," Amadori informed him. "And your driver has already confessed to his part in exchange for immunity from prosecution."

"Then he lies," Serrador said dismissively. A plug of something caught in his throat. He swallowed it. "I still have a strong and loyal constituency. I'll beat this."

Amadori's smile returned. "No, you won't."

"You unremarkable *pig!*" Serrador flushed as fear shaded to indignation. "Who are you?" It was a slur, not a question. "You bring me here late at night and you force me to listen to a tape recording of questionable merit. Then you call me a traitor. I will fight for my life and for my honor. You won't win this."

Amadori smirked. "But I already have won." He stepped back, drew his own gun, and held his arm out straight. The pistol was pointed down at Serrador's forehead.

"What are you talking about?" Serrador demanded. His stomach was liquid. Sweat glistened across his forehead now.

"You took the gun from me," Amadori said. "You threatened me with it."

"What?" Serrador looked at the gun. And then he

realized what had happened, why he had been brought here.

Serrador was right. He could very well have argued that the Catalonians had set him up. That they'd bribed his driver to testify against him. Had he been allowed to defend himself he might have persuaded people that he wasn't involved in the death of the American. With the help of a clever attorney he might have convinced a court that he was being framed. That this was an attempt to turn people against him and his Basque supporters. After all, Ramirez and the others were dead. They couldn't defend themselves.

But that wasn't what Amadori wanted. He needed Serrador to be what he really was: a Basque who had joined with the Catalonians to overthrow the government of Spain. Amadori needed a Basque traitor for his plans.

"Wait a minute—please," Serrador said.

The deputy's frightened eyes turned toward the gun on the table. He had touched it. That was something else the general had needed. His fingerprints on the damn—

The general pulled the trigger. The slightly turned head of Deputy Isidro Serrador snapped back as the bullet pierced his temple. He was dead before his brain could process the pain, before the sound of the blast reached his ears.

The force of the impact knocked Serrador backward onto the floor. Even before the sound of the shot had died, Amadori had picked up the gun from the table, inserted a full clip, and placed it on the floor beside Serrador. He stood for a moment and watched as

Serrador's dark blood formed a red halo under his head.

A moment later the general's aides and police officers crowded into the small room. A beefy police inspector stood behind him.

"What happened?" the inspector demanded.

Amadori holstered his pistol. "The deputy grabbed my gun," he said calmly, pointing to the weapon on the floor. "I was afraid that he might try to take hostages or escape."

The police inspector looked from the body to Amadori. "Sir, this matter will have to be investigated."

Amadori's face was impassive.

"Where will you be—for questioning?" the inspector asked.

"Here," Amadori replied. "In Madrid. With my command."

The inspector turned to the men behind him. "Sergeant Blanco? Telephone the commissioner and let him know what has happened. Tell him I await further instructions. Let his office handle the press. Sergeant Sebares? Notify the coroner. Have him come to handle the body."

Both men saluted and left the room. Amadori turned and walked slowly after them. He was followed by the major general.

He was also followed by the stares of men who clearly feared him, whether they believed his story or not. Men who apparently sensed that they had just witnessed a purge. Men who had watched a military general take the first, bold steps to becoming a military dictator.

FOURTEEN

Tuesday, 2:00 A.M.
Madrid, Spain

María Corneja was already waiting in a dark, grassy corner of the airfield when Aideen, Luis García de la Vega, and Darrell McCaskey arrived in an unmarked Interpol car. The helicopter that would ferry them north was idling some two hundred yards away on the tarmac.

Air traffic was extremely light. In his speech to the nation in six hours, the prime minister would announce that flights to and from Madrid were going to be cut by sixty-five percent in order to ensure the security of planes leaving the airport. But foreign governments had been informed of the plan shortly after midnight and flights were already being canceled or rerouted.

Aideen had gone back to her hotel room and pulled together some clothes and tourist accoutrements—including her camera and Walkman tape recorder, both of which could be used for reconnaissance. Then she went to Interpol headquarters with Luis while McCaskey phoned Paul Hood. Luis reviewed maps of the region in addition to briefing her on the character of the people up north and providing her with up-to-the-minute intelligence. Then they went back to the hotel, collected McCaskey—who had obtained an okay from Hood for Aideen's participation in the mission—and drove out to the airport.

Aideen didn't know what to expect from María. Little had been said about her, apart from the brief exchange in the hotel room. She didn't know whether she'd be welcomed or whether being an American and a woman would work for her or against her.

María had been sitting astride her ten-speed bicycle, smoking. Flicking the cigarette onto the asphalt, she dropped the kickstand of the bicycle. She walked over slowly, with an athlete's easy grace. She stood about five-foot-seven but seemed taller because of the way she held her square jaw high: high and set. Her long brown hair hung down her neck, the fine strands stirred by the wind. The top two buttons of her denim shirt were open over her green wool sweater and the bottoms of her tight jeans were tucked into well-worn cowboy boots. Her blue eyes swept past Luis and Aideen and came to rest on McCaskey.

"Buenas noches," she said to him in a husky voice.

Aideen didn't know whether that was intended as a greeting or a dismissal. Obviously McCaskey wasn't sure either. He stood stiffly beside the car, his expression blank. Luis hadn't wanted him to come to the airport, but he insisted that it was his duty to see Aideen off.

They watched María as she approached. Her eyes didn't flinch or soften. Luis put his hand around Aideen's arm. He stepped toward María, drawing Aideen with him.

"María, this is Aideen Marley. She works with Op-Center and was present at the shooting."

María's deep-set eyes shifted to Aideen but only for a moment. She walked past her and stopped in front of Darrell.

Luis called after her. "María, Aideen will be accompanying you to San Sebastián."

The thirty-eight-year-old woman nodded. But she didn't take her eyes off McCaskey. Their faces were only inches apart.

"Hello, María," McCaskey said.

María was breathing slowly. Her thick eyebrows formed a hard, rigid line like a bulwark. Her pale, sensuously arched lips formed another. "I prayed that I would never see you again," she said. Her accent, like her voice, was thick and deep.

McCaskey's own expression hardened. "I guess you didn't pray hard enough."

"Maybe not," she replied. "I was too busy crying."

This time McCaskey did not respond.

María's eyes ranged over him. Other than that, her features didn't change. It seemed to Aideen that the woman was looking for something. A man she once loved, memories to soften the hate? Or was she searching for something different? Something to revitalize her anger. The sight of arms, a chest, thighs, and hands she had once held and caressed.

After a moment María turned and walked back to her bicycle. She snatched her grip from the basket behind the seat.

"Keep this for me, Luis," she said, indicating the

bicycle. She walked over to Aideen and offered her hand. "I apologize for my rudeness, Ms. Marley. I'm María Corneja."

Aideen accepted her hand. "Call me Aideen."

"I'm glad to know you, Aideen," María said. She looked at Luis. "Is there anything else I need to know?"

Luis shook his head. "You know the codes. If something comes up, I'll call on your cellular phone."

María nodded and looked at Aideen. "Let's go," she said and started toward the helicopter. She made a point of not looking at McCaskey again.

Aideen slung her own backpack over a shoulder and scurried after her.

"Good luck to both of you," McCaskey said to the women as they passed.

Aideen was the only one who turned and thanked him.

The Kawasaki chopper revved up as the women approached. Though they wouldn't have been able to hear one another over the din, Aideen found the bitter silence awkward. She also felt torn. As McCaskey's colleague she felt she should say something on his behalf. But as a woman she felt like she should have ignored him too—and, while she was at it, used her own eyes to curse all men. Curse her father for having been an abusive alcoholic. Curse the drug dealers who ruined lives and families and made widows and orphans in Mexico. Curse the occasional gentleman caller in her own life who was only a gentleman for as long as it took to become an intimate.

They climbed on board and were airborne in less

than a minute. They sat close beside each other in the small, noisy cockpit, the silence continuing until Aideen finally had had enough of it.

"I understand you were out of the police business for a while," she said. "What did you do?"

"I managed a small legitimate theater in Barcelona," she said. "For excitement I took up skydiving. For even more excitement I acted in some of the plays. I've always loved acting, which is why I loved undercover work." Her tone was personable, her eyes unguarded. Whatever memories had troubled her back at the airfield were passing.

"That was your specialty?" Aideen asked.

María nodded. "It's very theatrical and that's what I enjoy." She tapped her duffelbag. "Even the codes are from plays. Luis uses numbers which refer to acts, scenes, lines, and words. When I work out of town he phones them. When I work in town he often leaves slips of papers under rocks. Sometimes he even writes them in the open as graffiti. He once left me—what do you call them? Good-time numbers on a telephone booth."

"That's what they call 'em in the States," Aideen said.

María smiled a little for the first time. With it, the last traces of her anger appeared to vanish. Aideen smiled back.

"You've had a terrible day," María said. "How are you feeling?"

"Still pretty shell-shocked," Aideen replied. "All of this hasn't really sunk in yet."

"I know that feeling," María said. "For all its fi-

nality death never seems quite real. Did you know
Martha Mackall well?''

"Not very," Aideen replied. "I'd only worked with
her a couple of months. She wasn't a very easy woman
to get to know."

"That's true," María said. "I met her several times
when I lived in Washington. She was intelligent but
she was also very formal."

"That was Martha," Aideen said.

Mentioning her stay in America seemed to bring
María back down again. Her little smile evaporated.
Her eyes darkened under her brow.

"I'm sorry about what happened back there,"
María said.

"It's all right," Aideen said.

María stared ahead. "Mack and I were together for
a while," she continued as though Aideen had not
spoken. "He was more caring and more devoted than
any man I've ever met. We were going to stay together
forever. But he wanted me to give up my work. He
said it was too dangerous."

Aideen was starting to feel uncomfortable. Spanish
women talked openly about their lives to strangers.
Ladies from Boston didn't.

María looked down. "He wanted me to give up
smoking. It was bad for me. He wanted me to like jazz
more than I did. And American football. And Italian
food. He loved his things passionately, including me.
But he couldn't share all of that the way he wanted
to, and eventually he decided he'd rather be alone than
disappointed." She looked at Aideen. "Do you understand?"

Aideen nodded.

"I don't expect you to say anything critical," María said. "You work with him. But I wanted you to know what that was about back there because you'll be working with me, too. I only learned he was here when I learned you would be coming with me. It was a difficult thing to accept, seeing him again."

"I understand," Aideen said. She practically had to shout to be heard over the roar of the rotor.

María showed her a little half-smile. "Luis tells me you worked to bring in drug dealers in Mexico. That took courage."

"To tell you the truth," Aideen said, "what it took was indignation, not courage."

"You are too modest," María shot back.

Aideen shook her head. "I'm being truthful. Drugs helped to wreck my neighborhood when I was a kid. Cocaine killed one of my best friends. Heroin took my cousin Sam, who was a brilliant organist at our church. He died in the street. When I got some experience under my belt, I wanted to do more than wring my hands and complain about it."

"I felt the same way about crime," she said. "My father owned a cinema in Madrid. He was killed in a robbery. But both of our desires would have been nothing if they weren't backed by courage and resolve. And cunning," she added. "You either have that or you acquire it. But you need it."

"I'll go along with resolve and cunning," Aideen said, "and one thing more. You have to learn to stifle your gag reflex in order to learn."

"I don't understand."

"You have to close down your emotions," Aideen explained. "That's what allowed me to walk the streets undercover—to observe dispassionately and to learn. Otherwise, you'd spend all your time hating. You have to pretend not to care as you talk to hawkers, learn the names of the 'houses' they represent. In Mexico City there were the Clouds, who sold marijuana. The Pirates, who sold cocaine. The Angels, who sold crack. The Jaguars, who sold heroin. You have to learn the difference between the users and the junkies."

"The junkies are always the loners, no?"

Aideen nodded.

"It's the same everywhere," María said.

"And the users always travel in packs. You had to learn to recognize the dealers in case they didn't open their mouths. You had to know who to follow back to the kingpins. The dealers were the ones with their sleeves rolled up—that was where they carried the money. Their pockets were for guns or knives. But I was always scared in the field, María. I was scared for my life and scared of what I would learn about the underbelly of someone else's life. If I hadn't been angry about my old neighborhood, if I weren't sick for the families of the lost souls I encountered, I could never have gone through with it."

María let the smile blossom fully now. It was a rich smile, full of respect and the promise of camaraderie. "Courage without fear is stupidity," María said. "I still believe that you had it, and I admire you even more. We're going to make a very good team."

"Speaking of which," said Aideen, "what's the

plan when we reach San Sebastián?'' She was anxious
to turn the conversation away from herself. Attention
had always made her uneasy.

''The first thing we'll do is go to the radio station,''
María told her.

''As tourists?'' Aideen said, perplexed.

''No. We have to find out who brought them the
tape. Once we do that, we find those people and watch
them as tourists. We know that the dead men were
planning some kind of conspiracy. The question is
whether they died because of infighting or because
someone found out about their plan. Someone who
hasn't come forth as yet.''

''Meaning we don't know if they're friend or foe.''

''Correct,'' María said. ''Like your government,
Spain has many factions, which don't necessarily
share information with other factions.''

As she was speaking, the pilot turned the stick over
to the control pilot and leaned back. He removed his
headset.

''Agent Corneja?'' he shouted. ''I just got a message from the chief. He said to tell you that Isidro
Serrador was killed tonight at the municipal police station in Madrid.''

''How?''

''He was shot to death when he tried to take a gun
from an army officer.''

''An army officer?'' María said. ''This case doesn't
fall under military jurisdiction.''

''I know,'' he replied. ''The chief is looking into
who it was and what he was doing there.''

María thanked him and he turned back to the controls. She looked at Aideen.

"Something is very wrong here," María said gravely. "I have a feeling that what happened to poor Martha was just the first shot of what is going to be a very long and very deadly enfilade."

FIFTEEN

Tuesday, 2:55 A.M.
San Sebastián, Spain

The *familia* is an institution that dates back to the late nineteenth century. It is part of the same Mediterranean culture that gave rise to crime families in Sicily, Turkey, and Greece. The variation created by the Spanish was that a member's loyalty was to a legitimate employer, usually the owner of a plant or labor group like bricklayers or icemen. To keep the employer's hands unsullied, a cadre of employees was selected and trained to perform or protect the owner against acts of violence or sabotage and to execute the same against rivals. The targets were almost always business sites; attacks against home and members of one's personal family were considered uncivilized. Occasionally, *familia* members engaged in smuggling or extortion, though that was rare.

In return for their services, *familia* members were occasionally rewarded with extra wages. Perhaps a college education for their children. Usually, however, their loyalty earned them only the thanks of their employer and guaranteed lifetime employment.

Juan Martinez considered the attack against the yacht to be uncivilized. Certainly the scope of it was unparalleled—so many *familia* members killed at once. Juan had never shied from violence during his years of service to Señor Ramirez. The violence committed against the boating concern, especially in the early years, was usually directed at ships or machines or buildings. Once or twice a worker was attacked, but never the owners or senior management. What had been done tonight demanded a response in kind. Juan, a street kid from Manresa who had worked for Señor Ramirez for twelve years, was eager to deliver it. But first he needed a target. The radio station was a good place to start looking for one.

Juan and three coworkers drove out to the small broadcast facility. It was located on a nine-hundred-foot-high hilltop, one of three hills located just north of La Concha Bay in San Sebastián. A narrow paved road led halfway to the summit. Near the top, an enclave of expensive, gated homes had been built overlooking the bay.

How many heads of familias *live here?* Juan wondered, sitting in the passenger's side of the car. He was carrying a backpack, which he'd packed at the factory. He had never been up this way before and the view of the coastline, spectacular and serene, made him uncomfortable. He was a man who enjoyed work and activity. He felt as out of place here as he would have in the moonlit gardens that were visible just past the gates.

A narrower dirt road, typically traveled by motorbikes and hikers, led the rest of the way. The view of the bay was blocked by a turn in the hill; the grasses were not clipped and lush but scrublike and sparse.

This was Juan's kind of place again. He looked up the road toward the low-lying cinderblock building at the end. It was surrounded by a chain-link fence just over eight feet high, with barbed wire strung thickly across the top.

Radio Nacional de Público was a small, 10 kw station that reached as far south as Pamplona and as far north as Bordeaux, France. The RNP typically broadcast music, news, and local weather during the day and matters of interest to the Basque population in the evening. The owners were avowed antiseparatist Basques who had endured gun attacks and a firebombing. That was why the building was made of cinderblock and was set well back from the fortified fence. The broadcast antenna stood in the center of the roof. It was a tall, skeletal spire made of red and white girders. It stood approximately one hundred fifty feet tall and was topped by a winking red light.

The *familia* driver, Martín, had cut the headlights as the car approached. He pulled over three hundred yards from the gate and parked beside the domed crest of the hill. The four men got out. Juan pulled a bicycle from the trunk, slung a backpack on his shoulder, and sprinkled water from a bottle on his face. The water trickled like sweat along his cheeks and down his throat. Then he walked boldly toward the gate. The other three men fixed silencers to their pistols and followed one hundred feet behind him. Juan huffed and walked loudly, partly to cover the footsteps of the others, and partly to make sure he was heard.

As Juan had expected, there were guards inside the perimeter. They were three men with guns, not professional security people. They had undoubtedly been brought here to keep an eye on the station in the aftermath of the broadcast. Juan and the others had decided ahead of time that if there were people patrolling the grounds, they would have to be taken out quietly and simultaneously.

Juan forced himself to relax. He couldn't afford to let the men see him shiver. This was his operation and he didn't want the other members of the *familia* to think he was nervous.

Juan stopped when he saw the gate. "Son-of-a-bitch," he said loudly.

One of the guards heard him. He walked over urgently while the other two stayed back, covering him.

"What do you want?" the guard asked. He was a very tall, lanky man with a curly spray of thinning brown hair.

Juan stood there for a long moment, apparently dumbfounded. "I want to know where the hell I am."

"Where the hell do you want to be?" the guard asked.

"I'm looking for the Iglesias campground."

The guard snickered mirthlessly. "I'm afraid you've got a bit of a ride ahead of you. Or more accurately, behind you and to the east."

"What do you mean?"

The guard jerked a thumb to the right. "I mean the campground's on the top of that next hill over there, the one with the—"

There was a dull series of *phup-phup-phups* behind Juan as the other *familia* members fired at the guards.

The men dropped silently with red, raw holes in their foreheads.

As the *familia* members moved forward, Juan set the bicycle down, pulled off his backpack, and went to work.

The easiest way to get in was to announce yourself on the intercom and wait for the gate to be buzzed open. But that wasn't an option nor was it the only way in. Juan removed a cloth from the backpack as well as a crowbar. His undershirt was heavy with sweat and the cool air chilled him as he climbed halfway up the fence to the left of the gate.

He flung the crowbar over the top while holding the free sleeve of his shirt. The shirt landed on top of the barbed wire. Juan reached his index and middle fingers through the nearest link, grabbed the crowbar, and pulled it back through. Then he removed the iron bar and tied the shirt sleeves together. When he was finished, he took the shirt belonging to Ferdinand, the muscular night watchman. He repeated the procedure so that there were two layers of fabric over the barbs. When he was finished, the men climbed over the safe zone they'd created on top of the fence. They dropped quietly inside the perimeter and then waited a moment to make sure no one had heard them. When they were certain no one had, they walked swiftly toward the metal door in front. They walked carefully, crossing the open area in relative silence.

The other three men had crowbars as well and Ferdinand had a .38 revolver in his deep-cut right pants pocket. There were extra shells in his left pocket, wrapped in a handkerchief so they wouldn't jangle.

Juan and his people did not want to kill any more people. But after what had been done to Señor Ramirez, they would not hesitate to do anything that was necessary to complete their mission.

They knew that the door would be locked and had planned accordingly. Juan was the tallest of the men and he placed his crowbar on the top left side of the door, between the door and the jamb. Martín bent low and put his bar on the bottom left side. The other man, Sancho, inserted his crowbar to the left of the knob. Ferdinand pulled the gun from his pocket and stood back, ready to fire in case they were attacked.

The men wedged the prongs of the crowbars in as far as they would go. If they didn't get it open on the first try they would push them back in unison and try again. They figured that two strong pulls should do it. Martín had worked in construction and said that even if the door were double-bolted, the jambs wouldn't be steel reinforced. Grounded metal like that would wreak hell with the radio broadcasts, he said.

The men pulled hard on Juan's count of three. The door flew open on the first try, large wood splinters fracturing up and down the jamb. As soon as Ferdinand gave them the all-clear they ran in.

There were three people inside. One man was inside a soundproof booth and two people, a man and a woman, were seated at a control panel. As planned, Martín sought out the fuse box. He found it quickly and killed the electricity. The station died before the announcer could report what was happening. Under the brilliance of two battery-powered emergency lights mounted on the ceiling, Juan and Sancho ran over to the technicians. They clubbed each one hard across the collarbone. They fell to the ground, the woman moaning and the man shrieking. While Ferdinand covered them, Juan entered the booth. He walked calmly toward the announcer.

"I want to know who gave you the tape you played earlier," Juan said.

The slender young man, bearded and indignant, moved back on the rolling chair.

"I'll ask you one more time," Juan said, raising the crowbar. "Who gave you the tape recording?"

"I don't know who he was," the man said. His voice was high and squeaky. He cleared his throat. "I don't know."

Juan swung the crowbar against the man's left tricep. The man grabbed his arm as his mouth dropped open and let out air, like a furnace. Tears formed in his wide eyes.

"Who gave you the tape?" Juan repeated.

The man tried to close his mouth. It didn't seem to want to work. The chair thumped up against the wall and stopped.

Juan continued toward him. He looked at the fingers of the man's right hand. They were wrapped around his upper arm. He swung the crowbar again, at the fingers.

The iron bar smashed the back of his hand, just below the lower knuckles. There was an audible crack, like the snap of dry chicken bones. The hand dropped onto the man's lap. Blood pooled and caused the skin to bulge at once. This time the victim was able to scream.

"Adolfo!" he shouted from that wide, open mouth.

"Who?" Juan repeated.

"Adolfo Alcazar! The fisherman!" The man provided Juan with the address and Juan thanked him. Then he swung the crowbar one more time, just hard enough to break the man's jaw. Juan looked out at Martín and Sancho, who did likewise. There wasn't time to check for cellular phones and he didn't want them calling ahead to warn the fisherman.

Five minutes later the four *familia* members were driving back down the road toward San Sebastián.

SIXTEEN

Monday, 8:15 P.M.
Washington, D.C.

When Hood called home, neither Sharon nor the kids picked up the phone. The answering machine message came on after four rings; it was Harleigh's from the day before.

"Hi. You've reached the Hood family. We're not home right now. But we're not going to tell you to leave a message because if you don't know that, we don't want to talk to you."

Hood sighed. He'd asked the kids not to leave smart-ass messages like that. Maybe he should have insisted on it. Sharon had always said he wasn't strict enough with them.

"Hey, guys, it's me," Hood said. The conviviality in his voice was difficult, forced. "I'm afraid I'm going to be at the office a while longer. I hope you all had a good first day of spring vacation and that you're out at the movies or the mall or something fun. Sharry, would you please give me a call when you get back? Thanks. Love you all. Bye."

Hood felt a flash of desperation as he hung up. He wanted very badly to talk to Sharon. He hated having this barrier between them and he wanted to make things better. Or at least to make peace until he could sit down, talk to her, and make things better. He tried Sharon's cellular phone but got kicked into the answering system. He decided not to leave a message.

Almost the moment he put the phone in the cradle his private line rang. It was Sharon. He smiled and a weight seemed to rise from his chest.

"Hi there," he said. This time the conviviality was effortless, genuine. There was noise behind her—loud talking and garbled announcements. "You guys at the mall?"

"No, Paul," she said. "We're at the airport."

Hood had been slumped back tiredly in his big leather chair. He sat up. He didn't say anything for a moment; it was a good habit he'd picked up during his political career.

"I've decided to take the kids to Connecticut," Sharon continued. "You won't be seeing them much anyway this week and my folks have been asking us to come up."

"Oh," he said. "How long do you intend to stay?" His voice was calm but his insides weren't. He was looking at the framed family photograph on his desk. The picture was three years old but the smiles on the four faces suddenly seemed to belong to another lifetime.

"I honestly don't know," she answered.

Ron Plummer and Bob Herbert arrived then. Hood held up a finger. Herbert saw that he was on his private line. He nodded and the men turned their backs to the doorway. Ann Farris arrived a moment later. She joined the two men waiting in the hall.

"I guess that depends on—" Sharon said, then stopped.

"On what?" Hood asked. "On me? On whether I want you here? You know the answer to that."

"I know," Sharon said, "though I don't know why. You're never around. We go on vacations and you leave the first day."

"That happened once."

"That's only because we haven't even tried to take another vacation," Sharon said. "What I was going to say is, my coming back to Washington depends on whether I want to watch the kids get disappointed over and over again—or whether I want to put a stop to it altogether."

"That's what *you* want," Hood said. He had raised his voice and lowered it quickly. "Have you asked them what they want? Does that matter?"

"Of course it matters," she said. "They want their father. And so do I. But if we can't have him, then maybe we ought to settle that now instead of letting this drag on."

Herbert turned back toward the office. His lips were pursed and his eyebrows were raised. Whatever he had was important. As Herbert turned back around, Hood found himself wishing that he could start everything over again. The day, the year, his entire life.

"Don't go up there," Hood said. "Please. We'll figure something out as soon as the situation is under control."

"I figured you'd say that," Sharon replied. Her voice wasn't hard, just final. "If you want to figure it

out, Paul, you know where we'll be. I love you—and
I'll talk to you, okay?''

She hung up. Hood was still looking out the door
at the backs of the heads of his subordinates. He had
always regarded Bob and Mike and Darrell in particular as a special kind of family. Now, suddenly, they
were his only family. And it wasn't enough.

He hung up the phone. Bob heard it and turned. He
wheeled in followed by the others. His eyes were on
Hood.

"Everything okay?" Herbert asked.

It suddenly *hit* him. His wife had just left their home
and taken the kids with her. He half had it in mind to
send someone to the airport to stop them. But Sharon
would never forgive him for muscling her. He wasn't
sure he'd be able to forgive himself.

"We'll talk later," Hood said. "What've you got?"

"A major crapstorm, as they say back in my home-
town of Philadelphia, Mississippi. I've just got to
make sure you still want Darrell and Aideen in the
middle of it.''

"Paul," Ann said, tapping her notebook in her open
hand, "if I could just steal a minute I can be out of
here."

Hood looked at Herbert.

The intelligence chief nodded. "Okay if I stay?"

Ann nodded.

"Okay," Hood said to Ann.

"Thanks," she said.

Hood's eyes dropped briefly to Ann's fine-boned
fingers under the notepad. The long, red fingernails
seemed very feminine. He looked away. He was angry

at Sharon and was drawn to Ann, who wanted him. He hated feeling that way but he didn't know what to do about it.

"I've just had a call from the BBC," Ann said. "They obtained a tourist's videotape of the scene around the Congress of Deputies in Madrid. It shows Martha's body being removed—"

"Freakin' ghouls," Herbert complained.

"They're newspeople," Ann countered, "and whether we like it or not, this is news."

"Then they're ghoulish newspeople," Herbert said.

"Let it go, Bob," Hood said. He wasn't in the mood for another family squabble. "What's the bottom line, Ann?"

She glanced at her notes. "They pulled an image of Martha's face," she continued, "ran it through their data base, and came up with a picture of Martha when she met with Nelson Mandela's Zulu rival Chief Mangosuthu Buthelezi in Johannesburg in ninety-four. Jimmy George at the Washington *Post* says he's got to run with what he knows tomorrow before the BBC story gets out."

Hood pressed his palms into his eyes and rubbed. "Does anyone know about Aideen being there with her?"

"Not yet."

"What do you recommend?" Hood asked.

"Lie," Herbert offered.

"If we try and fudge this," Ann replied with a hint of annoyance, "if we say something like, 'She was a diplomatic troubleshooter but she was really there on vacation,' no one'll believe us. They'll keep on digging. So I suggest we give them the bare bones truth.''

''How bare bones?'' Hood asked.

''Let's say that she was there to lend her experience to Spanish congressional deputies. They were concerned about rising ethnic tension and she's had experience in that area. True, end of story.''

''You can't tell the press that much,'' Herbert pointed out.

''I have to,'' Ann said.

''If you do that,'' Herbert said, ''they may figure out that she wasn't there alone. And then the bastards who shot Martha might come back for a second try at Aideen.''

''I thought the killers were all at the bottom of the sea,'' Ann said.

''Maybe they are,'' said Hood. ''What if Bob's right? What if they're not?''

''I don't know,'' Ann admitted. ''But if I lie, Paul, then that could be deadly too.''

''How?'' Hood asked.

''The press'll find out that Martha was there with a 'Señorita Temblón,' and they'll try to track her down. It won't take them long to figure out that there *is* no Señorita Temblón. Then they'll try to find the mystery woman themselves. They'll also try to figure out how she got into the country and where she's staying. Their search could help lead the killers right to her.''

''That's a good point,'' Herbert had to admit.

''Thanks,'' Ann said. ''Paul, nothing is optimal. But if I give out this much, at least the press'll be able to verify that what we're giving them is the truth. I'll admit there was someone else and I'll tell them that because of security considerations her associate left the country quietly. They'll buy that.''

"You're sure?" Hood said.

Ann nodded. ''The press doesn't always tell everything. They like the feeling of being in on something secret. Makes them feel important at cocktail parties, part of the inner workings.''

''I was wrong,'' Herbert said. ''They're not just ghouls. They're *shallow* freakin' ghouls.''

''Everybody's something,'' Ann said.

Herbert scrunched his brow at that but Hood understood. His own integrity had taken a few good hits over the last few hours.

''All right,'' Hood said. ''Go with it. But contain it, Ann. I don't want the whereabouts of Darrell or Aideen found out. Tell the press that they're being brought back here under very tight security.''

''I will,'' she said. ''What do I say about a successor to Martha? Someone's bound to ask.''

''Tell them that Ronald Plummer is Acting Political and Economics Officer,'' Hood said without hesitation.

Plummer thanked him with his eyes. Acknowledging that in an official statement, without attaching another name to the office, was a vote of confidence in Plummer. The job was his to lose.

Ann thanked Hood and left. He didn't watch her go. He turned to Herbert.

''So what's your crapstorm?'' he asked.

''Riots,'' Herbert said. ''They're bustin' out everywhere.'' He hesitated. ''You okay?''

''I'm fine.''

"You look faraway."

"I'm fine, thanks, Bob. What's the overview?"

Herbert gave him a you-ain't-foolin'-me look and moved on. "The riots are no longer contained in the Ávila, Segovia, and Soria corridor of Castile," Herbert said. "Ron, you've got the latest."

"This just came via fax from the U.S. consulate in the city," Plummer said, "though I'm sure several news services must be on it by now. Word of the Barcelona soccer cancellation got out—not surprising when the German players quietly tried to skip town. Angry fans actually blockaded the motorway with their cars as the bus headed to the El Prat airport. The *policía nacional,* Spain's state troopers, came to try and rescue them. When the *policía* were hit with rocks, the Mossos d'Escuadra were called to help them."

"They're the autonomous police of Catalonia," Herbert said. "They're mostly responsible for government buildings and have a take-no-prisoners attitude."

"Except that prisoners were taken," Plummer said. "Over twenty. When the Mossos d'Escuadra contingent brought them in, the police station was attacked by a mob. Martial law is about to be declared in the city, which is where we're at right now."

"Now, Barcelona's about two hundred miles from San Sebastián," Herbert said, "and it's an urban center as opposed to a resort. I'm not worried that the rioting is going to spread there quickly." He hunched forward and folded his hands. "But I am worried, Paul, that when martial law is declared it's going to have a very, very strong impact on the collective Spanish conscience."

"How so?" Hood asked.

"One word," Herbert replied. "Franco. There are strong and bitter memories of his militant, fascist Falange party. The first time government sponsored militancy surfaces in nearly a quarter of a century, you can bet there's going to be very fierce resistance."

"The irony," said Plummer, "is that the Germans helped Franco win the Spanish Civil War. Having Germans as a flashpoint here is going to make the resentment even tougher to put down."

"What does this have to do with our people?" Hood asked. "Are you saying they should lay low until we see what happens?"

Herbert shook his head. "I'm saying that you should get them out, recall Striker, and urge the President to evacuate all nonessential American personnel. Those who stay in Spain should button up tight."

Hood regarded him for a long moment. Herbert was not a man prone to overreaction. "How bad do you think it's going to get?" Hood asked.

"Bad," Herbert said. "Some major political fault lines have been activated here. I think we may be looking at the next Soviet Union or Yugoslavia."

Hood looked at Plummer. "Ron?"

Plummer folded the fax and creased it sharply with his fingertips. "I'm afraid I'm with Bob on this one, Paul," he said. "The nation of Spain is probably going to come apart."

SEVENTEEN

Tuesday, 3:27 A.M.
San Sebastián, Spain

Adolfo Alcazar was exhausted when he got into
bed.

He slept on a small, flat mattress in a corner of the
one-room apartment. The sagging mattress rested on a
metal frame not far from the stove; still lit and glowing
dimly, the stove provided the only light in the small
room. The old frame was rusted from the sea breeze
that blew through the window.

He smiled. The mattress was the same one he'd
bounced on when he was a boy. It occurred to him
now as he lay down, naked, how pure an act that had
been—to bounce on the bed. It was an activity that
didn't give a damn about what went before or what
was coming next. It was a complete, self-contained
expression of freedom and joy.

He remembered having to stop when he grew a little
and made more noise. The people who lived downstairs complained. It had been a harsh thing for a child
to learn, that he wasn't free. And that was only the
first lesson in his lack of liberty. Until he met the
General his life had been a series of surrenders and
retreats that made others happy or rich. As he lay

down in bed, in the bed that used to make him feel so free, Adolfo felt a taste of what it was like to be free again. Free of government regulations that told him what he could fish and fishing magnates who told him when and where he could fish so as not to interfere with them and recreational boats clogging his harbor because the boating industry had more influence in Madrid than small fishermen had. With the help of the General he would be free to make a living in a nation that once again belonged to the people. To *his* people. The General didn't care if you were Castilian like Adolfo or Catalonian or Basque or Galician or whatever. If you wanted to be free from Madrid, if you wanted self-rule for your people, you followed him. If you wanted to maintain the status quo or profit from the sweat of others, you were removed.

Lying on his back, staring into the darkness, Adolfo finally shut his eyes. He had done well today. The General would be pleased.

The door flew inward with a crack, startling him. Four men rushed toward him before he was fully awake. As one man shut the door the others pulled him facedown on the floor. His arms were stretched out from his sides and his palms were pressed down on the floor. They pinned him in that position with their knees and with their hands.

"Are you Adolfo Alcazar?" one of them demanded.

Adolfo said nothing. He was looking toward the left, toward the stove. He felt the middle finger of his right hand pulled back slowly until it broke with a single, flashing snap.

"*Yes!*" he shrieked. Then he moaned.

"You killed many men today," one of them said.

Adolfo's head was cloudy with thought but clear with pain. Before he could clear his mind his right index finger was pulled back and broken. He screamed as the pain raced up to his elbow and back again. He felt something—one of his socks—stuffed roughly between his teeth.

"You killed the head of our *familia,*" the man said.

His ring finger was drawn back until it popped. They released it and the three broken fingers sat side by side, bloated but numb. His hand was trembling as they twisted back the pinky finger. It flopped down, shattered like the others. Then he felt something hard and cold on his thumb. His head was forced around and he saw a crowbar, held vertically. The curved end was resting on top of his thumb. It was raised straight up and brought down hard. The thumb burned as the skin ripped and bone cracked. The crowbar went up again and then came down, this time on the wrist joint. It came down once in the center, once on the left, and once on the right. Each blow sent a swift, hot wave of pain up his arm to his shoulder and along his neck. When it passed there was only a deep throbbing weight on his forearm, like an anvil was sitting on it.

"Your hand will never again be raised against us," the man said.

With that, they released Adolfo and turned him over. He tried to control his right arm but it flopped as though it were asleep. He caught a glimpse of blood as it trickled down his forearm. He didn't feel it until it reached his elbow.

Struggling weakly, Adolfo was dragged several feet and then they pinned him again, on his back. The sock was still jammed in his mouth. It was dark and tears of pain filled Adolfo's eyes. He could not see the faces of his captors. He fought to get free again but his efforts were like the wriggling of a fish in one of his nets.

"Save your strength," the man said. "You're not going anywhere—except to hell if you don't tell us what we wish to know. Do you understand?"

Adolfo looked up at the dark face. He tried to spit out the sock, not to respond but in defiance.

The man grabbed a fistful of hair and pulled Adolfo's head toward him. "Do you understand?"

Adolfo didn't answer. A moment later the man nodded to someone kneeling on Adolfo's knee. A moment after that he felt his right leg being lifted. Every part of him screamed as his bare foot was placed into the open grate of the oven, above the dying fire. He came violently alive and screamed into the sock and tried to withdraw. But the men held him there.

"Do you understand?" the man above him repeated calmly.

Adolfo nodded vigorously as he kicked and rocked and tried to get away. The man turned toward the others. They withdrew his foot and set it back down. The flesh screamed and he was viciously awake. But the pain focused his mind. He was panting through the sock and squirming under their grip. He looked up wide-eyed at the one dark face.

The man removed the sock and held it over Adolfo's mouth. "Who do you work with?" he asked.

Adolfo was panting heavily. His foot felt icy-hot, like ocean spray on a bad sunburn.

He felt them lift up the other leg.

"Who do you work with?"

"A general," Adolfo gasped. "An Air Force general named Pintos. Roberto Pintos."

"Where is he stationed?"

Adolfo didn't answer. It was time to wait a little before lying again. The one time Adolfo had met General Amadori—the real general, not this imaginary General Pintos—was at a meeting of nonmilitary aides in an airplane hangar in Burgos. There, the General had warned everyone that this day might come. That they might be found out and interrogated. He said that once the war had begun, it wouldn't matter what they said. But he cautioned them to hold out as long as possible for their own sense of honor.

Most men can be broken, he had said. *The trick is not to be broken without confusing the enemy. If you are captured, there is nothing you can do to prevent being tortured. What you must do is talk. Tell the enemy lies. Keep on lying as long as you can. Lie until the enemy cannot tell the true from the false, the good information from the bad.*

"Where is General Pintos stationed?" the torturer continued.

Adolfo shook his head. The sock was crushed back into his mouth and he felt himself jerked forward on the left and his foot placed into the ferocious heat. His struggles were as frantic as before. But while the pain was awful and it drew sweat from every inch of him, there was one thing comforting. The pain in his right foot was not so blinding anymore. He held on to that thought until the pain in his left foot tore it from his mind and sent sheets of anguish up and down his entire body. Except for his right hand. He felt nothing there. Nothing at all, not even pain—and that scared him. It made him feel a little dead.

They pulled his foot from the fire and dropped it back down. They pinned him again. The dark face came close to him again. The tears in Adolfo's eyes smeared the black shape.

"Where is Pintos stationed?"

The sheets of pain had become a constant burning, but it was less intense. Adolfo knew that he could hold out until the next round—whatever the next round was. He was proud of himself. In a strange way he felt free. Free to suffer, free to resist. But it was his choice.

"Ba—Barcelona," Adolfo moaned.

"You're lying," the torturer replied.

"N-no!"

"How old is he?"

"F-fifty-two."

"What color is his hair?"

"Brown."

The torturer smacked Adolfo. "You're lying!"

Adolfo looked up at the face and shook his head once. "No. I speak . . . the truth."

The face hovered a moment longer and then the sock was shoved back down. Adolfo felt himself tugged to the side. They grabbed his left arm and held it and pushed his hand into the opening.

He screamed in his throat as his fingers curled into

a fist and fought to get out of the heat. And then everything went dark.

He woke bent over the sink with water rushing
down over the back of his head. He coughed, vomited
up the stew, then was dropped onto his back on the
floor. Every patch of flesh on his feet and left hand
throbbed hotly.

The sock was thrust back in his mouth.

"You're strong," the dark face said to him. "But
we have time and I have experience. The first things
men always give up are lies. We will continue until
we have the truth." He bent closer. "Will you tell us
who you work with?"

Adolfo was trembling. The parts of him that weren't
burned or broken were chilly. It seemed very odd to
feel something so trivial as that. He shook his head
twice.

This time he wasn't moved. The sock was pushed
harder into his mouth and held there. One of the crowbars was raised over Adolfo's right shoulder and was
swung down hard. The bone broke audibly under the
blow. He cried into the sock. The crowbar was raised
again and struck lower, between the shoulder and elbow. Another bone broke. He cried again. Each blow
brought a burst of agony and a yelp and then numb-
ness.

Each scream was a rent in his will. The pain was
just pain but every scream was a surrender. And as he
surrendered those pieces of his fighting spirit, he had
less to draw on.

"When you talk, the beating will stop," the voice
said.

Someone started working on his left side and he jumped and howled with each strike. He felt the wall of resistance crumble faster now. And then something surprising happened. He didn't feel like himself anymore. His body was broken; that wasn't him. His will was shattered; that wasn't him. He was someone else. And that someone else wanted to talk.

He said something into the sock. The face came down and the beating stopped. The sock was removed.

"Am . . . Am . . ."

"What?" said the dark face.

"Ama . . . dori."

"Amadori?" the face repeated.

"Am . . . a . . . do . . . ri." Each syllable rode out on a breath. Adolfo couldn't help himself. He just wanted the pain to stop. "Gen . . . er . . . al."

"General Amadori," the face said. "That's who you work with?"

Adolfo nodded.

"Is there anyone else?"

Adolfo shook his head once. He shut his eyes.

"Do you believe him?" someone asked.

"Look at him," someone replied. "He hasn't got the wits left to lie."

Adolfo felt himself being released. It felt good just to lie there on his back. He opened his eyes and stared up at the dark figures gathered around him.

"What do we do with him?" one man asked.

"He killed Señor Ramirez," said another. "He dies. Slowly."

That was the final word on the matter—not by concensus but because the man swung his crowbar down on Adolfo's throat. The fisherman's head jerked up and then fell back as his larynx shattered; his dead arms didn't move. Then he lay there tasting blood and wheezing. He was able to draw just enough breath to remain conscious but not enough to satisfy his lungs.

The pain settled into a steady roar, which helped to keep him conscious. He was Adolfo Alcazar again but the agony in his limbs and in his throat made it difficult to string thoughts together. He couldn't decide whether he'd acted courageously by holding out for as long as he did or cowardly for having succumbed at all. Flashes of thought said yes he'd been brave, then no he hadn't. And then it didn't seem to matter as he shivered and the pain suddenly attacked him. Sometimes it came in like the tide, engulfing him. Sometimes it lapped at him like tiny breakers out at sea. The small swells he could manage. But the big ones tortured him. God, how they made him shake all over.

He had no idea how long he lay there and whether his eyes had been open or closed. But suddenly his eyes were open and the room was brighter and there was a figure bending beside him.

It was his brother, Berto.

Norberto was weeping and saying something. He was making signs over his face. Adolfo tried to raise his arm but it didn't respond. He tried to speak—

"A . . . ma . . . do . . . ri."

Did Norberto hear? Did he understand?

"City . . . chur . . . church."

"Adolfo, lie quietly," Norberto said. "I've telephoned for a doctor—oh, God."

Norberto continued saying a prayer.

"*Warn . . . Gen . . . er . . . al . . . they . . . know. . . .*"

Norberto laid a hand on his brother's lips to silence them. Adolfo smiled weakly. His brother's hand was soft and loving. The pain seemed to subside.

And then his head rolled to the side and his eyes shut and the pain was gone.

EIGHTEEN

Tuesday, 4:19 A.M.
San Sebastián, Spain

The helicopter set María and Aideen down south of the city. It landed atop a hillock along a deserted twist in the Rio Urumea, the river that ran through the city. A rental car, reserved by a local police officer who worked with Interpol, was waiting for them near the road. So was the police officer, thick-mustachioed Jorge Sorel.

During the helicopter trip, María had studied a map she'd brought with her. She knew the route to the radio station and Aideen could tell that she was anxious to get there. Unfortunately, as María lit a cigarette, Jorge told her there was no reason to go.

"What do you mean?" she demanded.

"Someone attacked the staff a little over an hour ago," he said.

"Someone?" María said. "Who?"

"We don't know yet," admitted the officer.

"Professionals?" she said impatiently.

"Very possibly," he acknowledged. "The attackers seemed to know exactly what they were doing. There were numerous broken limbs and everyone had a broken jaw."

"What did they want?" María asked.

Jorge shook his head. "Again, we can't even begin to speculate. The only reason we went up there was because the station suddenly went off the air."

María swore angrily. "This is *maravilloso*," she said. "Marvelous. Are there *any* leads?"

Jorge was still shaking his head. "The victims were unable to speak and now the doctors have them sedated. We assume the attackers were looking for whoever provided them with the audiotape."

"The idiots," María snarled. "Didn't they anticipate that? Didn't they take precautions?"

"Yes," said Jorge. "The irony is they were very well prepared. The station has always been a target for malcontents. Their politics, you know—very antigovernment. The facility is surrounded with barbed wire and is constructed like a bunker. It even has a metal door. The employees keep guns inside. But deterrents only sway the timid hearted. And these attackers were not timid."

"Constable," Aideen said patiently, "do you have any idea who it was that provided the tape?"

Jorge snuck an uncomfortable look at María. "I'm afraid the answer is once again no," he said. "We have two patrols going through the surrounding villages. They're looking for groups of people who may be searching for the person or persons who provided the tape. But we came to this relatively late. So far, we've found no one."

"The attackers would probably separate once they left here," María said. "They wouldn't want to risk everyone getting caught. They also wouldn't stay together after they found whoever they were looking for,'' María said. She drew on her cigarette and exhaled through her nose. She regarded Jorge intently. ''Are you sure that's all you can tell us?''

''I'm sure,'' he replied. His gaze was equally intent.

''What are the chances that the person who had the tape was from this area?'' Aideen asked.

''Very good,'' said María. ''Whoever planned this would have wanted someone who knew the waters where the yacht was destroyed. Someone who knew the town and the people at the station.'' She looked at Jorge. ''Give me a place to start looking.''

Jorge shrugged. ''The town is small. Everyone knows it. For someone who knows the waters, talk to the fishermen.''

María looked at her watch. ''They'll be going out in about an hour. We can talk to them at the docks.'' She pulled hard on her cigarette. ''Who blesses the waters for the fishermen?''

''That would be Father Norberto Alcazar,'' Jorge said. ''He will only do it for the old families, not the companies.''

''Where is he?''

''You will probably find him at the Jesuit church in the hills south of Cuesta de Aldapeta,'' Jorge said. ''That's on the west side of the river just outside of San Sebastián.''

María thanked him. She took one last drag from her cigarette, then she dropped it and crushed it hard under her heel. She let out the smoke as she walked toward the car. Aideen followed her.

''Father Alcazar is a very pleasant man,'' Jorge said

after them. "But he may not be forthcoming about his flock. He is very protective of them."

"Let's hope that he wants to protect one of them from being murdered," María said.

"You have a point," Jorge said. "Call on your cell phone when you are ready. The helicopter will come back for you here. The airport is small and has been reserved for military business—as a precaution."

María acknowledged brusquely as she got behind the wheel of the car and started it up. Dirt and clods of grass spit behind them as the car tore away from the foot of the hillock.

"You're not happy," Aideen said as she took the map from her backpack and unfolded it. She also had a loaded .38 in the backpack which María had given her during the flight.

"I wanted to kick him," María grumbled. "They only went up there because the station went off the air. The police should have *known* that someone would go after the radio crew."

"Maybe the police wanted the station to be attacked," Aideen said. "It's the same way with gang wars. The authorities stand back and let the bad guys kill each other."

"It's more likely that they were told to stay out of it," María said. "The men who were killed on the yacht were influential businessmen. They headed devoted *familias*—employees who will do anything for them, including murder. The police are paid to stay out of such things."

"Do you think the constable—"

"I don't know," María admitted. "But I can't be sure. One can never be sure in Spain."

Aideen thought back to what Martha had said about the police in Madrid cooperating with the street extortionists. *That might be diplomacy,* she thought, *but it stinks.* She was forced to wonder if even the government police in Madrid were giving the investigation of Martha's assassination their all.

"That's one of the reasons I left Interpol," María went on as she headed north along the river. "Dealing with these people is more frustrating than it's worth."

"But you came back," Aideen said. "For Luis?"

"No," María replied. "I came back for the same reason I left. Because there is so much corruption the rest of us can't afford to give up. Even to manage my small theater in Barcelona, I had to pay fees to the police, to the sanitation workers, to everyone but the postal workers. I had to pay them to make sure that they did the jobs they were already paid to do."

"So the government workers have their cushion and the industrial workers belong to families," Aideen said. "Independent workers end up paying extortion to one or fighting the strength of the other."

María nodded. "And that is why I'm here. It's like love," she said. "You can't give up because it doesn't work the first time. You learn the rules, you learn about yourself, and you get back in the arena for another run at the bull."

The first pale red light of dawn began to brighten the skies. The hilltops started to take shape against the lighter sky. As she glanced eastward, Aideen thought how funny it was that she liked and admired María.

The woman was no less confident and aggressive than Martha had been. But except for when she'd had to face Darrell back at the airport, there was something selfless about María. And Aideen could hardly blame María for throwing a little attitude Darrell's way. Regardless of who was right and who was wrong, seeing him again had to be rough.

They reached the outskirts of San Sebastián in less than thirty minutes and crossed the bridge at María Cristina. Then they headed southwest toward the church. They stopped to ask a shepherd for directions and were at the church just as the rim of the sun flared over the hill.

The small stone church was open. There were two parishioners inside, a pair of fishermen, but not the priest.

"Sometimes he goes to the bay with his brother," one of the fishermen told the women. The men told them where Adolfo lived and the route Father Alcazar usually took to get there. They got back in the car and headed north, María opening the window, lighting another cigarette, and puffing on it furiously.

"I hope this doesn't bother you," María said of the cigarette. "They say that the smoke is bad for others but I can assure you that it saves lives."

"How do you figure that?" Aideen asked.

"It keeps me from getting too angry," María replied. She did not appear to be joking.

They found Calle Okendo and drove two blocks to the southeast. The street was narrow; when they reached the two-story apartment building María had to park half on the sidewalk. Otherwise there wouldn't have been room for another vehicle to get by. Aideen put her .38 into the pocket of her windbreaker before she slid from the car. María tossed her cigarette away and slid her gun into the rear waistband of her jeans.

The downstairs door did not have a lock on it and they entered. The dark stairwell smelled of a century of fishermen and dust, which tickled Aideen's nose. The steps creaked like dry old trees in a wind and listed toward the dirty white wall. There were two apartments on the second floor. The door to one of them was slightly ajar. María gave it a push with her toe. It groaned as it opened.

They found Father Alcazar. He was kneeling beside the naked body of a man and weeping openly. His back was toward them. María stepped in and Aideen followed. If the priest heard them he made no indication of it.

"Father Alcazar?" María said softly.

The priest turned his head around. His red eyes were startling against his pale pink face. His collar was dark where it was stained with tears. He turned back to the body and then rose slowly. Backlit by the sharp morning light his black robe looked flat, like a silhouette. He walked toward them as though he were in a trance. Then he removed a jacket from a hook behind the door, went back to the dead man, and laid it across his body.

As he did, Aideen had a chance to study the body. The victim had been tortured, though not out of vengeance. There were no burn or knife marks on his torso. His eyes, ears, breast, and groin appeared to be intact; only his limbs had been worked over. He'd been tortured for information. And his windpipe had been smashed; to kill him slowly, as opposed to a blow to the head. Aideen had seen this before, in Mexico. It wasn't pretty, but it was prettier than what the drug lords did to people they tortured for betraying them. Strangely enough, it never stopped other people from betraying the Mexican *señoríos,* as they called them. The dead men and women always believed that they were the ones who would never be caught.

The priest turned back toward the women. "I am Father Alcazar," he said.

María stepped toward him. "My name is María," she said. "I'm with Interpol."

Aideen wasn't surprised that María had told him who she really was. The killings were escalating. This wasn't the time to go undercover.

"Did you know this man?" María asked.

The priest nodded. "He was my brother."

"I see," María said. "I'm sorry we couldn't have gotten here sooner."

Norberto Alcazar gestured weakly behind him as fresh tears spilled from his eyes. "I tried to help him. I should have tried harder. But Adolfo—he knew what he had gotten himself into."

María stepped up to the priest. She stood as tall as he did and looked flush into his bloodshot eyes. "Father, please—help us. What *had* Adolfo gotten himself into?"

"I don't know," the priest said. "When I arrived here he was hurt and talking wildly."

"He was still alive?" María asked. "You've got to

try to remember, Father, what he said! Words, names, places—anything.''

"Something about the city,'' Norberto said. "About a church. He said a place or a name—Amadori.''

María's eyes burned into his. "General Amadori?''

"It could be,'' Norberto said. "He . . . he did say something about a general. I don't know. It was difficult to understand.''

"Of course,'' María said. "Father, I know this is difficult. But it's important. Do you have any idea who might have done this?''

He shook his head. "Adolfo was going to the radio station last night,'' he sobbed. "That is all I know. I do not know what business he had there other than to deliver a tape recording. I came back this morning on my way to bless the waters. I wanted to see if he was all right. I found him like this.''

"You saw no one coming or leaving?''

"No one.''

María regarded him for a moment longer. Her brow was deeply knit, her eyes smouldering. "One question more, Father. Can you tell us where to find the Ramirez boatworks?''

"Ramirez,'' the priest said. He took a long tremulous breath. "Dolfo mentioned him. My brother said that Ramirez and his friends were responsible for killing an American.''

"Yes,'' said María. She cocked a thumb over her shoulder. "They killed this woman's partner.''

"Oh—I'm so sorry,'' Norberto said to Aideen. His eyes returned to María. "But Ramirez is dead. My brother—saw to that.''

"I know," María said.

"What do you want with his people?"

"To talk to them," María said. "To see if they were involved in this." She nodded toward Adolfo. "To see if we can prevent more murders, stop the fighting from escalating."

"Do you think that's possible?"

"If we get to them in time," María said. "If we learn what they know about Amadori and his people. But please, Father. We must hurry. Do you know where the factory is?"

Norberto took another deep breath. "It's northeast along the shore. Let me come with you."

"No," said María.

"This is my parish—"

"That's right," she said, "and your parish desperately needs your help. I don't. If the people panic, if their fear frightens away tourists, think what will happen to the region."

Norberto bowed his forehead into his hand.

"This is a lot to ask of you now, I know," María said. "But you have to do this. I'm going to go to the factory to talk with the workers. If what I think is happening *is* happening, then I know who the enemy is. And maybe it's not too late to stop him."

Norberto looked up. He pointed behind him without turning. "Dolfo thought he knew who the enemy was. He paid for that belief with his life. Perhaps with his soul."

María locked her eyes on his and held them. "Thousands of others may join him if I don't hurry.

I'll phone the local police from the car. They'll take care of your brother.''

"I'll stay with him until then.''

"Of course,'' María said, turning toward Aideen.

"And I will pray for you both.''

"Thank you,'' María said. She stopped and turned back. ''While you're at it, Father, pray for the one who needs it most. Pray for Spain.''

Less than two minutes later they were back in the car and heading northeast across the river.

"Are you really just going to talk to the factory workers?'' Aideen asked.

María nodded once. ''Do me a favor?'' she said. "Call Luis. Autodial star-seven. Ask him to locate General Rafael Amadori. Tell him why.''

"No encryption?''

María shook her head. ''If Amadori is listening somehow and comes after us, so much the better. It'll save us the trouble of finding him.''

Aideen punched in the code. Luis's cellular beeped and he answered at once. Aideen passed along María's request and told him about Adolfo. Luis promised to get right on it and call them back. Aideen folded away the phone.

"Who is Amadori?'' she asked.

"A scholar,'' she said. ''He's a military general too, but I don't know much about his career. I only know him as a published author of articles about historic Spain.''

"Obviously, they alarm you.''

"Very much so,'' María said. She lit a cigarette. "What do you know about our national folk hero El Cid?''

"Only that he beat back the invading Moors and helped unify Spain around 1100. And there was a movie about him with Charlton Heston."

"There was also an epic poem and a play written by Corneille," María said. "I staged it once at my theater. Anyway," she went on, "you are partly right about El Cid. He was a knight—Rodrigo Díaz of Vivar. From around 1065 to his death in 1099 he helped the Christian king, Sancho II, and then his successor, Alfonso VI, regain the kingdom of Castile from the Moors. The Moors called him *el cid*—'the lord.'"

"Honored by his enemies," Aideen said. "Impressive."

"Actually," María said, "they feared him, which was his intention. When the Moorish stronghold of Valencia surrendered, El Cid violated the peace terms by slaughtering hundreds of people and burning the leader alive. He was not the pure knight that legend has made him—he would do anything to anybody to protect his homeland. It's also a myth that he fought to unify Spain. He fought for Castile. As long as the other kingdoms remained at peace with Alfonso, as long as they paid him tribute, neither Alfonso nor El Cid cared what happened to them.

"General Amadori is an authority on El Cid," María continued. "But I've always detected in his writings the desire to be something more."

"You mean, to be El Cid," Aideen said.

María shook her head. "El Cid was a glorified soldier of fortune. There is something more to General Amadori than waging war. If you read his essays in the political journals you'll find that he is a leading proponent of what he calls 'benevolent militarism.' "

"Sounds like a fancy name for a police state," Aideen said.

"It is," María agreed. She took a long drag on her cigarette then flicked it out the window. "But he has given the models of Nazi Germany and Stalinist Russia a new-old twist: militarism without conquest. He believes that if a nation is strong, there is no need to conquer other nations. Those nations will come to him to trade, to seek protection, to be aligned with greatness. His power base will grow by accretion, not war."

"So General Amadori doesn't want to be like Hitler," Aideen said. "He wants to be like King Alfonso."

"Exactly," María replied. "What we may be seeing is the start of an effort to make Amadori the absolute leader of Castile and to make Castile the military hub of a new Spain. A hub which will dictate to the other regions. And Amadori has chosen this time—"

"Because he can move troops and influence events while appearing to stop a counterrevolution," Aideen said.

María nodded.

Aideen looked out at the brightening sky. Her eyes lowered and her gaze ranged across the beautiful fishing village. It seemed so peaceful, so desirable, yet it had been corrupted. Here, in less than a day, over a dozen people had already died or been brutally injured. She wondered if there had ever been a time, since people first descended from trees and began despoiling Eden, if manifest destiny had ever come cheaply.

"The price in blood will be very high before

Amadori can realize his dream,'' María said, as though reading Aideen's mind. "I am Andalusian. My people and others will fight—not to keep Spain unified but to keep Castile from becoming the heart and soul of a new Spain. It's a rivalry which dates back to the time of El Cid. And unless we find a way to stop men like Amadori, it will continue long after we're gone."

No, Aideen decided. There had never been a time when people graciously accomodated other people and other ways. We were still too close to the trees for that. And among us, there were too many bull-apes who were unhappy with the size and makeup of the tribe.

But then she thought about Father Alcazar. There was a man still trying to do God's work while in the grip of his own suffering. There *were* good people among the territorial carnivores. If only they had the power.

But if they did, Aideen asked herself, *wouldn't they wield it like all the rest?*

She didn't know—and after being awake for nearly twenty-four hours this wasn't the best time to ponder the question. However, as she sat there squinting out at the blue-gold sky, thinking about what María had just said, she was reminded of another question.

Think about it, Martha had said to her when they were still back in the U.S. *Think about how you handle someone's agenda.*

Just the way Rodgers had said, Aideen thought: with a better agenda.

The trick now was to come up with one.

NINETEEN

Monday, 9:21 P.M.
Washington, D.C.

Intellectually, Paul Hood knew that the United Nations was a good idea. But emotionally, he did not have much respect for the institution. It had proven itself ineffective in war and largely ineffective in peace. It was a forum for posturing, for making accusations, and for getting a nation's views into the press with the best possible spin.

But he had a great deal of admiration for the cool-headed new Secretary-General, Massimo Marcello Manni of Italy. A former NATO officer, senator in the Italian parliament, and ambassador to Russia, Manni had worked mightily the previous year to keep Italy from tumbling into the kind of civil war for which Spain seemed headed.

At Manni's request, a teleconference had been arranged for 11:00 P.M. by National Security head Steve Burkow. Secretary-General Manni had been talking to the intelligence and security chiefs of all the Security Council nations to discuss the deteriorating situation in Spain. Burkow, Carol Lanning at the State Department, and new Central Intelligence Director Marius Fox—the cousin of Senator Barbara Fox—would be in on the call.

Shortly before Burkow's office called at 8:50, Hood had already informed Bob Herbert and Ron Plummer that he wanted Darrell to remain in Madrid and Aideen to stay in the field.

"If Spain is coming apart," Hood told his team, "then HUMINT is more important than ever." Hood asked Herbert to make sure that Stephen Viens remained in contact with his loyal colleagues at the Pentagon-based National Reconnaissance Office. Viens was a longtime friend of Op-Center's Matt Stoll and had always been a steadfast ally during all previous surveillance efforts. Though Viens had been temporarily relieved of his NRO duties because of an ongoing Senate investigation into funding abuses, Hood had quietly given him an office at Op-Center. Unlike most people in Washington, Hood believed in repaying devotion. The NRO had begun conducting satellite reconnaissance of military movements in Spain some forty minutes before. Hood wanted that photographic surveillance to become part of Herbert's database. He also wanted copies of the pictures sent to McCaskey in Spain, via the U.S. Embassy in Madrid, and to the Striker team, which was airborne. At other intelligence organizations in Washington, department heads tended to covet information to give their groups an edge. But Hood believed in sharing information among his people. To him and to the unique personnel working with him, the job was not about personal glory. It was about protecting Americans and national interests.

In addition to satellite reconnaissance, Op-Center drew on international news reports for information.

Raw TV footage was especially valuable. It was plucked from satellite feeds before it could be edited for broadcast. The uncut footage was then analyzed by Herbert's team and also by Laurie Rhodes in the Op-Center photographic archives. Often, camouflaged weapons bunkers were constructed well prior to military actions. While these facilities might not always be visible from space, they often showed up in slightly altered topography, which could be seen in comparative studies from the ground.

Hood took a short dinner break in the commissary, where he read the Sunday comics someone had left lying around. He hadn't looked at them in a while and he was amazed at how little they'd changed from when he was a kid. *Peanuts* and *B.C.* were still there, along with *Tarzan* and *Terry and the Pirates* and *The Wizard of Id*. It was comforting, just then, to visit with old friends.

After dinner, Hood had a short briefing from Mike Rodgers in the general's office. Rodgers told him that Striker would reach Madrid shortly after 11:30 A.M., Spanish time. Options for Striker activities would be presented to Hood as soon as they were available.

After the briefing, Hood checked in with the night crew. While the day team continued to monitor the Spanish situation, Curt Hardaway, Lt. Gen. Bill Abram, and the rest of the "P.M.Squad," as they called themselves, were overseeing the routine domestic and international activities of Op-Center. Lieutenant General Abram, who was Mike Rodgers's counterpart, was especially busy with the Regional Op-Center. The mobile facility had been returned from its Middle East shakedown and was undergoing repair work and fine tuning. Everything was under control. Hood returned to his office to try to rest.

He shut off the light, threw off his shoes, and lay back on his couch. As he stared at the dark ceiling his mind went to Sharon and the kids. He glanced at his luminous watch—the one Sharon had bought him for their first anniversary. They would be coming into Bradley International soon. He played with the notion of borrowing an army chopper and flying up to Old Saybrook. He'd buzz his in-laws and use a megaphone to beg his wife to come home. He would be dismissed for all that but what the hell. It would give him plenty of time to stay home with the family.

Of course Hood had no intention of doing that. He was romantic enough to want to play the modern-day knight, but he wasn't reckless enough. And why bother going up to Old Saybrook if he couldn't promise to slow down? He *liked* his work. And shorter hours were something the job just wouldn't permit. Part of him felt that Sharon was being vindictive because she'd had to cut way back on her career activities in order to raise the kids. But even if he'd wanted to stop working and raise a family—which he didn't—they couldn't have lived on Sharon's salary. That was a fact.

He shut his eyes and dropped his arm across them. *But facts don't always matter in situations like this, do they?*

Hood's mind was too busy to allow him to sleep. He alternated between feeling angry, guilty, and utterly disgusted. He decided to give up trying to rest.

He made himself a pot of coffee, poured it black into his memorial WASHINGTON SENATORS baseball mug, and went back to his desk. He spent some time with the computer files of Manni's Italian secessionist movement. He was curious to see what, if any, intelligence work had been done to stopgap the collapse of Italy.

There was nothing on file. It was a nearly six-year-long process, which began in 1993 as an offshoot of voter unhappiness over increasing political corruption scandals. Smaller communities claimed that they weren't being adequately represented and so members of parliament were elected from individual districts rather than through proportional representation as before. That caused a fragmentation of power among the major parties which allowed smaller groups to flourish. Neo-Fascists came to power in 1994, business interests of the Forza Italia party wrested power from them a year later, and then the fall of Yugoslavia caused unrest all along the Istrian Peninsula in the north—unrest that the Rome-based Forza Italia was ill equipped to handle. For help the premier turned to parties that had a power base there. But those groups were interested in building their own strength and fanned the rebelliousness. Violence and secessionist talk flourished in Trieste and moved west to Venice and slingshot south as far as Livorno and Florence.

The Milan-born Manni was recalled from Moscow to try to negotiate a fix to the deteriorating situation. His solution was to draft a pact that made northern Italy a largely autonomous political and economic region, with a congressional government in Milan to replace the bloc in the parliament in Rome. Both groups worked independently with the elected premier. While the Italians above the Northern Apennines paid taxes to their own capital, they used the same currency as the south; the two regions remained militarily intact; and the nation was still referred to as Italy.

No military action was taken by Rome and no foreign intelligence services were involved to any great extent. The Italian Entente, as it was called, provided no model for the situation in Spain. And they lacked the one thing that had made Manni's efforts workable: he was only dealing with two factions, north and south. The Spanish conflict involved at least a half dozen ethnic groups who had rarely if ever been comfortable together.

The call came through ten minutes late. Hood called Rodgers in to listen on the speakerphone. As Rodgers arrived and took a seat, Manni was explaining in English that the reason he was late was because Portugal had just asked the United Nations for help.

"There has been violence along the border between Salamanca and Zamora," Manni said.

Hood glanced at the map on his computer. Salamanca was located just below Zamora in central and northwestern Spain. Together, the regions shared about two hundred miles of border with Portugal.

"The unrest began about three hours ago when anti-Castilians held a candlelight rally at the Postigo de la Traición—the Traitor's Gate. That's the spot by the city wall where the Castilian king Sancho II was assassinated in 1072. When police attempted to break up the rally, stones and bottles were thrown and the police fired several shots into the air. Someone in the crowd fired back and an officer was wounded. The police are mostly Castilian and they immediately turned on the ralliers—not as peacekeepers but as Castilians.''

''With guns?'' Hood asked.

''I'm afraid so,'' said Manni.

''Which is like dropping a lighted match on gas,'' said hawkish National Security advisor Burkow.

''Mr. Burkow, you are correct,'' said Manni. ''Like a firestorm, riots spread westward to Portugal. The police called for military help from Madrid and it is being provided. But Lisbon is concerned that they may not be enough to contain the fighting and also to stop refugees from crossing the border. They've just asked the United Nations to create a buffer zone.''

''How do you feel about Portugal's request, Mr. Secretary-General?'' Carol Lanning asked.

''I am opposed,'' he replied.

''I don't blame you,'' said Burkow. ''Lisbon's got an army, an air force, and a navy. Let them field a force.''

''No, Mr. Burkow,'' Manni said. ''I am uneasy about having *any* army on the border. Placing a force there would legitimize the crisis. It would acknowledge that a crisis exists.''

''Doesn't it?'' Lanning asked.

''It does,'' Manni agreed. ''But to millions of Spaniards the crisis is still a highly localized one. It's a provincial matter, not a national or international one. And officially, it is still under control. If they learn that an army is gathered on the border—any army— there will be misinformation, confusion, and panic. The situation will become even worse.''

"Mr. Manni," Burkow said tensely, "this may all be academic. Are you aware that Prime Minister Aznar has spoken with President Lawrence and asked for a U.S. military presence offshore?"

"Yes," Manni said, "I am aware of this. Ostensibly, the force is there to defend and evacuate American tourists in the wake of the killing."

"Ostensibly," Burkow agreed.

"Has the President made a decision?"

"Not yet," said Burkow, "but he's leaning toward it. He's waiting for intelligence to determine whether American interests are, in fact, in danger. Paul? Marius? Do either of you have anything to say about that?"

Being the senior official, Hood answered first. "Except for the attack against Martha—or perhaps because of it—there have been no reports of additional hostilities against American tourists," he said. "Nor do we expect there to be. The people of Spain will be extremely sensitive about straining relations further. Besides, whatever the region, Spain's economy depends upon tourism. It's very unlikely that they'll want to do anything to jeopardize that. As for additional political attacks against Americans, we all know that Martha was assassinated because she worked for Op-Center. We believe that she was murdered as a singular warning to the United States not to do exactly what we're discussing: become involved in Spanish politics. As long as we keep our distance, politically and militarily, we don't expect any more such attacks."

"Paul's on the money about the tourist situation," Marius said. "We've been very carefully monitoring the actions of the Spanish police and military. They respond very quickly to put down violence in popular tourist centers. Of course,'' he added, ''that may change if the conflict takes on a life of its own or if the police are provoked the way they were at the Traitor's Gate.''

"Which," Burkow interrupted, "is the heart of the matter. It's the reason the President is considering sending troops. There's a point in every internal conflict when protest becomes open warfare. When emotion takes over from common sense. When expectations change from 'I want to preserve my economy' to 'I want to preserve my life.' When that happens—"

"*If* it happens," Manni pointed out.

"Fine," Burkow said. "If it happens, tourists—American and otherwise—will have no one looking out for them."

As Burkow was speaking, Hood received a secure e-mail message from McCaskey. He motioned Rodgers over as it came through. They read it together.

Paul, it read. *Field Ops report Basque yacht bomber murdered by Catalonian team. FOs going to talk to hit squad. Assessment: motive was revenge, not politics. I've warned FOs that one of them may still be in danger if she's recognized as survivor of the MM situation. She doesn't think these people are carrying on that agenda. I'm inclined to agree that circumstances have changed. Inform if you want her recalled.*

The yacht bomber apparently was backed by army general named Amadori. Checking on him now. Not surprisingly, local NATO files on the general appear to have been purged.

Hood sent an acknowledgment along with his congratulations to Aideen and María for their intelligence work. He didn't like the idea of her being out there with members of the team that had had Martha killed. Especially after having inadvertently left her and Martha open to the attack in the first place. But María was a crack agent. With her there to back Aideen—and vice versa—Hood informed Darrell to let the women make the call.

"Mr. Burkow," Manni said, "your concerns are well founded. But I believe we should wait to see whether the Spanish government can put this down themselves."

"So far, they haven't exactly instilled confidence," Burkow said. "They couldn't even keep Deputy Serrador alive long enough to interrogate him."

"Mistakes were made," Manni agreed. "Everyone was caught off guard. But we mustn't compound those mistakes."

"Paul Hood here. What do you recommend, Mr. Secretary-General?"

"My advice, Mr. Hood, is to give the prime minister another day to work things out. He has called in his military advisor on civil unrest and they're drawing up a plan to deal with all possible contingencies."

Rodgers leaned toward the phone. "Sir, this is General Mike Rodgers, Deputy Director of Op-Center. If the prime minister or his officers need any military or intelligence support, my office is prepared to offer it very, very quietly.''

"Thank you, General Rodgers," said Manni. "I will certainly inform Prime Minister Aznar and General Amadori of your generous offer.''

Hood was looking at Rodgers as Manni spoke. Something passed between them at the mention of Amadori's name—a rapid and unexpected deflation of spirit visible in their eyes, a moment of numb paralysis in their limbs. Hood felt like a predator who suddenly realized that his prey was much smarter, more feral, and far deadlier than he'd expected.

The paralysis passed quickly. Hood hit the mute button. "Mike—"

"I know," Rodgers said, already rising. "I'm on it.''

"If it's the same man," Hood said, "they've got some very serious problems over there.''

"Spain does," Rodgers said, "along with every nation that's going to want to get its people out of there in a hurry.''

As Rodgers hurried from the office Hood listened, disinterested, to the political jabber between Manni, Burkow, and Lanning. They agreed about how they needed to let Spain solve this situation themselves but with a level of vocal support from the U.S. which would be heard by the feuding factions and could be ratcheted up to a military presence if necessary. A military presence that could become defensive action but that was actually offense designed at helping to preserve the legitimate government of Spain—

It was all very necessary, Hood knew, but only in

terms of posturing—like the United Nations itself. The
real work was going to be done over the next few
hours as they tried to figure out whether Amadori was
behind the unrest. And, if so, how far he had gone in
undermining the government. If he hadn't gone too
far, U.S. intelligence and the military would have to
work with Spanish leaders to figure out how to stop
him. That would be difficult to do quietly, but it could
be done. There were templates for that kind of con-
tainment in Haiti, Panama, and other nations.

But it was the alternative that concerned Hood. The
possibility that, like a cancer, Amadori's influence had
spread far into the workings of the nation. If that were
the case, then it might not be possible to remove the
general without killing the patient. The only model for
that was the collapse of Yugoslavia, a struggle in
which thousands of people died and the sociopolitical
and economic ramifications were still being felt.

Spain had nearly four times the population of Yugoslavia. It also had friends and enemies in neighbor-
ing nations. If Spain came apart the unrest could easily
spread throughout Europe. The breakup could also set
an example for other melting-pot nations such as
France, the United Kingdom, and Canada.

Perhaps even the United States.

The call ended with an agreement that the
Secretary-General's staff would provide hourly updates to the White House, and that Burkow would
inform Manni of any changes in administration policy.

Hood hung up the phone feeling more helpless than
he had since he'd first joined Op-Center. He'd had
missions go right and missions go wrong. His team

had thwarted terrorists and coups. But he'd never faced a situation that threatened to set the tone for a new century: the idea that fragmentation was the norm rather than the exception and that nations as the world knew them could very well be on the brink of extinction.

TWENTY

Tuesday, 4:45 A.M.
Madrid, Spain

Word of Adolfo Alcazar's brutal death traveled quickly from María Corneja to Luis García de la Vega to Darrell McCaskey. As he was required to do by law, Luis conveyed news of the homicide to the Ministry of Justice in Madrid. There, a high-ranking officer on the night staff quietly passed the information to General Amadori's longtime personal aide, Antonio Aguirre. Aguirre—a former staff officer to Francisco Franco—personally went to the General's office, knocked once on the door, and waited until he was invited in. Then he gave the news to the General himself.

Amadori did not seem surprised to learn of Adolfo's death. He also did not mourn Adolfo. How could he: the General had not known the man. It had been imperative that the two men be together and communicate with one another as little as possible. That way, if Adolfo had been arrested and forced to talk, there was nothing but his own testimony to link him to the General. There were no telephone records, notes, or photographs. To Amadori, Adolfo Alcazar was a loyal soldier of the cause, one of the many revolutionaries whom the General did not and could not know.

But what the brave and devoted Adolfo Alcazar had done was a flashpoint that had helped to make this revolution possible. The General vowed aloud to Antonio Aguirre that his murder would be avenged and his killers eliminated. He knew exactly who to go after: the Ramirez *familia*. No one else would have a reason or the means to eliminate Adolfo. Their deaths would be an example to others that he intended to treat resistance with terminal force.

And, of course, as the General told Antonio, the roundup and execution of the Ramirez *familia* would serve one other purpose. It would frighten and scatter other *familias* that might be inclined to oppose him. Which was why the strike had to be very public and very dramatic.

The General gave Antonio the order to make that happen. Antonio saluted smartly, turned, and left without saying a word. He went directly to his desk and phoned General Americo Hoss at the Tagus Army Air Base outside of Toledo. The General's orders were communicated verbally. Like Adolfo, General Hoss would do whatever was necessary to serve the General.

It was still dark when the four aging HA-15 helicopters lifted off. Like most of the helicopters in the Spanish army, the HA-15s were transport choppers rather than gunships. The thirty-year-old aircraft had been outfitted with a pair of side-door-mounted 20mm cannons, which had been fired only in practice missions.

This was not a practice mission.

Each helicopter carried a complement of ten soldiers, each of whom was armed with a Z-62 submachine gun or a Modelo L-1-003 rifle adapted to accomodate standard M16 magazines. Mission commander Major Alejandro Gómez had orders to take the factory and to use whatever means were necessary to obtain the names of the killers.

Gómez was expected to return with prisoners. But if they refused to come, he was expected to return with bodybags.

TWENTY-ONE

Tuesday, 5:01 A.M.
San Sebastián, Spain

María pulled up to the security booth at the Ramirez factory and flashed her Interpol credentials. She'd decided en route that she didn't want to be a tourist here. She was relatively confident that the guard would phone ahead to warn the plant manager that she and Aideen were coming in. The manager, in turn, would inform any of the murderers who might be on the premises. Ordinarily, the killers would probably have hidden or fled. That was why María had taken the precaution of informing the guard, "We have no jurisdiction here. We only want to talk to members of the *familia.*"

"But Señorita Cornejas," the burly, gray-bearded sentry replied, "there is no *familia.*"

It was a cool disavowal. It reminded Aideen of the drug dealers in Mexico City who had always insisted that they never heard of *el señorío*—"the lord of the estate"—the drug lord who provided them with all the heroin sold in the nation's capital.

"Actually, you're a little premature," María replied, gunning the car engine in neutral. "I have a very strong suspicion that in just a little while there *will* be no *familia.*"

The guard gave her a veiled but puzzled look. He wore a ribbon for valor and had the gruff, immutable bearing of a drill sergeant. In Spain, as elsewhere, security positions were a haven for former soldiers and police officers. Very few of them appreciated being ordered around by civilians. And far, far fewer liked being lectured by women. As María had suspected when she first set eyes on him, this one was going to need another little push.

"Amigo," she said, "trust me. There *won't* be a *familia* unless I get to talk to them. A few of them took it upon themselves to kill a man in town. That man has some very powerful friends. I don't think those friends are going to let this matter sit."

The sentry looked at her for a long moment. Then, turning his back to them, he made a phone call. His voice did not carry outside the booth. But after a short conversation the sentry hung up, raised the bar, and admitted the car to the parking lot. María told Aideen that she was convinced now that one or more members of the *familia* would see them. And, Aideen knew, María would press them to tell her whatever they knew about General Amadori. With Ramirez and his people dead, their plan—whatever it had been—was probably dead as well. Amadori was the one they had to worry about. She needed to know, as fast as possible, how *much* they needed to worry about him.

Two men met María and Aideen at the front door of the factory. The women parked the car nose in and emerged with their arms extended downward, their hands held palms forward. María stood by the driver's side, Aideen by the passenger's door, as the men walked over. They stopped a few yards away. While one man watched, the other—a big, powerfully built fellow—took the women's guns and telephone and tossed the items in the car. Then he checked them for wires. His check was thorough but completely professional. When he was finished, the two men walked in silence to a large van parked nearby. The women followed. The four of them climbed into the back and sat on the floor amid cans of paint, ladders, and drop cloths. The men sat beside the door.

"I am Juan and this is Ferdinand," said the man who had watched the frisking. "Your full names, please."

"María Corneja and Aideen Sánchez," María said.

Aideen picked up on the "change" in her own nationality. It was an inspired move on María's part. These two might not trust fellow Spaniards right now but they'd trust foreigners even less. Internal warfare was a perfect environment for foreign powers to spread weapons, money—and influence. Roots like that were often difficult to dislodge.

Aideen looked from one to the other of the men. Juan was the older of the two. He looked tired. The skin was deeply wrinkled around his nervous eyes and his slender shoulders were bent. The other man was a colossus whose eyes were deep-set under a heavy brow. His flesh was smooth and tight like the face on a coin and his broad shoulders were straight.

"Why are you here, María Corneja?" Juan asked.

"I want to talk to you about an army General named Rafael Amadori," María said.

Juan looked at her for a moment. "Go ahead."

María pulled the cigarettes from her jacket. She took one and offered the pack around. Juan accepted one.

Now that they were here, it bothered Aideen that they were collaborating with killers. But as Martha had said, different countries had different rules. Aideen could only trust that María knew what she was doing.

María lit Juan's cigarette and then she did her own. The way she lit his smoke—cupping the match under Juan's cigarette, inviting him to take her hands and move them toward the tip—made the action very intimate. Aideen admired how she used that to establish a rapport with the man.

"Señor Ramirez and the heads of other business groups and *familias* were slain yesterday by a man working for Amadori," María said. "I believe you've met him. Adolfo Alcazar."

Juan said nothing.

María's voice was softer than Aideen had ever heard it. She was wooing Juan.

"Amadori is a very powerful officer," María continued, "who appears to hold a key place in the food chain of what's been going on. Here's how it looks to me. Ramirez had an American assassinated yesterday. Amadori knew this was going to happen and let it happen. Why? So that he could present an audiotape to the nation implicating Deputy Serrador. Why? So that Serrador and the Basques he represents would be discredited at home and abroad. Then he had Alcazar murder your employer and his coconspirators. Why? To discredit the Catalonians and destroy their power-base. If Serrador and the business leaders were planning some kind of political maneuver, that's finished now.

"More importantly," María went on, "the presence of a conspiracy weakens the government considerably. They don't know who they can trust or who to turn to for stability. Words won't reassure the people. They're fighting each other from the Atlantic to the Mediterranean, from the Bay of Biscay to the Strait of Gibraltar. The government needs someone strong to establish order. I believe that Amadori has orchestrated things to make himself that man."

Juan stared at her through the smoke of his cigarette. "So?" he said. "Order will be restored."

"But maybe not as it was," María said. "I know a little about Amadori—but not enough. He's a Castilian nationalist and, from all I can determine, a megalomaniac. He appears to have used these incidents to put himself in a position to have martial law declared throughout Spain—and then to run that martial law. I'm concerned that he won't step down after that. I need to know if you have or can get any intelligence that will help me stop him."

Juan smirked. "You're suggesting that Interpol and the Ramirez *familia* work together?"

"I am."

"That's ridiculous," Juan said. "What will stop you from gathering intelligence on us?"

"Nothing," María admitted.

Juan's smirk wavered. "Then you admit you might."

"Yes, I admit that," María said. "But if we don't stop General Amadori, then whatever intelligence I happen to gather on the *familia* will be useless. The general will hunt you people down and destroy you. If not for killing his operative, then for the threat you represent. The possibility that you could rally other *familias* against him.''

Juan looked at Ferdinand. The granite-solid watchman thought for a moment and then nodded once. Juan regarded María. So did Aideen. María had played Juan honestly—and beautifully.

''Adversity has made stranger trenchmates,'' Juan said. ''All right. We've been looking into Amadori since we returned to the factory.'' He snickered. ''We still have some allies in government and the military, though not many. The death of Señor Ramirez has scared people.''

''As it was meant to,'' María remarked.

''Amadori is based in Madrid, at the office of the Defense Ministry,'' Juan said. ''But we hear he has established a headquarters elsewhere. We're trying to find out where. He has powerful Castilian allies in the Congreso de los Diputados and in the Senado. They're backing him with deeds and with silence.''

''What do you mean?''

''The prime minister has the right to declare martial law,'' Juan said, ''but the parliament can effectively block him by cutting off funds if they don't approve of the measure or the leader.''

''And they haven't done that here,'' María suggested.

''No,'' Juan said. ''I've been told by an informer from the Ruiz *familia*—''

''The computer makers?'' María asked.

"Yes," Juan said. "I've been told that the funding was actually above what the prime minister had requested. By fivefold."

María whistled.

"But why wouldn't they back him?" Aideen asked. "Spain is facing great danger."

Juan looked from María to Aideen. "Usually, the money is approved in parcels. That's done as a means of preventing exactly this kind of coup. Powerful people are behind this. Perhaps they or their families have been threatened. Perhaps they've been promised positions of greater authority in the new regime."

"Regardless," María said, "they've given Amadori the power and the money to do whatever he deems necessary." She drew slowly on her cigarette. "Simple and brilliant. With the army under his control and the government crippled by acts of treason, General Amadori can't be stopped by any legal means."

"Exactly," Juan said. "Which is why the *familia* has had to work on this in our own way."

María looked at Juan then ground her cigarette on the floor. "What would happen if he were removed?"

"Do you mean dismissed?" Juan asked.

"If I'd meant dismissed I would have said dismissed," the woman replied sharply.

Juan turned and put his cigarette out against the metal wall. He shrugged. "We would all benefit. But it would have to be done quickly. If Amadori has time to establish himself as the savior of Spain, then whatever momentum he creates will continue with or without him."

"Granted," María said. "And he will move quickly to present himself as a hero."

Juan nodded. "The problem is, it won't be easy getting close to him. If he stays in one place, there will be security. If he moves around, his itinerary will be classified. We'd have to be very lucky just to—"

Aideen held up her hand. "Quiet!"

The others looked at her. A moment later María obviously heard it too. By then they could feel it in their gut—the low beat of distant rotors.

"Helicopters!" Juan said. He jumped to the back of the van and opened the door.

Aideen looked past him. Coming in over the nearby hills were the navigation lights of four helicopters. They were about a mile away.

"They're coming toward the factory," Juan said. He turned toward María. "Yours?"

She shook her head. She pushed past him and jumped onto the asphalt. She stood watching the choppers for a moment. "Get your people out of here or into safe areas," she said. "Arm them."

Aideen slid out around the men. "Hold on," she said. "Are you telling him to shoot at Spanish soldiers?"

"I don't know!" she snapped. She started running toward the car. "These are probably Amadori's men. If any of the *familia* members are captured or killed, it accomplishes what we're afraid of. By shutting down pockets of dissent, he's strengthened in the eyes of the people."

Aideen jogged after her. She was trying to imagine some other scenario. But there were no riots in San

Sebastián and the police were handling the inquiry into the explosion in the bay. There were only small homes and fields between this spot and the mountains: the Ramirez factory was the only target large enough to merit four helicopters.

This is a civilized nation preparing to make war on itself, she told herself. Though it was difficult to accept that fact, it was becoming more and more real by the moment.

Juan stepped from the van. He was followed by Ferdinand.

"Where are you going?" Juan shouted after the women.

"To call my superior!" María shouted back. "I'll let you know if I find out anything."

"Tell your people that we will not fight back unless we're attacked!" Juan yelled as he and Ferdinand started running toward the factory. The helicopters were less than a quarter mile away. "Tell them that we have no quarrel with the honest soldiers or people of—"

His words were drowned out by the rattling drone of the rotors as the choppers bore down on the factory. An instant later the crisp chatter of the airborne Modelo L-1-003 guns was added to the din and both Juan and Ferdinand fell to the ground.

TWENTY-TWO

Tuesday, 5:43 A.M.
Madrid, Spain

Darrell McCaskey couldn't sleep.

After bringing Aideen to the airfield, he'd returned with Luis to Interpol's Madrid office. The small complex occupied a single floor of the district police station. The turn-of-the-century brick building was located just off the broad Gran Vía on Calle de Hortaleza. The ride back to the city had been a quiet one as McCaskey reflected on his months with María.

Suddenly exhausted when they returned, McCaskey had lain down on a soft sofa in the small dining room. But while he'd gladly shut his heavy eyelids, his heavy heart had refused to shut down. María's anger had disturbed him, though it was not unexpected. Worse than that, though, was simply seeing the woman again. It reminded McCaskey of the biggest mistake of his life: letting her go two years before.

The sad thing was, he'd known it then.

Lying there, McCaskey remembered vividly all the differences that had come up during her stay in America. She had a live-for-today attitude, not worrying very much about health or money or the danger of some of the assignments she took. They had different tastes in music and in the sports they liked to watch or play. She liked to bike everywhere, he liked to walk or drive. He loved cities and high energy places, she loved the country.

But whatever their differences, and they were considerable, one thing was true. They had loved each other. That should have counted for more than it did. It sure as hell did now.

McCaskey could still remember her face when he told her the relationship wasn't working for him. He would always see that face, hard but deeply hurt—like a soldier who'd been wounded but refused to believe it and was determined to keep going. It was one of those snapshots that stayed in the soul and came back from time to time, as vivid as the moment it happened. "Emotional malaria," Op-Center psychologist Liz Gordon had once called it when they were talking about failed relationships.

She got that right.

McCaskey gave up trying to keep his eyes shut. As he lay staring up at the fluorescent lights, Luis came running in. He hurried to a phone on one of the four round tables in the dining room. He snapped his fingers and motioned for McCaskey to pick up another one.

"It's María," Luis said. "On line five. They're under attack."

McCaskey swung from the sofa and rushed to the nearest table. "Are they okay?"

"They're in a car," Luis said. "María said she thinks it best to stay where they are." He scooped up a phone.

McCaskey did likewise and punched line five.

"María?" Luis said. "Darrell is on the phone and Raul is checking on the helicopters. What's happening now?"

McCaskey decided not to ask for an update. If he missed anything Luis would fill him in.

"Two of the helicopters are circling low over the factory grounds," María said. "The other two are hovering just above the roof. Troops are climbing out. Some of the soldiers are taking up positions on the edge of the roof. Others are using aluminum ladders to climb down toward the doors. All of them are armed with submachine guns."

"You said they already shot two men—"

"They shot at two members of the Ramirez *familia,* Juan and Ferdinand," María said. "Both men had taken part in the retaliation for the yacht attack. But they hit the ground and surrendered—I think they're all right."

Her voice was calm and strong. McCaskey was proud of her. He had a deep desire to take back those stupid, selfish words he'd once uttered to her.

"We were meeting with the men when the attack began," María continued. "I don't know if the troops targeted them specifically or if the helicopters opened fire on the nearest target."

"The sentry—" Aideen said.

"Yes, that's right," María added. "Aideen noticed that the guard at the factory was gone when the attack began. He's former military. He could have pointed the men out to the helicopters."

A tall, muscular officer ran into the dining room.

Luis turned and looked at him. The man shook his head.

"No flight plan was filed for the helicopters," he said.

"Then this isn't going through the regular military chain of command," Luis said into the phone.

"I'm not surprised," María said.

"What do you mean?" Luis asked.

"I'm convinced that General Rafael Amadori is running this put-down operation as a private war," María said. "It appears that he's engineered events so that parliament has granted him emergency powers. He also has a very narrow window in which to eliminate opposition. By the time anyone decides to try and stop him it will be too late."

"Do we know where the general is based?" McCaskey asked.

"Not yet," the woman replied. "But I'm sure he's made it difficult for anyone to get near him. I'll have to give Amadori this much: he appears to be very well prepared."

McCaskey noticed a change in María's voice. He recognized it because it had always made him feel a little jealous. She did not approve of Amadori's motives or actions, but there was a trace of admiration for the man.

María fell silent as gunfire erupted in the distance.

Aideen said something McCaskey couldn't quite make out.

"María!" McCaskey yelled. "Talk to me!"

It was several seconds before she came back on. "Sorry," she said. "The troops have entered the factory. We were trying to see what they were doing—there are parked cars in the way. We heard a few bursts of fire from the soldiers and then—*damn!*''

''What?'' McCaskey said.

There was a peppering of loud reports followed by the unbroken drone of automatic fire.

''*María!*'' McCaskey shouted.

''They let the soldiers provoke them,'' she said.

''Who did?'' Luis demanded.

''Probably some of the *familia* members and maybe some of the other workers,'' María said. ''There was gunfire from inside the factory. They must have shot at the soldiers. Workers are running out—falling out. The ones with guns are being cut down. Juan is yelling for them to surrender.''

McCaskey looked over at Luis. The Interpol officer seemed pale as he looked back at McCaskey.

''This is incredible,'' María said. ''The soldiers are shooting anyone who doesn't put down their weapons. Even if they're just goddamned crowbars! People are shouting inside. It sounds like they're warning people to surrender.''

''How near are the soldiers to your position?'' McCaskey asked.

''About four hundred yards. But there are other cars around—I don't think they know we're here.''

Perspiration collected on McCaskey's upper lip. The law was collapsing. He wished there were some way he could get the two women out of there. He looked over at his companion. Luis's eyes were moving quickly without focusing on anything. He was anxious too.

"Luis," McCaskey asked thickly, "what about the police chopper?"

"It's still there—"

"I know. But can you get permission for it to go in?"

Luis lifted his hands helplessly. "Even if I could, I doubt they'd go. The soldiers might suspect a *familia* ruse."

A strong military offensive and paranoia. It was a combination that caused leaders to shut themselves off from all but their closest advisors. It was also a mix that could turn soldiers into indiscriminate executioners. McCaskey wished that Striker were here instead of over the Atlantic, hours away.

No one spoke for a long moment. McCaskey continued to regard Luis. There were three options. The women could stay where they were; they could try to get out; or they could attempt to surrender. If they tried to sneak away and were spotted, they'd probably be cut down. If they attempted to surrender they might also be shot. The safest course seemed to be to stay where they were and use their fake IDs if they were discovered. McCaskey wondered if Luis were going to make the call for them. The Interpol officer was big on taking responsibility for his people's actions and then taking any heat those actions generated. But this wasn't about blame or credit. This was about lives.

"María," Luis said into the speaker, "what do you want to do?"

"I've been wondering about that," María said. "I don't know what the attackers are after. We're seeing prisoners coming out now. Dozens of them. But we have no idea where they're going to be taken. Possibly to be interrogated. I wonder—''

''What do you wonder?'' Luis asked.

There was muted conversation on María's end. Then silence except for faint gunfire.

''María?'' Luis said.

The conversation stopped. There was only gunfire.

''María!'' Luis repeated.

After a moment Aideen came on. ''She's not here.''

''Where is she?'' Luis asked.

''On her way to the factory with her hands raised,'' Aideen replied. ''She's going to try to surrender.''

TWENTY-THREE

Monday, 10:45 P.M.
Washington, D.C.

The phone call from National Security Chief Steve Burkow was brief and surprising.

"The President is considering a radical shift in Administration policy toward Spain," Burkow informed Paul Hood. "Be at the White House situation room at eleven-thirty tonight. And would you please have the latest intelligence on the military situation sent over?"

It was less than an hour since the conference call with U.N. Secretary-General Manni. It had been decided, then, that the status quo was going to be maintained. Hood had been able to lie down and take a short nap. He wondered what could have changed since the call.

Hood said he'd be there, of course. Then he went into the small private washroom in the back of his office. He shut the door. There was a speakerphone set in the wall under the light switch. After splashing water on his face he called Bob Herbert. Herbert's assistant said that he was talking to Darrell McCaskey and asked if this were a priority call. Hood said it wasn't and asked for Herbert to call back when he got off.

Hood had already finished washing his face and straightening his tie when the internal line beeped. Hood was glad to hear it. Like a scavenger drawn to carrion, his tired mind had padded back to Sharon and the kids. He didn't know why—to punish himself, he wondered?—but he didn't want to think about them now. When a crisis was pending, it was not the best time to reassess one's life and goals.

Hood hit the telephone speaker button and leaned on the stainless steel sink. "Hood," he said.

"Paul, it's Bob," Herbert said. "I was going to call you anyway."

"What's Darrell's news?"

"It's pretty grim," Herbert said. "NRO intelligence has confirmed that four helicopters, apparently sent by General Amadori, attacked the Ramirez factory at 5:20 A.M., local time. Aideen Marley and María Corneja were in the parking lot, hunkered down in their car, during the attack. The Spanish troops gunned down about twenty people before taking control of the factory and rounding up others. According to Aideen—who's still in the car and in contact with Darrell—María surrendered to the soldiers. Her hope is that she can find out where Amadori is headquartered and get that information back to us."

"Is Aideen in any immediate danger?"

"We don't think so," Herbert said. "The troops aren't making a sweep of the parking lot. It looks to her like they want to finish rounding up a few people and get the hell out."

"What about María?" Hood asked. "Will she try

to stop Amadori?'' He knew that the White House would have some of this information. That was probably one of the reasons for the hastily called meeting. He also knew that the President would ask the same question.

"Truthfully, I don't know,'' Herbert admitted. ''As soon as I hang up I'm going to ask Liz for the psychological workup she did when María was working here. Maybe that'll tell us something.''

"What does Darrell think?'' Hood asked impatiently. ''If anyone would know María Corneja, he's the man.'' Hood didn't put much trust in psychoanalytical profiles. Cold, paint-by-number studies were less valuable to him than human feelings and intuition.

"What man knows any woman?'' Herbert asked.

Hood was about to tell Herbert to spare him the philosophy when his mind flashed to Sharon. Hood said nothing. Herbert was right.

"But to answer your question,'' Herbert continued, ''Darrell says he wouldn't put it past her to kill him. She can be single-minded and very, very focused. He says she could find a handy pen or paperclip and rip a hole in his femoral artery. He also says he could see her hating his barbarity but also applauding his courage and strength.''

"Meaning?''

"She could think too much or too long,'' Herbert said. ''Hesitate and miss an opportunity.''

"Would she ever join him?'' Hood asked.

"Darrell says no. Emphatically no,'' Herbert added.

Hood wasn't so sure, but he'd go with Darrell on this one. Herbert didn't have any additional information on Serrador's death or outside confimation of his involvement with Martha's murder. But he said he'd keep working on both. Hood thanked Herbert and asked him to send all of the latest data to the President. Then he headed out to the White House.

The drive was relaxed at this hour and he made the trip in just under a half hour. Hood turned off Constitution Avenue, turned onto 17th Street, and made a right onto the one way E Street. He made a left and stopped at the Southwest Appointment Gate. He was passed and, after parking, he entered the White House through the West Wing. He walked down the spacious corridors.

Whatever his state of mind, whatever the crisis, whatever his levels of cynicism, Hood never failed to be moved and awed by the power and history of the White House. It was a nexus for the past and future. Two of the Founding Fathers had lived here. Lincoln had preserved and solidified the nation from here. World War II had been won from here. The decision to conquer the moon was made here. Given the right mix of wisdom, courage, and savvy, this pulpit could drive the nation—and thus, the world—to accomplish anything. When he was here, it was difficult for Hood to dwell on the failings of any of our nation's leaders. There was only the fire of hope fueled by the mighty bellows of power.

Hood rode the main access elevator down to the situation room on the first sublevel. Beneath this level were three other subbasements. These included a war room, a medical room, a safe room for the first family and staff, and a galley. Hood was greeted by a sharp young guard who checked his palm print on a horizontal laser scanner. When the device chimed, Hood was allowed to pass through the metal detector. A Presidential aide greeted him and took him to the wood-paneled situation room.

Steve Burkow was already there. So were the imposing Chairman of the Joint Chiefs of Staff General Kenneth VanZandt, Carol Lanning—sitting in for Secretary of State Av Lincoln, who was in Japan—and CIA Director Marius Fox. Fox was a man in his late forties. He was of medium height and build, with close-cropped brown hair and well-tailored suits. There was always a brightly colored handkerchief in his breast pocket, though it never managed to outshine his brown eyes. He was a man who truly enjoyed his work.

But he's new at the job, Hood thought cynically. It would be interesting to see how long it took for the bureaucracy and the pressures of the job to wear him down.

There was a long, rectangular mahogany table in the center of the brightly lit room. An STU-3 secure telephone and a computer monitor were positioned at each of the ten stations, with slide-out keyboards underneath the table. The computer setup was self-contained. Software from outside, even from the Department of Defense or State Department, was debugged before it was allowed into the system. On the ivory-colored walls were detailed color maps showing the location of U.S. and foreign troops, as well as flags denoting trouble spots. Red flags for ongoing problems and green for latent. There were no flags in Spain and a single green one offshore. Apparently, the change in Administration policy did not include sending American land troops to the region. The offshore marker was most likely for a carrier to airlift U.S. officials if it became necessary.

No one had had a chance to do more than say hello to Hood before the President arrived.

President Michael Lawrence stood a broad-shouldered six-foot-four. He both looked and sounded presidential. Whatever combination of the three Cs—charisma, charm, and calm—created that impression, Lawrence had them. His longish silver hair was swept back dramatically and his voice still resonated as though he were Mark Antony on the steps of the Roman Senate. But President Lawrence also looked a great deal wearier than he had when he took office. The eyes were puffier, the cheeks more drawn. The hair looked silver because it was more white than gray. That was common among U.S. presidents, though it wasn't just the pressures of the office which aged them tremendously—it was the fact that lives were deeply and permanently affected by every decision they made. It was also the steady flow of early morning and late night crises, the exhausting travel abroad, and what Liz Gordon once described as ''the posterity effect'': the pressure of wanting to secure a positive review in the history books while pleasing the people you were elected to serve. That was a tremendous emotional and intellectual burden that very few people had to deal with.

The President thanked everyone for coming and sat down. As he poured himself coffee, he offered his condolences to Hood on the death of Martha Mackall. The President commented on the loss of a young and talented diplomat, and said that he had already assigned someone the job of organizing a quiet memorial tribute to her. Hood thanked him. President Lawrence was very good and also very sincere when it came to human touches like that.

Then he turned abruptly to the business at hand. The President was also very good when it came to shifting gears.

"I just got off the phone with the Vice-President and with the Spanish ambassador, Señor García Abril," the President said. He took a sip of the black coffee. "As some of you know, the situation in Spain is very confused from a military standpoint. The police have been putting down some riots while ignoring others. Carol, you want to quickly address that?"

Lanning nodded. She consulted her notes. "The police and the army have been ignoring riots by Castilians against other groups," she said. "Churches all across the nation are being forced to cope with literally thousands of people coming to them for sanctuary."

"Are they providing it?" Burkow asked.

"They were," she replied, rifling through her papers, "until the crowds became too great in some locations—like Parroquia María Reina in Barcelona and Iglesia del Señor in Seville. Now they've literally locked the doors and are refusing to admit anyone else. In a few cases the local police have been called in to remove people from churches—a move, I should add, which is being privately denounced by the Vatican although they're going to urge 'restraint and compassion' in a public statement later today.''

"Thank you," the President said. "There seem to be three entirely separate factions running Spain at the moment. According to Ambassador Abril—who has always been very frank with me—the representatives in parliament are working their districts very hard, asking them to stay out of the fighting and to continue doing their jobs. They're promising the people anything in exchange for their support after the crisis. They're hoping to come out of this with blocs of voters to use as leverage in forming a new government.''

"You mean, forming a new government within the present system?" Lanning asked. "Or are they talking about creating a new government with a different system?"

"I'm getting to that," the President said. "The prime minister has virtually no support—in the parliament or among the people. He's expected to resign within a day or two. Abril says that the king, who is at his residence in Barcelona, will be able to count on the support of the church and most of the population apart from the Castilians.''

"Which is somewhat less than a majority," Burkow pointed out.

"About forty-five percent of the people," the President said. "Which puts the king in a very shaky position. We're told that his palace in Madrid is thick with soldiers, though no one's sure whether the troops are there to protect the place or to keep him from coming back.''

"Or both," Lanning remarked. "Just like the Winter Palace when Czar Nicholas was forced to abdicate.''

''Quite possibly,'' the President said. ''But it gets worse. Paul—Bob Herbert and Mike Rodgers have sent over the latest data on the military. You want to address that?''

Hood folded his hands on the table. ''There's a general who appears to be running this show—Rafael Amadori. According to our intelligence, he orchestrated the destruction of the yacht in the Bay of Biscay, which killed several leading businessmen who were also planning to bring down the government. He also appears to have been responsible for the death of Deputy Serrador. That's the man who my political chief Martha Mackall was on her way to see when she was killed this morning.'' Hood's voice dropped along with his eyes. ''We have reason to believe that Serrador set her up with the help of the party on the yacht.''

''Bob Herbert said he's working to confirm that,'' the President said. ''The problem is, even if we found out that part of the government was involved in a conspiracy, the rest of the lawfully elected government may not be around to hear our complaint. Now the policy of the United States, and of this Administration, has always been not to interfere in the internal affairs of a nation. The exceptions, like Panama, like Grenada, involved issues of national security. The problem here, and what General VanZandt is especially concerned about, is that Spain is a NATO ally. The outcome of the current strife will probably cause a reshaping of the government—but we can't afford to have a tyrant running the nation. We left Franco alone because he didn't have designs on other nations.''

"That's only because he saw from the sidelines what we did to Mussolini and Hitler,'' Burkow pointed out.

"Whatever the reasons, he stayed put,'' the President said. "That may not be the case here. General VanZandt?''

The tall, distinguished African-American officer opened a folder in front of him. "I have here a printout on the man's career. He signed up with the army thirty-two years ago and worked his way through the ranks. He was on the right side—or rather the left side—of the right-wing coup which attempted to overthrow the king in 1981. He was wounded in action and received a medal for bravery. After that he rose quickly. Interestingly, he never opposed NATO but he didn't participate in joint maneuvers. In letters to superior officers he advocated a strong national defense which didn't rely on outside help—"interference,'' he called it. He did, however, spend a lot of time entertaining and being entertained by Soviet troops during the 1980s. CIA intelligence puts him in Afghanistan in 1982 as an observer.''

"No doubt he was observing how to oppress people,'' Carol Lanning suggested.

"It's very possible,'' VanZandt replied. "During this time Amadori was also heavily involved in Spanish military intelligence and appears to have used his trips abroad to establish contacts there. His name came up in at least two CIA debriefings of captured Soviet spies.''

"In what context?" Hood asked.

VanZandt looked down at the printout. "In one case as a man whom the spy had seen at a meeting with a Soviet officer—Amadori was wearing his nameplate—and in the second case as someone to whom intelligence was to be reported in a matter involving a West German businessman who was trying to buy a Spanish newspaper."

"So," the President said, "what we're dealing with here is someone who's familiar with a failed coup in his own country and with antirebel tactics in other nations. He also has a lifetime of contacts, intelligence gathering capability, and virtual control of the Spanish military. Ambassador Abril fears, and not without some justification, that both Portugal and France are at risk. Running Spain as a military state, Amadori would be ideally positioned to undermine both governments over time and move troops in."

"Over NATO's dead body," VanZandt said.

"You forget, General," the President replied. "Amadori appears to have engineered this takeover as a progovernment action. He allowed a conspiracy to get going and then crushed it. It's a brilliant strategy: let an enemy show itself then crush it. And while you're crushing it, make the government look corrupt and crush them too."

"Whether he runs France or Portugal personally or puts in a puppet regime," Lanning said thoughtfully, "he still calls the shots."

"Exactly," said the President. "What came out of my conversation with Abril and the Vice-President is that there's going to be a new government in Spain.

There's no dispute about that. But we also agreed that whoever comes to power in Spain, it mustn't be Amadori. So the first question is, do we have the time and sufficient manpower to turn anyone there against him? And if not, is there any way that we can get to him ourselves?"

VanZandt shook his head and sat back. "This is a rotten business, Mr. President," he said. "A dirty, rotten business."

"I think so too, General," the President replied. He sounded surprisingly contrite. "But unless anyone's got any ideas, I don't see any way around it."

"How about waiting?" CIA Director Fox asked. "This Amadori may self-destruct. Or the people may not buy him."

"Every indication is that he's getting stronger by the hour," said the President. "It may be by default: he's killing the opposition. Am I wrong about that, Paul?"

Hood shook his head. "One of my people was there when he executed factory workers who may—*may*—have opposed him."

"When did this happen?" Lanning asked, openly horrified.

"Within the hour," Hood told her.

"This man has the makings of a genocidal maniac," she said.

"I don't know about that," said Hood, "but he certainly seems determined to seize Spain."

"And we're determined to stop him," the President said.

"How?" asked Burkow. "We can't do it officially.

Paul, Marius—have we got people underground there that we can count on?''

''I'll have to ask our contact in Madrid,'' Fox said. ''That kind of work hasn't been a part of our repertoire for a while.''

Burkow looked at Hood. So did the President. Hood said nothing. With Fox effectively out of the front line, he knew what was coming.

''Paul, your Striker team is en route to Spain,'' the President said, ''and Darrell McCaskey is already there. You're also working with an Interpol agent who surrendered to the troops at that factory massacre. What about her, Paul? Can she be counted on?''

''She surrendered to try and get to Amadori,'' Hood acknowledged. ''But we don't know what she'll do if and when she gets to him. Whether she'll reconnoiter or try and neutralize him.''

Hood hated himself for using that euphemism. They were talking about assassination—the same thing they'd all deplored when it happened to Martha Mackall. And for exactly the same reason: politics. This was, truly, a dirty, stinking business. He wished that he were with his family instead of here.

''What's this woman's name?'' the President asked.

''María Correja, Mr. President,'' Hood replied. ''We have a file on her. She was attached to Op-Center for several months when we were first commissioned. She learned from us and we from her.''

''What would Ms. Correja do if she had the support of a team like Striker?'' the President asked.

''I'm not sure,'' Hood answered honestly. ''I'm not

sure it would even make a difference. She's tough and pretty independent.''

''Find out, Paul,'' the President said. ''But do it quietly. I want this to stay at Op-Center from now until it's finished.''

''I understand,'' Hood said. His voice was a low monotone. His spirits were even lower. No one else had even offered to jump in with him.

He wasn't a boy. He knew that there might come a time when it would be necessary to stage a black-ops action like this—the use of Striker or one of his people to target and take out an enemy. Now that it was here he didn't like it. Not the job and not the fact that Op-Center was on its own. If they succeeded, a man was dead. If they failed, this would be on their consciences for the rest of their lives. There was no clean way out of it.

Carol Lanning must have understood that. She and Hood remained seated at the table, side by side, as the President and the others left. The men all said good-night to Hood but nothing more. What *could* they say? Good luck? Break a leg? Shoot him once for me?

When the room was empty, Carol put her hand on Hood's.

''I'm sorry,'' she said. ''It's no fun being disavowed.''

''Or set up,'' Hood said.

''Hmmm,'' she replied. ''You don't think anyone else knew what the President was planning?''

Hood shook his head. ''And when they leave here, they'll forget he ever suggested it. Like he said, this is Op-Center's play.'' He shook his head again. ''The damn thing is it's not even retribution. The men who killed Martha are dead.''

''I know,'' Carol said. ''Nobody ever said this business was fair.''

''No, they didn't.'' Hood wanted to get up. But he was too damn tired and way too disgusted to even think about moving.

''If I can do anything for you, unofficially, let me know,'' she said. She squeezed his hand again and rose. ''Paul—it's a job. You can't afford to look at it any other way.''

''Thanks,'' Hood said. ''But if I do that I can't see how I'll be any different than Amadori.''

She smiled. ''Oh, you will be, Paul. You'll never try to convince yourself that what you're doing is right. Only necessary.''

Hood didn't really see the distinction, but this wasn't the time to try to find it. Because, like it or not, he *did* have a job to do. And he was going to have to help Striker and Aideen Marley and Darrell McCaskey do their jobs as well.

He rose slowly and left with Carol. It was ironic. He once thought that running Los Angeles was difficult: angering special interests with everything you did and living in the public eye. Now he was working undercover and feeling as alone—personally and professionally—as a person could be.

He didn't remember who had said that in order to lead men you had to turn your back on them. But they were right, which was why Michael Lawrence was President and he wasn't. That was why someone like Michael Lawrence *had* to be President.

Hood would do this job because he had to. After that, he vowed, he would do no more. Here in the White House—which had awed him less than an hour before—he vowed that however this ended he would leave Op-Center . . . and get his family back.

TWENTY-FOUR

Tuesday, 6:50 A.M.
San Sebastián, Spain

Sleepy San Sebastián had been roughly awakened by the sounds of gunfire at the factory.

Father Norberto had remained at his brother's apartment long after the police had come for his body. He had stayed there, kneeling on the hardwood floor, to pray for Adolfo's soul. But when Father Norberto heard the gunfire, followed by the cries of people in the street and shouts of *"la fábrica!"*—"the factoᵣy!"—he headed directly back to the church.

As Norberto neared St. Ignatius he looked across the long, low field. He could see the helicopters hovering over the factory in the distance. But there was no time to wonder about them. The church was already filling with mothers and young children as well as the elderly. Soon the fishermen would arrive, returning to shore to make certain their families were safe. He had to attend to these people, not to his own wounds.

Norberto's arrival was heralded by the relieved cries of the people outside the church and thanks to God. For a moment—a brief, soul-touching moment—the priest felt the same love and compassion for the poor that the Son of Man Himself must have felt. It didn't alleviate his pain. But it did give him renewed strength and purpose.

The first thing Father Norberto did upon arriving was to smile and speak softly. Speaking softly made the people quiet down. It forced them to control their fear. He got everyone inside and into pews. Then, as Norberto lit the candles beside the pulpit, he asked white-haired "Grandfather" José if he would usher newcomers inside in an orderly fashion. The former salvage ship captain, a pious Catholic, accepted the task humbly, his gray eyes gleaming.

When the candles were lit and the church was awash with their comforting glow, the priest went to the altar. He used it to steady himself for just a moment. Then he led the congregation through Mass, hoping that they would take comfort as much in the familiar ritual as in the presence of God. Norberto hoped that he, too, would find solace there. But as he proceeded through the Liturgy of the Word, he found little for himself. The only consolation he had was the fact that he was giving comfort to others.

When Father Norberto finished the service, he turned to the uneasy crowd, which was already over one hundred strong. The heat of their bodies and their fear filled the small, dark church. The smell of the sea air came through the open door. It inspired Father Norberto to speak to the crowd from Matthew.

In a loud and strong voice he read for the parishioners. " 'And He saith unto them, Why are ye fearful, O ye of little faith? Then He arose, and rebuked the winds and the sea; and there was great calm.' "

The words of the Gospel, along with the need of

the people, gave strength to the priest. Even after the gunfire had stopped, more and more of them came into the church seeking comfort amidst the confusion.

Father Norberto didn't hear the telephone ringing in the rectory. However, Grandfather José did. The elderly man answered it and then came running up to the priest.

"Father!" José whispered excitedly into his ear. "Father, quickly—you must come!"

"What is it?" Norberto asked.

"It is an aide to General Superior González in Madrid!" José declared. "He wishes to speak with you."

Norberto regarded José for a moment. "Are you certain he wants to talk to me?"

José nodded vigorously. Puzzled, Norberto went to the pulpit and collected his Bible. He handed it to the elder member of the church and asked him to read to the congregation more from Matthew until his return. Then Norberto left quickly, wondering what the leader of the Spanish Jesuits wanted with him.

Norberto shut the door of the rectory and sat at his old oak desk. He rubbed his hands together and then picked up the phone.

The caller was Father Francisco. The young priest had phoned to inform Norberto that his presence was required—not requested, but *required*—in Madrid as soon as he could get there.

"For what reason?" Norberto asked. It should have been enough that General Superior González wanted him. González reported directly to the Pope and his word carried the authority of the Vatican. But when it came to matters involving this province and its five thousand Jesuits, González usually consulted his old friend Father Iglesias in nearby Bilbao. Which was the way Norberto preferred it. He cared about ministering to his parish, not his own advancement.

"I can only say that he asked for you and several others specifically," Father Francisco replied.

"Has Father Iglesias been sent for?"

"He is not on my list," the caller replied. "An airplane has been arranged for you at eight-thirty A.M. It is the General Superior's private airplane. Can I tell him that you will be on it?"

"If I'm so ordered," Norberto said.

"It is the General Superior's wish," Father Francisco gently corrected him.

When it came to ecclesiastic euphemisms, Norberto knew that that was the same thing. The priest said he would be there. The caller thanked him perfunctorily and hung up. Norberto returned to the church.

He took the Bible from Grandfather José and continued reading to the congregation from Matthew. But while the words came, warm and familiar, Father Norberto's heart and mind were elsewhere. They were with his brother and with his congregation. Most of the members were here now, cramming the pews and standing shoulder to shoulder along the three walls. Norberto had to decide who would help the people through the day and night. This would be especially important if friends or relatives had been lost at the factory—and if the fighting were only the start of something terrible. From the way Adolfo had been speaking the night before, the strife was just beginning.

When a calm had come over the congregation—
after seven years, Norberto could sense these things—
he closed the Bible and spoke to them in general terms
about the sorrows and dangers that might lie ahead.
He asked them to open their homes and hearts to those
who had suffered a loss. Then he told them that he
must go to Madrid to confer with the General Superior
about the crisis that was facing their nation. He said
he would be leaving later that morning.

The congregation was silent after he made his an-
nouncement. He knew that the people were never surprised when they were abandoned by the government.
That had been true when he was growing up during
the Franco years; it had been true during the rape of
the coastal seas during the 1970s; and from all ap-
pearances it was true now. But for Father Norberto to
be leaving them at a time of crisis had to come as a
shock.

"Father Norberto, we need you," said a young
woman in the first row.

"Dear Isabella," Norberto said, "it is not my desire
to go. It is the General Superior's wish."

"But my brother works at the factory," Isabella
continued, "and we have not heard from him. I'm
frightened."

Norberto walked toward the woman. He saw the
pain and fear in her eyes as he approached. He forced
himself to smile.

"Isabella, I know what you are feeling," he said.
"I know because I lost a brother today."

The young woman's eyes registered shock. "Father—"

Norberto's smile remained firm, reassuring. "My dear Adolfo was killed this morning. It is my hope that by going to Madrid I can help the General Superior end whatever is happening in Spain. I want no more brothers to die, no more fathers or sons or husbands." He touched Isabella's cheek. "Can you—*will* you—be strong for me?"

Isabella touched his hand. Her fingers were trembling and there were tears in her eyes. "I—I did not know about Dolfo," she said softly. "I'm so sorry. I will try to be strong."

"Try to be strong for yourself, not for me," Norberto said. He looked up at the fearful eyes of the young and old. "I need *all* of you to be strong, to help one another." Then he turned to Grandfather José, who was standing in the crowd along the wall. He asked the old sailor if he would remain at the church as a "caretaker priest" until his return, reading from the Bible and talking to people about their fears. He had come up with the term on the spot and José liked it. Grandfather José bowed his head and accepted gratefully and humbly. Norberto thanked him and then turned to his beloved congregation.

"We face difficult times," he said to the people. "But wherever I may be, whether in San Sebastían or in Madrid, we'll face them together—with faith, hope, and courage."

"Amen, Father," Isabella said in a strong voice.

The congregation echoed her words, as though one great voice were filling the church. Though Norberto was still smiling, tears spilled from his eyes. They weren't tears of sadness but of pride. Here before him was something the generals and politicians would never obtain, however much blood they spilled: the trust and love of good people. Looking at their faces, Norberto told himself that Adolfo had not died in vain. His death had helped to bring the congregation together, to give the people strength.

Norberto left the church amidst the good wishes and prayers of the parishioners. As he stepped into the warm daylight and headed toward the rectory, he could not help but think how amused Adolfo would have been by what had just happened. That it had been he, a disbeliever, and not Norberto who had inspired and unified a frightened congregation.

Norberto wondered if God had provided this sanctifying grace as a means for Adolfo to overcome his mortal sin. The priest had no reason to believe that, no theological precedent. But as this morning had proved, hope was a powerful beacon.

Perhaps, he thought, *that's because sometimes hope is the only beacon.*

TWENTY-FIVE

Tuesday, 8:06 A.M.
Madrid, Spain

Once the soldiers had secured the Ramirez boat factory, they lined up the three dozen surviving employees and checked their IDs. As she watched the soldiers pick out people, María realized that all of the core leaders of the *familia* were still alive. The factory guard and other informants must have kept careful records, including photographs. Amadori would have the cream of the *familia* for show-trials. He could show the nation, the world, that ordinary Spaniards were plotting against other Spaniards. That he had brought order to impending chaos. The people who were gunned down were probably not guilty of anything. In life, they could have insisted that they were not members of the *familia*. In death, they could be whatever Amadori wanted them to be. The care with which he had planned even this relatively small, remote action was chilling.

Those factory workers whose names were on the army's list were brought to the rooftop. One of the helicopters was used to ferry prisoners to the small airport outside of Bilbao. There, fifteen workers plus María were held inside a hangar at gunpoint.

Juan and Ferdinand were among the captives. They were tightly bound. Neither man spoke and neither man looked at her. She hoped they didn't suspect her of having set them up.

María couldn't address that right now. Time and deeds, not protests, would clear her. She was just glad to be here. When she'd surrendered, María still had no idea whether prisoners were being taken at all. She had approached the factory with her arms raised, hoping that the soldiers would hold their fire because she was a woman. María may have had a rocky history where relationships were concerned, but she'd never gone wrong betting on the pride of Spanish men. As soon as she was spotted—halfway across the parking lot—she was ordered to stay where she was. Two soldiers came rushing from inside. One of them frisked her with enthusiasm until she informed them that she had something to tell General Amadori. She wasn't sure what she had to tell him, but she'd think of something. The fact that she knew the general's name seemed to catch the men off guard. They didn't treat her gently after that, but they refrained from abusing her.

The prisoners stood in a bunch quietly, some of them smoking, some of them nursing lacerations, waiting to see whether they were being taken away or whether someone was coming. When a prop plane arrived from Madrid, the group was led onboard.

The flight to Madrid took just under fifty minutes. Though the prisoners' wounds were dressed, none of the captives spoke and none of the soldiers addressed them. As she sat in the twenty-four-seater, staring out at the bright patchwork of farms and cities, María played scenarios out in her mind. She would talk to no one but Amadori, who would see her—she hoped—because she could tell him how much the world intelligence fraternity knew about his crimes. Perhaps an arrangement could be reached wherein he would restrict his ambitions to becoming part of a new government.

She also imagined the general not caring what anyone knew or thought. Whether he wanted to rule an independent Castile or all of Spain, he had the guns and he had the momentum. He also had *familia* members not just to interrogate but to hold as hostages if he wished.

There was another consideration. The very real possibility that simply by talking to Amadori María might fuel his ambition. The hint of a threat, of a challenge, could cause him to become defensive, even more aggressive. After all, he too was a proud Spanish man.

The airplane taxied to a deserted corner of the airport—ironically, to a spot not far from where she had departed earlier in the day. Two large canvas-backed trucks were waiting to meet the plane. In the distance, María could see busy pockets of jeeps, helicopters, and soldiers. Since she and Aideen had left here seven hours before, portions of Barajas Airport seemed to have been turned into a staging area for other raids. That made tactical sense. From here, every part of Spain was less than an hour away.

María had a sick feeling deep in her belly. A feeling that whatever had been set in motion could not be stopped. Not without shutting down the brain behind

it. In that case, the question María had to ask was
Could General Amadori be stopped? And if so, how?

The eight prisoners sat in facing rows of benches
and the trucks headed into the heart of the city. Four
guards watched over them, two at each end of the
truck. They were armed with pistols and truncheons.
Traffic was unusually light on the highway, though the
nearer they got to the center of Madrid the thicker the
military activity became. María could see the trucks
and jeeps through the front window. As they entered
the city proper the traffic was heaviest near key government buildings and communications centers. María
wondered if the soldiers were there to keep people out
or to keep them in.

The small, anonymous caravan drove slowly along
Calle de Bailén and then came to a stop. The driver
had a brief conversation with a guard and then the
trucks moved on. María leaned forward and a guard
warned her back. But she had already seen what she
wanted to see. The trucks had arrived at the Palacio
Real, the Royal Palace.

The palace had been erected in 1762, constructed
on the site of a ninth-century Moorish fortress. When
the Moors were expelled, the fortress was destroyed
and a glorious castle was built here. It burned down
on Christmas Eve, 1734, and the new palace was built
on the site. More than any place in Spain, this
ground—considered holy, to some Spaniards—sym-
bolized the destruction of the invader and the birth of
modern Spain. The location of Nuestra Señora de la
Almudena, the Cathedral of the Almudena, just south

of the palace completed the symbolic consecration of the ground.

Four stories tall and built of white-trimmed granite from the Sierra de Guadarrama, the sprawling edifice sits on the "balcony of Madrid," a cliff that slopes majestically toward the Manzanares River. From here, the views to the north and west are sweeping and spectacular.

General Amadori was setting himself up in style. This wasn't the king's residence. His Highness lived in the Palacio de la Zarzuela, at El Pardo on the northern outskirts of the city. She wondered if the king was there and what he had to say about all of this. She had a sharp sense of déjà vu as she thought of the monarch and his young family locked in a room of the castle— or worse. How many times in how many nations had this scenario been acted out? Whether the kings were tyrants or constitutional monarchs, whether their heads were taken or just their crowns, this was the oldest story in civilization.

She was sickened by it. And just once she'd like to see the story end with a twist.

They were driven around the corner to the Plaza de la Armería. Instead of the usual early-morning lines of tourists, the vast courtyard was filled with soldiers. Some were drilling and some were already on duty, guarding the nearly two dozen entrances to the palace itself. The trucks stopped beside a pair of double doors set beneath a narrow balcony. The prisoners were led from the trucks into the palace. They shambled down a long hallway and stopped just beyond the grand staircase, in the center of the palace. A door opened;

María was standing near the front of the line and looked in.

Of course, she thought. They were at the magnificent Hall of the Halberdiers. The axlike weapons had been removed from the walls and racks, and the room had been turned into a detention center. A dozen or so guards stood along the far wall and at least three hundred people sat on the parquet floor. María noticed several women and children among them. Beyond this chamber was the heart of the Royal Palace: the throne room. There were two additional guards, one on either side of the grand doorway. María did not doubt for a moment that behind the closed door was where General Amadori had established his headquarters. María was also convinced that more than vanity had brought him to this spot. No outside force could attack the general without coming through the prisoners. The detainees formed a thick and very effective human shield.

A sergeant stepped from the room. He shouted for the new group to enter. The line began to move. When María reached the door, she stopped and turned to the sergeant.

"I must see the general at once," she said. "I have important information for him."

"You'll get your turn to tell us what you know," the gaunt soldier said. He grinned lasciviously. "And maybe we'll get a turn to thank you."

He grabbed her left arm just above the elbow and pushed her. María took a step forward to regain her balance. At the same time she turned slightly and slapped her right hand hard on the backs of the fingers that were holding her. The shock of the slap caused the sergeant's grip to loosen momentarily. That was all the time María needed. Grabbing the fingers in her fist, she spun around so that she was facing the soldier. At the same time she turned his hand palm up, bent the fingertips back toward his elbow, and snapped all four fingers at the knuckles. As he shrieked with pain, María's left hand snaked down. She snatched the 9mm pistol from his holster. Then she released his broken fingers, grabbed his hair, and yanked him toward her. She put the barrel of the pistol under his right ear. His forehead was against her chin and his legs were shaking visibly.

The entire maneuver had taken less than three seconds. A pair of soldiers who were standing just inside the hall started toward her. But she backed against the doorjamb, her body shielded by the sergeant. There was no way to get at her without killing the sergeant.

"Stop!" she snapped at the soldiers.

They did.

The prisoners who had been shuffling along behind María froze. Juan was among them. Several prisoners cheered. Juan appeared confused.

"Now," María said to the sergeant, "you can listen carefully or I'll clean your ears for you."

"I—I'll listen," he replied.

"Good," María said. "I want to see someone on the general's staff." She didn't really. She wanted to see the general. But if she demanded that right away she'd never get it. She had to give someone more information than they could handle so that she was moved along the chain of command.

A door opened a short way down the wide corridor. A young captain with curly brown hair stepped from a room on the other side of the detention area. As he emerged, his expression quickly shaded from puzzlement to annoyance to anger. He began walking toward her. He wore a .38 on his hip.

María looked at him. His green eyes held hers. She decided not to say anything to him; not yet. Hostage negotiations were the opposite of chess: whoever made the first move was always at a disadvantage. They gave up information, even if it was just their tone of voice telling an opponent their level of confidence in a situation. Quite often that information was enough to let you know whether they were ready to kill you, ready to negotiate, or hoping to delay things until they could decide their next step.

The officer's tan uniform was extremely neat and clean. His black boots shone and the fresh soles clicked sharply on the tile floor. His hair was perfectly combed and his square jaw was closely shaved. He was definitely a desk officer. If he had any field experience, even in war games, she would be surprised. That could work in her favor: he wasn't likely to make an important decision unless he checked with a superior officer.

"So," he said. "Someone does not wish to cooperate."

His voice was very strong. María watched his hand. She didn't think he was going to reach for his gun. Not if he were a desk officer who'd never had to look into someone's eyes while he pulled the trigger. On the other hand, he might want to impress his soldiers and the prisoners by making an object lesson of her. If he did, she'd shoot him and head toward the staircase.

"To the contrary, Captain," María replied.

"Explain," he snapped. He was less than three yards from her.

"I'm with Interpol," she said. "My ID is in my pocket. I was working undercover and was accidentally rounded up with the rest of this *familia*."

"Working undercover with whom?" he asked.

"With Adolfo Alcazar," she said. "The man who destroyed the yacht. He was murdered this morning. I was on the trail of his killers when I was apprehended."

That much was true, of course. She didn't say she was looking for information about Amadori.

María had spoken loudly and, as she'd planned, Juan had overheard.

"*¡El traidor!*" he shouted, and spat. "Traitor!"

The captain motioned to a soldier, who struck Juan in the small of the back with his truncheon. Juan groaned and arched painfully but María didn't react. The captain had been watching her.

"You know who committed the crime?" the captain asked.

"I know more than that," María replied.

The captain stopped just a few feet from María. He studied her for a long moment.

"Sir," she said. "I'm going to release the sergeant and turn over his weapon. Then I have a request to make."

María didn't give the officer time to think. She lowered the gun, pushed the sergeant away, then handed the pistol grip first to the captain. He motioned for the sergeant to accept it. The man took the gun and hesitated before returning it to his holster.

The captain's eyes were still on María. "Come with me," he said.

He'd bought it. He turned and María followed him toward his office. She'd moved up the ladder. They entered the Hall of Columns, which was exactly that. Desks, chairs, telephones, and computers were being moved in. The large room was being turned into a command center. As soon as they were inside, the captain turned to María.

"What you did out there was very bold," he said.

"My mission demanded it," she replied. "I can't afford to be stopped."

"What is your name?" he asked.

"María Corneja," she replied.

"I had heard that the bomber was dead, María," the captain said. "Who killed him?"

"Members of the *familia*," she replied. "But that's a small problem. They weren't in it alone."

"What do you mean?"

"They are being supported by the United States," she said. "I have names and I have details of what they're planning next."

"Tell me," he said.

"I will tell you," María said, "at the same time that I tell the general."

The captain sneered. "Don't haggle with me. I could turn you over to my interrogation group and have the information myself."

"Perhaps," she replied. "But you'd be losing a valuable ally. And besides, Captain, are you so sure you'd get the information in time?"

The sneer remained on his face as he considered what she'd just said. Suddenly, he motioned to a soldier who was carrying in a pair of chairs. He set them down, ran over, and saluted.

"Stay with her," the captain said.

"Yes, sir," the young soldier replied.

The captain left the room. María lit a cigarette and offered the soldier one. He declined, respectfully. As she inhaled, María considered what she'd do if the captain said the general wouldn't see her. She'd have to try to get away. Let Luis know somehow where the madman-who-would-be-king was hiding. Then hope that someone could get in here and dethrone him.

Try to get away, she thought. Let Luis know *somehow*. *Hope* that someone could get in. There were a lot of "maybes" in all of that. Perhaps too many on which to hang the fate of a nation of over forty million.

She wondered what her chances would be of getting the captain's gun, making her way through the detention room, forcing herself into the throne room, and putting a bullet in Amadori's forehead.

Probably not very good. Not with twenty or so soldiers between here and there. Somehow, she had to get in there legitimately and talk to the general. Tell him something that would slow him down. Then get back to Luis and help figure out some way of toppling the bastard.

The captain returned before María had finished her

cigarette. He strode through the doorway of the Hall of Columns and stopped. He smiled sweetly and she knew then she'd won.

"Come with me, María," he said. "You have your audience."

María thanked him—always thank the messengers in case you need a favor later—and lifted her shoe. She extinguished the cigarette on her sole. As she walked toward the captain she slipped the cigarette back in the pack. He gave her a curious look.

"It's a habit I picked up in the field," she said.

"Don't waste your resources?" he asked. "Or don't risk starting a fire, which can attract attention?"

"Neither," she replied. "Don't leave a trail. You never know who's going to come after you."

"Ah," the captain smiled knowingly.

María smiled back, though for a different reason. She'd just tested the officer with a heads-up and he'd failed. She'd hinted that she was schooled at infiltration, that she knew more than he did, and the captain had let it go. He didn't stop and take a second look at her. He was leading her right to the general.

Perhaps Amadori had made a few other mistakes in getting his coup underway. With any luck, María would be able to find them.

And then somehow, some way, get out to report them.

TWENTY-SIX

Tuesday, 8:11 A.M.
Zaragoza, Spain

The C-141B transport set down heavily on the long runway at the Zaragoza Airbase, NATO's largest field in Spain. The four twenty-one-thousand-pound Pratt & Whitney turbofans howled as the aircraft rolled to a stop. The plane had made a refueling stop at the NATO base in Iceland before completing the eight-hour trip against daunting headwinds.

During the flight Colonel August and his Striker team had received regular updates from Mike Rodgers, including a complete rundown on the White House meeting. Rodgers said that Striker's orders vis-à-vis General Amadori would be given to them by Darrell McCaskey. Receiving them face-to-face wasn't so much a security issue as an old tradition among elite forces: if you were sending a team on a hazardous mission, it was customary to look the leader in the eyes. A commander who couldn't do that did not have the mettle, and thus the right, to send anyone into danger.

Colonel August had also spent a few hours going through NATO's dossier on General Amadori. Though Amadori had never participated in any NATO maneuvers, he was a top-ranked officer of a member nation. As such, his file was short but complete.

Rafael Leoncio Amadori had been raised in Burgos, the one-time capital of the kingdom of Castile and the burial place of the legendary hero El Cid. Amadori joined the army in 1966, when he was twenty. After four years he was moved to Francisco Franco's personal guard, the result of a longtime friendship between Franco and Amadori's father, Jaime, who was the Generalissimo's bootmaker. By the time Amadori was made a lieutenant in 1972, he was one of the top men in charge of Franco's counterintelligence team. That was where he met Antonio Aguirre, ten years his senior, who was to become his top aide and most trusted advisor. Aguirre was Franco's advisor on domestic affairs.

Once he had joined the inner circle, Amadori was personally responsible for sniffing out and eliminating opponents of Franco's regime. With the death of Franco in 1975, Amadori moved back into the general military. However, his years in intelligence had not been wasted. Amadori rose quickly. More quickly than his accomplishments would suggest. If August had to guess, his promotions were probably the result of having collected compromising data on everyone who had been in a position to help or hinder his advancement.

August was convinced that if a coup were in progress—and it certainly looked as if one were—it had not simply happened overnight. Like the American kid who grew up wanting to be President, General Amadori obviously grew up wanting to be Franco.

August and six other Strikers had made the trip to Spain. Because a situation was developing in Cuba which could require HUMINT, Sgt. Chick Grey had been left behind with a contingent of Strikers in the event they were needed. Grey was a bright and highly capable leader who was due to get his second lieutenant's stripes very soon.

In Spain, August's second-in-command would be Corporal Pat Prementine. The serious young NCO, an expert at infantry tactics, had distinguished himself in the rescue of Mike Rodgers and his team during the Bekaa Valley operation. Prementine would be more than able to step in if anything happened to August. Privates Walter Pupshaw, Sondra DeVonne, David George, and Jason Scott had performed brilliantly in that operation as well, just as they had on previous missions. Communications man Ishi Honda was also on hand. Neither Colonel August nor his predecessor, the late Lt. Col. Charles Squires, would have gone anywhere without their ace radio operator.

The Strikers changed to civilian clothes before landing. They were met at the airbase by an unmarked Interpol helicopter, which flew them directly to the airport in Madrid. Their uniforms and gear, carried in oversized duffelbags, went with them. At the airport they boarded a pair of vans and were driven to the office of Luis García de la Vega. August and his team were greeted by Darrell McCaskey, who was awaiting the return of Aideen Marley.

McCaskey and August retired to the small, cluttered office of an agent who was on assignment. McCaskey had appropriated a portable coffeemaker and moved it in here.

"It's good to see you," McCaskey said, shutting the door.

"Likewise," August replied.

"Sit," McCaskey said.

August looked around. The two chairs beside the door were full of overstuffed folders so he perched himself on the corner of the desk. He watched as McCaskey went to the coffeemaker and poured Colonel August a cup.

"How do you take it?" McCaskey asked.

"Black, no sugar," August replied.

McCaskey handed him the cup then poured some for himself. August took a sip and set his cup on the mousepad.

"That's some pretty shitty stuff, isn't it?" McCaskey said, pointing to the coffee.

"Maybe," August said. "But at least the price is right."

McCaskey smiled.

It hadn't taken long for August to determine that McCaskey was what the elite forces called "TBW." Tired but wired. The former G-man was exhausted but anxious, running on adrenaline and caffeine. When the rush ended, McCaskey would crash big-time.

"Let me bring you up to date," McCaskey said. He sipped his own coffee and sat heavily in the swivel chair. Matt Stoll's small electromagnetic egg was between them, ensuring the security of the conversation. "Aideen Marley is on the way back to Madrid. She was up at the Ramirez boat factory in San Sebastián when it was attacked by General Amadori's forces. You know about that?''

August nodded.

McCaskey looked at his watch. "Her chopper should be landing in about five minutes and she'll be brought back here. She went up to find out more about the forces that are rallied against Amadori. He beat her to them. Aideen's partner on the mission, María Corneja, managed to get herself captured by Amadori's soldiers. We don't know exactly where Amadori is based. We're hoping that María can find out and somehow let us know. Have you spoken with Mike?''

August nodded.

"Then you have some sense of what your mission is.''

August nodded again.

"Once Amadori is found,'' McCaskey said, his gaze locked on August, "he must be captured or removed by terminal force.''

August nodded a third time. His face was impassive, as though he'd just been given the day's duty roster. He had killed men in Vietnam and he'd been tortured nearly to death when he was a POW there. Death was extreme, but it came with the uniform and it was the coin of war. And there was no doubt that Amadori was at war.

McCaskey folded his hands. His tired eyes were still on August.

"Striker's never had a mission like this,'' McCaskey said. "Do you have a problem with it?''

August shook his head.

"Do you think any of your team will have a problem with it?"

"I don't know," August said. "But I'll find out."

McCaskey looked down. "There was a time when this kind of thing was standard operating procedure."

"There was," August agreed. "But back then it was a first-strike option rather than a last resort. I think we've found the moral high ground."

"I suppose so," McCaskey said. He rubbed his eyes. "Anyway, you guys hang loose in the commissary. I'll let you know as soon as we have anything."

McCaskey rose and drained his coffee cup. August stood and took a sip from his own cup. Then he handed it to McCaskey. McCaskey smiled and accepted it. He took a swallow.

"Darrell?" August said.

"Yeah?"

"You're looking pretty close to flameout."

"I'm gettin' there," he admitted. "It's been a long haul."

"You know," August said, "if we have to go in I need you to be sharp. I'd feel a lot more comfortable if after Aideen arrives, you lay down somewhere. I can debrief her, talk to Luis, come up with a few scenarios."

McCaskey walked around the desk. He slapped August on the back. "Thank you very much, Colonel. I believe I will take that rest." He grinned. "You know what sucks?"

August shook his head.

"Not being able to do the things that you were able to do easily in your twenties," McCaskey said. "That sucks. All-nighters used to be a breeze for me. So was eating junk food and not having my stomach burn like a son-of-a-bitch.'' The grin faded. ''But age makes it different. Losing a coworker makes it different. And something else makes it different. The realization that just being right doesn't matter. You can have law and treaties and justice and humanity and the United Nations and the Bible and everything else on your side, and you can still get your ass handed to you. You know what the moral high ground has cost us, Colonel? It's cost us the ability to do the right thing. Pretty damn ironic, huh?''

August didn't answer. There was no point. Soldiers didn't have philosophies; they couldn't afford to. They had targets. And the failure to achieve them meant death, capture, or dishonor. There was no irony. At least, not in that.

The officer headed toward the commissary, where his team was waiting. When he arrived, he turned on the computerized ''playbook'' he carried. He indicated the plan McCaskey had presented, then he polled the team to make sure everyone was willing to be on the field, ready to play.

They were.

August thanked them, after which the team hung loose. All except for Prementine and Pupshaw, who figured out where and how hard to hit the soda machine so it would dispense free cans.

August accepted a 7-Up and then sat back in the plastic chair. He drank the soda to wash away the bitter coffee taste. As he did, he thought about what had happened over the past day. The fact that the politicians in Spain had turned to Amadori to stop a war. Instead, he used it as a primer to start a bigger war. Now the politicians were turning to more soldiers to stop that war.

August was a soldier, not a philosopher. But if there were an irony in all this, he was pretty sure he'd find it in there.

Written in blood and bound in suffering.

TWENTY-SEVEN

Tuesday, 1:35 A.M.
Washington, D.C.

Hood awoke with a jolt.

He had returned from the White House and immediately called Darrell McCaskey to relay the President's orders. McCaskey had been silent and accepting. What else could he be? Then, knowing he'd want to be awake whenever the Striker operation commenced, Hood shut the lights off and lay down on his office couch to try to rest.

He started to think about Op-Center's unprecedented two-tiered involvement in the operation. First there was the elimination of Amadori. Then there was the aftermath, helping to manage chaos. With Amadori gone many politicians, businesspeople, and military officers would fight to fill the power vacuum. They would do that by seizing individual regions: Catalonia, Castile, Andalusia, the Basque Country, Galicia. Bob Herbert's office was compiling a list for the White House. So far, there were at least two dozen viable contenders for a piece of the power. Two *dozen*. At best, what used to be Spain would become a loose confederation of states similar to the former Soviet Union. At worst, those states would turn on each other like the former republics of Yugoslavia.

His eyes were heavy and his thoughts became disjointed and Hood drifted off quickly. But his sleep was troubled. He didn't dream about Spain. He dreamt about his family. They were all driving together and laughing. Then they parked and walked down an anonymous Main Street somewhere. The kids and Sharon were eating ice cream cones. They continued laughing. The ice cream was melting fast and the more it dripped over their fists and clothes the more they laughed. Hood sulked beside them, feeling sad and then angry. Suddenly he stopped behind a parked car and slammed his fists on the trunk. His family continued to laugh, not at him but at the mess the ice cream was making. The three of them were ignoring him and he started to scream. His eyes snapped open—

Hood looked around. Then his eyes settled on the illuminated clock on the coffee table beside the couch. It had been only about twenty minutes since he'd shut his eyes. He lay back down, his head on the cushioned armrest. He closed his eyes again.

There was nothing quite like waking from a bad dream. He always felt a tremendous relief because that world wasn't real. But the emotions it aroused were genuine and that kept the sense of well-being from seeping deep inside. Then there were the people he dreamt about. Dreams always made them more real, more desirable.

Hood had had enough. He needed to talk to Sharon. He got up, turned on the desk light, and sat down. He ground the heels of his palms into his eyes then punched in her cell phone number. She answered quickly.

"Hello?"

Her voice was strong. She hadn't been sleeping.

"Hi," Hood said. "It's me."

"I know," Sharon said. "It's kind of late for anyone else to be calling."

"I guess it is," Hood said. "How are the kids?"

"Good."

"And how are you?"

"Not so good," Sharon told him. "How about you?"

"The same."

"Is it work," she asked pointedly, "or us?"

That pinched. Why did women always assume the worst about men, that they were always preoccupied and upset about their jobs?

Because we usually are, Hood told himself. Somehow, when it was this late and this dark and this quiet, you just had to be honest with yourself.

"Work is what it always is," he answered. "We've got a crisis. Even with that, what I'm most upset about is you. About us."

"I'm *only* upset about you," Sharon replied.

"All right, hon," Hood said calmly. "You win that one."

"I don't want to 'win' anything," she said. "I just want to be honest. I want to figure out what we're going to do about this. Things can't continue the way they are. They just can't."

"I agree," Hood said. "That's why I've decided to resign."

Sharon was silent for a long moment. "You'd leave Op-Center?"

"What choice do I have?"

"The truth?" Sharon asked.

"Of course."

"You don't need to resign," she said. "What you need to do is spend less time there."

Hood was really annoyed. He'd been sincere. He'd played his hole card—a big one. And instead of giving her husband a big wet kiss, Sharon was telling him how he'd done *that* all wrong.

"How am I supposed to do that?" Hood asked. "Nobody can predict what's going to happen here."

"No, but you have backups," Sharon said. "There's Mike Rodgers. There's the night team."

"They're all very capable," Hood replied, "but they're here for when things are running smoothly. I have to be on top of a situation like this one, or like the one we had last time—"

"Where you were nearly killed!" she snapped.

"Yes, where I was nearly killed, Sharon," Hood said. He stayed calm. His wife was already getting angry and his own temper would just fuel that. "Sometimes there's danger. But there's danger right here in Washington."

"Oh, please, Paul. It isn't the same."

"All right. It *is* different," Hood admitted. "But there are also rewards from what I do. Not just a good home but experiences. The kids have gone overseas with us, been exposed to things other people never get to do or see. How do you break that all out? How do you decide, 'This trip to a world capital wasn't worth missing ten dinners with Paul.' Or, 'Okay, we got to visit the Oval Office but Dad couldn't be at a violin concert at school.' ''

''I don't know,'' Sharon admitted. ''But I do know that a 'good home' is more than just a nice house. And a family is built by a lot of little things, ordinary things. Not just big, showy things.''

''I've been there for a lot of that,'' Hood said.

''No, Paul,'' Sharon countered. ''You *were* there for a lot of that. Things have changed. When you took this job most of the work was going to be domestic. Remember?''

''I remember.''

''Then your first international situation happened and everything changed.''

Sharon was right. Op-Center was established primarily to handle domestic crises. They jumped into the international arena when the President named Hood to head up the task force investigating a terrorist attack in Seoul, Korea. Hood had never been flattered by the appointment. Like the assassination of Amadori, it was a job no one else had wanted.

''So things changed,'' Hood admitted. ''What was I supposed to do, walk away from it all?''

''You did in L.A., didn't you?'' Sharon asked.

''That's right,'' Hood said. ''And it cost me something.''

''What? Power?''

''No,'' Hood replied. ''Self-respect.''

''Why? Because you gave in to your wife?''

Aw, Jesus, Hood thought. He gives her what she wants and he still can't win. ''That is absolutely not the reason,'' Hood replied. ''Because as much of a pain in the ass as politics was, and as long as the hours were, and even though privacy was nonexistent, I gave up something where I felt I was making a difference." His voice was tense. He was angrier about that than he'd thought. "So I quit politics and I got caught up in long hours all over again. Do you know why? Because once again I'm making a difference. Hopefully making things better for people. I like that, Sharon. I like the challenge. The responsibility. The sense of satisfaction."

"You know, I liked what I did too before I became a mother," Sharon said. "But I had to cut way back on that for the sake of the kids. For our family. At least you don't have to do anything that extreme. But you also can't micromanage, Paul. You have backups. Let them help you so that you can give us what we need to remain a family."

"You mean by your definition—"

"No. We need you. That's a fact."

"You *have* me," Hood said. He was growing angry now.

"Not enough," Sharon shot back. Her voice was clipped and firm. Here they were again, in the roles they always assumed when well-meaning discussions degenerated into unpleasant debates. Paul Hood playing the angry offense, his wife playing the cool defense.

"Jesus," Hood said. He wanted to lay the phone aside and scream. He settled for squeezing the receiver. "I've promised to quit, I've got a crisis here, and I can't sleep without thinking about all of you. And you tell me all the things I'm doing wrong while you're up there holding the kids hostage."

"I'm not holding them hostage," Sharon said curtly. "We're yours whenever you want us."

"Sure," Hood said. "On your terms."

"These are *not* 'my terms,' Paul. This isn't about me winning and you losing. It's not about you giving up a job or career. It's about making a few changes. Asking for a few concessions. It's about the *kids* winning."

The interoffice line beeped. Hood looked at the LCD: it was Mike Rodgers.

"Sharon, please," Hood said. "Hold on a sec." He put her on mute and picked up the other phone. "Yes, Mike?"

"Paul, I'm here with Bob Herbert. Check the computer. I'm sending over a picture from the NRO. We need to talk, now."

"All right," Hood said. "I'll be right with you." He returned to Sharon. "Hon, I've got to go. I'm sorry."

"I know you are," she said softly. "But you're not as sorry as I am. Goodbye, Paul. I do love you."

She hung up and Paul spun toward the computer monitor on the adjoining stand. He didn't want to think about what had just happened. About how his family was slipping away and there didn't seem to be a damn thing he could do about it. What rankled him most was Sharon seemed to believe that having him none of the time was better than having him some of the time. That made no sense.

Unless she's trying to pressure me, he thought.

He resented that. But then, what other weapon did

Sharon have? And she was right: he had screwed up, and more than once. He'd abandoned them on day one of their vacation in California. He'd forgotten birthdays and anniversaries and school concerts. He'd neglected to ask about report cards and doctor's appointments and God knows what else.

Hood picked up the interoffice line as the black-and-white satellite photo was downloaded. This was not the time to beat himself up. Tens of thousands of lives were at risk. He still had responsibilities, however distasteful Sharon had managed to make the word sound.

"Mike, I'm here," Hood said. "What am I looking at?"

"The Royal Palace in Madrid," he said. "The effective view is from twenty-five feet up looking down from about two o'clock. That's the main courtyard of the palace."

"I don't suppose those are tourist vans," Hood said.

"No," Rodgers said. "Here's how we got there. After the attack on the Ramirez factory, Steve Viens had an NRO satellite follow the prisoners. They went from the parking lot to the airport in Bilbao to the airport in Madrid. Then they were bused from there to the palace. We think that woman near the front of the line is María Corneja."

Hood enlarged the figure in the center. The computer automatically cleaned up the image for him. He hadn't known María well and he wasn't sure he'd recognize her if she hadn't been pointed out. But it certainly could be her, and it was the only woman in view.

The screen cleared. Other photographs began to appear.

"These are higher level views," Rodgers said. "Fifty feet, one hundred feet, two hundred feet. From the number of soldiers there and the top-level brass who are coming and going we think that that's where Amadori may be. But there's a problem."

"I see it," Hood said as the higher views appeared. "A square building with a courtyard in the center and nothing higher around it. Infiltration during the day is going to be a problem."

"Bingo," Rodgers said. "And waiting twelve hours until dark may not be acceptable."

"What about Spanish uniforms?" Hood asked. "Can't Striker wear those to get inside?"

"In theory, maybe," Rodgers said. "The problem is it doesn't look like any of the soldiers who bring prisoners to the palace or patrol the grounds are actually going inside. That's another reason we think General Amadori's there. He's probably got an elite guard inside, patroling the halls and taking care of security. They're the only ones who'll have access."

"Are there any underground passageways?"

"We're looking into that now," Rodgers said. "Even if there are, coming up inside those big sunlit corridors is going to be risky."

Hood's eyes burned and his mind was whirling. Part of him wished he could just bomb the palace, fly up to Connecticut, and collect his family. Maybe stay there and open a fish-and-chips stand on the seashore.

"So we wait?" Hood asked.

"No one here or in Madrid's in favor of that,"

Rodgers said. "But Aideen just arrived at the Interpol office. She and Darrell are talking the situation over with Brett and members of the Interpol team, adapting their playbook for the palace. There's a team of Interpol spotters on the roof of the Teatro Real, the opera house, on the other side of the avenue. They're scanning the entire palace with an LDE trying to pick out Amadori's voice."

The LDE—the Long Distance Ear—was a funnel-like dish that collected all the sounds from a narrow area and keyed in on those of a specific decibel range. In the case of a room inside a castle, it would automatically filter out external sounds such as cars, birds, and pedestrians. It would only "hear" very low intensity sounds inside walls. It would then compare the sounds to whatever was digitally stored in its memory—in this case, Amadori's voice.

"How long will it take them to scan the entire castle?" Hood asked.

"Until about four o'clock," Rodgers said.

Hood looked at the computer clock. "That's nearly two hours from now."

"I don't like the idea of Striker sitting around and getting stale either," Rodgers said, "but it's the best they can do."

"How far is the palace from the Interpol office?" Hood asked.

"I'm checking a map now," Rodgers said. "It looks to be about fifteen minutes by car—if there's no traffic or military checkpoints."

"Which means that if they sit and wait for the LDE findings they're as much as two hours and fifteen minutes away,'' Hood said. "If Amadori decided to leave the area before we pinpoint him, we'd have a problem.''

"True,'' Rodgers said. "But even if the Strikers were at the palace, there's nothing they can do. They can't choose a game plan without knowing exactly where he is. Besides, if Amadori isn't there we may be sending them off in the wrong direction.''

Hood looked at the high-resolution photograph of the troops in the courtyard. There were at least two hundred of them, broken into small groups. The soldiers looked as though they were drilling—perhaps to defend the compound, perhaps to serve as firing squads. In any case, it reminded Hood of the pictures he'd seen of Saddam Hussein's Republican Guards drilling in front of *his* residence before Desert Storm. Muscle flexing.

Amadori had to be there.

"Mike,'' Hood said, "we're responsible for María being in on this. She's got no backup. I can't have that.''

Rodgers was silent for a moment. "I don't disagree. But we've been over these photographs and we're going through floor plans of the palace now. Getting in there isn't going to be easy.''

"They don't have to go in,'' Hood said. "I just want some firepower in the area. Darrell can be in touch with them through Ishi Honda.''

"That's right,'' Rodgers said. "But the mission is still Amadori and we don't know for sure that he's there. We haven't been able to pick up any ELINT yet. It'll be another hour or so before we can start getting that.''

Hood was not getting impatient with Rodgers. The general was doing exactly what he was supposed to be doing. Pointing out options and possible pitfalls.

"If Amadori's somewhere else we'll pull Striker off,'' Hood said. "And who knows? Maybe the son of a bitch will decide to show himself and save us the trouble of going in.''

Rodgers exhaled audibly. "That's not likely, Paul. But I'll tell Brett to move out. I also want to remind you that, while we brought María into this, she acted without orders,'' Rodgers said. "She put herself in this situation. And not for our benefit, but for the benefit of her country. I will not be in favor of risking team lives to evacuate her.''

"Noted,'' Hood said. "And thanks.''

Rodgers clicked off and Hood hung up. He dumped the photos from the monitor and turned off the desk lamp. He shut his eyes.

It made no sense; none at all. Clinging to a job that by its very nature left you alone, cut off from your family and often cut off from subordinates. Maybe that's why he felt drawn to María's situation. She was alone too.

No, Hood wouldn't forget the mission. And he wouldn't forget what Mike Rodgers had been too respectful to point out: that the Strikers had lives and loved ones, just like María.

But Hood also couldn't forget Martha Mackall. And he'd be damned if he did nothing while another unarmed colleague faced danger in the bloody streets of Madrid.

TWENTY-EIGHT

Tuesday, 8:36 A.M.
Madrid, Spain

María followed the young captain into the corridor, confident that she could trust the officer to bring her to Amadori. Neither the captain nor the general had anything to gain by tricking her. They had to be curious about the information she said she possessed. And if he didn't trust her, he wouldn't be in front of her. He'd be behind her, with a gun.

Nonetheless, she was startled by the relative ease with which she'd been able to bully the captain. Either he was inexperienced or far more clever than she gave him credit for.

He turned to the left. María stopped.

"I thought we were going to see the general," she said.

"We are," the captain replied. He extended his arm down the hallway—away from the Hall of Halberdiers.

"Isn't he in the throne room?" she asked.

"The throne room?" The captain laughed loudly. "Wouldn't that be somewhat presumptuous?"

"I don't know," she replied. "Isn't being in this palace somewhat presumptuous?"

"Not when the king returns to Madrid and we need to protect him," the captain said. "We intend to secure both of the royal palaces."

"But there were guards—"

"Protecting the chamber from the prisoners." The captain bowed his head in the direction of his outstretched hand. "The general is in the state dining room with his advisors."

María looked at him. She didn't believe him. She didn't know why; she just didn't.

"But the question is not where the general is located," the captain continued. "The question is whether you have something to tell him or not. Are you coming, Señorita Corneja?"

María looked down. For now, she had no choice but to do what she was told. "I'm coming," she said, and walked toward the captain.

The officer turned and strode briskly along the brightly lit corridor, and then around the corner. María walked a little slower, remaining several steps behind him. Other soldiers moved quickly along the corridor. Some of them had prisoners, others were on field phones. A few were carrying computer equipment into rooms. None of them was paying her any attention.

This didn't feel right but María had to play it out. Yes, she was coming—but not without precautions.

"Would you like a cigarette?" she asked the captain. She was already reaching into the breast pocket of her blouse. She removed the pack and took one of the cigarettes out. She tore a match from the book of matches.

"Thank you, no," said the captain. "Actually, we'd

appreciate it if you didn't smoke here. So many treasures. A careless flick—''

"I understand," she said.

The captain had said exactly what María had expected him to say. She began to replace the pack but first palmed the cigarette. Because the captain was facing forward he didn't see her poke the match into the tobacco of the palmed cigarette. Then she put the cigarette down the front of her pants, into the crotch, and put the pack back in her blouse pocket.

Now, at least, she had a weapon.

The state dining room was on the other side of the music room overlooking the Plaza Incógnita. On the other side of the plaza was the Campo del Moro, the Camp of the Moors. The park marked the site where the troops of the powerful emir Ali bin-Yusuf camped in the eleventh century during the Moorish attempt to conquer Spain.

They reached the door of the music room and the captain knocked. He looked at María and smiled. She reached his side but she didn't return his smile. The door opened.

The captain extended a hand inside. "After you," he said.

María took a step toward it and looked in.

The windowless room was dark and it took a moment for her eyes to adjust. Something moved toward her from the shadows to the right. She backed away only to bump into the captain, who was standing directly and solidly behind her. Suddenly, he pushed her inside. At the same time, two pairs of hands grabbed her forearms. She was pulled off her feet and landed facedown on the floor. Boots were planted firmly on her shoulder blades.

A light came on, casting a soft amber glow throughout the room. María looked out at a pastoral mural as a third set of hands groped her legs, waist, arms, and chest, searching for concealed weapons. Her belt and watch were removed and they took the pack of cigarettes.

When the search was finished, the extra set of hands suddenly pulled back on María's hair. The tug was rough and she found herself looking up. With her shoulders pushed down and her head drawn back, the pain in her neck was intense.

The captain walked over and looked down at her. He smirked and put the hard heel of his boot against her forehead. He leaned into it and her head went back further.

"You asked me if I were sure I would get the information in time," the captain said. He grinned cruelly. "Yes, *señorita*. I am sure. Just as I am certain that many of the people we've brought to the palace will be purged from the system. Just as I am sure that we will win. A new nation isn't born without blood, sacrifice, and one thing more: willingness. The willingness to do whatever is necessary to get what you want."

María's vocal cord strained against the tightening flesh of her throat. Thick cables of pain twisted along her body from the front of her ears to the small of her back.

"I could snap your neck," the captain said, "but then you would die and that wouldn't help me. Instead, I will give you five minutes to reflect on the situation and then tell me what you know. If you talk, you will remain our guest but you will be unharmed. If you choose not to talk, I will leave you to these fine men. Believe me, *señorita*. They are very good at what they do.''

The captain released her forehead. María gagged horribly as her throat relaxed. The pain in her back was replaced by a cool, tingling sensation up and down her spine. She swallowed hard and tried to move, but the men were still standing on her back.

The captain looked at the men. "Let her taste some of what she can expect," he said. "Then maybe she will think differently."

As he backed away, María felt the boots lifted from her shoulders. She was hoisted up by the arms. As she was getting her footing a fist was driven hard into her belly. She doubled over, the air rushing from her lungs. Her legs went out from under her but the men held her up. One of them grabbed her hair from behind, pulled her erect, and she was punched again. María actually felt the contours of the fist against the small of her back. Her legs wobbled like ribbon and she moaned loudly. The next blow came up from under her chin. Fortunately, her tongue wasn't between her teeth as they clacked loudly and painfully. After a second blow, which knocked her head toward the right, her lower jaw hung down. She felt blood and saliva roll along her extended tongue.

The men released her and she dropped to the floor. She landed on her back with her arms splayed and her knees raised. Slowly, her bent legs rolled to the right.

María didn't hurt; she knew that the pain would come later. But she felt utterly spent, the way she did when she bicycled up a hill and had no strength left in her limbs. Yet as weak as she was she forced herself to open her eyes and look at the men. She wanted to see where they wore their guns.

They were all right-handed. That would make things easier.

The soldiers stepped into the hallway, splitting up her cigarettes. They shut the door and turned off the light. She knew this drill: break the body and then leave the shocked, disoriented mind a few minutes alone to contemplate mortality.

Instead, she forced her trembling hand down the front of her jeans. She found the cigarette and she drew it out. She rolled onto her side and peeled the paper away to get at the match. It was a trick she'd come up with years before when she worked undercover. Being frisked usually cost her her cigarettes. This way she got to keep a match. In a bind, fire was an ideal offensive weapon.

Her eyes were adjusted to the dark and she looked around. There was a group of music stands in the corner. She looked overhead and saw what she'd expected to see: a pair of sprinklers. There was one by the door in front and the other by the door that led to the dining room.

Perfect.

She crawled over to the stands. Her limbs were still shaking. She promised that she wouldn't ask much of them; only the strength to get her through the next hour or so.

When she reached the corner she got to her knees and then stood. She was wobbly but able to remain on her feet. Her jaw was beginning to ache and she was glad for that: the pain kept her alert. She staggered toward the door, set the stand down, and removed her sweater. She took off her denim shirt, put the sweater back on, then dropped the shirt a few feet from the door.

Once, when she had gone undercover to expose police abuses in Barcelona, María was arrested with a group of hookers. She had used her hidden match to melt the soles of her shoes. The smell brought the guards as they were about to rape a woman in a cell down the corridor. She literally arrested one of them with his pants down. This time she needed more than the stench of burning rubber. She needed something that would catch their eye.

She set the stand beside the door then knelt beside the shirt. Carefully, she struck the match against the bottom of her shoe. It occurred to her how useful shoe bottoms had been this morning. The match flared. She shielded it as she moved it toward the shirt. She touched it to the collar and the garment began to smoulder. A moment later it erupted in flame.

María crept back to the music stand. Struggling to her feet, she picked up the stand and leaned against the wall beside the door. She was breathing heavily to fight down the rising nausea caused by the blows to her belly. This wasn't the first time María had been punched. She'd been hit by rioters, junkies, an angry motorist, and once—only once—by a jealous lover. She'd struck most of them back; she'd sent her lover to the hospital. But this was the first time she'd been held and beaten. The indignity of the attack and the cowardice of the attackers tasted worse than the blood that formed a shallow pool in her cheeks.

Flames consumed the shirt quickly. A thick column of dark, gray smoke rose behind the door. But the smoke wasn't going high enough, fast enough. So María stretched the music stand out and jostled the burning pile. There was a soft hiss. Fiery shards and dark, red-rimmed ash flew from the shirt in all directions. They winked out after a moment and drifted to the ground. But the smoke from the stirred shirt swirled higher and higher.

Now it was high enough. An instant later an alarm went off, followed by the two sprinklers.

As soon as the water sprayed down, María stuck the music stand back in the shirt. She pushed it around like a mop. The shirt came apart in small pieces and she spread the ash over the floor.

She heard footsteps and moved back beside the door—on the right side. She was still holding the stand. The footsteps stopped.

"You two wait here," said one of the men, "in case she tries to get out."

Good, María thought. One soldier was coming in alone. That would make this easier. The door flew out and the soldier ran in. As he did he slid on the wet ash and landed on his back, hard. María immediately raised the music stand above her head. She drove the short, metal tripod legs into his face and he screamed. His fall and shriek were a blur of action. They obviously surprised the soldiers in the corridor and caused them to hesitate.

That was the beauty of elite soldiers, she thought. They were young, fit, and nowhere near as experienced as ragged old warriors.

Their hesitation was all María needed. She tossed the music stand away and let her weak legs have their way: she literally fell over, face first, onto the soldier. She landed across his waist.

Across the holster.

María knew that the two men in the hallway wouldn't shoot her. Not yet. As the fire bell clanged and water rained down on María, the two soldiers rushed forward. At the same time, swearing viciously and vowing to rape her, the hurt soldier tried to push María off. She let him. As she rolled over, she slid the 9mm pistol from his holster. She released the safety and without hesitation fired a shot into his knee. He screeched and blood splattered her face. But María didn't seem to notice as she got up on one knee, aimed low at the other two soldiers, and fired. The pistol coughed twice and blood splashed outward from their knees. The men cried out and crumpled in the doorway.

As water continued to sprinkle down on her, María stuck the pistol in her waistband. Then she waddled over on her knees and relieved the writhing soldiers of their weapons. The knee wounds pleased her. There wouldn't be a day in the lives of these men that they didn't think of her. The pain and disability would be a constant reminder of their brutality.

She pulled off the soldiers' neckties and quickly bound their wrists. Then she stuffed unburned sections of her shirt into their mouths. The bonds and gags weren't as secure as she'd have liked, but there wasn't a lot of time. She used the jamb to help her stand. As soon as she was sure her legs would hold her, she started shuffling quickly down the hall in the opposite direction from which she'd come. The corridor enclosed the main floor in the center of the palace. Continuing in this direction would bring her back to the Hall of Halberdiers and the throne room.

As she released the safeties of the two pistols in her hands, she vowed that this time she would have her audience with Amadori.

TWENTY-NINE

Tuesday, 9:03 A.M.
Madrid, Spain

Luis García de la Vega strode into the commissary. With him was his father, retired General Manolo de la Vega of the Spanish Air Force. Because Luis couldn't be sure who on his staff might be sympathetic to the rebel faction, he wanted someone behind him he knew he could rely on. As he'd told McCaskey, he and his tall, white-haired father rarely agreed on political issues. Manolo leaned to the left, Luis to the right.

"But in a crisis," he said, "where Spain itself is at risk, I trust no one more."

The room was empty except for the seven Strikers, Aideen, and McCaskey. The Interpol officer walked over to Darrell McCaskey, who was helping Aideen put together her grip. The Strikers had already packed their gear and were marking and examining tourist maps of the city.

"Anything new?" McCaskey tiredly asked Luis.

"Yes," Luis said as he pulled McCaskey aside. "A fire bell went off at the palace approximately ten minutes ago."

"Location?"

"A music room in the southern wing of the palace," Luis said. "The palace called the fire department to say it was a false alarm. But it wasn't. One of our spotters used heat-goggles and found the hot spot. The fire was extinguished, according to the spotter."

"Whoever's running things in the palace took quite a risk," McCaskey said, "considering all the treasures in there. I don't assume that's standard operating procedure."

"Not at all," said Luis. "The bastards didn't want anyone coming in. A half hour before, they also turned away a Civil Guard patrol when it attempted to make its daily inspection of the grounds."

"If Amadori is there, they won't turn away Striker," McCaskey vowed. "Hell, they won't know what hit them. What does the prime minister's office have to say about the situation?"

"They're still not acknowledging, officially, that Amadori has effectively seized power," Luis replied.

"What about unofficially?"

"Most of the top government officials have already sent their families to France, Morocco, and Tunisia." Luis frowned. A moment later the frown became a smirk. "You know, Darrell—I'll bet my family and I could get a table at the best restaurant in town tonight."

"I'll bet you could," McCaskey said, smiling weakly. He walked back to the table where Aideen was checking the equipment Interpol had provided for her. These included a camcorder—which was linked to a receiver in the communications office—a first-aid kit, a cellular phone, and a gun.

Aideen made sure the camcorder battery was fully charged. As she did, McCaskey checked the clip of the 9 × 19 Parabellum Super Star pistol she'd been issued. Aideen had already inspected it. But she realized that McCaskey was probably anxious and needed to keep busy. After examining the weapon he returned it to her backpack.

As the Strikers pulled on their backpacks, McCaskey studied Aideen to make sure that she looked like a member of a tour group. She wore Nikes, sunglasses, and a baseball cap. In addition to the backpack, she carried a guidebook and bottled water. She *felt* like a tourist—right down to the jet lag. As McCaskey looked at her, Aideen gazed longingly at the empty table behind him. She'd been able to sleep on the return flight from San Sebastián. But all the nap had done was take the edge off her exhaustion, and she knew it was just a matter of time before she crashed. She glanced behind her at the vending machines and contemplated a Diet Pepsi. She weighed the value of the caffeine against the risk that she'd have to find a bathroom before the mission was completed. That was something she'd learned to take into consideration during long, daytime stakeouts in Mexico City. Two hours could seem very, very long when you couldn't leave your post.

She decided to forgo the beverage.

McCaskey, on the other hand, looked as though he were ready to crash now. When she'd first briefed him about Martha's assassination, she remembered thinking how calm he sounded. She realized, now, that it wasn't calmness: it was focus. She doubted whether he'd shut his eyes since Martha Mackall's death. She wondered whether this reflected his determination to avenge her death, determination to punish himself, or both.

When McCaskey was finished with Aideen he turned to Colonel August. The officer was chewing gum and wearing a stubble. Sunglasses with Day-Glo green frames and reflective lenses were propped on his forehead. He was dressed in khaki-colored Massimo shorts and a wrinkled, long-sleeved white shirt with the sleeves rolled up just one turn. He looked like a very different man than the quiet, conservative soldier Aideen had met a few times back in Washington. August had a radio disguised as a Walkman to communicate with McCaskey. The volume dial was actually a condensor microphone. The colonel also carried bottled water. If it were poured onto the cassette in the Walkman, the tape—which was coated with diphenylcyanoarsine—would erupt into a cloud of tear gas. The dispenser would remain operational for nearly five minutes.

"All right," McCaskey said. "You're going to wait at the east side of the opera house. And if you get chased away?"

"We go to Calle de Arenal to the north," August replied. "We follow it east around the palace and enter the Campo del Moro. If that's blocked off, the fallback position is the Museo de Carruajes."

"If you get shooed from there?"

"We go back to the opera house," August said. "North side."

McCaskey nodded. "As soon as I hear from the spotters, I'll let you know where Amadori is. You'll consult your map and let me know which page of the playbook you're on."

McCaskey was referring to the Striker SITs and SATs "playbook"—Standard Infiltration Tactics and Standard Assault Tactics. Colonel August and Corporal Prementine had adapted these plays for the palace. There were a total of ten options in each category. Which option they selected would depend upon the time they had available as well as the amount and type of resistance they expected. However, one thing was constant in each scenario: not everyone went inside. After the death of Striker leader Lt. Col. Squires, August retooled every play to make certain there was a crew to assist with the exit strategy.

"As you know," McCaskey went on, "Aideen is going along solely to identify María and assist with her rescue. She won't be a combatant unless it becomes necessary. We've got a chopper on the roof and will be ready to move in with extra police if things get out of hand. Luis tells me that once you're inside, the only serious security problem you may face is the RSS."

"Damn," August said softly. "How does he know Amadori's got one of those?"

"The king had the system installed in all of the palaces," McCaskey said. "Bought it from the same American contractor who installed them up and down the Beltway. That's probably one of the reasons Amadori chose the palace for his headquarters.''

The RSS—Remote Surveillance System—was a goggle-like visor that tapped into the video security system of a building. There was a keypad built into the side of the goggles and a black-and-white liquid-crystal display in the eyepieces. Together, they allowed the wearer to see what any of the security cameras were seeing. Small videocameras mounted to some of the newer units also enabled guards to share audio-visual information.

"Brief your team," McCaskey warned. "If Amadori gets out of the throne room, pursuit's going to be very, very risky."

August acknowledged.

The other six Strikers were lined up behind Colonel August. McCaskey looked at them as he spoke. His eyes settled on Private DeVonne, who was at the end of the line. The African-American woman was wearing tight jeans and a blue windbreaker. It suddenly struck Aideen—as it must have struck McCaskey—how much she looked like a young Martha Mackall.

McCaskey looked down. "You men and women know the mission and you know the risks. Colonel August tells me you also know the legal and moral issues involved. The President has ordered us to remove a frightening despot from power. We are to use any means at our disposal. We do not have his public support. Nor do we have the support of the lawful Spanish government, which is in chaos. If anyone is captured, he or she will not be acknowledged or assisted by either country, except through the traditional diplomatic channels. However, we do have this much:

the opportunity as well as the duty to save thousands of lives. I view that as a privilege. I hope you do as well.''

Luis stepped forward. ''You men and women will also have the gratitude of many Spaniards who will never know what you did for them.'' He smiled. ''And you already have the gratitude and thanks of the few Spaniards who *do* know what you're about to undertake.'' He stood beside McCaskey and saluted them all. *''Vaya con Dios,* my friends. Go with God.''

THIRTY

Tuesday, 9:45 A.M.
Madrid, Spain

Father Norberto flew to Madrid in the General Superior's private plane. It was a twenty-year-old Cessna Conquest decorated in lavender and red with darkened windows and a small sacristy in the back. The eleven-seat two-prop aircraft was very noisy and very bumpy.

Like almost everything in Spain these days, Norberto thought bitterly as he squeezed the thickly padded armrests.

Yet even as he thought it, Norberto knew that that wasn't true. Not entirely. Norberto was accompanied by five other priests from villages along the northern coast. While his own soul was in turmoil, these men were calm.

Norberto breathed deeply. He wished that their composure was enough to steady him. He wished that he could somehow turn away from his private loss and focus on the monumental task ahead. Helping to keep the spiritual peace in a city of over three million people was a challenge unlike any he had ever faced. But maybe that was what he needed now. Something to keep him from dwelling on the terrible loss he'd endured.

The elderly Father Jiménez was sitting beside Norberto in the back row. Jiménez came from the village of Laredo, which was farther west along the coast. Not long after they were airborne, Jiménez turned from the window and leaned close to Norberto.

"I hear that we will be meeting with prelates from other denominations," Jiménez said. He spoke loudly in order to be heard over the growling engines. "There will be at least forty of us."

"Do you have any idea why he selected us?" Norberto asked. "Why not Father Iglesias in Bilbao or Father Montoya in Toledo?"

Jiménez shrugged. "I suppose it's because our parishes are very small. Our parishioners know one another and can help each other in our absence."

"That's what I thought at first," Father Norberto said. "But look around. We are also the oldest members of the order."

"Therefore the most experienced," said Jiménez. "Who better to entrust with such a mission?"

"The young?" Norberto said. "The energetic?"

"The young question much too much," Jiménez said. He poked Norberto's arm. "They're a little like you, my old friend. Perhaps the General Superior wants men. Men he can trust. Men whom he can tell to do a thing and it will be done, without delay or complaint."

Norberto wasn't so sure of that. He didn't even know why he felt this way. Maybe it was his awful grief or the overbearing manner with which he'd been ordered to Madrid. Or maybe, he thought portentously, God was poking him the same way Jiménez just had.

"Do you even know where we'll be gathering?" Norberto asked.

"When Father Francisco telephoned," Jiménez replied, "he said that we would be taken to Nuestra Señora de la Almudena." The priest's soft, white cheeks framed a gentle smile. "It feels strange, leaving a small parish for a place like that. I wonder if Our Lord felt the same way when he set out from Galilee? 'I must preach the Kingdom of God to other cities also, for therefore am I sent,' " he said, quoting the Gospels. Then he sat back, still smiling. "It feels strange, Norberto, but it also feels good to be sent."

Norberto looked ahead at the other priests. He didn't share Jiménez's optimism. The priests' ministrations should have come before the people turned on one another. Before they turned to rioting—and murder. Nor did Norberto presume to know what Jesus felt when He went into the wilderness. However, as he thought about it, Norberto imagined that Jesus was probably disturbed and overwhelmed by a society polluted with prejudice and mistrust, violence and immorality, greed and discord. Faced with that, there was only one place Jesus could have turned to for strength.

In his distress, Norberto had momentarily lost sight of that place. Closing his eyes and bowing his head, Father Norberto prayed to God for the courage to take on this burden. He prayed for the wisdom to know what was right and for the strength to overcome his own sudden rancor. He needed to hold on to the faith that was fast slipping away.

The plane arrived in Madrid early but was forced to circle for nearly half an hour. Military traffic had priority, they were informed. From what they could see through the window there was a great deal of that. When they were finally able to land at ten o'clock, the group entered terminal two, where they joined priests from around the country. Father Norberto recognized a few of the clergymen—Father Alfredo Lastras from Valencia, Father Casto Sampedro from Murcia, and Father Cesar Flores from León. But he didn't have time to do more than shake some hands and exchange a few words of greeting before the group was ushered onto an old bus and taken to the Cathedral of the Almudena. Norberto sat by the open window and Father Jiménez sat beside him. Traffic into the city was extremely light along the Avenue de America and they reached the famous—as well as infamous—cathedral in just under twenty minutes.

The sprawling Cathedral of the Almudena was begun in the ninth century A.D. Little more than the foundation was completed before work was halted due to the arrival of the Moors. The invaders raised their mighty fortress beside it. When the Moors were driven from Spain and the fortress was dismantled to make way for the Royal Palace, work was also scheduled to resume on the cathedral. However, the powerful and jealous Archbishop of Toledo did not want any church to be more imposing than his own. Individuals who gave money to finish a church on a site made unholy by the Moors faced both excommunication and death. It was nearly seven hundred years before work continued on the church. Even then, money and resources were scarce. Sections were completed and then work was abandoned, resulting in a chaotic variety of styles.

Finally, in 1870, the patchwork church was pulled down and a new Neo-Gothic church was planned. Construction began in 1883, though funds ran out with regularity and the effort was finally abandoned in 1940. It wasn't until 1990 that work was undertaken to finish the cathedral in earnest. Yet once again the billions of pesetas needed to execute the job were not forthcoming. Ironically, it was just three weeks ago that the last of the paint was applied to the friezes in the main entablature.

The gears complained loudly as the bus suddenly slowed. They had just turned off Calle Mayor and swung onto Calle de Bailén, where literally thousands of people were gathered outside the twin spires of the church. Beyond them were groups of reporters and TV cameras. The print journalists were on foot and the TV crews were on the backs of parked vans. Though the crowd was being kept away by a phalanx of metropolitan police, the arrival of the bus and the glimpse of the priests seemed to enflame them. The people began crying loudly for help and sanctuary. The heat inside the crowded bus seemed to enhance their voices and carry them to every ear, like a church bell in the still of morning. These were not political refugees but elderly men, mothers with babes, and schoolchildren. They were panicked and their numbers—like their passion—seemed to swell as the bus crept toward the front of the church. The priests regarded one another in silence. They had expected need, but not this kind of desperation.

Linking their arms, a line of police officers was finally able to get between the bus and the crowd. Father

Francisco came from the church and used a megaphone to implore the group to be patient. As he did,
he motioned for the forty-four priests to come inside.
They moved slowly, crowded into a tight, single-file
line by the surging mob. They reminded Father Norberto of the hungry masses he had once helped feed
in Rwanda and the homeless he'd served in Nicaragua.
It was astonishing the power the weak could have en
masse.

When all the priests were inside, the doors were
shut behind them. After the plane ride and the grinding
of the gears and the shouts of the crowd, the heavy
silence was welcome.

But it isn't real, Norberto reminded himself. The
fear and pain outside—*that* was real and it was growing. It needed to be addressed very soon.

General Superior González was already in the apse
of the cathedral, praying silently. As the group filed
down the nave the only sound was the scraping of
shoes and the rustling of robes. Father Francisco was
at the head of the line. When they reached the transept,
he turned and held both hands toward them. They
stopped. Father Fernandez walked forward alone.

Norberto was not a great admirer of General Superior González. Some argued that the fifty-seven-
year-old Jesuit leader was good for the order because
he courted the favor of the Vatican and the attention
of the world. But unless the priests of Spain preached
his views and advocated his conservative political
candidates and collected onerous donations from the
parish, none of the wealth and support he attracted
found its way to them. Norberto believed that General

Superior González was interested in extending the power and influence more of Orlando González than of the Spanish Jesuits.

González was the General Superior and Norberto would never defy him or criticize him openly. But standing in his presence, in an old and magnificent church, Norberto didn't feel the soul-warming piety he wanted to feel—that he *needed* to feel. He was still anguished and cynical and now he was also suspicious. Was González concerned for the people? Was he worried that the revolution would weaken his power? Or did General Superior González hope that a new leader would turn to him to help win the support of the nation's Jesuits?

After three or four minutes of silent prayer, González turned suddenly and faced the priests. They crossed themselves as he offered a benediction. Then he walked toward them slowly, his long, dark patrician face with its pale eyes turned toward the heavens.

"Forgive us, O Lord," he said, "for this day was the first day in over one thousand years that the doors of this cathedral have been barred from the inside." He regarded the priests. "In just a moment I am going to open those doors. I must leave, but Father Francisco will assign each of you to a different section of the cathedral. I ask you to talk to the people in turn, assuring them that this is not their struggle. That God will take care of them to trust in the leaders of Spain to restore peace." He stopped when he reached Father Francisco's side. "I thank every one of you for coming," he continued. "The people of Madrid need spiritual guidance and reassurance. They need to know that in this time of turmoil they have not been abandoned. Once Madrid has been quieted, its faith restored, we can move outward and bring peace to the rest of Spain.''

General Superior González moved past the priests. His black robe swung heavily from side to side as he walked toward the door. His step was confident and unhurried, as though everything was under control.

As Norberto watched the General Superior go, he realized with sudden horror that perhaps it was. That maybe this mission was not about ministering to the frightened or needy—not for their sake, anyway. He looked around him. Could it be that the most serene and devoted, the most *trusted* of the nation's priests had been brought here for one purpose only—crowd control? Create a demand for comfort, whip it to a frenzy by keeping the doors locked, and then dispense it generously?

Father Norberto was scared. He also felt dirty. General Superior González was not looking to gain favor with the leaders of this revolution. Norberto suspected that the General Superior was already part of this process to secure a new government for the nation.

A new government for Spain with himself as its spiritual head.

THIRTY-ONE

Tuesday, 10:20 A.M.
Madrid, Spain

María was convinced that General Amadori was, in fact, in the throne room of the Royal Palace. However, she did not go there directly after escaping from the soldiers. She needed a uniform and she needed an ally.

The uniform had to come first.

María got it in a stall in the men's latrine. The latrine was formerly—and formally—*el carto de cambiar por los attendientes del rey*—the changing room for the attendants of the king. Now soldiers were tramping in and out with disregard for its history or status. María was not a royalist but she was a Spaniard and this place had played a large part in the history of Spain. It deserved more respect.

The large white room had marble cornices and appointments. It was located in the southeastern sector of the palace, not far from the king's bedchamber. María reached it by moving cautiously from doorway to doorway. Most of the rooms along the way were unoccupied; those that were, she skipped. If an alarm of any kind had been raised about her escape, the search was confined to the area around the music room and the throne room. It was an appropriate use of manpower. They knew she had to try to get to Amadori eventually. The trick was to make sure they didn't notice her.

The uniform came to her courtesy of a young sergeant. He had entered the changing room with two other men.. When he opened the door, María was crouched on the toilet with both pistols pointed toward him.

"Come in and lock the door," she snarled in a low voice. The hum of the ceiling fan prevented her voice from carrying outside the stall.

There's a moment when most people who are confronted with a gun will freeze. During that brief time, the individual holding the weapon must give an instruction. If the command is given immediately and emphatically it will usually be obeyed. If it isn't, if the target panics, then the decision must be made whether to withdraw or fire.

María had already decided that she'd shoot to disable everyone in the room before allowing herself to be caught. Fortunately, the wide-eyed soldier did as he'd been ordered.

As soon as the door had been locked, María motioned the soldier over with one of the guns. She held the other one pointed up, toward his forehead.

"Lock your fingers behind your head," she said. "Then turn around and back toward me."

He clasped his fingers tightly behind his cap. María reached behind her without taking her eyes from him. She put one of her guns on the toilet tank, relieved him of his pistol, and tucked it in her belt, behind her. Then she retrieved the gun she'd put on the toilet.

María stepped back on the seat.

"Drop these." She poked his butt with the gun. "Sit on the edge on your hands."

The soldier obeyed.

"When your friends leave," she whispered in his ear, "tell them to go without you. Otherwise, you all die."

María and the sergeant—his nameplate said García—waited. She swore she could hear his heart-beat. He did as he was instructed when the others called to him, and when they were gone María told him to rise. Still facing front, he was told to take off his uniform.

He did. María then turned him around so he was facing the toilet. She told him to kneel in front of it.

"Please don't shoot me," he said. "Please."

"I won't," she said, "if you do as you're told."

There were two things she could do. One was to stuff his mouth with toilet paper, break his fingers so he couldn't take it out, then tie him to the heavy tank lid. But that would take time. Instead, she executed a tight front-kick to the back of his head. That drove his forehead into the ceramic tank and knocked him out. He'd probably suffered a concussion, but there was no way to avoid injuries in this situation. Grabbing the uniform and guns, she changed quickly in the adjoining stall. The uniform was baggy, but it would have to do. Tucking her hair into the snug pillbox cap, she holstered the sergeant's gun and hid the extra pistols under the front of her shirt.

She stuffed her clothes into the wastebasket—everything except the shoes. She rubbed the soles on her cheeks to give herself "stubble." When she was finished, she threw the shoes out as well. Then she went to the mirror to give herself a final check. As she did, two other sergeants entered. They were in a hurry.

"You're late, García!" one of them barked. He walked past María, following the other man toward the urinal. "The lieutenant gave each group five minutes to get in and—"

The sergeant stopped and turned. María didn't wait for him to act. She faced him and placed her right knee behind his left knee. Then she hooked her right arm, locked it around his neck, and threw him over her leg. He fell in front of her, lengthwise. Because her weight was on her right leg, she was able to lift her left leg. She stomped hard on his chest, breaking ribs and knocking the wind from him. His companion was facing the urinal. He turned but María had already stepped over the sergeant and was moving toward him. Lifting her right leg without breaking her stride, she drove her right knee hard into the small of his back. He was slammed against the urinal and fell back. As the soldier hit the tiled floor María kicked him in the temple with her heel. He went out immediately. The other man was still moaning so María pivoted gracefully and kicked him squarely in the side of the head. He, too, fell unconscious.

María stumbled back. She had marshaled the energy she'd needed for the attack, but the effort had drained her. The blows she'd suffered in the music room ached wickedly and this activity hadn't helped. But there was still a mission to complete and María intended to finish it. Staggering to the sink, she cupped water in her hands and drank.

Then she remembered something the man on the floor had said. Soldiers were being allowed to come in here at five-minute intervals. She'd just eaten up nearly two of those. There was no time to delay.

Pulling herself erect, María turned and started toward the door. Then, without hesitation, she stepped into the hallway. She turned right and then turned left a few doors down. She was back in the corridor leading to the throne room.

There were soldiers stationed here but she moved quickly, as though she were hurrying somewhere. Whenever she worked undercover María had found that two things were necessary for a successful infiltration. First, you had to act like you belonged wherever you were. If you did, no one questioned you. Second, you had to act as though you had somewhere to go—immediately. If you moved fast and with assurance, no one stopped you. She was certain that those qualities, plus the uniform, would get her back to the Hall of the Halberdiers. They might even get her inside. After that, María would need four things in order to get to Amadori.

The guns, wile—and two special allies.

THIRTY-TWO

Tuesday, 4:30 A.M.
Washington, D.C.

Mike Rodgers joined Paul Hood in his office to await word on Striker's deployment. Shortly after Rodgers arrived, Steve Burkow phoned with news from the White House. Hood hoped the call was only to give him the news. The hawkish National Security chief had a way of using calls like these to push the President's agenda.

According to Burkow, the king of Spain had phoned from his residence in Barcelona and spoken with the President. Officers loyal to the king had confirmed that General Rafael Amadori, head of military intelligence and one of the most powerful officers in Spain, had relocated his command center to the throne room of the Royal Palace.

Hearing that, Hood and Rodgers exchanged glances. Without a word, Rodgers went to a phone by the couch to inform Luis at Interpol that they had positively located their target. Hood allowed himself a little smile. He was pleased that they'd gotten that one right.

''There's now no doubt about what this General

Amadori is planning," Burkow continued. "The President has informed the king about the presence of the Striker team in Madrid. His Majesty has given us his approval to take whatever action is necessary."

"Of course he did," Hood said. The President's action was expedient and probably necessary, but it made him uneasy.

"Don't be so quick to judge the king," Burkow said. "He has also acknowledged that it probably won't be possible to hold Spain together. He said that too many long-simmering ethnic demons have been let loose. He also told the President that if the U.N. and NATO will assist in an orderly disassembling of the nation, he will abdicate."

"What good would that do?" Hood asked. "The king's powers are only ceremonial."

"That's true," Burkow said. "But he's prepared to use his abdication as a gesture to the people of Spain. He wants to show them that if they want autonomy, he won't stand in their way. However, he's adamant about not handing over power to a tyrant."

Hood had to admit that even though the king probably had a fortune hidden in foreign banks, there was an admirable if grandstanding logic to what he had proposed. "When will the king be making this gesture?" Hood asked.

"When Amadori is no longer a threat," Burkow replied. "Speaking of which, what's the status of your team?"

"We're awaiting word," Hood said. "Striker should be arriving at the target any mo—"

"They're there," Rodgers said suddenly.

"Hold on, Steve," Hood said. "Mike, what've you got?"

"Darrell just heard from Colonel August," Rodgers said, the phone still pressed to his ear. "Striker has successfully deployed along the east side of the opera house. They have the palace in view and so far no one has bothered them. The soldiers seem to be concentrating on the palace and nothing more. Colonel August is awaiting further instructions."

"Thank Darrell for me," Hood said, and repeated the information to Burkow. As he spoke, he brought up the mission profile McCaskey had filed a half hour before. There was a map of that section of Madrid as well as a detailed map of the Royal Palace, along with various assault and infiltration configurations. According to McCaskey, the estimate from the Interpol spotter put the palace strength at four or five hundred troops. Most of them were clustered outside the southern end, where the throne room was located.

"What would the plan and timing be if they had to go in now?" Burkow asked.

Rodgers had come over to the desk. He looked over Hood's shoulder. Hood put the phone on speaker.

"There's a sewer on the northwest corner of the Plaza de Oriente," Hood said. "It connects to a catacomb which used to be part of an old Moorish fortress. It's used to store rat poison now."

"Hold it," Burkow said. "How do they get into the sewer?"

"They use an old French Resistance trick," Rodgers replied. "Create a diversion and hit the main target. Nothing lethal—just lots of smoke."

"I see," Burkow said.

"The catacomb connects to a palace dungeon, which hasn't been used for that purpose in over two centuries," Hood said.

"You mean it's just sitting there?" Burkow said.

"That's correct," Hood replied.

"Given Spain's history vis-à-vis the Inquisition," Rodgers said, "I'm not surprised it hasn't been restored and opened to the public."

"Entering the dungeon will bring the Strikers right below the Hall of Tapestries," Hood continued. "From there, it's a short trip to the throne room."

"A short trip as the crow flies," Rodgers said, "though there are probably troops up and down the corridor. If they go in a three-cut mode, there'll definitely be casualties among the Spaniards."

"Three-cut mode?" Burkow said.

"Yes, sir," Rodgers said. "Cut through any resistance, cut down the target, then cut out. In other words, if they don't bother to obtain uniforms and sneak up on Amadori and take pains to minimize casualties—on either side."

"I see," Burkow said.

"We intended to wait and see if we hear from our person inside," Hood said.

"The Interpol agent who allowed herself to be captured," Burkow said.

"That's right. We don't know whether she'll try to

reach us or try to take out the target herself," Hood said. "But we thought it best to give her time."

Burkow was silent for a moment. "While we wait, we run the risk of Amadori growing exponentially stronger. There's a point at which a usurper ceases to be regarded as a rebel and becomes a hero to the people. Like Castro when he overthrew Batista."

"That is a risk," Hood agreed. "But we don't think Amadori is at that point yet. There are still dozens of riot zones and Amadori hasn't been named as an interim leader in any of the newscasts we've monitored. Until a few major figures join him—not just politicians, but business and religious leaders—he's probably going to lay low."

"He's already started leaning hard on industrial leaders," Burkow pointed out. "The men on the yacht and the *familia* members he rounded up—"

"He probably will scare others into line," Hood agreed, "but I doubt that'll happen within the next hour or two."

"So you think we should wait."

"Striker's on alert and ready," Hood said. "The delay isn't likely to do much harm and it *may* give us some valuable onsite intel."

"I disagree that the delay isn't likely to do much harm," Burkow said. "General VanZandt believes that it may also give Amadori a chance to punch up his own security. And getting him is the *primary* objective."

Hood looked up at Rodgers. They both knew what Burkow was implying: this wasn't the time to be cautious.

Hood agreed, to a point. The blitzkriegs, purges, and murders seemed to put Amadori in a class with Hitler and Stalin, not Fidel Castro or Francisco Franco. He couldn't be allowed to rule Spain.

"Steve," Hood said, "I agree with you. Amadori is the primary objective. But the Strikers are the only resource we have. If we use them recklessly, that'll endanger their lives and also jeopardize the mission." He looked at the computer clock. His assistant Bugs Benet had programmed it to give him the local time as well as the time in Madrid. "It's nearly eleven A.M. in Spain," he continued. "Let's see what the situation is at noon. If we haven't heard anything from María Corneja by then, Striker will move in."

"A lot can happen in an hour, Paul," Burkow complained. "A few key endorsements could make Amadori unstoppable. Remove him then and you kill a world leader instead of a traitor."

"I understand that," Hood replied. "But we need more information."

"Look," Burkow pressed, "I'm starting to get pissed off. Your team is one of the best strike forces in the world. Don't sit on them. Let them loose. They'll collect their own intel as they proceed."

"No," Hood said emphatically. "That isn't good enough. I'm going to give María the extra hour."

"*Why?*" Burkow demanded. "Listen, if you're afraid to give the order to waste that son-of-a-bitch general—"

"Afraid?" Hood snapped. "That bastard sat back

and let one of my people die. I can eat what's on the plate. Gladly.''

"Then what's the problem?"

"The problem is we've been so damned target focused we haven't worked out an exit strategy for Striker."

"You don't need María for that," Burkow said. "They go out the same way they go in."

"I don't mean we need an exit strategy from the palace," Hood said. "I'm talking about culpability. Who's going to take the heat for this, Steve? Did the President work that out with the king?"

"I don't know. I wasn't in on the conversation."

"Are we supposed to disavow Striker if they're caught?" Hood asked. "Say they're mercenaries or some kind of rogue operation and then let them twist in the wind?"

"Sometimes that has to happen," Burkow said.

"Sometimes it does," Hood agreed. "But not when there's an alternative. And the alternative we have here is to let a Spaniard be involved somewhere. A patriot. Someone Striker is there to support, even if that's just smoke-and-mirrors for public consumption."

Burkow said nothing.

"So I'm going to wait until noon to see if we get anything from María," Hood said. "Even her whereabouts in the palace will do. If Striker can scoop her up on the way to Amadori, then no—I won't have any problem giving the order to waste the son-of-a-bitch."

There was a long moment of thick silence. Burkow

finally broke it.

"I can tell the President it'll happen at noon?" he asked.

"Yes," said Hood.

"Fine," Burkow said coldly. "We'll talk then."

The National Security chief hung up. Hood looked up at Rodgers. The general was smiling.

"I'm proud of you, Paul," Rodgers said. "Real proud."

"Thanks, Mike." Hood closed down the computer file and rubbed his eyes. "But God, I'm tired. Tired of all of this."

"Close your eyes," Rodgers said. "I'll take the watch."

"Not till this is over," Hood said. "But you can do me a favor."

"Sure."

Hood picked up the phone. "I'll get on top of Bob Herbert and Stephen Viens, tell them I want that woman found and pinpointed. Meantime, see if there's anything else Darrell can do. An hour's not much time, but maybe somebody once bugged the palace. See if he can scare up any enemies of the king."

"Will do."

"And make sure he briefs Striker about what we're waiting on."

Rodgers nodded and left, shutting the door behind him. Hood made the calls to Herbert and Viens. When he was finished, he folded his arms on his desk and rested his forehead on them.

He *was* tired. And he wasn't particularly proud of

himself. To the contrary. He was disgusted by his eagerness to tear down Amadori as payback for Martha Mackall—even though it was someone else who had planned and carried out her murder. It was all part of the same inhuman tableau.

Eventually, though, it would all be over. Amadori would be dead or Spain would be Amadori's—in which case it was the world's problem and not his. Then Hood would leave here and go home to nothing. Nothing but a few private satisfactions, some awful regrets, and the prospect of more of the same for as long as he stayed at Op-Center.

That wasn't enough.

He would never get Sharon to see things his way. But as he sat there, his mind fuzzy and his emotions clear, he had to admit that he was no longer sure his way was right. Was it better to have big professional challenges and the respect of Mike Rodgers? Or was it better to have a less demanding job, one that left him time to enjoy the love of his wife and children and the small satisfactions they could all share?

Why should I have to choose? he asked himself. But he knew the answer to that.

Because the price of being one of the power elite in any field was time and industry. If he wanted his family back he was going to have to take back some of those things. He was going to have to join a university or a bank or a think tank—something that left him time for violin recitals and baseball games and snuggling in front of the boob tube.

Hood raised his head and turned back to his computer. And as he waited for news from Spain, he typed:

Mr. President:

I herewith resign the office of Director of Op-Center.

Sincerely,
Paul Hood

THIRTY-THREE

Tuesday, 10:32 A.M.
Madrid, Spain

When María finally reached the corridor outside the Hall of the Halberdiers, she was no longer able to proceed cautiously. The room was located toward the near end of the long hallway. The corridor was crowded with groups of soldiers, who were methodically searching the palace rooms. She had no doubt that they were looking for her.

It had been relatively easy getting this far. There were a number of interconnected rooms along the way and she'd been able to stay out of the corridor. The only stop she'd made was to try to telephone Luis to brief him. But the palace phones had been disconnected and she didn't want to risk trying to get a radio from one of the communications officers.

Swallowing her pain, she marched ahead quickly, purposefully. Her arms swung stiffly at her sides, her cap was pulled low, and her eyes peered straight ahead. *Look official*, she kept reminding herself.

María believed that in most cases an infiltration should be done quietly. The rules were enter in the dark, don't make noise, and blend in with the shadows. In the present situation she wouldn't be able to sneak through. The only approach to take was to act as though she belonged. Unfortunately, while there were women in the Spanish army, none of them were assigned to combat units. And as far as María could tell, none of them were here. Which is why she jogged toward the Hall of the Halberdiers. The cap hid her hair and the tunic hid her arms and chest. All she wanted to do was to get back to the room. If she could get inside, she had a plan that might get her through to the throne room.

If she ran too fast, María knew that she'd attract attention. If she ran too slowly, she was afraid that someone would stop her and ask why she wasn't with her unit. Her heart seemed to be pounding in all directions at once. Her body ached from the beating and she was frightened for Spain. But the danger and hurt and most of all the responsibility made her feel alive. These moments were like the instant before pulling a parachute ripcord or stepping onstage. They were hyperintense and unlike anything else in life.

A few heads turned to look at her but she was gone before anyone had a chance to see her face.

As María was about to turn into the doorway of the Hall of the Halberdiers, a familiar figure strode out, nearly colliding with her. It was the captain who had had her beaten. The officer stopped and glowered at María as she saluted and sidled past him. She tried to hide her face with the salute and didn't look up. All she needed was a few more seconds.

María saw Juan and Ferdinand ahead. They were sitting cross-legged along the near side of the crowd, looking down. The number of prisoners had thinned somewhat since she was last here. The prisoners were also more restless. That was probably a result of concern over where the others had been taken and the fact that the ranks of guards also had thinned. María assumed the soldiers were out looking for her. None of the guards in the room looked at her as she made her way toward the two Ramirez *familia* members.

"Wait!" the captain's voice broke loud and hard from the doorway behind her.

Juan and Ferdinand looked up. María continued walking toward them.

"I said *you!*" the captain bellowed into the room. "*Sergeant!* Stop where you are!"

María was about twenty paces from Juan. She wasn't going to make it before she had to deal with the captain. She swore silently and continued walking toward Juan. The prisoner was looking directly at her. It was frustrating that the captain may have recognized her but Juan didn't. The door to the throne room was about forty feet straight ahead, through the crowd. There were still guards on either side of the door. They were looking at her now, too. She had to get there and she wouldn't be able to do it alone.

"Sir, I have a report for the general," she said angrily without stopping or turning.

Right now, seconds mattered. She needed to get closer to Juan. She also wanted him to hear her voice and know who she was. The captain would know who she was too, for certain, but there was no way of avoiding that.

"It *is* you!" the captain roared when María spoke. "Stop at once and raise your arms!"

María slowed but she didn't stop. She needed to be in front of Juan.

"I said stop!" the captain cried.

María reached the edge of the crowd. She stopped.

"Now," the captain said, "raise your arms slowly with your hands out. If you make any sudden motions you will be shot," the captain said.

The young woman did as she'd been told. She watched Juan's eyes as they widened with surprised recognition. The soldiers stationed around the room still hadn't gone for their own weapons. She only had a few moments before they would be ordered to do so.

"You," the captain barked. "Corporal."

One of the noncommissioned officers standing beside the throne room door came to attention. "Sir?"

"Take her weapon!" the captain ordered.

"Yes, sir!"

"My—my legs," María said. She stopped in front of Juan and started to wobble. "May I sit down?"

"Stand where you are!" the captain snarled.

"But they were hurt when I was beaten—"

"Silencio!" he yelled.

María trembled for a moment more. The soldier had entered the crowd of prisoners on the opposite side and was making his way toward her. She couldn't wait any longer. She didn't think they would shoot her here, especially if she were down. That might start a riot. Moaning loudly, she dropped to her knees and fell forward against Juan.

"Get up!" the captain yelled.

María attempted to rise. As she pretended to struggle back to her feet, she drew the guns from her waistband. She shoved them into Juan's hand.

He took them clandestinely. Ferdinand had leaned over to help María. Juan slid a gun under his bent knee.

"Amadori's in the throne room," María whispered as hands helped her to her knees.

"We'll never make it—" Juan whispered back.

"We must!" she hissed. "We're dead anyway!"

Just then, the guard finished making his way through the crowd. He bent over María and yanked her up by the collar. She grunted as she stood and then pretended to stumble to one side. As soon as she was out of the way, Juan raised his gun, pointed at the soldier's thigh, and fired. The guard shrieked and staggered backward on a spray of blood. His gun dropped to the floor and one of the prisoners snatched it up. Regaining her balance, María unholstered her own weapon and turned toward the captain.

But the captain had already drawn his own weapon. He fired two rounds, one of which struck María in the left side. She twisted in pain and her own shot went wide. She landed on the man who had picked up the gun. Her hat tumbled off and her hair spilled out.

Juan rose as María fell. "*¡Asesino!*" Juan shouted. "Assassin!"

Before he could fire, a bullet struck him in the left shoulder. He twisted as he fell, his arms flying outward. His gun went spinning along the floor toward the hallway. The captain picked it up as he stalked toward them. The man who had fired, the other soldier standing guard at the throne room, came forward.

"Stay at your post!" the captain yelled.

The crowd of prisoners began to murmur loudly and the guards unholstered their weapons. Suddenly, the throne room door opened. General Amadori's personal aide, Major General Antonio Aguirre, stepped out. He was holding a 9mm automatic, which looked only slightly less intimidating than his scowl. The tall, lean, broad shouldered man took a moment to look around the room.

"Is there a problem, Captain Infiesta?" he asked.

"No, sir," the captain replied. "Not any longer."

"Who is he?" Aguirre asked, pointing the gun toward the man he'd shot.

He pointed to María. "Her accomplice," he said.

Aguirre's dark eyes settled on the woman. "Who is she?"

"I believe she's a spy," the captain informed him.

María stood unsteadily. "I am not . . . a spy, Major General," she insisted. She was clutching her side just below her ribs and leaning into the wound. It was bloody and it throbbed hotly. "I am María Correja from Interpol. I came here with information for the general. Instead of listening to me, this man had me beaten." She raised a hand weakly and gestured toward the captain.

"I will listen to you," said the major general. "Talk."

"No," María said. "Not here—"

"Here and now," Aguirre said curtly.

María shut her eyes for a moment. "I'm dizzy," she said truthfully. "Can I sit down somewhere?"

"Certainly," Aguirre said. His scowl remained

fixed. "Captain—take her and her accomplice outside. Let her talk and then conclude your business with her."

"Yes, sir," the captain said.

María turned. "Sir!" she shouted and started limping through the crowd, toward the major general. She was still thinking that if she could get into the throne room there might be something she could do—

She felt herself yanked back by the hair.

"You'll come outside as you've been ordered," the captain said as he tugged her from the crowd.

María was too weak to argue. She stumbled and nearly fell as she was pulled toward the hallway door.

"Bring him as well," the captain commanded, pointing to Juan.

Two of the guards came forward and grabbed Juan under the armpits. The Ramirez *familia* member grimaced with pain as they hoisted him to his feet and dragged him forward.

Behind them, the major general returned quietly to the throne room. He shut the door.

The click of the latch was the only sound in the otherwise silent hall. To María it was a noise as loud as the closing of a tomb door. It not only marked the end of her efforts to get inside the throne room, very possibly it marked the end of Spain itself. She was angry at herself for having blown the mission. For having gotten so damn close and screwing up.

The captain turned María around. Still holding her by the hair, he walked her toward the door. She went painfully, each step sending a lance of pain up her left side from heel to jaw.

"What—what are you going to do?" María demanded.

"We're going to take you outside to see what you know."

"Why outside?" María asked.

The captain didn't answer, and that in itself was an answer. They were being taken outside because that was where the plain, unadorned walls were.

The walls which condemned prisoners were put against to be shot.

THIRTY-FOUR

Tuesday, 10:46 A.M.
Madrid, Spain

As soon as he heard gunshots inside the palace, Colonel August casually removed his cellular phone from his deep pants pocket. He punched in Luis's office number but kept his face turned toward the warm sun as it crept over the buildings—soaking it up like any young vacationer. Behind him, except for Private Pupshaw, the other Strikers were pretending to study a tour book. Pupshaw was down the street, tying his shoe on the fender of a car. One of the aglets at the end of his shoelace contained a highly compressed irritant agent, primarily Chloroacetophenone—a mild but smoky form of tear gas. The other aglet contained a tiny heating coil that was activated when removed from the shoelace. It would cause the gas to be released two minutes after being placed inside the other aglet.

"This is Slugger," August said. "We've just heard from three of the players in the stadium." That meant he'd heard three shots in the palace. "Sound like they're pretty close to the spot where we want to go."

"Could be our teammate warming things up," Luis said. The line was quiet for a moment. Then Luis came back on. "Coach says to go to second base and put on your uniforms. He'll call the upper deck to see what they know."

Second base was the dungeon directly below the Hall of Tapestries. The upper deck was the spotters.

"Excellent," August said. "We're on our way." He turned the phone from ring to vibrate and returned it to his pocket. He told the other Strikers to follow him and then he raised his arm for Pupshaw to see. August crossed his second and third fingers.

The young private extended two crossed fingers and waved back. The two crossed fingers meant to put the aglets together.

August led his team quickly toward the sewer on the northwest corner of the Plaza de Oriente. They had videotaped the manhole cover when they'd first arrived and studied the playback as they stood around. Corporal Prementine and Privates David George and Jason Scott had their Walkman headsets in hand, ready to slide into the holes in the cover and lift it up. The headsets were actually made of titanium and would be able to handle the weight of the iron lid.

August put his arm around Sondra DeVonne as though she were his traveling companion. The two laughed as they walked. But when August looked at her he was actually looking past her at the traffic. It was virtually nonexistent due to all the military activity in the area. When Sondra looked at August she was keeping an eye on pedestrians. Like the streets, the sidewalks were relatively deserted.

They reached the corner and waited. Pupshaw had run over and caught up to them. No sooner had he

arrived than the middle of the street erupted into a
bright billowing cloud of orange smoke.

The wind blew the smoke toward them, which was
why they had selected that site. Before it arrived,
George, Scott, and Prementine had walked into the
middle of the street. They stopped and knelt and
pointed toward the smoke with their right hands. As
they did, they lowered one end of the headphones into
the manhole cover holes. A few seconds before the
smoke reached them, they hoisted it up and moved it
aside. Sondra whipped a palm-sized flashlight from the
pocket of her windbreaker and shined it down. The
light was not only for illumination: once the operation
was underway, hand signals and on/off signals from
flashlights would be their normal form of communication.

As the Interpol street plans had indicated, there was
a ladder just inside. She went down quickly, followed
by August, Aideen, and Ishi Honda. The other four
men went down next, the burly Pupshaw waiting on
the ladder to pull the lid back over the hole.

The entire operation took less than fifteen seconds.

The sewer was approximately ten feet tall and it was
easy to walk through it. The system was flushed at
noon and one A.M., and refuse was slightly more than
knee-deep. But the relief of being inside and on the
way compensated for the discomfort of the viscous
liquid and its stench. They followed Sondra's flashlight to the west and the catacombs.

As they walked, August put in his EAR plug—Extended Audio Range. This device looked like a hearing
aid and allowed secure audio reception within a two

hundred mile range. A Q-tip–shaped microphone taped to his chest allowed him to communicate with Interpol headquarters.

The sewer turned to the north at a brick wall that stood almost shoulder-high. There was a nearly three-foot gap at the top—the entrance to the catacombs. DeVonne handed the flashlight to Private George while Private Scott boosted her up and over. It had been agreed ahead of time that she would handle point for the mission. August was next in line followed by Aideen, with Corporal Prementine bringing up the rear. Private DeVonne was still suffering from occasional emotional slumps over Lt. Col. Squires's death. That had occurred during her first mission with Striker. However, August was pleased to see that she'd been completely focused since they'd reached Madrid. And she was even more so down here—moving like a cat, quiet and alert. Since they'd entered the sewer, not a rat had passed that she'd failed to notice.

After the seven Strikers and Aideen had gone over the brick wall, they pressed on following a map Luis had had printed out. It wasn't as easy moving in here. The roof was only five feet high here, and the rubble and dirt crunched loudly under their feet. Their clothes were clammy at first, then thick and hard as they dried in the cool, extremely musty air.

Suddenly, August stopped.

''Incoming message,'' he whispered to the others.

The Strikers formed a tight circle around him. Sondra reminded in front and Corporal Prementine stayed behind. The other Strikers and Aideen had gathered close in on either side. Their proximity would enable Colonel August to speak quietly if there were new orders.

"Are you in?" Luis asked.

"We're about fifty feet into the catacombs," August replied. Since the audio line was secure, scrambled on both ends, there was no chance of it being intercepted and no reason to speak in code. "We should reach the dungeon in about three minutes."

"You'll probably get the go-ahead then," Luis informed him. "We've just heard from the spotters."

"What's happening?" August asked.

"María Cornejas has been taken outside, into the courtyard," he said. "It looks like she's bleeding."

"Those shots we heard—?"

"Very possibly," Luis agreed. "The problem is, it doesn't look like those will be the last ones."

"What do you mean?"

"It looks as if one of the officers is selecting men for a firing squad," Luis told him.

"Where?" August asked.

"Outside the chapel," he said.

August snapped his fingers at Sondra and pointed to the map. She immediately brought it closer and turned the flashlight on it. He indicated for her to turn it over to the blueprint of the palace.

"I'm looking at the map now," August said. "What's the most direct route to the—"

"Negative," Luis replied.

"Sir?"

"This update is *not* to be acted upon. We wanted you to know what was going on in case you hear the volley. Darrell has already consulted with General Rodgers and Director Hood at Op-Center and they concur that your target must remain Amadori. If he's beginning to execute prisoners, it's vital that he be contained as soon as possible.''

"I understand," August said, and he did. The mission objective was crucial. But the colonel felt the same nauseating kick in the gut he'd experienced in 1970 when his battle-weary company engaged a vastly superior North Vietnamese force outside of Hau Bon on the Song Ba River in Vietnam. August needed to cover the company's retreat and selected two men to stay behind with a pair of standoff rifles and hold the road as long as possible. He knew he would probably never see those two soldiers again, but the life of the company depended upon them. He also knew he would never forget the crooked half-smile one of the men gave him as he looked back at the company. It was a boy's smile—a boy who was struggling very hard to be a man.

"As soon as you're in position under the Hall of Tapestries," Luis said, "Darrell wants you to get into gear. He expects to give you the go command within the next ten to fifteen minutes."

"We'll be ready," August replied.

He briefed the team succinctly and then ordered them forward. There was no extraneous conversation. The Strikers reached their target in just over two minutes, after which Colonel August ordered them to remove their outer clothes. Beneath their damp jeans and jackets were kevlar-lined black jumpsuits. Reaching into their grips, the Strikers traded their Nikes and sandals for black ''grippers,'' high-top sneakers with deeply ridged hard-rubber soles. The customized soles were designed to keep the wearer from slipping on slick surfaces and to enable them to stop suddenly and with precision. They were backed with kevlar to help prevent anyone from shooting up through a floor to bring the soldiers down.

The Strikers also strapped black leather sheaths around their thighs; the sheaths contained eight-inch-long serrated knives. A loop around the other thigh contained a pencil-thin flashlight. They tucked Uzis under their arms and pulled black ski masks over their heads. When they were ready, August moved them from the catacombs to the dungeon. Six of the Strikers went ahead two at a time, the middle group of two leapfrogging over the first pair and the last pair moving up to take their place. Aideen was teamed with Ishi Honda. This allowed the two stationary pairs to cover the front and rear, respectively. They reached the dungeon in slightly over three minutes. It looked exactly like it had in the photographs they'd seen back at Interpol.

The one exit from the dungeon was an old wooden door at the top of the long and very narrow staircase. The only light came from Sondra's flashlight and from the imperfect fit of the door. August motioned for Privates Pupshaw and George to check the door. August was prepared to blow it if they had to, though he'd prefer to enter with a little less thunder.

After a minute, Pupshaw came running back. ''The hinges are rusted all to hell,'' he whispered into August's ear, ''and the MD's giving me a reading of some kind of lock on the handle on the outside.''

The MD was the metal detector. Slightly larger than a fountain pen, the MD was primarily used to find and define landmines. However, it could also ''see'' through wood.

''I'm afraid we're going to have to go through the door, Colonel,'' Pupshaw said.

August nodded. ''Set it up.''

Pupshaw saluted and ran back upstairs. Prementine joined them. Together, the men rigged a thumbnail-sized amount of C-4 around the handle and around each hinge. They stuck a remote-control detonator, about the size of a needle, into each wad.

As they were working, August received word from Luis. María was being interrogated by an outside wall and a firing squad had been assembled. It was time to move out.

Luis thanked them again and wished them luck. August promised to contact Luis when it was all over. Then he disconnected the microphone and stowed it in his grip. The action must not be broadcast, even to Interpol. The United States could not be connected with what was about to transpire and even an inadvertent recording or misrouting of the signal would be disastrous.

Like the other Strikers, August slipped the grip on his back. It was flat and lined with kevlar; the bulletproof material provided extra cover for the soldiers. Joining the others, August gave Pupshaw the order to proceed. Once the door was opened they'd proceed in serpentine fashion, Sondra still at point, Prementine at the rear. The object was to get to the throne room as

quickly as possible. They were authorized to shoot—
arms and legs if possible, torso if necessary.

The Strikers stood at the foot of the steps and covered their ears as Pupshaw twisted the top of what
looked like an elongated thimble. The three small
charges erupted with a bang like a popped paper bag.
Door planks flew apart in jagged fragments, carried in
all directions by three thick, gray, lumpy clouds.

"Go!" August shouted even before the echo of the
blast had died.

Without hesitation Private Sondra DeVonne bolted
up the stairs, followed in a tight line by the rest.

THIRTY-FIVE

Tuesday, 11:08 A.M.
Madrid, Spain

There is no way in hell that I'll allow this to happen, thought Darrell McCaskey.

McCaskey had one thing in common with Paul Hood. The two men were among the very few Op-Center executive officers who had never served in the military.

No one held that against McCaskey. He'd joined the New York City Police Academy straight out of high school and spent five years in Midtown South. During that time he did whatever was necessary to protect the citizens of the city he served. Sometimes that meant repeat felons would "trip" down the concrete steps of the precinct house when they were being booked. Other times it meant working with "old school" mobsters to help keep the rough new gangs from Vietnam and Armenia out of Times Square.

McCaskey received several commendations for bravery during his tenure and was noticed by an FBI recruiter based in Manhattan. He joined the agency and after spending four years in New York was moved to FBI headquarters in Washington. His specialty was foreign gangs and terrorists. He spent a great deal of time overseas, making friends in foreign law enforcement agencies and contacts in the underbellies of other nations.

He met María Corneja on a trip to Spain and fell in love with her before the week was out. She was smart and independent, attractive and poised, desirable and hungry. After so many years undercover—pretending to be hookers and school teachers and countless flower delivery women—and even more years competing with men on the police force, she welcomed McCaskey's genuine interest in her thoughts and feelings. Through Luis, she arranged to come to the U.S. to study FBI investigative techniques. She had a hotel room in Washington for three days before she moved in with McCaskey.

McCaskey hadn't wanted the relationship to end. God, how he had not. But McCaskey made the rules in the relationship, just as he did in the street. And he tried to enforce them. Like his street rules, they were designed to be beneficial. But whether he was trying to get María to stop smoking or to accept less dangerous assignments, he stifled the character, the recklessness that helped make her so extraordinary. Only when she left him and returned to Spain did he see the things she'd added to his life.

Darrell McCaskey had lost María once. He had no intention of losing her again. There was no way in hell that he was going to sit at Interpol headquarters, safe and comfortable, while General Amadori had her executed.

As soon as he'd finished talking with Paul Hood and Mike Rodgers on the secure line in Luis's office,

McCaskey turned to the Interpol director. Luis was sitting at the radio waiting to hear from Striker. His father was seated beside him. McCaskey informed Luis that he wanted the Interpol chopper.

"For what?" Luis asked. "A rescue attempt?"

"We have to try," McCaskey said as he rose. "Tell me you disagree."

Luis's expression indicated that he didn't—though he didn't appear comfortable with the prospect.

"Give me a pilot and a marksman," McCaskey said. "I take full responsibility."

Luis hesitated.

"Luis, *please*," McCaskey implored. "We owe this to María and there isn't time to debate it."

Luis turned to his father and spoke briefly in Spanish. When he was finished, he buzzed his assistant and gave him an order. Then he turned back to McCaskey.

"My father will be the liaison with Striker," Luis said, "and I told Jaime to have the helicopter ready to go in five minutes. Only you won't need a marksman and you won't take responsibility. Those jobs, my friend, are mine."

McCaskey thanked him. Luis left to oversee the preparations while McCaskey lingered in the room for two minutes. That was how long it took for him to make preparations of his own. Then he ran up the stairwell to the rooftop. Luis met him a minute later.

The small, five-person Bell JetRanger rose into the clear late morning sky from the roof of the ten-story building. The Royal Palace was just under two minutes away. The pilot, Pedro, was ordered to fly directly to it. He was patched in to the spotters, who told him exactly where María was. The spotters also informed him that it looked as if a five-man firing squad was being marched in her direction. The pilot passed the information on to McCaskey and Luis.

"We're not going to be able to talk them out of this," Luis said.

"I know," McCaskey replied. "And I don't care. The woman has guts. She deserves our best effort."

"That isn't what I mean," Luis said. A small gun rack in the rear held four weapons. Luis eyed them unhappily. "If we shoot only to chase them off, they'll return fire. They could bring us down."

"Not if we do it right," McCaskey said. Off in the distance the high, white engirdling balustrade of the palace, with its statues of Spanish kings, appeared over the surrounding treetops. "We go in as quickly as we can. I don't think they'll shoot at us until we're down. They won't want to bring a chopper down on their heads. When we touch down, you fire to clear the field. The soldiers will run for cover. When they do, I go and get María before they can regroup."

"Just like that," Luis said doubtfully.

"Just like that," McCaskey nodded. "The simplest plans always work best. If you cover me and keep the soldiers ducking, I should be able to get in and out in about thirty seconds. The courtyard's not that big. If I can't get back to the chopper, you abort and I'll try to get her out some other way." McCaskey sighed and dragged his fingers through his hair. "Look, I know this is dangerous, Luis. But what else can we do? I'd want to do this if any of our people were in trouble. I *have* to do it because it's María.''

Luis took a deep breath, nodded once, then turned to the gun rack. He selected a NATO L96A1 sniper rifle with an integral silencer and a Schmidt & Bender telescope. He handed McCaskey a Star 30M Parabellum pistol, the standard issue of the Guardia Civil.

''I'll have Pedro swing over the palace and then come straight down in the courtyard,'' Luis said. ''As soon as we touch down I'll try to drive the firing squad back. Maybe I can hold them back without having to kill anyone.'' Luis's face fell slightly. ''That's *maybe*, Darrell.''

''I know,'' McCaskey said.

''I don't know if I'll be able to shoot a Spanish soldier, Darrell,'' Luis admitted. ''I honestly don't know.''

''They don't seem to have a problem with that,'' McCaskey pointed out.

''I'm not them,'' Luis replied.

''No, you're not,'' McCaskey said apologetically. ''For what it's worth, I'm not sure I could shoot one of my own people either.''

Luis shook his head. ''How did it ever come to this?''

McCaskey checked the clip and sat back. He thought bitterly, *It came to this the way it always does. Through the fierce hate harbored by a few and the complacency displayed by the rest.* There were signs of that in the United States. McCaskey knew that if Striker succeeded the real work was just beginning— here and elsewhere. People like General Amadori had to be stopped before they got this far. McCaskey wasn't as versed in aphorisms as Mike Rodgers, but he did remember hearing someone say once that all it took for evil to flourish was for men of conscience to do nothing. If he survived this, Darrell McCaskey vowed that he would not be one of those who did nothing.

They would be passing over the northeastern corner of the palace in approximately fifteen seconds. There were no military helicopters in the immediate area though trucks and jeeps were coming and going along Calle de Bailén just below them.

McCaskey was calm now after his initial urgency. Part of that was because he hadn't slept in over a day. Sitting still allowed a relaxing torpor to wash over him. Though his mind was sharp and his purpose true, the anxious finger-drumming, foot-tapping and cheek-biting that were a part of his impatient nature were missing. Part of his composure was also due to María. Relationships can be problematic and mistakes will be made and hindsight is frustrating. McCaskey didn't punish himself for being human. But it was rare and comforting to have an opportunity like this to set a wrong right. To tell someone you're sorry and to show them you care. Whatever it cost, whatever it took, McCaskey was determined to get María out of the courtyard alive.

While McCaskey sat looking out his window, Luis leaned forward and spoke to Pedro. The pilot nodded, Luis squeezed his shoulder appreciatively, and then sat back.

"Are you ready?" Luis asked McCaskey.

McCaskey nodded once.

The helicopter descended and flew low over the eastern wall of the palace. Then it banked to the south and sped toward the courtyard between the Royal Palace and the Cathedral of the Almudena.

There was a megaphone built into both sides of the chopper. Luis slipped on the headset, adjusted the mouthpiece, then lay the rifle across his lap. He looked outside and tapped McCaskey on the leg.

"There!" Luis said.

McCaskey looked over. He saw María being held against a fifteen-foot-tall pedestal, which was supporting four massive columns. The square, grayish pedestal projected about five feet out from the long, unbroken wall to the left. To the right was a short expanse of wall and then a series of arches that swept away from the wall at a right angle. The low, darkly shadowed arches formed the eastern boundary of the courtyard. Beyond them was the eastern wing of the palace which contained the royal bedchamber, the study, and the music room.

There were two soldiers on either side of María, clasping her arms. An officer was standing in front of her. About one hundred fifty feet to the south, a line of military vehicles separated the courtyard from the church. There were no civilians in the courtyard and roughly sixty or seventy soldiers. Six of them were walking toward María in a line.

"We'll land with those arches on your side," Luis said. "They may provide you with cover."

"Right!"

"I'm going to try and focus on the officer in front

of María," Luis said. "If I can control him, maybe I can control the group."

"Good idea," McCaskey said. He held the Parabellum in his right hand, pointing upward. He put his left hand on the door handle. Pedro slowed the chopper's forward motion and they began to descend. They were less than one hundred feet above the courtyard.

The soldiers were looking up now, including the officer in front of María. He wasn't moving; no one was. As McCaskey had suspected, they weren't going to shoot at a chopper bearing directly down on them. When they landed, though, he suspected it would be a much different matter. He looked over at María. Because there was an iron streetlamp between them and the pedestal, the chopper wouldn't be able to get as close as McCaskey would have liked. He'd have to cross about thirty feet of open courtyard to get to María. At least it didn't look like she was tied up though it did appear as though she might be hurt. There was blood on her left side and she was leaning in that direction. She wasn't looking up at the helicopter.

The Spanish army officer—he was a captain, McCaskey could tell now—was swinging an arm at them to take off again. As they continued to descend, he unholstered his pistol and motioned more wildly for them to leave.

The soldiers of the firing squad were on Luis's side. They stopped their approach as the chopper set down. The captain was on McCaskey's side. McCaskey watched him closely as he stalked toward them. He was shouting but his words were swallowed by the din of the rotor. Behind him, the two soldiers were still holding María.

"I'm going to open the door," McCaskey said to Luis when the captain was about fifteen feet away.

"I'm with you," Luis said. "Pedro—be ready to lift off again at my command."

Pedro acknowledged the order. McCaskey put his hand on the latch, pulled, and threw open the door.

McCaskey got exactly what he was expecting. As soon as he placed one foot on the ground the captain lowered his gun without hesitation and fired at the helicopter. The bullet struck the rear of the cabin, just aft of the fuel tank. If it was a warning shot, it was a dangerous one.

McCaskey didn't have the same reservations as Luis. McCaskey knew that if he shot the captain he would make Luis an accomplice. But they had to defend themselves.

With the cool of a seasoned G-man putting in time at the shooting range, McCaskey swung his Parabellum around, leveled it at the captain's left leg, and fired two rounds. The leg folded inward, blood spitting from two wounds just above the knee. Ducking low, McCaskey jumped from the cabin and ran forward. Behind him, he heard the distinctive *phut, phut* of the silenced sniper rifle. He didn't hear any return fire and imagined that the soldiers of the firing squad, as well as the other soldiers in the rear of the courtyard, were doing just as Luis had predicted. They were scattering for cover.

The soldiers holding María released her and ran toward the nearest arch. She dropped to her knees and then onto her hands.

"Stay down!" McCaskey yelled as she tried to rise.

She looked at him defiantly as she turned a shoulder toward the pedestal. Leaning against it, she got her legs beneath her and stood slowly.

Of course she did, he thought. Not because he told her she shouldn't but because she was María.

The gun had fallen from the captain's hand. He was attempting to get it back as McCaskey raced past him. He snatched it up and continued ahead. The officer's cries of rage and pain were quickly drowned by Luis's voice coming over the megaphone.

"*Evacúen la área,*" Luis warned them. "*Más helicópteros están de tránsito!*"

McCaskey had had four years of Spanish in high school but he got the gist of what Luis was saying. He was telling the soldiers to get out, that more helicopters were on the way. It was an inspired maneuver that could buy them the little extra time they needed. McCaskey didn't doubt that the soldiers would resist. If they were ready to execute Spanish prisoners, they wouldn't hesitate to attack Interpol operatives. But at least they wouldn't charge recklessly back into the courtyard.

Occasional bursts of fire were met by Luis's rifle fire. McCaskey didn't look back but he hoped the chopper wasn't damaged.

As he came closer to María, he saw that her side was thick with blood and that her face was bloody as well. The bastards had beaten her. Reaching her side, he ducked a shoulder under her arm.

"Can you make it back with me?" he asked. He took a moment to look at her. Her left eye was bloody and swollen shut. There were deep cuts on both cheeks and along the hairline. He felt like shooting the bastard captain.

"We can't go," she said.

"We can," he insisted. "A team's inside hunting for—"

She shook her head. "There's another prisoner in there." She pointed toward a doorway some thirty feet away. "Juan. They'll kill him. I won't leave without him."

That too was María, McCaskey thought.

McCaskey looked back at the chopper. Flashes of fire were increasing as soldiers got inside the palace and took up positions by the windows. Luis was able to drive them back but he wouldn't be able to hold them for long.

McCaskey picked María up. "Let me take you to the chopper," he said. "Then I'll go back and get—"

Suddenly, there was a loud report from somewhere directly above them. It was followed by a gurgled cry from the chopper megaphone. A moment later Luis stumbled from the open door on McCaskey's side. He was holding the rifle in one hand and clutching a wound in his neck with the other. McCaskey looked up. A sharpshooter on top of the arches had managed to get a clear shot through the open door of the helicopter. McCaskey was furious with himself for having anticipated only groundfire. He should have had the goddamn chopper drop him off and then get the hell out of there.

Luis walked forward haltingly. The rifle clattered from his hand and he left it where it fell. His goal was obviously the captain, who was writhing painfully. Luis took two steps more and then fell across him. No one risked shooting at him now.

Pedro looked desperately toward McCaskey, who waved him off. There was nothing else the pilot could do. A couple of bullets *pinged* off the rotor as the helicopter rose, but it wasn't severely damaged. The chopper headed away from the palace, toward the cathedral, and was quickly out of range.

They, unfortunately, were not.

THIRTY-SIX

Tuesday, 11:11 A.M.
Madrid, Spain

To reach the throne room from the Hall of Tapestries, it was necessary to exit the long but narrow hall, go around the grand staircase, then pass through the Hall of the Halberdiers. Altogether it was a journey of slightly more than two hundred feet. The Strikers would have to cover the distance quickly, lest the noise of the explosion send General Amadori into hiding.

For the seven soldiers and Aideen, however, it was also a foray against more than two hundred years of American tradition. Although the United States had clandestinely assisted or encouraged assassination attempts against the likes of Fidel Castro and Saddam Hussein, only once in its history had the military targeted a foreign leader for assassination. That was on April 15, 1986, when U.S. warplanes took off from England to bomb the headquarters of Libyan despot Muammar al-Qaddafi. The attack was in retaliation for the terrorist bombing of a West Berlin discotheque frequented by American soldiers. Qaddafi survived that assault and the U.S. lost an F-111 and two airmen. Three hostages were murdered in Lebanon in reprisal for the American air raid.

Col. Brett August was aware of the lonely significance of the mission they were undertaking. In Vietnam, the base "padre," Father Uxbridge, had a word for it. The priest tried to keep the mood light by giving all his sermon themes a military-style acronym. He called ethical ambiguities like these M.I.S.T.: Moral Issues Sliced Thick. That meant there was so much to chew on that you could think about it forever and never do anything because you could never reach a satisfactory intellectual resolution. The priest's advice was to do what felt right. August hated bullies—especially bullies who imprisoned and killed those who disagreed with him. This felt right. The irony was that if they succeeded, credit for the deed would go to Spanish patriots loyal to the king, whose identities must be kept secret for security reasons. If they failed, they would be described as rogue operatives who had been hired by the Ramirez clan to avenge his death.

When the dungeon door blew open, the Strikers found themselves behind what was left of a three hundred year old arras. The bottom of the tapestry had been torn off in the explosion and the top was still fluttering as they rushed through. The Strikers' orders were to disable opponents wherever possible and they were ready for the first wave of soldiers that came to investigate the blast. The Strikers' ski masks contained goggles and mouth filters which would protect them from the Orthochlorobenzylidene malononitrile grenades Privates DeVonne and Scott were carrying. The fast-acting agent caused burning eyes and retching. In an enclosed area like the palace rooms, the gas would disable an opponent for up to five minutes. Most people couldn't stand the effects for more than a minute or two and attempted to get to fresh air as quickly as possible. During the leapfrog approach, DeVonne and then Scott would take alternate tosses as necessary.

The first group of Spanish soldiers was swallowed in a huge yellow-and-black cottonball of gas. They dropped where they stood, some in the doorway and a few just inside the room. Anticipating that the Spaniards wouldn't fire blindly into the thick cloud, the Strikers moved boldly through the doorway and proceeded along the southside wall. The door to the Hall of the Halberdiers was straight ahead, on the same side.

Soldiers were rushing toward them, guns raised. Scott's partner, Private Pupshaw, crouched and fired ahead knee high. Two soldiers fell and the rest went racing to doorways for cover. While they scattered, Scott rolled a grenade down the hall. There was a three second delay and then the hallway filled with smoke. August and Private Honda leapfrogged ahead, followed by Private DeVonne and Corporal Prementine.

The Strikers were halfway to the Hall of the Halberdiers when August heard shouts inside along with gunfire. As soon as August and Honda were back in front of the team, the colonel held up a hand to halt their progress. He didn't know how many people were inside the chamber or why there was shooting, but Striker was going to have to neutralize the entire room before they entered. He raised three fingers, then two—indicating attack plan thirty-two—then pointed at Privates DeVonne and Scott with the other hand. He motioned them ahead, Scott to the near side of the door,

DeVonne to the far side. As soon as they were in position, both rolled grenades into the Hall of the Halberdiers.

When he was helping to train NATO troops in Italy, August had described the effect of the OM gas as very much like pouring boiling water in an anthill. The targets went down where they stood and just squirmed. Here, as Striker moved from room to hall to room, the impression of moving through an anthill was especially strong.

August pointed back to Prementine and Pupshaw, who rejoined their partners on either side of the door. They heard coughing and vomiting inside. When no one came out, August and Honda went in. The two Strikers squatted low on either side of the door, weapons ready, and surveyed the room.

August wasn't quite prepared for the sight that greeted him: hundreds of bodies, mostly civilians and a few soldiers, writhing on the floor of the Hall of the Halberdiers. August knew that they wouldn't die. But his mind flashed to images of the Holocaust, to gas chambers from the Second World War, and he had a flash of guilt—one of Father Uxbridge's moral paradoxes.

He forced it aside. He had to. Once a tactical strike force set out, no member could afford to waver. The lives of the soldiers didn't depend upon a shared ideology. They did depend upon a shared commitment.

August motioned for Honda to go right around the mass of bodies. Still squatting, August went left. Both men stayed close to the wall. There were bullet knicks in the marble near the door. The soldiers had obviously fired in that direction when the grenades rolled in. Though they were in no condition to fire now, August watched them as carefully as he could through the yellow haze. There was always the possibility that someone might rally enough to fire off a few rounds. But no one did. When he reached the throne room door, Colonel August withdrew the flashlight from the loop around his thigh. He flicked it on and off twice to indicate that the next group should proceed. Private DeVonne, Aideen, and Corporal Prementine came in, moving low along the wall as August and Honda had done. Privates Pupshaw and Scott followed them in.

The other Strikers and Aideen entered the Hall of the Halberdiers. As they did, August kept the gagging soldiers covered while Private Honda attached a thumbnail-sized lump of plastique to the base of the doorknob. He inserted a fuse, which heated by turning the cap. Five seconds later the plastique would detonate. The door would open and Scott would roll in another gas grenade. According to the map, this door was the only exit from the throne room. Once the people inside were disabled, the Strikers would move against Amadori.

When everyone was in position, Honda activated the fuse. It glowed red and then the plastique blew outward in a narrow line parallel to the floor. The door flew open and Private Scott rolled in a grenade. There were shouts and gunfire aimed at the door and then the gas exploded with a bang and a loud *whoosh*. Then the gunfire stopped and the choking began. When he heard them, August motioned for Private DeVonne and Corporal Prementine to move in.

Still on point, DeVonne took the first shot in the chest. She stumbled when she was hit and fell backward, landing against Prementine. The corporal backed out, pulling her with him, and the Strikers fell back several paces. August knew that the kevlar lining would have kept the bullet from penetrating Sondra's chest, though she'd probably suffered a broken rib or two. She was moaning from the pain.

August motioned to Scott to roll in a second grenade. Then he crawled forward to DeVonne and pulled a grenade from her pouch. The gas was dissipating in the Hall of the Halberdiers and he threw one toward the mass of people. He had only two or three minutes to make a decision about whether to continue with the mission or to abort.

August crept toward the doorway. Someone had been waiting for them inside. Someone who was coherent enough to aim and fire a single shot at the first person in the door. He thought quickly. The security cameras wouldn't have given Amadori enough time to get out, but it might have told him how large the attacking force was. And given him time to put on a gas mask, if he had one. And he might.

He also might have sent for reinforcements. They couldn't afford to wait him out. August motioned to Pupshaw and Scott. The three of them went to either side of the door, August on the left, Pupshaw and Scott on the right. August held up four fingers then one. Plan forty-one was target-specific crossfire, with the third gunman covering the other two. August pointed to himself and Pupshaw, meaning that they'd take out Amadori. The entrance would be made using the Marine tactic of one soldier using a single somersault to get inside, then stretching out into a tight pencil-roll—the arms flat across the chest, holding the firearm, and the feet facing toward the target. The first soldier's entrance was designed to draw the fire to one side so the second soldier could enter. When the two men were in, they'd sit up—legs still extended—and fire ahead. Meanwhile, the soldier responsible for setting up the cover fire would remain outside the room. He'd pencil-roll in front of the doorway, remaining on the outside and facing the target. He'd stop on his belly with his weapon pointed ahead.

August pointed to himself. He'd go in to the left, followed by Pupshaw. By the time Scott rolled into view, the other two Strikers would have the target in their sights.

August doffed his backpack and sidled to the door. Pupshaw and Scott did the same on the right. August looked at Pupshaw and nodded. The colonel somersaulted in and cut to the left pencil-roll. There was gunfire, but it trailed him as he turned quickly to the left. Pupshaw went in and was in position before the gun could be turned toward him. Both men had their sights on the target as Scott rolled into position.

August's right hand shot up, the fingers splayed. That was the sign for the Strikers not to fire.

Neither of the other Strikers fired. August stared over his gunsight at a priest, gagging terribly. There was an automatic weapon jutting from under his right armpit, pointing toward the door. Behind him was a general wearing a gas filter and goggles. From his size and hair coloring, August knew that it was Amadori.

The general's left hand was around the priest's throat. Behind the general was another officer—a major general, August determined through the yellow haze. There were six other officers in the room, all of them high-ranking, all of them sprawled on the floor or leaning across a conference table in the center.

The general motioned up and down with the gun. He was telling the Strikers to stand. August shook his head. If Amadori fired, he might get one of them. But he wouldn't get all of them. And if the general shot the priest, then he had to know that he himself was dead.

It was a standoff. But the one running out of time now was Amadori. He had no way of knowing whether Striker was a SAT—a stand-alone team—or the first wave of a larger force. If it was the latter, then Amadori couldn't afford to be trapped here.

The general obviously made up his mind quickly, as August had expected him to. Amadori began walking the priest forward slowly. The older clergyman was having difficulty standing. But pressure from Amadori's fingers around his throat brought him upright each time he threatened to stumble. The major general walked with them, tight against Amadori's back. As they approached, August could see that the major general had a handgun. He suspected that the only reason these men hadn't fired was because they didn't know who or what was waiting for them outside the throne room.

August watched as the three men came forward. There was no doubt that the Strikers could take Amadori. The question was the pricetag for both sides. In situations like these, the decision was up to the commanding officer. For August, the question was the same as it was in chess: whether an exchange of high ranked pieces was worth it. For him, the answer had always been no. Depending upon who was sharper and better prepared, it was better to keep the game going and wait for the other player to make a mistake.

August held out his right hand, palm down. That meant to do nothing unless provoked. Outside the door, Scott passed the signal to the other Strikers. Scott wriggled back as Amadori approached. He didn't take his gun off him. As he stepped through the doorway into the Hall of the Halberdiers, the other Strikers also took aim at the general. The exception was Corporal Prementine, who was helping Private DeVonne.

The gas in the throne room was beginning to wear off. At August's signal, Scott threw another grenade to cover their retreat. They rose and exited after the general. Scott walked with his back pressed to August's back. The private was facing into the throne room, watching to make sure that none of the choking soldiers attempted to get off a shot. None did.

August couldn't afford to feel frustrated as Amadori walked toward the corridor. The general had had a gas filter with him: that was a reasonable precaution. The President of the United States had one in the Oval Office. They were kept in most rooms at 10 Downing Street. Boris Yeltsin had one in his desk and one in each of his cars. The surprise was that Amadori had had a hostage. The killing or even wounding of a hostage was always unfortunate; the killing or wounding of a Roman Catholic priest in Spain would be a disaster.

August considered the situation carefully. If they let Amadori out into the open, the general's army would be better able to protect him. And if he got away, this attack could make him a hero in the eyes of his people. But that wasn't the biggest problem. August had no idea if and when reinforcements might arrive. And if they did show up, they might also be equipped with gas masks.

My chess game be damned, August decided. He was going to have to go for the king. He couldn't get his head or torso, but he had a clear shot at his legs and could bring him to the ground. Even if the general or the major general turned on him, that would give the other Strikers a chance to take them out.

He raised his index finger once and then again. Number one was going after number one.

August and Scott were still standing back-to-back. August half-turned and whispered to the private as they walked toward the hallway.

"When I move, dive to your left."

Scott nodded.

An instant later, August fired.

THIRTY-SEVEN

Tuesday, 11:19 A.M.
Madrid, Spain

Father Norberto had heard the unmistakable sound of the helicopter flying low over the palace courtyard. It was followed soon after by the equally unmistakable crack of gunfire. He listened with one ear as he continued reading from Matthew 26 to the small group of people seated around him. It wasn't until one of the parishioners went out to check, then came running back, that the congregation learned that something dire was going on.

"There is gunfire outside," the man shouted into the church. "Soldiers are shooting at people in the courtyard."

The church was silent for a long moment after that. Then Father Francisco rose from the group he was counseling in the front of the nave. He raised his arms as though offering a blessing.

"Please remain calm," Francisco said, smiling. "No harm will come to the church."

"What about the General Superior?" someone shouted. "Is he safe?"

"The General Superior is at the palace," Francisco replied calmly, "hoping to secure a role for the mother church in the new Spain. I'm sure that God is looking out for him.''

Father Norberto found something very unnerving about Francisco's composure. Faith in God alone would not inspire such confidence. The feeling that Norberto had had earlier, that General Superior González was involved in the upheaval—that might be enough to give Francisco comfort. Especially if he had foreknowledge that there would be gunfire. But for what? There was only one thing Norberto could think of.

Executions.

The man ran back outside. The priests resumed counseling the people who sat before them, leading them in prayer or offering words of comfort. A few minutes later the man came back.

"There is yellow smoke coming from windows of the palace,'' the man yelled. ''And gunfire inside!''

This time, Father Francisco was not so composed. He left without a word, walking hurriedly toward the door behind the ambulatory, which opened into the courtyard of the Royal Palace.

Father Norberto watched him go. The silence of the church was even deeper now. Around them he could hear the crack of guns. Norberto looked down at the text then back toward the anxious faces before him. They needed him. But then he thought of Adolfo and of his dying need for absolution. Beyond these walls were times of trial and acts of sin. His place was with those who required the sacrament of penance, not comfort.

Norberto put his hand on the shoulder of a young

woman who had come in with her two little girls. He smiled at the mother and asked if, for a while, she would not mind reading in his place. He said that he wanted to see if Father Francisco required any assistance.

Walking quickly down the aisle, Father Norberto made his way to the ambulatory and out the large door into the courtyard.

THIRTY-EIGHT

Tuesday, 11:23 A.M.
Madrid, Spain

Colonel August had leaned to his left in order to get a clear shot at Amadori's leg. All he managed to get was the top of the general's foot, but it was enough. Amadori howled through his gas mask and fell against the major general. As he did, the general's gun discharged. The automatic was still poking out from under the priest's arm and it pumped several shots in August's direction. They traced a straight vertical line as the general stumbled back. But the colonel had already jumped to the left while Scott dove to the right. Screaming and covering his ears, the priest had fallen to his knees and remained there with his face between his legs. The bullets pinged off the marble wall but no one was hit.

The two Strikers hit the ground in perfect diving roll-outs, one shoulder connecting with the floor with the head tucked into the chest. The rest of the body followed in a somersault and the men ended up standing, facing in the direction of the dive. They turned quickly toward their targets as the other Strikers fanned into the hallway, making sure that the other soldiers were still on the ground. Private DeVonne emerged on her own, though she was stooped over and in obvious pain from the shot she'd taken.

During the time it had taken August and Scott to roll out, the major general had grabbed Amadori around the chest with one arm. Pulling hard, he helped the general stay on his feet. The two men retreated. As they did, they set up a spray of automatic fire that sent the Strikers dropping to the ground and rolling in all directions for cover. There were screams all around them as several of the Spanish soldiers were struck.

Throughout the exchange, Aideen had remained just inside the Hall of the Halberdiers. She didn't stay there because she was afraid. She stayed there because she didn't want to get in the way of the Striker game plan. She also wanted to be free to assist any of the Strikers who might go down. She'd tried to help Sondra into the hallway but the private had insisted that she was all right. For the moment, she probably was. Aideen knew from experience that at least there was one benefit to constant pain, like a broken rib or a nonlethal bullet wound. The mind had the ability to block that pain out, even when it was severe. It was the jab of recurring or steadily increasing pain that was difficult to deal with.

Now, standing beside the jamb, Aideen suddenly had another mission. The wounded Amadori had disappeared around the turn in the corridor to the east. At that moment she was the only team member who was still on her feet. From the western end of the corridor, straight ahead, she heard the distinctive stomp of boots. The smoke was still too thick for her to see that far, but she knew that reinforcements were on the way. The Strikers would have to release more grenades to deal with them. If the soldiers had been alerted by security cameras or by a call from the throne room, they might very well be wearing gas masks. If that were the case, the Strikers would have their hands full just getting out of there. And Colonel August would abort if he felt that the mission had been too severely compromised. In the meantime Amadori might get away.

Someone had to stay with the general, Remote Surveillance System or not. If Aideen kept her distance, Amadori might not spot her. Chances were he'd be watching the cameras ahead of him, not behind him. And keeping her distance until she had a clear shot at the general was doable. There was blood on the floor from the bullet wound in Amadori's leg. It would provide a trail she could follow easily. And if he stopped to bandage it, that was fine too. Perhaps Aideen would be able to get to him then.

Aideen looked back. The Spanish soldiers were wearing gas masks. August motioned his team back while he and Scott fired and drove the onrushing soldiers running for cover.

Aideen swore. Colonel August was going to call the mission off. But she wasn't a Striker. She didn't have to abort anything. This whole thing started when someone was encouraged to shoot at her and Martha Mackall. That seemed a fitting way to end it.

Aideen took a deep breath to still her trembling legs. The air tasted like charcoal through the mask, but she was getting used to that. Rolling off the jamb, she ran into the smoke-filled hallway, and followed the corridor to the east.

THIRTY-NINE

Tuesday, 5:27 A.M.
Washington, D.C.

Sitting back in his wheelchair, Bob Herbert reflected on the fact that there was nothing quite like this feeling. Waiting in Paul Hood's office with Hood, Mike Rodgers, and Op-Center's international legal expert, Lowell Coffey II, Herbert contemplated the mood that settles onto a room in which officials are waiting for news of a covert operation.

They're very much aware of the world going on around them, as usual. And they're envious of the people in that world, where the problems don't usually involve life and death and the fate of millions. They're also slightly condescending toward those people.

If they only knew what real responsibility was. . . .

Then there's the personal side of the situation. There's extreme tension over the fate of people everyone works with and cares about. It's not unlike waiting for a loved one to come out of life-threatening surgery. But it *is* worse in one key way. This is something *you* ordered them to do. And being good soldiers, they accepted the assignment with courage and poise.

Add to that the possibility that those heroic souls might have to be disavowed if captured, left to twist in the wind. That was good for a healthy helping of guilt. And there was more guilt over the fact that while their butts were on the firing line, yours was safe and secure. There was also envy—ironically for the same reason. There's no high quite like risking your life. Throw exhaustion into the mix, with eyes that fight to shut and minds too tired to process thoughts or emotions, and the mood was unlike any other.

Yet Herbert cherished that mood every time it came around. He cherished it without gloom and without pessimism. Occasionally their worst fears were realized. Occasionally there was death. A Bass Moore like in North Korea or a Lt. Col. Charlie Squires. But because of everything that was at risk in operations like these, Herbert never felt more alive.

Hood obviously didn't share his feelings. He had been extremely down since before the operation began, something Herbert had never seen before. Of all of them, Hood was usually the most even-keeled, always ready with an encouraging word or smile. This morning there was none of that. He had also become uncharacteristically angry when he learned that Darrell McCaskey had choppered over to the palace. And even worse, that McCaskey had taken Luis García de la Vega with him. Unlike Striker, McCaskey could easily be traced to Op-Center. Through Luis, Op-Center's involvement with Interpol on this mission could be ascertained. With all of the nations connected to Interpol—a few of which were not exactly America's best friends—the political mess could be horrendous. It was Hood, not By-the-Book Rodgers, who had thought out loud about disciplinary action against

McCaskey. It was the usually skittish Coffey who had pointed out that it might not be as bad as Hood thought. Since María Corneja was a prisoner at the palace, a rescue attempt might be entirely justified under Interpol's charter. Hood calmed down upon hearing that. The mood in the room returned to being merely apprehensive.

And through it all, through the heavy silence and gnawing concern, there wasn't a word from Spain or Interpol. Not until 4:30, when they got a call from a groggy Ann Farris at home. She told them to turn on the television and have a look at CNN.

Coffey hopped from the sofa and walked to the back of the room. While he opened the TV cabinet in the back of the office, Hood pulled the remote control from his desk. As everyone turned around, he punched the television on. At the top of the news on the half-hour was a report on a shootout at the Royal Palace in Madrid. An amateur videotape had captured the Interpol helicopter leaving the courtyard south of the palace while gunfire was heard in the distance. Then the report cut live to a camera crew on the scene in a helicopter. There were faint traces of yellow smoke rising from several windows.

"That's Striker's IA," Herbert said, referring to the irritant agent.

Rodgers was sitting in the armchair next to Hood's desk. He reached for the small color map that had been downloaded from the Interpol computer. Herbert rolled his chair over.

"That smoke on TV looks awfully close to the courtyard, doesn't it?" Rodgers asked.

"Right where the throne room should be," Herbert said.

"So the Strikers are definitely in there," Hood said. He looked at the clock on his computer. "And on time."

Herbert turned back to the TV and leaned an ear toward the screen. The onsite announcer had nothing to offer but dire superlatives about the event. The usual drone. There was no information about the cause or the nature of the struggle. But that wasn't what he was listening for.

"I'm hearing gunfire," Herbert said cautiously. "Muted—like it's not coming from the courtyard."

"Is that surprising?" Hood asked. "We knew that if the Strikers succeeded in getting Amadori there'd almost certainly be pursuit."

"Pursuit," Rodgers said. "Not resistance. The IA should have prevented that."

"Unless the gunfire's coming at 'em blindly," Herbert said. "People can do some weird stuff when they're choking."

"Could those shots be coming from the firing squad we were told about?" Coffey asked.

Rodgers shook his head. "This is individual fire and much too sporadic."

"The good news," Herbert said, "is if the Strikers had been caught, there wouldn't be any shooting at all."

The men were silent for a moment. Hood looked at the computer clock. "They were supposed to signal Luis's office once they got back into the dungeon." He looked at the phone.

"Chief," Herbert said, "it's an open line from here to there and my people are monitoring it. They'll let us know as soon as they hear anything."

Hood nodded. He looked back at the television. "I don't know where the Strikers get it," he said. "The courage to do these things. I don't know where any of you gets it. In Vietnam, Beirut—"

"It comes from a lot of places," Rodgers said. "Duty, love, fear—"

"Necessity," Herbert added. "That's a big one. When you don't have a choice."

"It's a combination of all of those," Rodgers said.

"Mike," Herbert said, "you know all about famous quotes. Who was it that said you can't fail if you screw your courage up—or words to that effect."

Rodgers looked at him. "I think the quote you're looking for is, 'But screw your courage to the sticking-place and we'll not fail.' "

"Yeah, that's the one," Herbert said. "Who said that? Sounds like Winston Churchill."

Rodgers grinned faintly. "It was Lady Macbeth. She was encouraging her husband to murder King Duncan. He did and then the whole plot came crashing down around him."

"Oh," Herbert replied. He looked down. "Then that's not the quote we want, is it?"

"That's all right," Rodgers said. He was still grinning slightly. "The regicide may have backfired badly but the play was a brilliant success. It all depends how you look at things."

"As I used to tell all my clients while the jury was deliberating," Coffey said, "trust in the system and in the people to whom we've entrusted it.'' He was still standing by the television, staring at the screen. ''Because as another great thinker once said, 'It ain't over till it's over.' ''

Herbert looked back at the television. The sounds of gunfire seemed to increase in frequency but not in volume. The announcer made an observation about that.

Herbert still felt alive. And optimistic, because that was his nature. But there was no ignoring the shadow that had fallen over the room. The unhappy truth that what they had all been quietly hoping for had not materialized: a call or broadcast declaring that a coup attempt in Spain had ended with the assassination of its leader.

The realization that the mission had not gone exactly as planned.

FORTY

Tuesday, 5:49 A.M.
Old Saybrook, Connecticut

Sharon Hood couldn't sleep. She was tired and she
was at her childhood home in her old bed but her mind
wouldn't shut down. She'd argued with her husband,
read one of her old Nancy Drew books until three,
then shut off the light and stared at the patterns of
moonlight and leaves on the ceiling for nearly two
hours. She looked around at the posters that had hung
there since before she moved out to go to college.

Posters of the movie *Doctor Zhivago*. Of the rock
group Gary Puckett and the Union Gap. A cover of a
TV Guide signed, "Cherish and Love, David Cas-
sidy," which she and her friend Alice had waited in
line three hours to get at a local shopping center.

How had she managed to be interested in all those
things, get high honors in school, hold a part-time job,
and have a boyfriend when she was sixteen and sev-
enteen?

You didn't need as much sleep then, she told herself.

But was that really what made it all mesh? Time
alone? Or was it the fact that if one job didn't work,
she got another. Or if one boyfriend didn't make her
happy, she got another. Or if one group recorded a

song she didn't like, she stopped buying their records. It wasn't a matter of energy. It was a matter of discovery. Learning about what she needed to be happy.

She thought she'd found it with that multimillionaire winemaker Stefano Renaldo. Sharon had met his sister in college and gone home with her one spring break and had been seduced by Stefano's wealth and his yacht and his attention. But—ironically, now that she thought about it—after two years she realized that she didn't want someone who'd inherited all his money. Someone who didn't have to work for a living. Someone who people came to for investment capital while he, depending upon his mood, yea'd or nay'd their hopes and dreams. That kind of life—that kind of man—was not for her.

She up and left the yacht one sunny morning, flew back to the United States, and didn't look back. The bastard never even phoned to see where she'd gone and Sharon didn't understand how she could ever have been with him—what the hell she'd been *thinking*. Then she met Paul at a party. It wasn't like being hit with a hammer. Except for Stefano, no man had ever struck Sharon that way—and Stefano's appeal was all on the surface. The relationship with Paul took time to develop. He was even-tempered, hard-working, and kind. He seemed like someone who would give her room to be herself, support her in her work, and be a nurturing father. He wouldn't smother her with gifts or jealousy the way Stefano had. And then one day, at a Fourth of July picnic a couple of months after they met, she happened to look into his eyes and it all clicked. Affection became love.

A branch scraped heavily against the window and Sharon looked over. The branch had certainly grown since she was a girl. That same branch used to scratch so gently against the same window.

It has grown larger, she thought, *but it hasn't changed.* She wondered if that was a good or a bad thing, being able to stay the same. *Good for a tree, bad for people,* she decided. But change was one of the most difficult things for anyone to do. Change— and compromise. Admitting that your way might not be the only way of doing things or even the best way.

Sharon gave up trying to sleep. She'd pull another Nancy Drew from her shelf. But first she slid from the bed, pulled on a robe, and went to look in on Harleigh and Alexander. The kids were sleeping in the bunk bed that used to belong to her younger twin brothers— Yul and Brynner. Her parents had met at a matinee of the original *The King and I.* They still sang "Hello, Young Lovers" and "I Have Dreamed" to one another, off-key but beautifully.

Sharon envied her parents the open affection they shared. And the fact that her father was retired and they got to spend so much time together and they seemed so thoroughly happy.

Of course, she thought, *there were times when Mom and Dad weren't so content—*

She remembered quiet tension when her father's business wasn't going so well. He rented bicycles and boats to people who came to the sleepy resort on the Long Island Sound, and some summers were bad ones. There were gas shortages and recessions. Her father had to put in long hours then, running his business during the day and working as a short-order cook at night. He used to come home smelling of grease and fish.

Sharon looked at her children's peaceful faces. She smiled as she listened to Alexander snore, just like his dad.

The smile wavered. She shut the door and stood in the dark hall, her arms folded around her. She was angry at Paul and she missed him terribly. She felt safe here, but she didn't feel at home here. How could she? Home wasn't where her possessions were. Home was where Paul was.

Sharon walked slowly back to her old bedroom.

Marriage, career, children, emotion, sex, stubbornness, conflict, jealousy—was it hope or arrogance that possessed two people and convinced them that all of those things could be melded into a working life?

Neither, she told herself. *It was love.* And the bottom line, however she got to it, was that as much as her husband frustrated her more than any man had or could, as much as he wasn't there as much as she or the kids wanted or needed, as much as she was angry at him almost as much as she felt affection for him, she still loved him.

Deeply.

Alone now in the small, quiet hours of the morning, Sharon felt that she may have come down too hard on Paul. Leaving Washington with the kids, snapping at him on the phone—why the *hell* wasn't she willing to cut him any slack? Was it because she was angry that he could take all the time he wanted for his career and she couldn't? Very possibly. Was it also because she keenly remembered missing her father during the summer busy season and when he had to hold a night job? Probably. She didn't want her kids to experience the same thing.

Sharon didn't feel that what she'd said to Paul was wrong. He *should* spend more time with his family and less time at work. His job required a greater commitment than nine-to-five, but Op-Center would continue to function if he came home for dinner *some* nights . . . if he went on vacation with them *once* in a while. But how Sharon had spoken to him—that was a different matter. She was frustrated and instead of talking to him she'd taken it out on him. After taking his kids away, that had to leave him feeling very much alone.

The woman took off her robe and lay down on the twin bed. The pillow was cold with her sweat and the branch was still scratching. She looked over. As she did, she saw her cellular phone on the night table. The black plastic glowed in the moonlight.

Rolling onto her side, Sharon picked up the phone, flipped it open, and began punching in Paul's private number. She stopped after the area code. She discontinued the call and set the phone aside.

She had a better idea. Instead of giving him a call— where even a small thing, like getting voice mail or hearing the wrong word could trigger a relapse—she'd give him an olive branch. Feeling guilty and forgiving at the same time, Sharon lay back, shut her eyes, and dropped almost at once into a contented sleep.

FORTY-ONE

Tuesday, 11:50 A.M.
Madrid, Spain

When the soldiers in the courtyard suddenly withdrew, Darrell McCaskey silently thanked Brett August. The Strikers had to be the reason for the abrupt pullback.

After the helicopter took off, the soldiers on the rooftop kept McCaskey and María pinned down. At the same time the scattered soldiers around the perimeter regrouped. It appeared as if they were organizing for an assault. But the attack never came. Everyone seemed riveted by loud pops from inside the palace.

"It's begun," McCaskey said to María.

Yellow smoke filtered through several of the windows along the wall beside the arches. There were shouted commands at the far end of the courtyard, near the western side of the palace. Though it was difficult to see because of the high, bright sun and deep shadows, the bulk of the soldiers seemed to disappear. Not long after that, McCaskey heard gunfire behind the ornate white walls.

"What's going on?" María asked. She was leaning against the inside of the arch closest to the palace wall. Her legs were stretched in front of her. McCaskey had placed his handkerchief across the gunshot wound in her side and was holding it in place.

"It's the countercoup," he replied. He didn't want to say much in case they were overheard. "How are you doing?"

"All right," she replied.

As they spoke, McCaskey had squinted across the wide, sunlit space. To the south—McCaskey's left—a tall iron gate separated the palace courtyard from the cathedral. The church doors had been shut before but now it looked as though people were beginning to emerge—priests as well as parishioners. He assumed that they'd heard the helicopter and the shots that had been fired at it. Within the courtyard itself Luis was still lying across the captain. The Interpol chief was silent but the Spanish officer was moaning.

"We have to bring him in," María said.

"I know," McCaskey said. He continued to peer into the sunlight. He was finally able to pick out at least three soldiers who had remained behind. Two of them were roughly four hundred feet away. They were crouched behind a post that supported the gate on the southern side of the courtyard. A third soldier was squatting behind an old lamppost about three hundred feet straight ahead, to the north.

McCaskey put his gun in María's hand. "Listen, María. I'm going to try and get Luis. I'll see if the soldiers will trade him for that captain."

"That is not a trade," María declared angrily. "Luis is a man. The captain is *una víbora*. A snake that crawls on the ground." She glanced out at the captain and her swollen upper lip pulled into a sneer. "He is lying there just as he should—on his belly.''

"Hopefully," McCaskey said evenly, "the soldiers won't see things quite the same way. Can you move around slightly so they can see the gun?"

María put her left hand on the bloody handkerchief and twisted slightly. She brought her right hand around.

"Hold it," he said before the gun came around. "I want to tell the soldiers something first. How do you say, 'Don't shoot'?"

"No disparar."

McCaskey leaned his head out from behind the arch. *"¡No disparar!"* he yelled. He kept his head exposed then asked María, "How do you say, 'Let's take care of our wounded'?"

She told him.

McCaskey shouted, *"¡Cuidaremos nuestros heridos!"*

There was no response from the soldiers. McCaskey frowned. This was one of those moves where you had to put everything on the table and pray.

"All right," he said to María as he rose. "Let them see the gun."

María twisted further until her right hand came from behind the archway. The gun glinted in the sun at the same time as McCaskey stepped into the open. He held his hands up to show that he was unarmed. Then, slowly, he began walking into the courtyard.

The soldiers did nothing. The sun felt savagely hot as McCaskey stepped closer to the wounded men. He was aware of continued gunfire from inside the palace—not a good sign. The Strikers should have been in and out without engaging the enemy.

Suddenly, a soldier stepped from behind the gate-post. He entered the gate and walked toward McCaskey. He was armed with a submachine gun. It was pointed directly at McCaskey.

"*No disparar,*" McCaskey repeated in case the soldier hadn't heard him the first time.

"*¡Vuelta!*" the soldier shouted.

McCaskey looked at him and shrugged.

"He wants you to turn around!" María yelled.

McCaskey understood. The soldier wanted to make sure he didn't have a weapon shoved in his waistband. McCaskey stopped, turned, and lifted his pants legs for good measure. Then he continued walking. The soldier didn't shoot him. He also didn't lower his weapon, which McCaskey now recognzied as an MP5 of Hong Kong origin. If he fired at this range, he'd cut McCaskey in half. McCaskey wished he could see the soldier's face beneath his cap. It would have been nice to have some idea what the man was thinking.

The walk to where Luis was lying took less than a minute but it felt much, much longer. When McCaskey arrived the Spanish soldier was still about thirty feet away. The soldier kept the gun pointed in McCaskey's direction. The American knelt slowly, keeping his arms raised. He looked down at the wounded men.

The captain was looking up at him, wheezing through his teeth. His lower leg was sitting in a deepening puddle of blood. If he didn't get help soon he'd bleed to death.

Luis was lying facedown across him, like an *X*. McCaskey bent his head and looked at Luis. His eyes were closed and his breathing was shallow. His normally dark face was pale. The bullet had struck the right side of his neck about two inches below the ear. Blood was dripping onto the stone blocks. It streamed toward the pool of the captain's blood and they mingled thickly.

McCaskey stood slowly and straddled the men. He put his arms under Luis and lifted him up. As he rose he heard a commotion at the gate. McCaskey and the Spanish soldier both looked over.

A sergeant at the gatepost had his hand around a priest's arm. The priest was speaking quietly and pointing toward the wounded men. The sergeant was yelling. After a moment, the priest simply wrested his arm away and stormed forward. The sergeant continued to yell at him. He shouted for the priest to stop.

The priest shouted back that he would not. He pointed toward the palace, where there were still the sounds of gunfire and clouds of yellow smoke. He said he was going to see if he could be of any assistance.

The sergeant warned him that there was danger.

The priest said he didn't care.

So that was what the debate was all about, McCaskey thought. The priest's safety. *Never assume.*

McCaskey didn't want to stand there while Luis bled. Cradling him gently to his chest, he turned and started walking toward the arches. The soldier let him go. McCaskey turned and saw him attending to the wounded captain.

McCaskey returned to the arch. Carefully, he set

Luis down beside María. He looked back. The priest was kneeling beside the captain. He turned back to the injured man.

"Poor Luis," María said. She set the gun down and touched his cheek.

McCaskey felt a pinch of jealousy. Not for María's touch but for the concern he saw in her eyes. The look came from deep inside her, pushing aside her own pain. He had been such a damn fool to lose her. He noticed, now, how pale she looked as well. He had to get help for her.

McCaskey unbuttoned his cuff and ripped off the bottom of his sleeve. He lay the cloth on Luis's wound.

"You both need medical help," McCaskey announced. "I'm going to try and get to a telephone—call for an ambulance. As soon as I do that, I'll look for your friend Juan."

María shook her head. "It may be too late—"

She tried to get up. McCaskey pushed down firmly on her shoulders.

"María—"

"Stop it!" she shouted.

"María, *listen* to me," McCaskey said. "Give me just a little time. With any luck this assault will make it unnecessary to rescue Juan or anyone else from General Amadori's thugs."

"I don't believe in luck," María said. She used her free hand to push aside his arms. "I believe in the lousiness of people. And so far I've never been disappointed. Amadori may execute his prisoners just to keep them from talking about what he's been doing—''

María stopped. She glanced past McCaskey. As she did, her eyes widened.

''What is it?'' McCaskey asked, turning around.

''I *know* that man,'' she said.

McCaskey gazed into the courtyard. The priest was hurrying toward them. He slowed as he neared. He obviously recognized her as well.

''María,'' the priest said as he reached the arch.

''Father Norberto,'' she replied. ''What are you doing here?''

''It was strange fortune brought me,'' he said. He squatted and touched her head comfortingly. Then he looked at her wound. ''My poor girl.''

''I'll live,'' she said.

''You've lost a lot of blood,'' Norberto said. He glanced at Luis. ''So has this man. Has a doctor been summoned?''

''I'm going now,'' McCaskey said.

''No!'' María shouted.

''It's all right,'' Norberto said, ''I'll stay with you.''

''It isn't that,'' María said. ''There's a prisoner— he must be helped!''

''Where?'' Norberto asked.

''He's in a room over there,'' she said. She pointed toward the doorway along the palace wall. ''I'm afraid they'll kill him.''

Norberto took her hand. He patted it as he rose. ''I will go to him, María,'' he said. ''You stay here and try not to move.''

María looked from the priest to McCaskey. The

concern McCaskey had seen in the woman's eyes was gone, replaced by contempt. His heart shattered, McCaskey left without a word. He was followed closely by Father Norberto.

The men entered the doorway together, McCaskey going in first. He'd left the gun with María in case the soldiers had a change of heart. He hoped he wouldn't need it here. The gunfire was louder, of course. But it was still far enough away so that McCaskey didn't think they'd get caught in a firefight. He looked at the old wooden cross hanging on the priest's chest. McCaskey's tired eyes lingered for a moment as he asked God to help his comrades who might be in the middle of the fighting.

There were eight doors along the short corridor. They were all shut. McCaskey stopped and turned to the priest.

Speaking in a very low whisper, he asked, "Do you speak English?"

"Some," Norberto replied.

"Okay," McCaskey said. "I'm not going to leave you alone."

"I'm never alone," Father Norberto replied, gently touching the cross.

"I know that. I mean—unprotected."

"But the wounded ones—"

"There may be a telephone in one of these rooms," McCaskey told him. "If there is, I'll make the call and stay with you. We'll find María's friend and take him out together."

Norberto nodded as McCaskey turned the first door-knob. The door opened into a dark study. After being out in the bright sun it took a moment for McCaskey's eyes to adjust. When they did he saw a desk at the far end of the chamber. There was a telephone in the near corner.

"That's a break," McCaskey said.

"You go," the priest said. "I'll continue searching for the woman's companion."

"All right," McCaskey said. "I'll join you as soon as I'm finished."

Norberto nodded and went to the next door.

Shutting the door, McCaskey went to the telephone. He lifted up the receiver and swore; there was no dial tone. He'd been afraid of that. Amadori's people must have shut down access to all outside lines. In case any of the prisoners got away they wouldn't be able to get intelligence out of here.

Returning to the corridor, McCaskey moved on to the next room. The door was opened and he looked in. It was a music room. It smelled faintly of smoke and then he noticed the ashes on the floor. This must have been where the fire alarm went off. Father Norberto was in the corner with a prisoner, whom McCaskey assumed was Juan.

"Father—how is he?" McCaskey asked.

Norberto didn't turn around. His shoulders slumping, he just shook his head gravely.

McCaskey turned. The only way he was going to be able to get help was if he found Striker. They could call Interpol and ask for medical assistance. Even if the strike force hadn't succeeded in killing Amadori, the general was going to have to allow medical assistance into the palace. His own people had been injured in the fighting.

McCaskey took a deep breath and started down the corridor.

FORTY-TWO

Tuesday, 12:06 P.M.
Madrid, Spain

The music room of the palace was dark. However, there was enough light coming in from the corridor to allow Father Norberto to see the man slouched in the corner on the floor. He was gravely wounded. There were splashes of blood on him, on his clothes, and on the wall behind him. Fresh blood continued to pour from gashes on his cheek, forehead, and mouth. There were several raw, bloody wounds in his legs and chest.

Father Norberto could literally feel the presence of Death—just as he had when he knelt like this beside his brother. The sensation was always the same, whether Father Norberto was ministering to the terminally ill or holding the hand of someone who had been fatally injured. Death had a sweet, vaguely metallic scent that filled the nostrils and poisoned the stomach. The priest could almost feel Death's touch. It was like a cool, invisible smoke chilling the air and seeping into his flesh, his bones, his soul.

Death had come for this man. As Norberto's eyes adjusted to the dark, he could see what a miracle it was that the man still lived. The monsters who had imprisoned him in this room had shot, beaten, and burned him without mercy or restraint.

For what? Norberto wondered with bitter indignation. *For information? For vengeance? For amusement?*

Whatever the reason, it couldn't justify this. And in a Catholic nation, a nation that purportedly lived by the Decalogue and by the teachings of Jesus Christ, what his captors had done was a mortal sin. For their crimes they would live outside of God's grace for eternity.

Not that that would help this poor man. Father Norberto lowered himself to his knees beside the dying prisoner. He pushed the man's sweat-dampened hair from his forehead and touched his bloody cheek.

The prisoner opened his eyes. There was no sparkle in them; only confusion and pain. They drifted down the priest's robe and then returned to his eyes. He tried to lift his arm. Father Norberto caught his trembling hand and held it between his own hands.

"My son," said Norberto. "I am Father Norberto."

The man looked up. "Father—what . . . is happening?"

"You've been hurt," Norberto said. "Just rest quietly."

"Hurt? How badly?"

"Be still," Norberto said softly. He squeezed the man's hand and smiled down at him. "What is your name?"

"I am Juan . . . Martinez."

"I am Father Norberto. Do you wish to make a confession?"

Juan looked around. His eyes were darting and afraid. "Father . . . am I . . . dying?"

Norberto did not reply. He only held Juan's hand tighter.

"But how can this . . . be?" Juan asked. "There is no pain."

"God is merciful," Norberto said.

Juan clutched the priest's fingers. His eyes shut slowly. "Father—if God is merciful, then I pray . . . He will forgive my sins."

"He will forgive only if you repent sincerely," Norberto replied. In the distance he heard guns popping with less frequency. There would be many others who needed God's comfort—and His forgiveness. Pressing his cross to the lips of the wounded man, Norberto asked, "Are you truly sorry for having offended God with all the sins of your past life?"

Juan kissed the cross. "I am truly sorry," he said contritely and with great effort. "I have killed . . . many men. Some at a radio station. Another in a room—a fisherman."

Norberto felt Death turn and laugh at him. He had never experienced anything so cruel or punishing as this moment—the realization that the hand nestled in his was the hand that had slain his brother.

Norberto's eyes were points of rage in a sea of ice. They burned into the man before him as though he were the Devil himself. Father Norberto wanted desperately to throw the man's hand aside and watch him slide into eternal damnation, unconfessed and unsaved.

This man murdered my brother—

"The killings had to be," Juan choked. His hand was shaking and he clutched Norberto's fingers harder. "But . . . I am truly sorry for them."

Norberto shut his eyes. His teeth were locked and trembling, his hand unresponsive to Juan's touch. Yet he fought the urge to drop this hand that had snuffed out Adolfo's life. As much as he was a grieving brother he was also a father ordained in the sight of God.

"Father—" Juan coughed. "Help . . . me to say . . . the words."

Norberto drew air through his teeth. *It is not necessary that I forgive him. Forgiveness is the province of God.*

The priest opened his eyes and glared down at the bruised face and broken body sprawled before him. "Father, forgive me my transgressions," Norberto said coldly, "for which I am truly repentant."

"I . . . repent," Juan rasped. "I . . . repent . . . truly." Juan shut his eyes. His breath came in short gasps.

"Sins forgiven are removed from the soul, restoring the sinner to a state of sanctifying grace," Norberto said. "May God forgive you your trespasses and deliver you unto salvation."

Juan's lips parted slowly. There was a short sigh. Then there was nothing more.

Norberto continued to stare down at the dead man. Juan's hand was cold. Blood continued to trickle from his chest and cheek.

Norberto could not justify or forgive what this man had done. But Adolfo had gone fishing in a sea where the prey fight back. If Juan had not slain his brother then someone else would have. Tears filled Norberto's eyes. He should have stopped it with Adolfo.

If only he had known about his brother's other life. If only he'd been less harsh then perhaps Adolfo wouldn't have been afraid to come to him. Why did he let him go out that night? Why didn't he stay with him when he went to deliver that audiotape, the tape that helped to start all of this. *Why didn't I act when there was still time?* And the worst punishment of all was that he had not been able to save his brother's soul—only that of his killer.

"Oh, God," Norberto said, letting his head roll back and tears fall freely. He set Juan's hand down beside his body and covered his own eyes.

As Father Norberto knelt there he felt Death leave— though it did not go very far. The priest forced himself to stop crying. This was not the time to mourn Adolfo or to damn his own failings. There were others who needed comfort or absolution—others who may have acted arrogantly in the bloom of life, only to find humility in the face of eternal damnation.

Father Norberto rose. He made the sign of the cross above Juan Martinez. "May God forgive you," he said softly.

And may God forgive me, Father Norberto thought as he turned and left the room. He hated the man who had just died. But in his heart, in the deepest and truest part of him, he hoped that God had heard his repentance.

There had been enough damnation for one day.

FORTY-THREE

Tuesday, 12:12 P.M.
Madrid, Spain

It was the policy of all American elite forces to leave nothing usable behind. In some cases, where the mission was covert-red—meaning that no one could know the forces had even been there—even shell casings were collected. In a covert-green raid like this one it was only necessary that the identities of the operatives never be revealed.

Colonel August was aware that Aideen Marley had peeled off from the group. She had no orders to do so, but he couldn't fault her initiative. As it stood, if she failed to get General Amadori the mission would be considered a partial success. Striker would have succeeded in flushing out the officer before he was ready. The firefight would force the municipal police and other officials to enter the palace. They'd find the prisoners and learn how they were forced to come here. Amadori might still be in a position to seize power, but this would make it a little more difficult. Certainly he'd find it tough to get support throughout Europe when news of his atrocities got out.

Still—

Colonel August didn't like partial successes. Aideen

had gone off to the southern wing of the palace in pursuit of Amadori. If Striker could keep the army off her back long enough, and if Amadori's wound kept his mind on escape instead of security, she might be able to finish the job they set out to do. If she succeeded, they could still spare Spain the months of violent conflict and ruthless purges that would ensue if Amadori survived.

There were approximately three hundred feet between the Strikers and the oncoming Spanish soldiers. Though Amadori's troops were wearing gas masks, the thick yellow smoke from the grenades had prevented them from proceeding more than a few yards every minute. Striker, meanwhile, had been able to keep up a steady retreat. They'd even helped several of the prisoners get out, those who had been kept in the Hall of the Halberdiers and had managed to make their way through the dissipating gas.

Striker was nearing the grand staircase of the palace. Behind it was the stairway to the dungeon. To the south was the corridor Amadori and Aideen had taken. Sidling up to Corporal Prementine, Colonel August instructed him to select one soldier to cover the retreat. Prementine was then to lead the other Strikers out of the palace.

"Sir," Prementine said, "one soldier won't be enough to do the job. I'd like to remain behind as well."

"Negative," August said. "That would make three of us."

"Sir?"

"I'll be here as well," August said.

"Sir—"

"Do it, Corporal," August said.

"Yes, sir," Prementine said, saluting.

The corporal informed Private Pupshaw that he'd be staying behind with Colonel August. The burly private responded with an enthusiastic salute and then reported to his commanding officer. August told Pupshaw that when they reached the staircase he was to take up a position just inside the corridor. August would handle the crossfire from the northern side of the staircase. If either of them were attacked from behind, the other would be in a position to cover him.

Privates Scott and DeVonne left behind their remaining supply of gas grenades. There were only three of them. August figured they would get five strong minutes of defense out of two of those grenades and cover fire. The last grenade would give them another two minutes for their own retreat. The timetable was snug, but it was doable. He only hoped that Aideen could catch up to her wounded prey, do what needed to be done, and exit cleanly.

Corporal Prementine wished the two men well. Silently, he and the other Strikers departed.

August thanked him then informed Pupshaw that they were to hold their positions for exactly five minutes from the time they reengaged the Spanish soldiers. At August's signal they would then follow their fellow Strikers back "down the hole," Pupshaw retreating first.

August and Pupshaw lay on their bellies and prepared to meet the assault. They would fire low, no higher than the knees. Pupshaw had a grenade ready to roll against the Spaniards. August raised his left arm.

Twenty seconds later the first Spanish soldier appeared through the thinning yellow cloud. August turned his left thumb down.

Pupshaw pulled the pin and rolled the grenade.

FORTY-FOUR

Tuesday, 12:17 P.M.
Madrid, Spain

As he moved down the corridor, Darrell McCaskey felt naked without a weapon. But it had been more important to him that María have one. It had been a while since he'd used the aikido skills he'd learned when he joined the FBI, but they would have to suffice.

McCaskey slowed as he neared the next corridor. He stopped at the corner and peeked around stealthily, the way he used to do when he was on stakeouts. He took a mental snapshot of the scene and then withdrew quickly, his heart jumping from slow to hyperactive.

There was a tall man standing part of the way down the corridor. He was a general with Francoesque layers of braid and an array of medals. He was armed with a handgun and he was wearing a gas filter and goggles. He was also bleeding from a wound in his leg.

It had to be Amadori.

The man had been looking behind him as he approached. McCaskey was sure Amadori hadn't spotted him. He swore at himself for having left his gun with María. He had nothing to use against the man. Nothing except his fists and the fact that Amadori didn't know he was here.

The FBI had taught McCaskey that if an agent didn't bring superior firepower to a situation he should back off until he could muster that firepower. A stand-off always favored the pursuer. Failure favored the pursued.

But with everything that was at stake, McCaskey couldn't take the chance of letting Amadori go.

McCaskey looked up and mustered his resolve. He listened to the general's limping footsteps. Amadori was approximately ten feet away. McCaskey would crouch and swing around, try to pin his legs to the wall, then grab his arm before he could fire.

Just then, McCaskey heard footsteps behind him. He turned and saw Father Norberto walking toward him. That wasn't all he saw. Above the music room, McCaskey noticed a red eye looking down from the ceiling.

It was a camera eye. And Amadori was wearing goggles—Remote Surveillance System goggles.

The footsteps stopped. McCaskey swore. He'd been too damn tired to think this through and now he was at a serious disadvantage. Amadori knew precisely where he was.

There was nothing to do but retreat. He turned and ran toward the door that led to the courtyard.

"What is it?" Father Norberto asked.

McCaskey motioned him back. The priest just stood there, confused.

"Jesus!" McCaskey cried in frustration. He didn't think Amadori would shoot a member of the clergy. But a Catholic priest would make the perfect hostage.

No one would dare order an attack for fear of hitting the priest.

McCaskey had to get the priest out of here. Reaching Father Norberto, he put his arms around him and tried to move him toward the courtyard door. A moment later he heard a shot and felt a punch in his back and then everything went blindingly red.

FORTY-FIVE

Tuesday, 12:21 P.M.
Madrid, Spain

It was easy for Aideen to follow the trail of blood. The drops were so close together they overlapped in spots. Amadori was losing blood quickly. What she hadn't anticipated was that the general would be alone when she caught up to him. Alone and waiting for her.

Amadori fired once as Aideen came around the corner. She jumped back as soon as she saw him and the bullet whizzed by. There was silence after the echo of the gunshot died. Aideen stood there listening, trying to determine if Amadori moved. As she waited, she felt something pressed hard against the small of her back. She turned around and saw a man step the rest of the way from a doorway. It was the major general. He was holding a gun on her.

Aideen cursed under her breath. The officer was wearing his RSS goggles. He must have been tuned in to the cameras behind them and spotted her. They'd separated and now she'd been snared.

"Face front and raise your hands," he commanded in Spanish.

Aideen did. He relieved her of her gun.

"Who are you?" he asked.

Aideen didn't answer.

"I don't have time to waste," the major general said. "Answer and I'll let you go. Refuse and I'll leave you here with a bullet in your back. You have a count of three."

Aideen didn't think he was bluffing.

"One," said the officer.

Aideen was tempted to tell him that she was an Interpol operative. She had never faced death that seemed so imminent. It had a way of weakening one's resolve.

"Two."

She doubted that the major general would spare her even if she told him who she was. But she would definitely die if she didn't.

Yet by telling the truth, she could very well ruin the lives and careers of María, Luis, and their comrades. And she would destroy countless other lives if she helped Amadori survive this assault.

Maybe she'd been meant to die in the street with Martha. Maybe there was no escaping that.

Aideen heard the gun bark behind her. She jumped. She felt blood on her neck. But she was still standing.

A moment later Aideen felt the major general stumble against her. She lurched involuntarily as he fell forward. The two guns clattered on the floor. She glanced back at the officer. Blood spurted like a water fountain from the back of his head. She looked up.

A familiar man was walking toward her, down the corridor. He was holding a smoking pistol and wearing a look of grim satisfaction.

"Ferdinand?" she said.

The *familia* member hesitated.

"No, it's all right," she said. She looked around quickly. Then she turned her back toward the surveillance camera behind her. Certain she wouldn't be seen, Aideen lifted her black mask just enough for him to see her face. "I'm here with others," she said. "We want to help."

Ferdinand continued walking toward her. "I'm glad to hear that," he said. "Juan and I doubted you back at the factory, after the attack. I'm sorry."

"I don't blame you. You had no way of knowing."

Ferdinand held up the gun. "This came to me when your friend caused an uproar before. They took her away, and also Juan. I want to find them—and I want to find Amadori."

"Amadori went this way," Aideen said. She pointed as she stopped to pick up her gun. She also picked up the major general's gun and goggles.

The dead man's blood was cooling on the back of Aideen's neck and she used the sleeve of her black shirt to wipe it off. She felt sick as she walked away. Not because the man had died; he'd been ready enough to kill her. What bothered her was that neither the general nor the major general had had a hand in the event that brought Op-Center into this situation in the first place, the murder of Martha Mackall. To the contrary. These people had killed the men behind the murder. The crime for which they were being hunted was having orchestrated a coup against a NATO ally—a coup that, ironically, a majority of the people in Spain might have supported had it been put to a vote.

Martha was wrong, Aideen thought miserably. *There are no rules. There's only chaos.*

Aideen and Ferdinand started off after Amadori. Aideen was in the lead, Ferdinand a few paces behind her. Aideen checked the gun she'd retrieved. The safety was switched off. That bastard of a major general *had* been ready to shoot her in the back.

The corridor ahead was empty. They heard a shot and quickened their pace. Aideen wondered if someone else—possibly María?—had found Amadori. The trail of blood continued around the corner. They followed it, stopping short as they entered the hallway leading past the music room. They saw General Amadori standing there with a gun in his white-gloved hand. The gun was being held to someone's head. It took a moment for Aideen to realize who the general was holding in front of him.

It was Father Norberto. And at his feet was another man lying faceup. He wasn't moving.

It was Darrell McCaskey.

FORTY-SIX

Tuesday, 12:24 P.M.
Madrid, Spain

When Father Norberto had entered the courtyard outside the palace, he didn't believe the soldiers were going to hurt him. He could see it in their eyes, hear it in their voices.

He had no such illusions about this man, the one who had just shot the American in the back. The officer had a gun pressed under his jaw and was holding his hair tightly with the other hand. The man was bleeding. He did not have the time or disposition to talk.

"Where is the major general?" Amadori shouted.

Aideen dropped the major general's goggles and gun and kicked them into the hallway. "He's dead. Now let the priest go."

"A woman?" Amadori yelled. "Damn you, who is making war on me? Show yourself *now!*"

"Let the *padre* go, General Amadori," Aideen said. "Release him and you can have me."

"I do not negotiate," Amadori yelled. He took a quick look behind him. The door to the courtyard was only a few yards away. He pulled off his goggles and threw them to the floor. Then he pressed the gun harder against Father Norberto's throat and continued

backing toward the door. "My soldiers are still outside, watching the perimeter while their brothers fight.
When I call them they'll come. They'll hunt you
down."

"You'll shoot me if I show myself."

"That is correct," said Amadori. "But I'll release
the priest."

The woman was silent.

Throughout his years in the priesthood, Norberto
had talked to grieving widows and parishioners whose
brothers or sisters or children had died. Most of them
had expressed the desire to die as well. Despite his
own loss, Norberto didn't feel that way. He did not
want to be a martyr. He wanted to live. He wanted to
continue helping others. But he wasn't going to let a
woman die for him.

"My child, leave here!" Norberto cried.

Amadori pulled tighter on his hair. "Don't talk."

"My brother, Adolfo Alcazar, believed in you,"
Norberto said. "He died in your service."

"Your brother?" the general said. He continued
walking. He was just a few feet from the door. "Don't
you realize that the people who killed Adolfo are
here?"

"I know," Norberto said. "One of them died in my
arms, just as Adolfo did."

"Then how can you take their side?"

"I haven't taken their side," Norberto said. "I am
on the side of God. And in His name I beg you to call
off this war."

"I don't have time for this," Amadori snapped.

"My enemies are the enemies of Spain. Tell me who the woman is and I'll release you."

"I won't help you," Norberto said.

"Then you'll die." Amadori groaned as he reached the door. He was obviously in pain. Still holding the priest, he stepped into the gleaming sunlight and turned toward the southern gate. "I need assistance!" he yelled. He looked back quickly to make sure Aideen hadn't moved.

The soldiers on the other side of the courtyard had their guns pointed toward the arches. They turned to look at the door. Suddenly, one of the soldiers stepped from behind the gatepost.

"Stay where you are, sir!" the soldier yelled.

Amadori glanced toward the arches. He saw two people crouched there, a bleeding man and a woman.

"Get your unit back out here," Amadori shouted. "Secure the courtyard!"

The soldier pulled the field radio from his belt and called for reinforcements. As he did, the woman behind the arch aimed at Amadori. The general angrily swung the priest around so he was facing her. The woman held her fire; gunshots from the soldiers quickly drove her back behind the arch. Amadori looked back into the palace to make sure the other woman hadn't come from around the corner.

She had not. She didn't need to.

Darrell McCaskey was lying on his side halfway down the corridor. He was facing Amadori and holding the gun Aideen had kicked into the corridor.

Father Norberto looked in as well. He didn't understand. There was no blood, yet he'd seen the general shoot this man in the back.

Amadori began to turn the priest around. But McCaskey didn't give the general a chance to maneuver Father Norberto between them. And he didn't fire to wound the general. He put two quick shots into Amadori's temple.

The general was dead before he reached the ground.

FORTY-SEVEN

Tuesday, 12:35 P.M.
Madrid, Spain

"You took one of the bulletproof vests," Aideen said as she ran toward McCaskey.

"Never travel without it," McCaskey said. He winced as she helped him to his feet. "I put it on before I came here. After he shot me—I figured I'd lie low and wait for something like this."

"Glad I didn't just kick out the goggles," Aideen said.

Ferdinand ran past them to the priest. Father Norberto was standing just inside the doorway, staring down at the body of General Amadori. He knelt and began to say a prayer over the dead man.

"Father, he doesn't deserve your blessing," Ferdinand said. "Come. We must go."

Norberto finished praying. Only when he made the sign of the cross over the general did he rise. He looked at Ferdinand. "Where are we going?"

"Away," Ferdinand said. "The soldiers—"

"He's right, Father," Aideen said. "We don't know what they're going to do. But we should be somewhere else when they do it."

McCaskey held onto Aideen's shoulder while he

drew several painful breaths. "We've also got to let the boss know what's going on as soon as possible," he said. "Where's the team?"

"They encountered some resistance after the flush-out," she said. "They withdrew."

"Can you get to them?"

Aideen nodded. "Can you walk?"

"Yes, but I'm not going with you," McCaskey said. "I can't leave María."

"Darrell, you heard what Amadori said," Aideen declared. "More soldiers are on the way."

"I know," McCaskey said. He smiled faintly. "All the more reason I can't leave her."

"He won't be alone," Father Norberto told her. "I'll stay with him."

Aideen regarded them both through her mask. "There isn't time to argue. I'll get the word out. You three take care."

McCaskey thanked her. As she turned and ran toward the grand staircase, McCaskey hobbled toward the priest.

"I'm sorry about this," he said in English, pointing to Amadori's body. "It was necessary."

Norberto said nothing.

Ferdinand put his gun in his waistband. "I'm going to look for my friend Juan," he said. He regarded McCaskey. "Thank you, sir, for ridding Spain of this would-be *caudillo.*"

McCaskey wasn't exactly sure what Ferdinand had said, but he got the gist of it. *"¡De nada!"* he said. "You're welcome."

Father Norberto suddenly put his hand around Ferdinand's neck. He squeezed hard.

"*Padre?*" Ferdinand said, confused.

"Your friend is in there," Norberto said. There were tears in his eyes as he pointed toward the music room. "He's dead."

"Juan dead? Are you certain?"

"I am certain," Norberto said. "I was with him when he died. I was with him when he confessed his sins. He died absolved of them."

Ferdinand shut his eyes.

Norberto squeezed harder. "Everyone has the right to absolution, my son, whether they have slain one or they have slain millions."

The priest released Ferdinand and turned away. He walked toward McCaskey, who had limped past them and was peering cautiously out the door. McCaskey didn't know what the exchange had been about, but it didn't sound pleasant.

"What should we do?" Norberto asked.

"I'm not sure," McCaskey admitted.

He watched the soldiers as they watched him. The reinforcements were just arriving from an entrance further along the courtyard. It looked to McCaskey as if they were carrying gas filters. They must have been part of the group that went after Striker.

Once again McCaskey felt helpless. The Interpol spotters might not realize that Amadori was dead, that a show of force from local police units might be enough to shut the heart of the revolution down. Especially if it came before the soldiers could rally behind a new leader.

''What if I go and speak with them,'' Norberto asked. ''Tell them that there is no longer any reason to fight.''

''I don't think they'd listen,'' McCaskey said. ''You may put some fear in some of them—but not all. Not enough to save us.''

''I've got to try,'' Norberto said.

He stepped around McCaskey and walked out the door. McCaskey didn't try to stop him. He didn't believe the soldiers would hurt the priest. And if he could buy them an extra minute or two, it was worth a try. At this point, he was willing to try anything.

McCaskey had no idea what was going to happen to the movement with Amadori dead. But from the way the three dozen or so soldiers were massing along the southern side of the courtyard, he had a good idea what was going to happen to him and María and all the prisoners who were being kept here.

They would become pawns in one of the most significant and dangerous hostage dramas of this century.

FORTY-EIGHT

Tuesday, 6:50 A.M.
Washington, D.C.

"Incoming from Striker," Bob Herbert said.

He was manning the phone in Hood's office while Hood and Rodgers were on a conference call with National Security head Burkow and Spanish ambassador García Abril in Washington. Attorney Lowell Coffey and Ron Plummer were also in the office.

The ambassador informed Washington that the Spanish prime minister and King had relieved General Amadori of his command. His forces were being turned over to General García Somoza, who was being flown in from Barcelona. In the meantime, the local police forces—which included the elite Guardia Real from the Palacio de la Zarzuela—were being organized for a counterattack to take back the palace.

Hood took the Striker call at once, patched through from Interpol headquarters. He put it on the speaker. The radio silence had been nerve-wracking, especially since the spotters and satellite reconnaissance had reported shots and tear gas from different parts of the palace compound. He was also afraid the police would move in before Striker could move out.

"Home run," August said as soon as Hood was on.

"We're out of the dugout and back in the street."

There were smiles around the room and fists raised in triumph. Rodgers informed Burkow and Ambassador Abril.

"Excellent," Hood said enthusiastically. Since Striker was out in the open, August would be forced to give his report in the baseball code they'd arranged. "Injuries?"

"A minor sprain," said August. "But we have a problem. The coach went in to get his lady. The lady's boss went with him. The coach is all right but the others are hurt. They should really see a doctor."

"Understood," Hood said. McCaskey was the coach. August was telling him that he and Luis had gone in to get María and that the condition of Luis and María was possibly life-threatening.

"One more thing," August said. "When we tried to pick off their ace player we got caught in a pickle. Coach was the one who ended up nailing him."

Hood and Rodgers exchanged looks. McCaskey was the one who had ended up getting to Amadori. That hadn't been the game plan. But if there was one thing Hood had discovered about his team—Herbert, Rodgers, and McCaskey in particular—they were very good at improvising.

"It's our feeling," August continued, "that the coach probably shouldn't stay in the stadium for any length of time. We don't really want the other team talking to him. Do you want us to try and get them out?"

"Negative," Hood said. Good as Striker was, he refused to send them back in without a rest—especially with a police force getting ready to move in. "Where are the coach and his people?"

"The coach is by the doorway at B1," August said. "The lady and boss are in seats V5, one and three."

"Very good," Hood said. "You did your job, slugger. Now go home. We'll talk when you get there."

Herbert had rolled his chair to the computer and punched in the map coordinates August had provided. He asked the computer for a satellite update of the spot. Stephen Viens had linked them directly to the NRO download and it came up in fifteen seconds.

"I've got visuals on María and Luis," Herbert said. He pulled back so he could see the entire courtyard. "I've also got about thirty soldiers getting ready to do something."

Rodgers updated Burkow and Abril. As he did, Lowell Coffey went to the coffee machine and poured a cup.

"Paul," Coffey said, "if Amadori's dead, those soldiers may not kill our people or anyone else. They'll hold them as hostages. Use them to bargain their way to some kind of amnesty."

"And they'll probably get it, too," Plummer pointed out. "Whoever ends up running the country won't want to further alienate the ethnic supporters these people may have."

"So if the authorities don't attack," Coffey went on, "we'll probably get everyone out in time—including Darrell. The soldiers don't gain anything by killing them."

"Except McCaskey," Herbert pointed out. "Colonel August is right. If the soldiers in the compound find out that he's the one who killed Amadori, they're going to want his blood. Bad.''

"How will they know he killed the general?" Coffey asked.

"The security cameras," Herbert said. He brought up the map of the palace. "Look where he is."

Coffey and Plummer gathered around the computer. Rodgers was still on the telephone with Burkow and the Spanish ambassador.

"There are cameras at both ends of the corridor," Herbert said. "Darrell may have been taped. When they find the general dead, his soldiers may take the time to watch and see who did it."

"Any chance of erasing the tape with some kind of electronic interference?" Coffey asked.

"A low-flying aircraft with a directed electromagnetic burst could do it," Herbert said, "but it would take time."

Rodgers hit the mute button and stood. "Gentlemen," he said, "it's unlikely we'll be able to do anything in time."

"Explain," Hood said.

"Interpol informed the prime minister of Striker's success," Rodgers said. "The ambassador has just informed me that they want to move the police in now, before the rebel forces have a chance to regroup."

Herbert swore.

"What are their orders if the soldiers take hostages?" Hood asked.

Rodgers shook his head. "There aren't going to be any hostages," Rodgers said. "The Spanish government doesn't want to give the rebels—which is how they're describing them—a forum that will keep them center stage.''

"Can't blame them for that,'' Herbert said.

"I can when one of my people is still in the compound,'' Hood said angrily. "We did a goddamn job for them—''

"And now they're marching down the road we paved for them,'' Rodgers said, "acting in the best interests of their nation. The job we were asked to do by the President of the United States was to help give Spain back to its elected officials. There weren't any guarantees, Paul, about how those officials were going to behave afterward.''

Hood pushed his chair back from the desk and stood. He put his hands on his hips, shook his head, then went to the shelf near the TV and got himself a cup of coffee.

Rodgers was right. Chances were good that the Spanish prime minister and possibly even the king wouldn't survive this debacle. They weren't acting in their own self-interest. They were trying to preserve Spain. And in the long run, that helped Europe and the United States. There wasn't a polarized nation on earth that would benefit if yet another country collapsed into smaller republics.

Yet it wasn't their actions that bothered him. It was their we'll-take-it-from-here attitude, now that the difficult work had been done. What about the lives that had been sacrificed to correct what had occurred during their watch?

"Paul,'' Rodgers said, "the Spanish government probably doesn't even know about Darrell's role in the action. They probably assume that Striker got in and out as planned.''

"They didn't bother to ask.''

"And if they did, nothing would be different,'' Rodgers said. "Nothing *could* be different. The government can't give us time to figure something out because they can't afford to give the rebels time.''

Hood took his coffee back to the desk.

"I've faced these things before,'' Herbert said. "They suck. But Darrell isn't green. He'll probably pick up on what's happening. Maybe he'll be able to get himself and the others to safety until the shooting's over.''

"I also informed Interpol about the situation,'' Rodgers said. "I didn't tell them about Darrell's actions. That can come out later, when—with luck— we'll have him back here.''

"Yeah,'' Herbert said. "Then we can at least have some fun denying that he was ever even there.''

"I told them where Darrell, María, and Luis are,'' Rodgers continued, "and that they need medical attention. Hopefully, the message will make its way through the bureaucracy.''

Hood sat. "*Probably, maybe,* and *hopefully.* I guess there are worse words.''

"A whole lot of them,'' Herbert said. "Like *never, impossible,* and *dead.*''

Hood looked at him and then at the others. He was going to miss these people when he submitted his resignation—these good patriots and dedicated professionals. But he wasn't going to miss the waiting and the grief. There had been enough of that to last him a lifetime.

He also wouldn't miss the loneliness and the guilt. Wanting Nancy Bosworth in Germany and Ann Farris in Washington. That kind of empty flirtation was never what he'd wanted his life to be about.

Hood found himself hoping that Sharon had had a change of heart—that maybe she'd decided to come back. And he had to admit that Herbert was right. *Hope* was a lot more satisfying than *never*.

FORTY-NINE

Tuesday, 12:57 P.M.
Madrid, Spain

Breathing proved extremely painful for McCaskey. But as his FBI mentor, Assistant Director Jim Jones, once pointed out, "The alternative is not breathing and that ain't better." Bulletproof vests were designed to stop slugs from entering the body. Vests couldn't stop them from impacting hard and breaking ribs or—depending upon the caliber and proximity of firing—from causing internal bleeding. Yet as much as McCaskey was in pain, his concern was not for himself. He was worried about María. He had delayed going out, to see if he could get into Amadori's uniform. But the general was too tall, the clothes were too bloody, and McCaskey couldn't speak Spanish. A bluff would only delay the soldiers for a moment or two—not worth the effort.

Suddenly, there was a beep down the hall. It was an incoming message on the major general's radio. McCaskey figured they didn't have long before the soldiers came to see why the man wasn't answering.

More soldiers began arriving in the courtyard. McCaskey poked his head out the door. To the east of the arches was Calle de Bailén—and freedom. But it was over one hundred yards to the road. Once María left the safety of the arches there would be nothing to shield her from the soldiers. And she'd be carrying Luis instead of her weapon. McCaskey didn't know whether the soldiers would cut her down. He did know that they'd be foolish to let her or anyone else go. Not after all they'd witnessed here about the treatment of prisoners.

McCaskey decided that he was going to have to try to get to María and cover her as she left. As he was about to ask Ferdinand for his help, the Spaniard said something and offered McCaskey his hand.

"Is he planning to leave us?" McCaskey asked.

"He is," replied Norberto.

"Hold on," McCaskey said. He refused to take Ferdinand's hand. "Tell him that I need his help getting to María. He can't go."

Norberto translated for McCaskey. Ferdinand answered, shaking his head while he did.

"He says he's sorry," Norberto informed McCaskey, "but his *familia* needs him."

"I need him too!" McCaskey snapped. "I've got to reach Luis and María—get them out of here."

Ferdinand turned to go.

"Dammit," McCaskey shouted, "I need someone to cover me!"

"Let him go," Norberto said flatly. "We'll both go to your friends. They won't shoot us."

"They will when they realize that their leaders are dead."

There were loud footsteps down the hall. They were followed by gunshots. Ferdinand screamed.

"Shit!" McCaskey yelled. "Let's go."

Father Norberto's face was impassive but he hesitated.

"You can't help him," McCaskey said and started toward the door. "Come on."

Norberto went with him. McCaskey moved as fast as he could, each step bringing sharp pain along both sides. He tried to raise his left arm; a blinding flash stabbed his lungs and arched his spine. He switched his gun to his other hand. He wasn't as good left-handed, but he'd made up his mind that he was going to get to María—crawling if necessary, but he was going to reach her.

The two men stepped outside with Father Norberto between McCaskey and the soldiers. McCaskey stumbled from the lingering pain of having tried to lift his arm. The priest grabbed his left arm. McCaskey leaned on him gratefully. As he did, Father Norberto took the gun from him.

"What are you doing?!" McCaskey shouted.

The priest held the gun butt-up. Then he bent and laid it on the courtyard. "I am giving them one reason less to shoot at us."

"Or one more!" McCaskey cried as they continued walking.

He tried not to think about it. He tried not to think about the soldiers shouting at them in Spanish. María was watching them from behind the base of the arch, her gun in sight.

There was a shot and a loud *chink* roughly a yard from Father Norberto. Stone chips flew toward them.

One of them struck the priest in the thigh. He winced but continued walking.

María returned fire. One of the soldiers shot at her and drove her back.

The soldiers fired again. This time the bullet hit closer, just inches from the priest. It kicked up a fresh spray of stone. Norberto jerked toward McCaskey as several shards struck him in the side.

"Are you all right?" McCaskey asked.

Norbert nodded once. But his lips were pressed together and his brow was creased. He was hurting.

Suddenly, there was shouting behind them. It was coming from the direction of the palace.

"*El general está muerto!*" someone shouted.

McCaskey didn't need Father Norberto to translate for him. The general was dead—and in a moment they would be, too.

"Come on!" he said, urging the priest forward.

But even as he did so, McCaskey knew they were never going to make it. Other soldiers picked up the cry. There were shouts of rage and disbelief.

Just then there was another sound. The sound of helicopters. McCaskey stopped. He looked to his left, toward the palace. The soldiers also looked over. A moment later six choppers flew over the southern wall. They hovered over the courtyard, blocking the sun and sending out an ear-splitting roar.

It was the sweetest sound McCaskey had ever heard. The sweetest sight McCaskey ever saw was what looked like police sharpshooters leaning from the open doors and aiming CETME assault rifles down at the soldiers.

McCaskey heard sirens along the avenues alongside the palace. Aideen and Striker must have gotten out and given the police enough intel to send in the cavalry—serious business cavalry.

McCaskey started walking again. "Come on, Father," he said. "They're on our side."

The dual air and land approach suggested to McCaskey that the police were waiting for the army to split up like this so they could pin both parts down. That would significantly weaken resistance.

McCaskey and Father Norberto finished crossing the courtyard as the sirens neared and the choppers held the soldiers back. McCaskey ached to embrace María. But in his present condition it would probably cost him his lungs. She was also hurt, and Luis needed attention.

"It's good to see you again," María said, smiling. "Did I hear correctly? About Amadori?"

McCaskey nodded as he looked at Luis. The officer was ashen, his breathing very shallow. McCaskey checked the improvised bandage. Then he took off his own shirt and began tearing it into fresh strips.

"Father," McCaskey said, "we have to get Luis to a hospital. Please—would you flag down a car?"

"I don't think that will be necessary," Norberto said.

McCaskey looked toward the street. A police car had pulled up to the curb and four men had gotten out. They were dressed in distinctive dark blue berets, white belts, and spats.

"The Guardia Real," María said. "The Royal Guard."

A fifth man got out as well. He was a tall, white-haired gentleman with a proud military bearing. He approached quickly.

"It's General de la Vega," McCaskey said. Then he shouted, "We need help here. Luis needs a doctor!"

"*¡Ambulancia!*" María added.

The Royal Guard members began running toward them. One of them shouted something to María.

She nodded then turned to McCaskey. "They're setting up a mobile field hospital in the Plaza de Oriente," she said. "They're going to take him there."

McCaskey looked down at Luis. He finished bandaging the Interpol officer then took his hand and squeezed it hard. "Hold on, partner," McCaskey said. "Help's here."

Luis squeezed back weakly. His eyes remained shut. Father Norberto knelt beside Luis to pray for him. The priest was obviously hurting. It was also obvious that he had no intention of letting that stop him.

A moment later gunfire erupted once again from inside the palace. McCaskey and María exchanged glances.

"Sounds like the government's playing for keeps," McCaskey said.

María nodded. "We're going to lose a lot of good people today. And for what? One man's insane vision."

"Or his vanity," McCaskey said. "I'm never sure which one motivates a dictator more."

As they spoke, the police arrived. Two men lifted Luis up gently and carried him toward the plaza. The general thanked McCaskey and María for all they had done, then ran after them. The other two Royal Guardsmen stopped and lifted María.

"An honor guard." She grinned.

McCaskey smiled and rose, assisted by Father Norberto. They walked alongside María as she was carried away. McCaskey felt a knifelike jab with every step he took. But he kept up with the guards. It was rare to get a second chance at anything, whether it was the opportunity to fix a wrong choice at a moment of crisis or to reclaim a lost love. McCaskey had experienced both. He knew what it was like to be tortured by events his indecision or fear or weakness had caused.

If María Corneja would have him, there was no way he intended to lose her again. Not even for a minute. The pain of blowing a second chance would be much, much worse.

María sought and found McCaskey's hand. A moment later her eyes found his. And at least one pain stopped when it became clear that she felt the same.

FIFTY

Tuesday, 7:20 A.M.
Washington, D.C.

Though he hadn't slept much over the past twenty-four hours, Paul Hood felt surprisingly refreshed.

He had spoken with Colonel August and Aideen Marley when they returned to Interpol headquarters. The fate of Darrell McCaskey, María Corneja, and Luis García de la Vega hadn't been known then—although General Manolo de la Vega had assured him that when the time was right, a police assault squad would be going in even if he had to kick each butt in personally.

McCaskey finally called from a field hospital only to say that they were all right. A more detailed report would have to wait until they were on a secure line back at Interpol.

Hood, Rodgers, Herbert, Coffey, and Plummer celebrated with a fresh pot of coffee and congratulations all around. There was a call from Ambassador Abril, who said that the king and the prime minister had been informed and would be addressing Spain at two P.M. local time. Abril could not tell them whether the Royal Palace had been taken from General Amadori's troops. He said that that information would be provided to the

White House when it was available and would have to make its way through channels.

Abril also could not tell them what the future of Spain might be—not only because it would be inappropriate to, but because he truly didn't know.

"Deputy Serrador and General Amadori both released some very powerful opposing forces," he said. "Ethnic and cultural differences have been inflamed. I hope—yet am not hopeful—that they can be doused."

"We'll all be praying for the best," Hood said.

The ambassador thanked him.

After Hood hung up, Herbert muttered a few graphic Southern expressions for the ambassador and his secrecy—though Ron Plummer reminded him that Abril was acting according to protocol.

"I remember how upset Jimmy Carter was when the American hostages were released from Tehran," he said. "The Iranians waited until Ronald Reagan had been sworn in to let them go. When former President Carter telephoned the White House to find out if the Americans were free, he was told that that information was classified. He had to find out about it much later."

Herbert was not appeased. He picked up the phone on the armrest of his wheelchair and called his office. He asked his assistant to phone Interpol and ask the spotters for an update on the situation at the palace. Less than two minutes later he was informed that the shooting had stopped and, in the few areas of the courtyard they could see, the police seemed to be in control. A call to Stephen Viens and a check with NRO satellites confirmed that soldiers were being disarmed in other parts of the compound and civilians were being led out to a Red Cross facility that was being set up outside the Cathedral of the Almudena.

Herbert grinned triumphantly. "What do you say we inform Abril that 'diplomatic channels' include a lot more stations than they used to."

The call from McCaskey finally came at seven-forty-five. Hood put it on the speakerphone. McCaskey said he was whipped and suffering from three broken ribs and a bruised kidney. Otherwise, he said, he was in good spirits. María and Luis were in surgery but both were expected to pull through.

"I'll be staying here for a while to recover," McCaskey said. "Hope that isn't a problem."

"No problem at all," Hood said. "Stay until you recover everything you feel you need."

McCaskey thanked him.

They did not discuss McCaskey's role in killing General Amadori. That would not be discussed until someone from Op-Center—probably Mike Rodgers—flew over to debrief him. It was understood among intelligence agents that assassination must be treated with an almost ceremonial reverence. Debriefing must be done face to face, like confession. That helped to ensure that killing a leader or spy, while sometimes necessary, would never be taken casually.

"There is one thing I'd like to do as soon as possible," McCaskey said.

"What's that?" Hood asked.

"There's been a lot of religious unrest here," McCaskey said. "General de la Vega tells me that it appears that General Superior González, leader of the

Jesuits in Spain, was a strong supporter of General Amadori. The General Superior was overcome with tear gas in Striker's assault—he'd been meeting with the general in the throne room. There is certain to be a Vatican investigation.''

"That's going to make a lot of Spaniards very unhappy,'' Rodgers said. ''Especially if the General Superior denies the charges and loyalties are strained between the Jesuits and other Roman Catholics.''

"It's all going to help contribute to the collapse of Spain as we knew it,'' McCaskey said, ''which everyone here believes is imminent. Someone who spoke directly with the prime minister told General de la Vega that a new constitution is already being worked on—one that will allow the different regions virtual autonomy under a very loose central government.''

Herbert folded his powerful arms. ''Why don't we call old Abril up and let him know what's gonna happen in his own country.''

Hood frowned and motioned him silent.

"The reason I mentioned General Superior González,'' McCaskey said, ''is that there is a Jesuit priest who helped to save our lives. His name is Father Norberto Alcazar.''

"Is he all right?'' Hood asked, writing down his name.

"He was hurt getting me safely to María's side— couple of heavy-duty bruises from gunfire chopping up the courtyard. Nothing serious, though. But I want to do something for him. He doesn't strike me as the kind of priest who'd want to be kicked upstairs or anything like that. Father Norberto was telling me at the field hospital that he lost his brother in this ordeal. He's had it pretty rough. Perhaps we can do something for his parish. Work it through the Vatican, if the White House can arrange that.''

''We'll certainly talk to them about that,'' Hood said. ''We can set up a scholarship somewhere in the brother's name.''

''Sounds good,'' McCaskey said. ''Maybe one for Martha too. Maybe from all of this madness a little good *will* come.''

After the other men in the room wished McCaskey well—''And I don't mean with just your health,'' Herbert added—Hood hung up. Father Norberto's story reminded him of something that tends to get lost in events like these. It isn't only a nation whose destiny is changed. The ripples go outward, affecting the world—and the ripples go inward, affecting every citizen. It was not only an awesome metamorphosis to behold. It was damn near overwhelming to have been an integral part of the process. And without having left this office.

It was time to hang that responsibility up.

Hood buzzed Bugs Benet and asked him to call his wife. She was at her parents' home in Old Saybrook, Hood told him.

Herbert looked at Hood. ''Sudden trip?'' he asked.

Hood shook his head. ''Long time in the works.''

Hood swung the computer monitor toward him. He went to his personal file.

Bugs buzzed. ''Sir?''

''Yes?''

"Mr. Kent says that Sharon and the kids left early this morning to go back to Washington," Bugs told him. "They were going to take the eight o'clock flight. Do you want to speak with him?"

"No," Hood said. He looked at his watch. "Thank him and tell him I'll call later."

"Shall I ring Mrs. Hood's cellular?"

"No, Bugs," Hood said. "I'll tell her when I meet her at the airport."

Hood hung up and finished his coffee. Then he rose.

"You're going to the airport now?" Herbert asked. "Chief, I'm sure you're going to have to brief the President."

Hood looked at Rodgers. "Mike, are you okay to handle that?"

"Sure," Rodgers said. He patted his bandages. "I got myself rewrapped before I came here."

"Good," Hood said. He took his cell phone out of his jacket pocket and put it in a drawer. "I'm going to get out of here before I get summoned."

"When will you be back?" Herbert asked.

Hood looked at the monitor. He stood over the keyboard. "I'll see you at the service for Martha," he said.

He looked at Rodgers then. The general's eyes were sharp and unblinking. He understood.

"I can tell you this, though," Hood continued. "Darrell was right. Good can come from madness. Through all the crises we've had to deal with, I couldn't have been blessed with a greater team."

"I don't like the sound of that," Herbert said.

Hood smiled. Still smiling, he e-mailed his resignation to the White House. Then he turned from his desk, threw a respectful salute at Mike Rodgers, and walked out the door.

ABOUT THE CREATORS

Tom Clancy is the author of *The Hunt for Red October, Red Storm Rising, Patriot Games, The Cardinal of the Kremlin, Clear and Present Danger, The Sum of All Fears, Without Remorse, Debt of Honor,* and *Executive Orders.* He is also the author of the nonfiction books *Submarine, Armored Cav, Fighter Wing, Marine,* and *Airborne.* He lives in Maryland.

Steve Pieczenik is a Harvard-trained psychiatrist with an M.D. from Cornell University Medical College. He has a Ph.D. in International Relations from M.I.T. and served as principal hostage negotiator and international crisis manager while Deputy Assistant Secretary of State under Henry Kissinger, Cyrus Vance, and James Baker. He is also the bestselling novelist of the psycho-political thrillers *The Mind Palace, Blood Heat, Maximum Vigilance,* and *Pax Pacifica.*

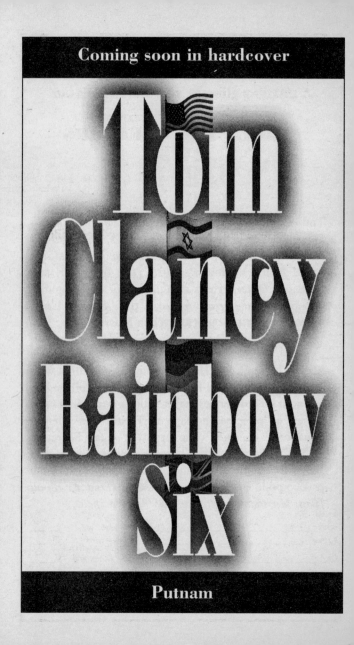

Tom Clancy's
Power Plays

POLITIKA

A new Soviet Union. A new political arena. A new adventure in military strategy that only Tom Clancy could have conceived...

0-425-16278-8/$7.50

Look for the next TOM CLANCY'S POWER PLAYS novel coming in December